THE
APOTHEOSIS

THE APOTHEOSIS

By
Darrell Lee

RISING PHOENIX PRESS ®

All rights reserved.
Published 2019 by Progressive Rising Phoenix Press, LLC
www.progressiverisingphoenix.com

ISBN: 978-1-946329-80-6

Printed in the U.S.A.

Edited by: Jody Amato

Cover photo "DNA Molecules On Abstract Technology Background, Concept Of Biochemistry And Genetic Theory" by WHITEMOCCA, used under license from Shutterstock.com.

Interior Illustration "DNA_312726" by BSGStudio, used with permission from all-free-download.com

Book and Cover design by William Speir
Visit: http://www.williamspeir.com

ACKNOWLEDGMENTS

It was a long and twisted road to get this story told. I didn't get it done by myself.

Thanks to the members of my critique group: Fern Brady and Mac Little you have helped my writing in countless ways. Thanks to my fellow writers that I spent the summer with in the Inprint workshop. I appreciate all your effort, patience, insights and suggestions. A special thank you to Catherine Blanchard for her help with Russian culture.

Thanks to my editors Monique Happy and Jody Amato for their experienced eyes. Yes, evidently, it takes two editors to keep my writing on track. In the end, any errors found on these pages are my responsibility.

Thanks to CEO Amanda Thrasher of Progressive Rising Phoenix Press for all your literary guidance.

For Yami
Because you are my advocate since the seed of this story germinated. Because this story made you cry, and because this story made you laugh. Because you gave all of that from your soul.

"Intellect distinguishes between the possible and the impossible; reason distinguishes between the sensible and the senseless. Even the possible can be senseless."

Max Born
1954 Nobel Prize Winner in Physics for
Fundamental Research in Quantum Mechanics

AUGUST 30, 2057

Despite what the Royal Bahamas Police Force may tell you, my name is John Numen. I was born on September 15, 1990 in Boston, Massachusetts. I obtained my Ph.D. at Harvard University in 2015, with my core training in contemporary genetics, biochemistry, and molecular, cellular, and mechanistic biology. I am also a self-taught computer programmer, with a few night classes in computer science thrown in when I could. I am a scientist, medical researcher, doctor, billionaire investor, fugitive on the FBI's Most Wanted list, and fledgling serial killer.

I don't know how many people you have to murder to qualify as a serial killer, but if my plans go as I hope, I will meet that number sooner or later. I consider it collateral damage for the advancements in science I have made. Tonight, I hope to justify the sacrifices I have already made and reach the apex of all my work.

I have kept all technical discussion of my research from this accounting. The technical documentation of my accomplishments is very extensive, stretching back over the past thirty-seven years. Those writings, along with all my equipment (some I have bought, some I have made), computers, and supporting data (stored on optical drives labeled and indexed to match the technical volume they supplement) can be found in my lab. At the moment, they are packed in crates that I have prepared for shipping in anticipation of my impending departure.

The other thing of importance, I suppose, is my considerable financial wealth, most of it acquired through my investment company. I am as proud of that as I am of my research. I doubt that all my investments and holdings can be discovered through the labyrinth of shell corporations,

*shady accounting firms, and bribed government officials that I have col-
lected in all the tax-haven countries around the world. The governmental
powers-that-be will want to confiscate all that they find to further line
their corrupt pockets. I have tolerated these parasites because I had no
other choice. I feel no need to make the work any easier for the authorities. I will simply wish them good luck.*

*The most likely reason somebody besides myself would be reading
these pages is because I have been found lying dead or in a vegetative
state on a gurney in the lab next to my house. There are plenty of reasons
for this to have happened; perhaps my theories are incorrect or simply
don't apply to a brain as complex as a human's. Maybe the hardware
isn't up to the task, or there is an undiscovered flaw in the software I built
that is running the whole thing or, since there is an ill-timed squall line
approaching, a lightning strike disabled the power generator midway
through the process. If a lightning strike is the reason, I would like to
stand corrected. God does exist. But not the way an ex-colleague once
insisted; God isn't the only one that can create human life. It is evident,
though, that his sense of humor is as black and his disdain for me as great
as I had feared.*

*I have placed this last entry at the beginning because I wanted to
save the reader from having to go through the pages that follow to answer
the immediate questions you are surely asking about the circumstances of
my death. As for my motivations, and the series of events that led to this
last entry, on this afternoon, you'll have to read further.*

*To be clear, the young man on the gurney next to me is a victim,
lured here under false pretenses for the completion of my grand experi-
ment. The young woman, who has been staying here for the last nine
weeks, though unharmed, is likewise a victim. I invited her here because I
was lonely and, unknown to her, had desires for her. She stayed here only
because I gave her a task she considered honorable, for a salary she
couldn't refuse. We became good friends, but our relationship was strictly
a professional one. She's not responsible for any illegal activities and was
unaware of mine.*

*I watched them sail away this morning to a small cay where I sug-
gested they spend the day so I could run my final test. The test was a success. It's getting late. Certainly, they know of the approaching weather by
now and will be hastening their return. I can hear the wind picking up*

outside. The radar on the laptop shows the storm approaching. I'll wait for them on the porch and, when they arrive, act as calmly as I am able. I'm nervous and excited. I hope I survive and can put this journal in its shipping crate. I am looking forward to my new life. I am looking forward to finally returning to Boston. If I am not too late, I have somebody I love very much there, and I have an old score to settle. After that last loose end is resolved, I am looking forward to the life I deserve.

FALL 2015

ETHAN

The meeting day with Dr. Ethan Shinwell took three interminable weeks to arrive. John waited, dressed in his best power suit, in the outer office with the administrative assistant for a half hour. The smell of musty wood-paneled walls, the click of the secretary's nails on the keyboard, and the hum of the printer down the short hallway behind her desk were all the same as when he last saw this part of the building. The afternoon coffee brewed on the small table, out of sight, by the printer. It was where he had gone to get a cup of coffee for his dad. Back then he was nine years old. Now he waited for an invitation to enter his father's old office from a man he'd met only once.

Finally, the dark oak door to the office opened. A thin man, dark hair protruding from under a navy-blue kippah, a full beard sitting on a gaunt face, stepped out. He looked at John through black-framed glasses that made his eyes look bigger than normal. A white dress shirt hung loosely from square shoulders. Black dress slacks clung to his hips with the help of a worn, overly tightened belt. *Had he been sick the last five years?*

"Good to see you again, Dr. Numen. Please come in."

John stood, shook hands. Ethan's grip was firm, his pale hand extending out from the sleeve of the dress shirt. John did not yet know that standing before him was a façade. The stone-hard bark of a tree that was rotting from the inside.

He entered the office. The walls were dark and wooden, like the door. A window to the right was the light source. The rich oak flooring was now covered with carpeting, a pale gray. In the center of the far wall sat a large desk covered with papers and a computer screen set to the side. It had the feeling of an old man's office, perhaps a high school principal about to retire. Not the office of a man in his thirties.

Ethan sat behind the desk. "Have a seat, please." He pointed to a chair opposite him. "Dr. Jones has told me quite a lot about you."

"He's an old friend of the family. So I am sure he embellished."

"He thought there may be some synergy with our current work and your research."

John sat back in the leather chair and crossed his legs. "That's the hope."

"I did some research of my own. You have an impressive academic record at Harvard." Ethan picked up an already opened folder on his desk. "I don't quite understand the software you developed or the device you engineered that's the subject matter of your dissertation."

"It's a computer-driven device that I developed to assist in somatic cell nuclear transfer to solve the replication of a key set of proteins during the cloning procedure for rhesus monkey embryos," John said.

Ethan flipped a page in the folder in front of him. "I see. The National Health Council Award for Medical Research, the J. Allyn Taylor International Prize in Medicine, and the Dana Award for Pioneering Achievement in Health, among others. This is an impressive list of awards, especially over such a short time."

"Thank you."

Ethan continued to examine the folder's contents. "Dr. Numen, this is a pharmaceutical research company, as you know. Your work is impressive; however, I really don't see how much of it applies to anything we are doing.

"I know of your father's legacy at this company. I'm in charge of the research activities that are done in this lab. Dr. Jones informed me that you talked of therapeutic cloning and that there could be an application. Looking at your work, I see mostly reproductive cloning. That's a bit out in left field for me."

"There really isn't much difference—"

"Yes, there is." Ethan looked over the top of the folder. "The creation of human life can only be done by God."

"Of course, Dr. Shinwell." John knew when there could only be one ego in a room, and if he wanted a discreet place to get his research done, he would have to give Dr. Shinwell's ego plenty of space.

"The federal government passed laws banning the cloning of humans just last fall." Ethan placed the folder on the desk. "Are you planning to change the direction of this company?"

"I think initially my work here will be outside the company's current business model. So, I should make no impact on your lab's activities," John said.

"That is nice to know. As long as it doesn't affect my budget or bring legal troubles, we should have no problems."

"I'll be paying for half the cost of equipping the new lab. Dr. Jones has agreed that the company will pay the other half. We didn't talk in detail about the budget structure. Just an educated guess, but I'd expect an impact to your budget for this year."

"How much will that be?"

"I'll write up a budget proposal for the next board meeting. I believe that is the standard protocol for budget issues. There's one other thing—" John leaned forward in his chair. "I know you're the director of the lab, but the one I'll be establishing will share the same building, yet will be physically separate. I'll have the final say on who has access to it, including you."

"We'll just see what Dr. Jones has to say about that. I don't think—"

"I have. He's given it his approval."

"I guess your 40 percent ownership in the company does bring privileges." Ethan picked up the folder on his desk and tossed it in the wastebasket behind him.

John stood from his chair. "Thank you for your time." *What a prick. Fuck you.* He headed for the door.

"Same here," Ethan replied.

JUNE 15, 2021

I decided to write this journal as sort of an insurance policy. Living such a reclusive life on an island all by myself, should some unforeseen accident or sudden heart attack end my life, it could be months or perhaps over a year before I am found. At least this will be my one chance to tell my story. I have kept this leather-bound, loose-leaf binder hidden in my dresser drawer with my shorts. Not very imaginative, I know, but it serves its purpose. Out of sight, but a place that will be eventually discovered, most likely by the police. However, I hope it will find its way to the scientific community, along with all my other writings. This is my story, written as accurately as my memory allows and as eloquently as I'm able.

I didn't have the understanding that I have today, but even then, I knew my family was wealthy. I remember my father, Sean Numen, as tall and muscular, as most boys see their dad. We spent at least one week in the summer on a deep-sea fishing trip in the Bahamas or Costa Rica and every Sunday afternoon we watched the Patriots play football on TV. My mother was a passing apparition, always off to a social event of one kind or the other. Most of my day-to-day caretaking was provided by the servants in the house. There was a definite upside: I learned how to cook from one of the best chefs on the East Coast.

My father had come far: medical school residency at John Hopkins in neurology and a move to Boston after residency, where he continued working on a new drug to treat depression. He formed his own company, found financial backing, and in five years had his new drug from "The Numen Company" on the market. That was the same year I was born.

In the first year, the company earned $300 million, more than any-

body at that time expected. Sales continued to climb every year thereafter, as new drugs were developed and brought to the market—all of them the brainchild of my dad. The year of my tenth birthday party, sales exceeded $15.7 billon.

All stories, just as all lives, have a beginning. My life has two beginnings. There is the obvious one, the day I was born. The second was on my tenth birthday. There is a before and an after, with this day in between. I was very advanced academically for my age by this time. I had begun taking high school-level courses the year before. Everyone else in my classes was five to seven years older than me. Without friends at school, my birthday parties became more sparsely attended. My parents tried to fill the gap with children of couples they knew from work or social events. They meant well, but you can't fake friendship. So, this celebration was like the one the year before—more routine tradition than a real party.

On a cloudless, warm September afternoon, under the shade of a large elm tree beside the pool, the table stretched out ten yards in front of me, half of its length covered with brightly wrapped presents. Everyone sang "Happy Birthday" and the gifts were opened. It was nice. But what I was waiting for was the annual football game.

"All right, let's see how many players we have," my father said as he stood by the table in his running shoes, blue jeans and t-shirt, holding a football in one hand. He counted out the children at the table. "Looks like ten. But I believe I can get Robert to join us, then I can play on the other team, giving us a decent six-man game." He winked at me. My dad loved the chance to play a game of backyard football.

"What do you say, Robert? Want to join the game?" My father looked over his shoulder at my Uncle Robert, who stood by the bar in the cabana. He was my mother's brother. Whatever maternal instincts she lacked he was gifted with.

Of course, I always played on my dad's team. The game went on for an hour. Uncle Robert's team was leading by a touchdown when the moment arrived. One of the boys on my team picked up the "kick-off" and started left. Heavily pursued, he could see his mistake, so he quickly tossed the ball backwards to me. I ran right, but two opposing players quickly converged on me, so in an instant I turned and threw the ball half the width of the field to my father, who was standing in the clear. He was as surprised as anybody to see the ball coming his way. Instinctively, he

9

caught the ball and began running upfield. Uncle Robert stood behind all the other players. He was the only one who would be able to catch my dad and so he began his pursuit.

My dad ran hard to his right, trying to get around the angle of pursuit. Uncle Robert gave chase, adjusting his original bad angle to reach for the flag dangling from my father's hip as he ran by, but he wasn't able to grab it. Now it was a foot race to the far goal line. I ran behind them as fast as I could. Uncle Robert slowly gained ground and reached for the flag on my dad's belt a second time, just as he crossed the goal line for the tying touchdown.

I cheered. All the kids on my team cheered. I was still running to him. Uncle Robert stopped and put his hands on his knees to catch his breath. I was almost to him. My dad walked slowly away from me, dropping the football from his hand. I stopped at his side. His hands came up to his chest and his shoulders hunched forward. He stumbled and pushed me out of the way as he fell. I watched his last breath go out of his body as I knelt in the grass beside him. My father was only forty-three.

The next six months were a blur. Much to my mother's surprise, I was to inherit 40 percent ownership of the company and a place on the board of directors upon my twenty-fifth birthday. She got 5 percent ownership. She took out her anger and shame on me at this revelation and numbed herself with alcohol. By the beginning of the next school year, I was living with Aunt Cathy and Uncle Robert. They didn't even have to fight for legal custody. She let me go. And I was better off for it, I am sure. They didn't have kids, so it was a good fit.

All my belongings were moved into an upstairs bedroom. That first day, I walked to the desk in front of the window that looked out to the large backyard. The yard was filled with trees, their leaves just starting to turn yellow and red. The afternoon sun came through and filled the room.

"All right, well, Robert and I will be downstairs if you need anything."

"Thanks, Aunt Cathy."

They didn't know their voices carried upstairs from the living room.

"Are we really doing the right thing?" Cathy asked.

"No doubt. I don't want him raised by their long-forgotten second cousin who lives in a God-knows-where little town in Iowa," Robert said.

"I guess," Cathy said. "But talk about a lot of changes for the poor child. I just hope we can get him through them all."

"There's a team of lawyers working it all out. He'll get a healthy chunk of money just from the selling of the house and furniture, not to mention John has 40 percent ownership in the company."

"I'm not talking about those changes! I mean living here, with us, in this house. The boy is going to feel like a stranger here. We're going to have to work very hard to make him feel welcome and at home," Cathy said. "I can only imagine how he feels basically losing both parents."

"We will, honey, we will. We owe it to him, and it's the least we can do for Sean."

I could tell that Uncle Robert and Aunt Cathy had tried their best to comfort and help me through the previous few months. I didn't feel bad about being there; I truly liked them and couldn't think of a better place to be, given the circumstance.

The stable home life enabled my academic work to pick up speed. Early graduation from high school, then Harvard. Again, an early gradu-ation with my Bachelor's and Master's degrees. I won't take up space here listing my academic achievements; they can be found online easily enough. Just before I started on my Ph.D., I made a trip home. Aunt Cathy insisted. I assumed it was because I'd been away for such a long stretch and she wanted to make sure to get some time before the Ph.D. work started. It was on my second night home, once we were seated at one end of the long dark mahogany table in the dining room, when Uncle Robert broke the news.

"I'm retiring."

I was stunned for a moment. "Well, well that is great! What are you now, forty-five? Still young, Aunt Cathy is even younger. You guys can travel the world, see some sights. God knows you have been working hard for the last twenty years. You've done well so you can do whatever you want. I have to say, though, I am surprised. A life-long workaholic like you, checking it in early." I smiled at Uncle Robert, who didn't smile, then at Aunt Cathy. She didn't smile back either. "So how come I'm the only one who seems to be happy about this?"

"I really didn't want to retire, but Cathy and I think it is the best decision considering... "

"Considering what?" I looked at Cathy, who was looking down at

her plate.

"I went to the doctor a few months ago, had some tests run. And the results weren't good news. They tell me I have cancer."

"What kind of—"

"In my brain."

I could feel a surge, something like fear and panic, but I could see no threat in front of me and my mind couldn't reconcile it. "Did you get a second opinion?" I asked.

"Three of them. They all said the same thing."

"What are they going to do? There must be something?"

"There is medication and radiation... because of where it's located, surgery isn't an option. We're going to fight it, but the doctors did not sound too optimistic. So, we thought it was important for you to know. Cathy is going to need your help one day. But who knows, maybe some brilliant doctor like yourself will come along and find a cure.

"The board has already picked my replacement. His name is Dr. Phillip Jones. I think you should meet him. You'll be on the board of directors soon enough, so I think it's important to start introducing you around."

"If you say so."

"Good, we'll go tomorrow."

I remember the next day, looking up at the three-story red brick building. The parking lot for employees was across the street. At the very top of the building, in shiny metallic letters, was written "The Numen Company." I hadn't been there since my father died.

"A lot has changed inside. We have a much bigger lab and a lot more people," Robert said.

The receptionist gave us a nod. Uncle Robert swiped his identification card over a gray pad next to a door on the left side of the lobby. He pulled the handle and we entered a hallway with doors to many offices. As I walked by each one, I saw one or two people seated at desks busily typing at the computer or talking on the phone. Near the end of the hall, where it made a right-hand turn, Robert opened a door with the nameplate "Dr. Phillip Jones." To the right a blonde secretary was typing away at her computer.

"Good morning, Elizabeth," Robert said.

"Good morning, Mr. Edward. Dr. Jones is expecting you."

Robert opened the oak door to the left of the secretary's desk, and we stepped into the office.

Dr. Jones sat behind a large dark oak desk with papers in disarray on top. He was older than Robert, with almost totally white hair and a receding hairline. He had a barrel-shaped upper body and almost no neck. He wore a white long-sleeved dress shirt, whose buttons were under a bit of a strain just above the belt, with a blue tie and dark dress pants. In front of the desk sat a young man in jeans and a brown tweed jacket, who appeared to be in his late twenties. He had thick glasses on his nose and a kippah on top of his head. Both men stood when the door opened.

"Hello, Robert," Dr. Jones said. "And this must be John Numen. It's a pleasure." Dr. Jones extended his meaty hand across the desk and I shook it. Dr. Jones nodded to the man in the thick glasses and said, "This is Dr. Ethan Shinwell. He's our newest and brightest biochemist at the company."

I felt like a teenager who had been set up on a blind date with his cousin.

"Dr. Shinwell has done some very interesting work at NYU. He has been with us about a year now and has really hit the ground running." I shook Ethan's hand. "Dr. Shinwell stopped by to talk about some matters with the lab. I suggested he stick around to meet you. I mean, after all, it won't be long before John here will be on the board of directors. You and John will be working here together some day."

"It's nice to meet you," I said. Have you ever met someone and you can tell right away they don't like you? That was what I felt from Ethan. I didn't know then that he treated the whole world like that, with a constant air of moral and intellectual superiority. He was always sure either in one or both of those ways he was superior to everybody else. I'm sure he wanted to work his way up in the company; he knew about me before I'd ever heard about him. He thought I would be an obstacle to his advancement. He didn't know how right he was.

"It was nice to meet you both, but I really need to get back to the lab. If you will excuse me." He left the room and closed the door. Dr. Jones motioned for me to sit in the chair Ethan had vacated, and Robert sat in the other chair.

"I like that young man, but he has the social skills of a seventh

grader," Dr. Jones said.

"Not everybody can be as charming as you," Robert said.

Dr. Jones smiled. "I sure am going to miss you blowing smoke up my ass around here. How old are you now, John?"

"Twenty-four."

"Robert tells me you are doing well at Harvard," Dr. Jones said.

"Yes, sir."

"Looks like this nut didn't fall far from the tree. Your dad was the same way, just as smart as could be. One helluva guy. You know you look a lot like your dad; tall, fit, same hair, but your eyes have the same shape as your mother's.

"I wanted to spend time with you and show you around myself to-day, but I have an important meeting with some customers. I'm sure Robert knows more about this place than I do anyway, so you'll be in good hands."

"No problem, Phillip," Robert replied. "I didn't bring him here to put a crimp in your day. I'll give him the tour. I just wanted you guys to meet face to face before John goes back to school next week."

We walked around the whole building. Most of it was boring offices, but on the third floor was the laboratory. Stepping off the elevator, we walked down a long hallway. Halfway down the hall were gray metal doors on each side. We stopped at the doors, and Uncle Robert swiped his card at the door to the right. A buzzer sounded and we walked in. It was one large room with tables gathered in groups in different areas and desks lined against the wall next to the windows. Men were working at different tables with equipment or computers. Ethan was there but at the far end of the long room. What he was doing wasn't very clear, but he looked focused on the task at hand.

"This is where all the real work gets done for the company. We don't want to bother any of these guys; I just wanted you to see it." Robert opened the door again and we walked out into the hall. I pointed to the other gray door across the hall.

"What's in there?"

Uncle Robert swiped his card across the door's pad and we stepped in. It was a large empty space, as large as half of the building, with a dirty, gray cement floor, unlike the white linoleum in the lab across the hall. It was dark and cold; a group of five narrow windows in the center of the far wall let in the only light.

"This is where we hope to expand one day." Robert's voice echoed. "If you come up with the right idea, it can be yours." I looked around the large, hollow space. Uncle Robert didn't know it, but I already had an idea for the space. That day I was introduced to two things that would change my life: the future home of my new lab and Ethan Shinwell.

There are a hundred things that make me think of her. Some don't occur very often, but some do. Just the name Ethan Shinwell reminds me of the first time I saw her.

DECEMBER 2018

HOLIDAY PARTY

John stepped off the elevator and walked down the same third-story hallway as he had every day for the past three years. When he got to the gray metal door, he swiped his access card. A buzzer sounded. Upon his entry, the overhead fluorescent lights hummed to life. John approached a large table covered with computer circuit boards and computer screens. He removed his coat and jacket and draped them over a chair. The lab was on his way to the party. Dr. Jones wouldn't take any excuse this year. John usually spent the holiday season in Europe. Not this year. There were pregnant monkeys to keep an eye on. He loosened his tie, looked at his watch. *I have enough time for a quick check.*

John passed a long row of tables covered with equipment. He passed his cloning device and the two freezers that kept their contents at eighty degrees below zero. At the far end of the lab, he swiped his card at another door and stepped into the primate area. Again, the overhead lights came on automatically.

To his right was a separate room with a large, glass window. An operating table occupied the center of the room. Surgical equipment in unopened packaging lay organized on tray carts lined against the wall. In the main room, stacked against the wall, were a half-dozen empty cages, two feet high by two feet wide and three feet long, solid metal, except for the barred front door. At the other end of the room, through a Plexiglas wall, a large metal apparatus with numerous ropes for the rhesus monkeys to climb on stood in the center of the confined space. A skylight lit the area with sunshine during the day. Sitting about, calmly grooming themselves or one another, were five female rhesus monkeys. Each had been implanted with an embryo the week before.

As John approached the glass wall, one of the monkeys, whom he had named Petri, came to a metal platform just inside the small glass door in the center of the wall. She had come to John's laboratory from the lab at Harvard University when she was three years old. She had never known life outside of a laboratory and looked to humans as caregivers. She had developed an attachment to John. He enjoyed spoiling her with treats he kept in his pocket. He unlatched the thick Plexiglas door and opened it. Petri hopped through and climbed on John's arm.

"How are you this evening, Ms. Petri?" John reached into his pocket, removed an almond and gave it to her. She quickly devoured the morsel. It had taken John three years to get to this point. These five primates were about to prove that he could clone a perfectly healthy primate 100 percent of the time. In the beginning, it took over one hundred attempts to produce just one embryo suitable for implantation. By the end of the second year, he had refined the technique so that every embryo was a good candidate. When he tried the first ten implantations, one produced a clone: Petri's clone. Now he believed his device was perfected; it was going to be 100 percent successful. John gave Petri his last almond and opened the Plexiglas door again.

"I must be going; I don't want to be late for the company holiday party." John placed his hand on the bottom edge of the doorway and Petri ran down his arm, back onto the platform inside.

From his lab, it was a short drive through the snow-plowed streets of Boston to the Four Seasons Hotel. When he got to the crowded conference room, the party was going strong. John looked around. Not a single familiar face. These people worked in the same building he did, but he knew only a dozen of them by face and a handful by name. Everyone else in the room was a stranger. John jostled through the crowd till he was at the bar. The bartender stood waiting.

"Old Fashioned," John said.

"Yes, sir."

"Angostura Bitters, please."

"Yes, sir."

John looked back at the expanse of tables in the room. That was when he first noticed her. She was halfway across the room, walking through the crowd. A full-length black evening dress fit her form well.

Not too tight. Bare shoulders of unblemished alabaster skin, like a satin sheet. The dress narrowed to her dainty waist and flowed over her hips to the floor. Ink-black hair fell to mid-back. She came closer. John faced the bar. The bartender came from the far end with his drink. As the bartender arrived, so did the woman, now standing beside him.

"Water, please," she said to the bartender. John looked at her. She noticed and smiled at him. Her eyes were a dark chocolate brown and her smile very polite and sexy at the same time.

"I don't believe we've ever met. I'm John."

She reached out with her hand as John extended his. Hers seemed half the size of his.

"Nice to meet you. I'm Amira."

"I've never seen you around the building. But I work in a lab on the third floor and don't get out very much."

"I don't work at the company. If you work in the lab, you probably know my husband, Ethan Shinwell?"

"Yes. I know Dr. Shinwell. I don't work in his lab, I work in one across the hall."

The bartender returned with her water. "Thank you," she said, taking a sip. Her eyes widened a bit.

"You work in the new lab near my husband?"

"Yes. Right across the hall."

"You must be Dr. John Numen, the son of the man who started the company?"

"Yes, I am," John said.

"Dr. Numen, it's a pleasure to meet you." She smiled wider.

"Please, call me John."

"I read your bio in the company brochure. All the board members are in there; they handed them out at the front door this evening."

"I'm in the company brochure?"

"Yes, but there wasn't a picture with it like the other board members, which is why I didn't know who you were. It's very nice to meet you in person. My husband mentioned you to me when you first came to the company."

John looked over Amira's shoulder and saw Ethan approaching.

"Dr. Numen, good to see you. I see you've met my wife?" Dr. Shinwell placed his arm around her waist. Amira stood rigid.

"We were just introducing ourselves. You're a lucky man, Dr. Shinwell. She's a beautiful woman."

Amira looked down at the floor.

"Thank you, Doctor. Sorry to interrupt. We must be going. If you don't mind, dear?" He nodded to Amira.

"Nice to meet you, Dr. Numen," she said, this time without a smile. In a moment, she had disappeared into the crowd with Ethan.

JUNE 20, 2021

During the summer, just a few months shy of my twenty-first birthday, Uncle Robert took me to Nassau to meet the tax attorney. I didn't even know I had a tax attorney, much less in the Bahamas. But I knew the trust fund left to me by my father had been growing, untouched, with investments and deposits from the company for the past eleven years. I had no idea how important this trip was to be to me later.

It was a small, brick, windowless building, standing alone on a block of a nondescript street in New Province. The only unusual things about it were the five satellite communication antennas on the roof and the thick, metal front door. We walked in and were immediately greeted by Lee Silkcox. Black as ink, almost two-dimensional. Salt-and-pepper hair and beard. His casual dress gave no hint of his wealth. To this day, he's one of the smartest men I have ever met.

He shook hands with Uncle Robert, and pleasantries were exchanged.

"Perhaps you should find a local bar to kill some time, Robert. I'll give you a ring when I am finished with Mr. Numen." With that, Uncle Robert was gone.

"Only a few months away now, Mr. Numen. I am very excited for you. Come with me so we can look at these computer screens together."

We moved to the back half of the building, through a doorway to a room whose walls were covered with flat panel TVs. All of them, except two with news channels, scrolled stock market information from around the world. Three computers with two monitors each sat on tables against the back wall. Multi-colored charts and graphs were displayed on these.

Every couple seconds they would update with real-time information. What they were analyzing I couldn't tell. We sat together, in plush leather chairs, at a large table in the middle of the room with three computer monitors on it. He pulled up a spreadsheet.

"I am told you are a very intelligent young man. That's good, it will make my job a lot easier. I don't suppose you know what a 'Double Irish with a Dutch Sandwich' is, do you?"

"No, sir."

"It's a tax-avoidance technique employed by certain corporations, in this case, The Numen Company, using a combination of Irish and Dutch subsidiary companies to shift profits to low- or no-tax jurisdictions. This financial... technique... involves sending profits first through one Irish company, then to a Dutch company, and finally to a second Irish company headquartered in a tax haven. This technique helps your company—I say 'your' because in a few months you will hold the largest portion—to reduce the overall corporate tax rates... significantly."

"Is that legal?"

"Yes, it is, for now. Your company is grandfathered in and can take advantage of this technique until 2020. After that, we'll have to get creative for your company's bottom line to remain unaffected. But don't worry, there's always another way."

"Does Uncle Robert know?"

"Yes. All board members know. But not all are going to know as much as you, once I am finished with you. Your father was very kind to me. Gave me a chance when none of the other white jerk-offs of a businessman would. I can never repay him. But I can try with his only son."

"When I was little my father brought me here during the summer to fish—"

"I know, he would use the same trips to come and see me. He usually had a large cash shipment to bring me. Not everything can, or should, be done electronically. But we aren't here to talk about just the company's money. I introduced you to the Irish-Danish as a simple example of the high-level concept of a financial tool to take advantage of the system in place on an international scale. Today we are really interested in your personal money. Do you know how much money you have?"

"I have a little over $3 million in a trust fund."

"You have the standard-looking trust fund back in America. True.

That's really for show. That $3 million is a very small portion of what your father left for you. I've done very well for you over the past eleven years. It has been pretty easy, though, since the only thing to pay for has been your education. But things are changing. Soon you'll have a place of your own, a car. You have a girlfriend?"

"I have a couple girls I'm seeing, but you know, it's casual."

"Casual or not, they cost money and the older the women, the higher the cost. After you are married, the cost of a girlfriend goes way, way up. Not worth the trouble or expense, if you ask me. As soon as the academia lets up, you'll be wanting to take a few of them on trips and such. It's normal."

"I am missing Rome."

"The unknown accounts I'm about to show you, even if you knew about them, you couldn't have found any information. Do you know why you wouldn't be able to find any information on your soon-to-be-gotten wealth?"

"No."

"Because it's all hidden."

"Where?"

"In shell corporations. Here in Nassau, Panama, The Cayman Islands, Swiss bank accounts… just to name a few."

"Why?"

"Your father was a very smart man. He began this system when the company was founded. He knew its potential and found every way possible to keep every dime he could. He was looking out for your future before you were even born. And I've been here every step of the way. Hell, I even taught him a few things he didn't know. And that's really saying something."

"Can you teach me?" I asked.

"Yes, I can. If you are sure you want to know."

"I am."

"People can be funny when it comes to money. I have seen multimillionaires get bent over $500, because it isn't about the amount, it's about how they must be more than everybody around them. And you never know how people will take it if they know how much you have. It's important for you to understand the things I tell you, and what I show you here can't be shared with anyone. Not Dr. Jones, not your aunt and uncle,

not a girlfriend and certainly not a wife, if you ever have one. You want to blend in like a chameleon. I have a safe here that is full of false identifications of all types from many different countries. YOUR identifications. We'll use them to make the many different accounts you'll be needing. A chameleon, yes, but you and I know you're much more. That's a significant advantage to have in life."

"I understand."

"You have no idea how much you remind me of him. I can see that brain of yours working. Just like your dad. Let's begin. Rule number one: don't ever send me an electronic message of any kind—phone, fax, email, or text message—that isn't encrypted. I have software you'll need to install on your personal computer and smartphone."

"Yes, sir."

"Do you want to continue to keep your wealth and have it grow?"

"Yes, sir."

"Rule number two: then don't flaunt it, especially in America. If you buy a big mansion in Beverly Hills with a gold-plated Rolls Royce and throw extravagant parties for people you don't know, get your picture taken by the paparazzi dating the latest supermodel, hanging out on your new yacht in Saint-Tropez—you'll get noticed. And you'll end up with a team of lawyers and a security detail just to go to the grocery store. That behavior is for movie stars and the simple-minded rich. Of the truly wealthy, the people in this world who have real influence, the large majority don't do that. Get noticed and that will be the beginning of the end of your free money."

"Yes, sir, Mr. Silkcox."

"You can call me Lee. We're going to be talking very often the next few years. Remember, I make my money by making sure you make the most money you can. We have something that is hard to find in the business world: a win-win relationship."

I couldn't have been in better hands. He was my mentor of the financial underworld. He opened a whole new universe to me. One that operates beneath the seen world. Wall Street is peanuts compared to the volume of money that's moved, unseen, by the tax authorities of the "free world" governments. These governments that tax over the purchase or sale of a stick of gum. Somehow, this has become acceptable to billions of people, to just give their money away to these entities.

My father wasn't a sheep in a herd. Neither am I. And neither is Lee Silkcox. I am proud to say that eventually, after many years, I was able to teach him a thing or two. And that's really saying something.

JANUARY 30, 2019

AMIRA

She hadn't wanted to move back to Boston. She wanted to be away from its neatly trimmed old houses on old shaded streets. It smelled of soccer games and PTA. A good place for a family. Not so much for an exciting life. Almost all her friends from high school had left. The few who remained had a couple of kids already and a schedule too packed with motherhood to socialize. Real friendships, ones close enough for her to share her problems, to find some sympathy, had been replaced with Facebook ones.

Amira liked New York. She liked the fast pace and busy streets and bustling restaurants. She enjoyed the cultural shiny side and reckless underside of the city at night. It took four breathtaking years at New York University to obtain her journalism degree. A position waited for her at *The New Yorker*, where she had interned for two summers. Anticipating her career and life in the big city experience, her mood soared. One day, she knew she would write something important. An investigative piece perhaps, or maybe a novel. For her, New York City pulsated. From The Big Apple, she could springboard to anywhere.

She met Ethan at the beginning of the last semester of her senior year. Unlike her friends who dreamt of meeting Mr. Right and marrying, she felt too young for long-term relationships. Life moved too fast for obligations. Certainly, Ethan wouldn't be anything but another quick fling. She studied him while they were in line at the cafeteria. Tall, fit, and awkward. He was Jewish, like her, the kippah always atop his head.

They lunched together for the next few days. Then a movie and dinner. His family had money. His body was muscular and lean. A touch socially awkward, but polite. Devoutly Jewish; his father was a rabbi in New York. He was graduating with his Ph.D. in Biomolecular Science at the same time as Amira. He had a job lined up in Boston. Perfect. She would be staying in New York. She knew she was out of his league; she would have the upper hand. She was sure the romance would be short-lived. The way she liked them. All her plans changed with two tiny pink lines on an early pregnancy test the week before graduation.

Ethan argued that he had a good job at a growing company. And it was a good job; however, it was in Boston. He looked at her earnestly and told her she would be happy back in Boston. This relieved Amira's parents, her mother really more than her father. One of her mother's constant worries was that Amira would meet a man outside their faith and culture. Amira came back. To have his child, to watch it grow. They would raise a family. Spend fall afternoons at football practices or buy a prom dress. Whichever would be required.

After Elona's birth, Ethan wanted her to remain at home with the child. She didn't have to worry, he would provide. Elona became Amira's one true bright spot. A child-sized image of herself, with cream-colored skin, big brown eyes, and a mane of black hair. Full of energy, enthusiasm, and love. Amira returned to Boston for Ethan; she stayed in Boston for Elona.

Slowly, over time, it became clear to her that Ethan expected her behavior to model the traditional housewife role. Dinner should be ready when he arrived home. He dictated the food acceptable in the house. Removing meat, eating only organically grown vegetables in very small portions. He said that through the pain of self-deprivation he desired to get closer to God. His hair and beard grew shabby.

She resented how Ethan restricted her interactions outside the home and her access to unsupervised funds. Sex became infrequent and mechanical. She battled him for the first four years, with many tears from her, and many apologies from him. However, nothing obtained resolution, nothing changed. Ultimately it wore her down, like the unrelenting current of a river. Pulling her down and keeping her from breathing. Now, it was a movie now and then, when the tension between them abated.

Her one time a year to dress up was the company's holiday party. Only held a month ago, it seemed like a year. Now that the holidays were over, the forced amicableness for the sake of the season no longer held sway. Yesterday's fight erupted over money she'd spent on makeup, or at least that was the pretense. But she knew the real reason, the root cause of all of Ethan's tirades: control. A cloud hung over her life, like being homesick for a place that never existed.

She looked around the dining room of the restaurant. Pale table-cloths, candle-lit tables, waiters in white jackets, crystal chandeliers, and tall wine glasses. She sat at a table alone, in her best cocktail dress, bought before she met Ethan. So stylish and trending then, but now it looked dated. She would order something expensive and have at least two glasses of wine. This passive-aggressive dinner would cost three times what she had spent on the makeup. That is what she had reduced herself to. She would deal with the consequences of an unapproved absence from the house later.

She looked up from the wine list and saw the maître d' leading him through the tables. He was dressed in a suit. She knew fashion and recognized an elegant designer suit when she saw one. She thought the same thing about the suit he'd worn at the holiday party. A red tie with that one; a light blue tie gave this one the right touch. He glanced around the room. Their eyes met for an instant, but his continued. She felt a twinge of disappointment. Then his head swung back to her and their eyes locked. He stopped, and a smile came to his lips. Hers too. He moved confidently through the tables to her. Soon he was standing on the other side of the table.

"Good evening, Amira. It's so good to see you again."

His eyes looked directly at her and her breathing paused for an instant. She felt the tension in her stomach she got when talking to a man she found attractive. She felt her face flush. *He remembered my name.*

"Good evening, John. Very nice to see you again, too."

The maître d' realized he'd lost his guest and made his way toward them. John noticed only one place setting.

"Dining alone?"

"Yes."

"Could I join you?"

Yes. No. What if someone who knows Ethan sees us? How will I explain? Certainly, nobody from our building would be at a restaurant this expensive on a weekday night. They're too busy paying for their kids' braces or college. "Yes. I'd like that."

He sat across from her. He moved with grace, even in the simple act of seating himself at the table. His shoulders were broad under the light gray silky jacket. His white shirt was neatly pressed. She liked his looks, that he was taller than she; the sharp bone structure of his face and his thick brown hair gave him a dignified demeanor. She couldn't discern any distinct feature about him. He was handsome just the same. Two waiters set his place and handed him a wine list. He didn't open it.

"Did you have any particular wine in mind?" John asked her.

Amira knew little about wines. In college she was too broke for anything but the cheap stuff. Ethan knew less than she did. He attempted to hide his ignorance with an attitude that it was superfluous.

"No."

"Can you provide us with a bottle of Crémant de Loire Brut NV?" John asked the waiter.

"Yes, Dr. Numen."

The waiter collected the wine list and left. They each studied the entrée menu. The waiter came to the table and opened the bottle John had ordered. He poured a small amount of it in the wine glass at John's setting. He took a small sip and set his glass back down—an act she could tell he had done countless times.

"It's fine, Victor, as usual."

The waiter filled his glass and then Amira's.

"To friends and life with passion," John said and lifted his glass for the toast.

Amira Shinwell, wife and mother, looped a strand of hair behind her ear, lifted her glass, touched it to John's with a smile, and had her first drink of sparkling wine since she'd left New York. It felt good.

"What is it you do—I mean in your lab?"

John looked at his wine glass for a moment then to her eyes again. "I'm doing research in cloning. That's what has been occupying all of my time lately. Hopefully this year I'll see the work I've been doing come to fruition.

"If it does, as I expect, there is another area of research I am working on that involves an extensive software system. I have been writing the core pieces of that also. At least that's the high-level description, suitable for dinner conversation. How about you?"

"I take care of our daughter and run the house. Nothing really suitable for dinner conversation either. But I have a plan I hope to implement this year."

"Care to share it?"

"I already have a degree in journalism from NYU. I'm thinking about trying to find a position with a local newspaper or do freelance writing."

"How old is your daughter?"

"A very precocious five."

"Do you have a picture?"

Amira removed her cell phone from her purse, flicked to her favorite picture, and turned the screen toward John. The screen was filled with the smiling face of a child. Big brown eyes, a mane of raven-black hair in a need of brushing, blushed cheeks on an ivory complexion. A miniature of Amira.

"She's beautiful."

"She's my whole world." Amira put the phone back in her purse. "But don't let that innocent face fool you. Yesterday I was driving her home from school. I ask the usual question. 'Anything interesting happen at school today?' She answered, 'My teacher asked me what I wanted to be when I grow up.'

'What did you tell her?'

'I told her I want to be just like my mommy.' So, you can imagine the pride swelling inside me. 'Really?' I said. 'Yep, I told her I want to drink wine and say bad words.'"

"Uh-oh."

"It gets worse."

"Worse?"

"I, of course, am about to wreck the car trying not to laugh when she says, in a casual sort of way, 'Oh, and you can't say *fucking cow* at school. The *cow* part is okay, just not the *fucking*.'"

"That is worse."

"You can imagine the shock. My jaw almost hit my lap. 'Elona!' 'I'm sorry, Mommy, I didn't mean to say it.' We both have to work very hard on not saying that word, I said. 'Okay... the teacher says she wants to have a conference with you next Thursday.'"

John choked on his wine. "So, journalism degree... interesting. Have anything published?"

"As an intern for *The New Yorker* I got a small piece published. That's the extent of my literary achievements. But I love fiction, I've been an avid reader as far back as I can remember. Two years ago, I started on a manuscript for a book but only got about one hundred pages done. It's hard with a toddler in the house."

"I can imagine it would be hard to get settled in behind a keyboard."

"I do all my creative writing longhand, in a notebook. The old-fashioned way. It slows my mind down enough to really think about what I'm writing, and, of course, I can then write anywhere. But even with that I just couldn't keep it up."

"That's a pure Boston accent you have. Do you like it here, in Boston?"

"The place is nice. The people are nice. Good place to raise a fam—." She paused. "May I have some more wine?"

He poured her some more from the bottle.

"I'm supposed to say, 'Great. A wonderful place to raise a family.' And that's true, mostly. It's a nice place for a family. But—being a housewife in Boston isn't what I dreamt about when I was at NYU." Finally, she'd said it out loud, the words she had held back for years. She said them now to a man with whom she hadn't spent twenty minutes.

John was silent for a minute. "Life can throw us curveballs. Taking our best swing at them is all we can do."

The waiter returned to the table. Amira hadn't looked at the menu enough to make a decision. John didn't need to.

"Did you have anything particular in mind?" John asked Amira.

"Not really."

"Do you mind if I order for you?"

"Be my guest."

"We'll spilt the pan-seared beef tenderloin medallions with mushrooms and Marsala sauce, baked au gratin with Romano and Fontina cheeses, accompanied with Vesuvio potatoes and vegetable of the day."

The waiter wrote the order, took their menus, and left.

It will be nice to eat a meal with a man who enjoys meat, Amira thought. *An articulate man, an elegant suit, and perfect wine.* On a cold Wednesday evening, this was a world of change for Amira.

"Your work sounds complicated," Amira said, feeling the need to keep the conversation going.

"Not as much as you might think. Science can involve a lot of boring repetition and mundane observations. But I like the excitement of discovery and doing things not done before. Having a passion, a theory, maybe just an insight that nobody else has and running with it."

Amira laughed quietly, thinking about a life with passion. She supposed John thought like this every day, lived his life like this every day. Spoke like this every day. In the Shinwell household, and in the house where she grew up, no such paradigm existed.

"When you were studying at NYU, what was your favorite modern piece of literature, one from an author still living today, the one that inspired you to write, that gave you passion?"

Amira hadn't expected the question. She hadn't thought about her inspiration for years, suppressing it along with the rest.

"*The Rest Was Folly and Ashes* by Joseph Clarke."

"His first novel, written when he lived in Prague, almost forty years ago," John said.

"Yes, that's right." Amira wasn't surprised he knew, she could feel the raw intelligence sitting across from her.

"Probably ranked top twenty of the most influential novels of the twentieth century. It has themes of love, death, renewal, and the fundamental nature of femininity and masculinity. Very interesting coming from a Jewish girl from Boston."

"Maybe there's more to Jewish girls from Boston than you're giving us credit for."

"Maybe."

"I remember the company brochure said you went to Harvard. I remember it said you have a Ph.D. What was your field of study there?"

"Medical science related."

"Medical science related? That's it? That's all I'm getting from you?"

John smiled and shrugged his shoulders.

"Oh no, I'm not letting you get away with that."

She took her cell phone from her purse and began searching on the internet. "Let's see what Harvard University's website has to say about you." Amira read and scrolled. She looked up from the small glowing screen. "No wonder you don't talk about it. Who would believe you? I don't even understand the titles of any of these papers you wrote."

John remained poker-faced.

Amira looked down at the screen again and read again. "I assume all these awards are a good thing."

"They sound fancy but don't really pay the bills."

"Like *you* have to worry about that."

The waiters came with their plates. Amira put the phone away. The plates of vegetables and potatoes they would share was placed in the middle of the table. One of the waiters refilled their glasses. Without windows to the outside, no indication of the pace of the day or passage of time, only the gentle light from the chandeliers and the candle on the table, reserved intimacy enveloped them. It came somehow with the food.

"Joseph Clarke seems to put a book out about every ten years. Do you like any of his other novels?" John asked.

"Of course, I love them all, but that one is my favorite. Since clearly we can't talk about whatever it is you do in your lab, I'm afraid you are going to have to tell me about yourself. I already know about your father founding the company and that you're on the board of directors. Just begin at the beginning."

"The real beginning happened when I was ten. My father died. We were close. Life was good. That seems like one part of my history frozen in time.

"After he died, my mother never recovered. Soon, I was living with my Aunt Cathy and Uncle Robert. They were great to me. Aunt Cathy couldn't have children, so they raised me as their own. My mother drifted farther and farther away. I guess she was guilt-free enough, knowing I was with good people. We spent summers in Europe. I love Rome. I think I really fell in love with the city when I was in my teens. It's alive, yet holds all this culture and history and priceless works of art. The people there work among mankind's greatest achievements in architecture, engineering, and art and still make time in their day to have a simple lunch at a sidewalk café.

"I acquired a large trust fund at twenty-one, and my ownership in the company when I turned twenty-five. After too many years in school to talk about, I returned to Boston to continue my research at the company. I've put in some long hours; it has been years of research, but I still treat myself to a Christmas-season vacation in Rome. I own an apartment there just outside Vatican City. From my second-story bedroom window, I bet you could shoot an arrow and hit the dome of St. Peter's Basilica."

"Sounds wonderful."

They ate their beef medallions, vegetables, and potatoes with small talk and familiarity. John ordered the perfect dessert. She could feel his eyes on her constantly, but never obvious. He poured the last of the wine into their glasses. She could tell John Numen had poured many servings of wine into many a girl's wine glass. She wondered how many meals in how many restaurants across Boston, Europe, or Rome there had been.

Amira felt good, like she did in her carefree days. However, their empty glasses testified to the length of the evening. The time to go had arrived. He rose from his chair. And moved to pull hers back.

"But they haven't brought my check," Amira said.

"I come here often. I've an understanding with them. If they see me dining with anyone else, I always get the bill, especially if it's a beautiful woman."

Amira blushed and stood. They walked through the tables and out into the wintry air. Amira handed the valet her ticket. His car arrived first. A long, sleek, black BMW coupe. Wide and low to the ground. The valet stopped the car in front of them. The engine purred with power, lazy steam rolling from the tailpipes.

John's eyes met hers. "Thanks for the conversation and the evening," he said. "It was very nice. You're a very lovely, intelligent woman. Treat yourself to a new dress and insist Ethan dine out once in a while. Maybe he isn't as stupid as I think. Maybe it'll work out."

She knew he knew. His words didn't hurt. She knew he was talking about romance and intimacy and passion. She could tell by his tone. John walked to the open driver's door.

"Goodbye," John said. He looked at her for a moment, then he was behind the wheel and shutting the door. The car shot forward out of the parking lot into the street, the red taillights disappearing into the traffic.

OCTOBER 21, 2021

The sun hadn't come up yet on that Sunday morning. I sat in the dark living room watching the news. It had been a long night. Uncle Robert was getting worse. Aunt Cathy was with him all night. She came in the room, sat down beside me, and laid her head on my shoulder.

"His last coherent sentence was about you," Cathy said.

"What did he say?"

"He wanted to know when you were coming home again. I think he could feel his mind slipping away and wanted to see you one last time."

I patted Cathy's hand. Neither of us spoke, content to let the drone of the television fill the void. The news program came back from commercial. "In international news, Cuba's dictator Raul Castro died yesterday from what government news sources say was natural causes. He came to power in 2008 when his brother Fidel Castro became ill. Over the last fifteen years, Raul has ruled the country in much the same way as his older brother, even after Fidel Castro's death in 2016. Many within the U.S. government had hoped for progress in Cuba on the human rights front and progress toward democracy, but little has changed since 1959. News of his death, as with Fidel's, has resulted in spontaneous street celebrations in Miami among exiled Cubans there." The screen showed people in the streets of Miami waving the Cuban and American flags. "Now, with the death of Raul, hope is higher in both the U.S. government and in underground democratic organizations inside Cuba that a democratic government will come to power. Raul Castro was ninety years old."

I turned the volume down with the remote.

"The world is changing," Cathy said. "You know Robert knew you

were doing your research at the company, like your dad. That made him very proud."

"Mrs. Edward!" called the nurse from the doorway of the bedroom. We rushed into the room to see Uncle Robert motionless on the bed, the heart monitor bedside the bed showing a straight line and solid tone. "I was just in the bathroom for a minute," the nurse explained.

"It's okay," Cathy said.

I walked over and turned off the monitor. Aunt Cathy began to sob. The world certainly was changing, and I would do my best to make it change the way I wanted.

FEBRUARY 12, 2019

THE GIFT

On a Tuesday afternoon, while Ethan was away at a conference in Balti-more, Amira sat on the couch at her parents' house watching television. Her cell phone rang. The number was local, but she didn't recognize it.

"Hello?" Amira said.

"Hi. This is John." Amira felt butterflies. "I hope I haven't caught you at a bad time."

"Hi. No, not at all," Amira answered. She rose from the couch and began casually walking through the kitchen to the door that led to the backyard.

"Sorry to call you like this, but I got your number from a service. I didn't know any other way to get in touch with you."

"It's okay, I don't mind."

"I wanted to tell you I enjoyed our dinner."

"Me too." Amira replied. Not saying she'd thought about it every day since.

"And I have something I'd like to give you. A gift. I was wondering if I could interest you in dinner again tonight?"

Yes. No. Wait, I can't think. Of course, he knows Ethan is out of town. Amira had reached the backyard undetected by her mother or Elona.

"I'm at my parents' right now. I don't think I could be dressed for a fancy dinner anytime soon."

"Nothing fancy, very casual. I'll cook you dinner at my place."

Amira's pulse doubled. It sounded like someone else saying, "Okay."

"Great. I'll text you my address and the entry code for the building.

About six o'clock?"

"Okay," was all Amira could get out again.

"See you then." John said and her phone went silent.

Amira looked at the time on her phone; it was three o'clock, her hair was a mess, and she had no makeup on. She walked back in the house. "Mom, can you watch Elona for a while?"

Amira parked her SUV across the street from John's building. The winter had been relatively snowless so the drive hadn't been bad. Blue jeans, boots, thin jade sweater and a brown leather jacket seemed appropriate to her. When she entered the code John had texted, the door opened. She took the elevator to the top floor, the penthouse, of course. John opened the door with a big smile. He looked handsome and relaxed in his blue jeans, socks, and Patriots T-shirt.

"Please, come in. I'm so glad you came."

Amira felt flushed again and stepped inside. She liked the way he looked at her. She let it soak in. John shut the door. She felt the uneasiness again, being alone with him.

The ceiling was high. A spacious living room area spread in front of her, a fireplace with a flat-screen TV above it. A bay window showcased downtown Boston in the distance. The sofa was leather and the coffee table in front had three stacks of books covering it. The walls on each side of the fireplace were shelved and filled with books. More books rested on a low shelf below the bay window. Beyond the living room she could see the kitchen. The walls and ceiling were painted taupe, and all the trimming around the rooms were white.

John led her to the kitchen. All the cabinets were aged white. A long counter with bar-height chairs separated the living room from the kitchen. The table, set for two, waited at the other end of the kitchen.

"Have a seat and watch me prepare the best iron-skillet rib-eye dinner you will ever have," John said, motioning to a chair at the counter. "Would you like some wine?"

"That would be great." She removed her jacket and placed it on the back of the chair at the end of the counter.

John poured them some wine from an open bottle sitting on the counter by the stove. He handed her a glass.

"To friends and life with passion," he said.

They touched glasses and took a sip. John moved back to the counter and continued to slice the mushrooms in a small pile. Resting on a metal pan were two marbled steaks covered with seasonings.

This was the first time she had taken a long look at him. His shoulders were broad, it hadn't been just the suit. His stomach was as flat as a board and his jeans fit him very nice and snug on his rear.

Why didn't she and Ethan cook this way? Part of it was certainly because of custom. Marriage is prone to be highjacked by custom and predictability. Custom carries its own security, its own comfort. It easily changes into laziness.

And then there was being Jewish. It came with its own set of rules, regulations, and social pressure and structure. And the overriding fear of change. Ethan feared change in their pre-defined roles more than anything else.

"I have salad, too. It's already done and sitting in the fridge."

She watched him now, how he moved, even the simple act of slicing mushrooms. He went to the cabinet to get a pan to sauté the mushrooms, then reached for the cooking wine. He moved with precision and grace. Strong and confident. For the first time in a long time Amira felt herself getting aroused from just watching a man. He was talking, but she wasn't paying any attention until he stopped.

"Would you?" John asked again.

"I—uh."

"Music?"

"Yes, I guess so."

John swiped at a screen on the wall near the refrigerator and low, smooth saxophone jazz came from nowhere. Amira had told herself on the drive to his apartment that she could stop this any time she wanted. Could still stop it even now. But it was becoming bigger than she was, gaining its own momentum. Picking her up and taking her to the place she wanted to go so badly, but was afraid of at the same time. She was also afraid of silence and realized she hadn't said much since she'd walked in.

"What's this gift you claim to have for me?"

"You want to know now?"

"Of course."

John stopped slicing mushrooms. "I was going to wait till after dinner, but if you insist."

He opened the cabinet near her and picked up two boxes wrapped in Valentine's Day motif wrapping paper. "Valentine's Day is only two days away, so they didn't even ask how I wanted it wrapped. Sorry." He handed her one of the boxes.

It wasn't light, but not heavy either. She pulled at the ribbon until it came loose, then tore away the red and white paper. She opened the box to find a book. She looked at the title and author: *In The Half Moon Light* by Joseph Clarke.

"I've never seen this book."

"I know. Nobody has. It's his latest. It won't be at the bookstores for another month."

"How?"

"I guess my parents got invited to some pretty exclusive parties. My dad met Joseph at one of them not long before his second novel was published. They were both big offshore fishing enthusiasts. So, my dad took him. They were great friends ever since. He spent many summer vacations and Christmas holidays at our house. If I hadn't gone to live with my aunt and uncle, I'd have probably have gone to live with him, in L.A."

"Why didn't you tell me?"

"I'm telling you now. Open the front cover and look inside."

Amira did. Handwritten on the inside of the cover, it read:

To Amira,

The thing that separates us from the apes isn't the invention of tools or machines. It is the invention of fiction. The world can always use another good writer.

Best Wishes,

Joseph Clarke

"Oh, my God. I don't know what to say. It's the best gift I've ever been given."

John handed her the second box.

"I don't know what's in here, but there's no way it can outdo that." She tore away the wrapping paper and opened the box. Inside was a leather-bound journal with three hundred lined blank pages and a single number-two pencil. Amira held it in her hands. She opened the cover and heard the new leather groan. She flipped the blank pages and the scent of the virgin paper brushed her face. Tears came to her eyes.

"I was wrong. This is the best gift."

John moved to her and took her hand. The tears came faster. She stood from the chair and he held her. He put his fingers under her chin and raised her face.

Over the years, John would think about this moment and remember it as when he fell in love with her, without even knowing it at the time. John's lips found hers. He kissed her gently and she moved her lips to kiss him back. They kissed and held each other tighter. Her breathing grew deeper and she let out a soft moan. They kissed again and John held her by the shoulders and covered her face with gentle kisses. He pulled away, took her by the hand, and led her past the living room, down the hallway to his bedroom.

Their lovemaking was passionate and fulfilling. Amira had found an oasis in her desert. When it was over, John pulled slowly away and looked at her as large gentle tears rolled out of the corners of her eyes and she buried her face on his shoulder. He held her and ran one hand over her until he could feel her shoulders relax and she had wiped away the tears.

Amira looked up at him. "I have these feelings for you... they don't match my knowledge of you. We've spent a couple of hours together over a dinner and I cannot stop thinking about you."

"I feel the same way. I've been thinking about you too." John took a deep breath and squeezed her tight for a moment.

Amira stared at the ceiling. *Now what?* She lay still and quiet for a long time. "So, where does that leave us?"

"Do you love him?"

"No, there hasn't been love in that relationship in a long time." Amira was embarrassed by her answer.

"That's all I need to know. I want to keep seeing you, whenever we can, and we'll see how it goes between us and where it leads." John meant what he was saying. He had her best interests in mind, and he didn't want to cause her any of the pain that he thought an affair would bring. "I've a very flexible schedule for my work. I'm sure we can find time to spend together."

"That sounds like a good start to me."

She relaxed. She was glad it wasn't over before it really began. She wanted badly to be with a man she desired. Even if it was stolen time together.

"I don't want to get out of bed with you to cook," John said.

"Me either."

John took his cell phone from the side table and punched up the app for Tung Tse Chinese Restaurant. "How about Chinese food?"

Amira looked around the room for the first time. Both bedside tables, the desk in the corner, the dresser, and the floor around the bed were covered in books.

"What do you like to read?"

"Everything."

"Ever heard of a Kindle?"

"I have a couple of those. Each one has about a thousand books on it… Chinese?"

"Sounds wonderful," Amira replied.

"Done. They say a forty-minute delivery time."

Amira slid over on top of him. "Just enough time."

Three hours later, empty cartons of Chinese food lay about John's bedroom, and the bottle of wine from the kitchen sat emptied. Amira had dressed, gathered herself, kissed John good-bye at the door, and left. He was back in bed. His phone rang. He looked, hoping it was Amira. He was disappointed.

"Hi, Mom."

"Hi, John. Did I wake you?"

Just from that short sentence John could tell that she had been drinking.

"I'm just watching TV."

"How have you been? Seems forever since I've heard from you."

"I've been good. You know, working hard."

"I like that you work at your father's place. It has been so long since I've seen it. I should come to Boston and visit soon."

John knew she wouldn't. A long silence followed.

44

"Or you could come to Manhattan and visit me."

"I will, next Christmas—I promise."

"You sound just like your father now over the phone. My God, next year you'll turn thirty. Where have the years gone?" Another long silence. "Me and Mark are going to Japan next week. Would you like to come with us?"

"Sorry, I have to work." John didn't know who Mark was. He didn't want to know.

"Oh yes, your research. I forgot. When we get back, I'll be sure to call and tell you about it." She slurred the last part. John knew by now how to pick out the words.

"I'll talk to you then." John took the opening to end the conversation.

"Bye, dear."

"Bye, Mom."

John opened a book to read. Then put it back down. He didn't need to read to sleep tonight. In his dreams, he was with Amira.

APRIL 10, 2022

The months following Amira's first visit to my apartment were the happiest I'd ever known. I diligently watched the monkeys' progress, and I finished the CAT scan system in anticipation of the new arrivals. Amira and I saw each other often, usually at lunch. I would return to work with the scent of her still on me and casually pass Ethan in the hallway. Sometimes she came to my apartment in the mornings after taking Elona to school and on Saturday afternoons when she could make an excuse to be out of the house.

One weekend in late April, when Ethan was away on business travel, we saw a movie while holding hands. It sounds so trivial now, but I remember it being a big deal. Out and about like a normal couple, doing normal date things. The times when we were together passed at twice the speed of a normal day. We talked about literature and philosophy and why the world was the way it was and how it could be better and how we would change it. I was not really much of a talker; I think I was a bit too practical to really be chatty. Except when I was around her. She inspired me and opened my mind to different subject matters, and we talked and talked for hours on end without any of it being forced or trite. She simply brought out the best in me. And I believed I did the same for her. We were happy and content and stimulated in each other's company. And that was all we needed. That night, we ate dinner at a restaurant before rushing back to my apartment. She always had to go too soon, leaving me there with the sweat-dampened sheets and silence.

By mid-June the five expectant monkeys had each given birth to healthy replicas of Petri. It was a time of great excitement, and I spent long hours in the lab studying and observing the mother-infant pairs and performing tests on the infants. By September the newborn monkeys were eating solid food and thriving. They were developing normally and I felt confident I had achieved a 100 percent success rate for embryo implantation.

Things were going well, but that was about to change. At first, I was sure it was for the better, only to find out it was for the worse.

SEPTEMBER 2019

SEPARATION

"Amira, come here."

Ethan's command came from the study. Supper baked in the oven. Elona was watching TV in the living room. It was early evening on a Friday. Amira stopped mid-stroke in ironing Elona's dress. She knew that tone all too well. Whatever Ethan wanted to talk about couldn't be good. Her hope for a peaceful weekend winked out of existence in an instant. She placed the iron on the counter. Her mind raced. *We've been very careful. No texts. No emails. I always call him, never the other way around. I always use the prepaid phone. It's still hidden in the lining of my purse. He hasn't found that, my purse is in here.*

Amira stood in the doorway of the study. Ethan sat at his desk, his laptop in front of him.

"Why is there an email here from *Boston Magazine* informing you that they have received your resume for a position there?"

"Where's the email? When did I get it?"

"In your inbox. It just arrived."

Damn it, of all the luck. I applied only yesterday.

Ethan checking Amira's email was nothing new. Some battles weren't worth fighting.

"Elona's been in school for almost a month now. I thought I'd try to find some part-time work. Like I said, use that journalism degree I have." And some battles are.

"Why do you insist on disobeying me? We have discussed this idea at least twice before and I told you that you will not work outside this house! I am the husband, I decide how this house is run! I am deleting

THE APOTHEOSIS

your email account!"

Delete my account, like I can't make another? A secret one. But I'm not hiding this from you. I'm not your slave. The ball of anger grew in Amira's chest. Down the hall, Elona peered around the corner. Amira sensed her and looked to her right. Their eyes met. Amira could see the dread on her child's face of another argument brewing. If it was about anything else she'd let it go, if only to save Elona from having to hear another one. To save the weekend and next week from having to watch Ethan brood about, silent and sulking. The anger in Ethan's eyes was as blatant as the sadness and fear in Elona's. But she was determined to stand her ground over this. Ethan and his threats had gone too far.

"Elona, go to your room and shut the door, please." Amira's voice was calm but forced. Elona stood silent and still. She dropped her eyes to the floor. Amira knew what she was contemplating: *If I don't go to my room, the fight won't happen.* "Now! Elona."

The child ran to her room.

The door shut.

Amira turned to glare at Ethan. The ball grew. *How dare you make me have to speak to Elona like that?*

🧬

John opened the door to Amira, red-eyed, red-nosed, clutching her purse and a tissue.

"It must be bad for you to drive here in the pouring rain. What happened?"

"Ethan took her." Amira came inside and sat on the couch.

"Elona?"

"Yes."

"Where?" John sat beside her.

"He didn't say, but I'd expect to his parents' apartment in New York. She doesn't even have a change of clothes."

"What was this fight over?"

"The job I applied for... and he threatened to delete my email account." Amira held her head in her hands. "There was a lot of yelling and screaming and him quoting scripture... I told him he could go fuck himself in the ass with that book."

John smirked.

"I don't know where that came from... I swore I'd quit talking like that."

"It's never too late to start again."

"It's not funny. I don't want every time Elona hears the F-word for it to have come from her mother."

"Sorry."

"Oh, God, I hope Elona didn't hear that... I was just so... so angry." Amira sighed and sat up straight. "He stormed out of the study to Elona's room and picked her up and headed for the door. I tried to stop him and he pushed me."

"He pushed you?"

"Yes... twice. Once inside the apartment and once in the hallway. Elona was crying. I was crying. I tried to stop him from getting on the elevator, and he pushed me to the floor. The neighbors came out. I was so embarrassed. The elevator opened and he was gone with her. I just sat there and cried."

"Are you hurt?"

"No, just my pride... and dignity. I don't know how I'll be able to look my neighbors in the eye again."

"I wouldn't worry about them. And if he's heading to the grandparents' place, I wouldn't worry about Elona either. At least not about being clothed, fed, bathed, and teeth brushed. From the stories you tell me, she has both sets of grandparents wrapped around her finger. And she knows it. They'll get her to feeling better and probably have her call you as soon as they understand what happened."

"You're right."

John wrapped an arm around her. She let out another deep breath and rested her head on his shoulder.

"Do you want something to eat?"

"I'm not hungry."

"Want to watch TV?"

Amira shook her head.

"Would you like to go to my lab and see my new baby monkeys?"

Amira had been hoping for weeks to see the new arrivals. She sat back to see his face.

"That's unfair for you to ask me that now; you've been putting me off all this time and now you're just using it as a ploy to get me to feel better."

"Nobody ever told me I had to be fair."

The slightest smile came to her lips.

🧬🧬🧬

When they entered the lab, the overhead lights came on. Cold air met Amira's face. The whirl of fans inside the rack of computers filled the space with an annoying hum. Amira gazed around in amazement. In the middle of the room, a large machine sat on top of a table. A bundle of multicolored wires came out of the gray metal housing and ran along the underside of a robotic arm. The arm extended out over the table to a work area with a large black metal cylinder that stood to the ceiling. A panel of switches, LED lights, and a flat-panel computer screen were mounted to the side, at the base of the cylinder. Underneath the screen, on the tabletop, sat a keyboard and a mouse. Amira looked at the computer monitor and could see a live video feed of the end of the robotic arm inside the cylinder. A mechanical hand, with a delicate gold needle-like tool extending from the center, showed on the screen. Amira looked back at the arm, where it came out of the cylinder, and followed it back to its base. She noticed the rack of four blank computer screens and a keyboard.

"This must be your miracle. The accumulation of all those IQ points bouncing around in that mind of yours. Your masterpiece."

"I've worked on it the last four years. It's the device that enables me to extract the nucleus from the donor cell and replace it with the nucleus of the clone cell in just the right way to get the key proteins in place. It constructs the internal working of the cell so that it's perfect, of course, using those computers on the wall behind you and software developed by yours truly. It stimulates the nucleus of the donor egg to begin cell division and building of the embryo. It begins there inside that cylinder."

Amira looked to the left of the table and saw a separate device. A table at one end and a vertical long, hollow cylinder at the other. She paused for a moment. "That is a CAT scan machine, right?"

"I use it to study the development of the brain in the cloned monkeys. I've a few ideas I'm researching. If you look at the computer screen behind the table, you can see the images. The software I created is making

52

a detailed analysis. It takes a while, so I let it run pretty much twenty-four hours a day."

John opened a drawer in the desk next to him and removed a bag of almonds. He opened the bag and placed half a handful into his right pants pocket. He held some out for Amira. "Put these in your pocket." She did. He placed the bag back in the drawer and closed it. John pointed to the far end of the room past the CAT scan. "It's through that door at the end; the monkeys are waiting."

From behind the Plexiglas, the monkeys screeched their excitement at having visitors. Petri ran to the platform in front of the door, her infant hanging onto her back. Amira noticed each adult monkey had a small infant clinging to her somewhere. Each infant had a different-colored plastic band around one of its wrists. John went to the door, unlatched and opened it. Petri scampered out onto John's shoulder. Her baby had a red wristband. The other monkeys moved toward the door. John closed it.

"Amira, this is Petri, and riding along with Petri is her baby, Petri Three. Petri, this is Amira."

Amira reached out slowly and stroked Petri on her shoulder.

"Give her an almond."

Amira did and laughed at the way Petri snatched it from her hand, bit it in half, and gave half to the baby she was carrying. The baby ate the almond with the enthusiasm of its mother.

"She's so stinking cute! Can I hold her?"

"Take a few almonds out of your pocket and hold them in the palm of your hand so she can see them. I'll move so she can get from my shoulder to yours. For almonds, she would let the devil himself hold her."

That was exactly what happened. A minute later Petri and Petri Three were sitting happily on Amira's shoulder eating every almond handed their way. Soon Amira's almonds were gone, and Petri returned to John's shoulder. John opened the Plexiglas door again and she hopped back inside. John threw the remaining almonds in to the other monkeys, closed the door, and locked the latch. Amira stood silently. The smile that had been on her face was gone. She stared at the monkeys inside the enclosed area. A lightening flash strobed through the overhead domed skylight and thunder cracked. Rain drummed on the roof.

"I'm leaving him." She didn't look at John standing behind her. "God knows I have tried to make it work, tried for Elona, tried for my parents—I just can't." A tear rolled down her cheek. She kept looking at the monkeys. "It's more than just the loss of love or passion or intimacy. He will not let me grow. He wants to keep me in a cage, just like these monkeys, and he'll never change."

"How can I help? What do you need from me?" John put his arms around her.

"Patience," she said. "I'm going to talk to him when he comes back. It's going to take a while for me to get my own place, as well as get Elona and myself settled there. We won't be able to see each other till the separation is complete."

"I understand."

"Thanks. There's one other thing you can do for me," Amira said.

"Anything."

She faced him. "Take me back to your place and bring me to your bed."

When Ethan returned the next evening, Amira felt ready. She spent the first hour with Elona, hearing about the new doll Grandmother bought her and the new clothes. Ethan didn't say a word to Amira the whole evening, or during dinner. When dinner ended, Ethan secluded himself in the study. Amira put Elona to bed.

Amira took a shower, changed into sweatpants and a T-shirt, and went to the study. Ethan sat at his desk reading the Tanakh. When she walked in, he continued reading as if she wasn't there.

"Ethan, we need to talk," Amira said.

"No, we don't. You are not working outside this house. That is my final word on the matter. I hoped time alone would help you understand that fact. Elona needs you at home." Ethan turned a page of the book, pressing it down firmly with his hand.

"I'm leaving," Amira said.

Ethan looked up from the book. "Leaving? Where're you going? It's ten o'clock at night."

"I mean I'm moving out, with Elona. I want a divorce."

"I forbid it."

"Ethan, please. We need to talk. We have to talk about how best to handle this for Elona." Amira kept her voice calm and her tone even.

Ethan stood from the chair and went around the desk. He pointed his finger at Amira's face. "I forbid it! You'll not destroy this family!"

She stood her ground. "I'm not your child. I'm not asking your permission. This is not a family. We're two people living separate lives within the same house. There's no love here." Amira raised her voice at the end. "You want to control me like I'm your servant, but I'm not going to live my life this way!"

Amira's defiance, in Ethan's eyes, was a defiance of God. God had ordained the husband as the authority in the marriage. It threatened him, but mostly it scared him. He was losing, or as he now realized, he had already lost her. Anger widened his eyes and veins protruded from his forehead. He didn't know how to stop it. His open hand came up out of frustrated reflex and landed sharply on the side of Amira's face before either of them knew it, leaving the red imprint of his fingers.

She gasped from the pain. He had never struck her before. Her eyes went back to his. She could see the outward expression of anger, but she could smell the fear. Her eyes did not flinch. Her stare never left his.

"I'm leaving. You can beat me if you want, but that fact will not change!"

He clenched his fist in front of Amira. Instead of striking her again, he grabbed the book from the desk and threw it against the wall behind her. "I'll not grant you a divorce, ever! You'll be back here in a week. Do you understand? I'll fight you every step of the way. I will not help you break up our family."

"I don't expect any help." Amira slammed the door on her way out.

The next morning, after she took Elona to school, as soon as the bank was open Amira withdrew half of the money in their checking and saving accounts. She opened up her own account at a different bank and calculated that she had enough money to last for a year. *By then I need to have a job.* From there, she took the laptop to a Starbucks to search for an apartment.

She settled at the table and opened the laptop. She took a sip from the latte and waited for the login screen. *I don't think Ethan would put spyware on my computer. But I can't be sure. I'll just have to risk it.* Into Google she typed "Craigslist Boston." Under "Housing" she selected "apt/housing." Next she selected "All Apartments."

The screen filled with pictures, sorted by newest to oldest. Amira scrolled through the page. *Something close to Elona's school.* Her attention was drawn to the picture of an empty living room, well-lit, an open kitchen with golden-oak flooring, and cabinets with black granite countertops at the far end.

Rent: $2,500 / Month
Broker Fee: One Month
Available Date: 09/12/2019
Beds: 2
Baths: 2
Pet: No Pets

Features: Central Air, Dishwasher, Eat-in Kitchen, Granite Countertops, Hardwood Floors, Laundry, Modern Bath, Modern Kitchen, Near T, New/Renovated Kitchen, Parking For Rent, Storage, Near Public Transportation

Spacious 2 bed 2 bath apartment located on Jacob Street. Gorgeous updated kitchen, granite, dishwasher. Modern bathroom, good closet space, windows, gleaming hardwood floor in kitchen and bath and crown moldings. Steps to Star Market and C-Line. Great restaurants within walking distance. Central A/C. Exclusive laundry and storage space right outside of unit.

Call or Text Lisa 508-516-3877

That is a very short drive to Elona's school. And it's available tomorrow. Amira punched the number on her phone.

"Hello?" a young woman's voice answered.

"Hi, I'm calling about the apartment you have for rent. Is it still available?"

"Yes, it is still available."

"I am very interested, can I come see it?"

"Great, I'm the broker. What time would you like the viewing?"

"Now?"

"I can't right now, but I could meet you there in an hour."

"Works for me."

Amira wrote the address on the Starbucks napkin.

"Thanks, see you soon."

Amira spent the next forty minutes making a to-do list and sipping her latte before leaving for the appointment. Like all of Boston, maple trees lined the sidewalks of Jacob Street. Metro bus tracks separated the two sides. Businesses and brick apartment buildings occupied most of the block. A Whole Foods wasn't far away.

The broker, a smartly dressed woman in her thirties, stood in front of a red brick building with rich-toned maple doors. The broker spotted her as soon as she stepped out of the car. They shook hands.

"Hi, I'm Lisa."

"Amira."

"Let me show you the place."

They proceeded to the door and the broker opened it with a security keypad. They took the stairs to the second floor. Just three doors down.

It was everything the ad claimed it to be. Stainless steel appliances, granite countertops, domed lights on the ceiling. The bedrooms were down a short hall. Amira fell in love with it immediately. It smelled of fresh paint, new carpet, and new life.

"I'll take it."

"When would you like to move in?"

"Day after tomorrow."

"That may be a challenge. There is paperwork for the lease agreement and a credit check. You must pay the first month's rent and the broker fee of $2,500."

"If I pay the broker fee in cash," Amira removed an envelope from her purse, "and made it $3,000, would that help to get the paperwork done in time?" She removed thirty $100 bills from the envelope.

Lisa took the money with a smile. "Yes, I'm sure we can find a way."

"And perhaps you know a moving company that can find a way to fit me in that day? There isn't that much to move and I'd being willing to pay extra for the inconvenience."

"I know just the company… my brother owns it."

Amira sat in her car, excited and nervous. *It's real and it's about damn time.*

THE PARENTS

Sharon and Guy Levitt were surprised to see Amira and Elona arrive un-announced. The first sign that something was wrong. After supper, with Elona out of earshot in the living room watching cartoons, Amira's mother seized the opportunity.

"Are you going to tell us or are we going to have to guess?" Sharon said.

"I'm leaving Ethan, divorcing."

Guy furrowed his forehead.

"All marriages go through rough times. Are you and Ethan sure about this?" Sharon asked.

"It's my idea, not Ethan's. As a matter of fact, he even said he would not grant me a divorce."

"Why do you want this?" Guy asked.

"I don't love him. The love is dead. It's been so for a long time. He just wants to keep me at home to do his laundry and cook his food. I want more out of my life. I want a career. I want to respect the man I love and I want to be respected and loved."

"Ethan's father is a rabbi and this would be a very big scandal for his family. You will be *mesorevet get*," Sharon said.

"I'll go to the rabbinical court; they can make him," Amira said.

"What if they don't? You can never remarry," Sharon said.

"Maybe I'll become Baptist!"

"Amira!"

"He actually slapped me and pushed me to the ground during our last fight. It will only get worse from here."

Everyone sat silently for a minute.

"Where will you stay? What will you do?" Sharon asked.

"I already have a deposit on an apartment, I did it this morning. I move in the day after tomorrow. I'll get a job. I have a degree and I did work while in college, I'm sure I can find work. Until then, I've half of the money Ethan and I have saved."

"Already you have an apartment and separated the money?" Sharon said.

Amira took a deep breath. "Mother, Father, please. I'm your daughter, you've raised me to do the right thing. I'd not do this if I didn't feel very strongly about it. I need you to trust me and trust my judgment... because... I'm going to need your support."

Sharon's eyes filled with tears. She stood up from the table without saying a word and went to the bedroom.

Amira's father cleared his throat. "It's okay, she just needs time. She's just worried about you. We love you, and you do have our support."

Amira smiled, got up and walked over to her still-seated father and gave him a hug. "Can we stay here for a few nights?"

"Of course. I need to call Ethan and tell him where you and Elona are, though."

"Thanks, Daddy." A kiss landed on his cheek.

Amira went to the living room and announced to Elona that they were spending the night at Grandmother and Grandfather Levitt's house and sleeping together in her old room. Elona squealed with excitement.

THE APARTMENT

The next day, after taking Elona to school, Amira stopped by the U-Haul office. She bought as many boxes as could fit in her SUV, four rolls of boxing tape, and a black Sharpie. When she arrived at her apartment building, instead of her usual reserved spot in the garage, she parked at the curb by the front entrance. She got out and walked to the front door. The doorman on duty, Frank, stood at his usual position. She liked him. He was about fifty, always polite, and looked to be in reasonable shape, so she didn't mind asking him to help with the groceries from time to time. He opened the door for her as she approached.

"Good morning, Mrs. Shinwell."

"Hi, Frank. I've a favor to ask you. I've a bunch of empty boxes in the back of my car. Do you think you could get a cart and bring them up to my apartment for me?"

"Of course, Mrs. Shinwell. David can tend to the front door while I do that."

"Here's the key to the car so you can get the back open."

"Yes, ma'am."

The solitary elevator ride felt odd. The same carpet on the floor, new, installed earlier in the year, same wood veneer paneling on all the walls except the one with the door. Same button panel, yet things felt different.

She opened the door to a quiet apartment. Dirty dishes sat in the sink and on the table. She packed a suitcase with clothes and toiletries for herself and Elona. As she finished, the front doorbell rang. She opened the door to find a solemn Frank standing with a cart full of her collapsed boxes.

"Are you and Mr. Shinwell moving, ma'am?"

"No, Frank, only me."

"That is too bad, Mrs. Shinwell. You're one of my favorite people in the building."

"Thank you, Frank. And you have always been one of mine." Amira handed him a ten-dollar bill. He handed her the keys to the car.

"I've told you before that you don't need to tip me."

"And I've told you I want to."

"Let me know if you need anything else," he said.

Amira ran out of boxes and made another trip to the U-Haul office to buy more. Frank again helped move them from the car to the apartment. As soon as the packing was finished, it was time to get Elona from school. She left the packed boxes stacked against a wall in each room, got the suitcase, and left before Ethan returned from work.

◗◖◗◖

After Amira picked Elona up from school, they made a trip to the mall for a new pair of shoes. She took Elona to the food court for an ice cream.

"How's the Rocky Road?" Amira asked as she sat across the table watching the wild-haired child concentrate on the tasty task at hand.

"It's so good. But you never let me have Rocky Road before. Why?"

"It's because of the marshmallows."

"But they are the BEST part! Why?"

"It isn't important. Just know, that from now on, when you are with me you can get Rocky Road any time you want."

"And when Daddy is with us?"

"You don't miss much, do you? No, I don't think your father will let you have Rocky Road."

"Okay," Elona said quickly between licks to keep the ice cream off the cone. She didn't like the cone to get soggy before she ate it. "Aren't you having any, Mommy?"

"No, I'm not hungry." Amira took a deep breath. "There's something I want to talk about with you. It's important."

"What?" Elona asked between licks.

62

"It's about me and Daddy. We're having problems."

"I heard you guys yelling again last night."

Amira cringed. "Well, Daddy and I are having a lot of arguments, and... well... I think it is best if you and I live somewhere else."

Elona stopped eating her ice cream. "Where?"

"In our own apartment, near Daddy, but not the same one."

"In the same building?"

"No."

"Are you and Daddy getting a divorce?"

"Where did you learn that word?"

"From school. Alex's parents are divorced and so are Cindy's. That means that the mommy and daddy don't live together any more, right?"

"Yes, that's what that means, and yes, I believe Daddy and I are going to get divorced. But you'll have your own room with the same things you have now."

"What about Daddy?"

"We won't be far from him and you can see him all the time."

"You promise?"

"Yes, I do. You'll have a room with him too, for when you are with him."

"And you promise I'll still have all my stuffed animals?"

"Yes, I do."

"Wait till I tell Alex!" Elona smiled and licked the ice cream off the cone.

🧬

Amira was chopping vegetables next to her mother in the kitchen when her cell phone, lying on the counter, chimed. She saw Ethan's number on the display.

"Hello," Amira answered.

"What do you think you are doing?"

"I'm getting mine and Elona's things ready to move," Amira answered, keeping her voice low so Elona, watching TV in the other room, couldn't hear. She glanced at her mother, who continued to chop carrots, her back turned. Obviously listening.

"You have no job, you aren't going to be able to pay rent or put food on the table. Where do you *think* you are moving?"

"I found an apartment. You may have changed the password to the online bank account, but I am on the account. You don't need a password if you withdraw in person. I took half the money from the checking and saving accounts. That will do until I find work." Silence from the other end of the phone. "Hello?"

"This childish tantrum you're throwing is hurting your daughter and your family. God has ordained the husband with total authority. I will not give you a divorce! You'll be back here, you'll see."

"No, I won't," Amira answered, but Ethan had already hung up.

Amira rolled out of bed before the alarm clock the next day. She waited outside Ethan's building in the crisp air as Boston started its workday, drinking coffee until the moving truck with three muscular men arrived. Amira rode with them and their dollies on the service elevator to the apartment. In less than two hours the furniture from Elona's room, the guest room, a couch and the television from the living room were moved from their places to the back of the moving van and covered with blankets. The boxes were next, which took less than thirty minutes.

When they arrived at the new apartment, the boxes were removed from the truck first and placed at one end of the living room. They occupied a quarter of the floor space, even though they were stacked three high. Amira directed the placement of each piece of furniture, including setting up a bed in each bedroom. It took half of the time to unload as it did to load. By lunchtime Amira stood alone in her very first apartment.

She estimated she had five hours before her mother showed up with Elona. She sorted through the boxes stacked in the living room and moved out the boxes marked "Elona's Room" and "Elona's Bath." She wanted Elona's space to be totally prepared when she arrived. In two hours, the bed was made, the clothes hung in the closet, and her toys and books placed just like they had been at the old apartment.

While she was in the kitchen sorting through the boxes labeled "Kitchen Stuff," the doorbell rang. She opened the door to see her father standing behind her mother, who was holding Elona by the hand. Elona, her hair tamed by a ponytail, gave a nervous smile. She stood in her favorite purple dress and shoes, unconcerned that it clashed dramatically with her green coat.

"Mommy!" Elona came to Amira.

"There's my baby."

She gave Elona a long hug and removed her jacket. Sharon stepped in and also gave Amira a hug. Amira could feel her mother's eyes moving around the apartment.

"She was dead set on the purple dress," Sharon said.

"I know, the coat for it was in a box here." Amira noticed her father carrying a pizza box. "Oh, Daddy, thank you so much. I'm starving." Amira took a long sniff over the box. "Cheese pizza, perfect!"

She gave her father a hug too. Turning to her daughter, she saw Elona studying the large stack of boxes in the living room. "Would you like to see your room?"

Elona nodded. Amira took her by the hand down the short hallway to the doorway on the right. Elona went into the room first. The lamps on each side of the bed were on and they gave the room a warm glow. Elona walked around, not saying anything, studying the room's contents. Amira opened the door leading to the bathroom.

"You even have your very own bathroom."

Elona looked through the doorway to see her toys already in the tub. She smiled and looked up at Amira.

"I like it."

Amira bent over and placed her hands on each side of Elona's face and gave her a big kiss on the forehead. "Good! Now let's eat. I'm starving."

Amira found the box with the plates and got out four. In a different box were the glasses.

"Sorry, I haven't made it to the grocery store yet. All we have is water from the tap." Amira pulled out three glasses and Elona's spill-proof plastic cup with a picture of Tweety Bird on the side.

Sharon pulled out a tablecloth from a box on the counter and spread it on the carpet where a table should be. "We'll go this week and find you a dining table," she said.

"A cheap one," Amira replied.

Guy put the pizza box in the center of the tablecloth and let out a grunt as he sat on the floor. Elona giggled and plopped down beside him.

"I hope the table is in place before I have to eat here again. My knees won't like this too much." He grinned and tousled his granddaughter's hair.

Elona clapped her hands. "I like eating on the floor, like the Japanese."

"That's right, Elona," Amira said, surprised. "The Japanese do sit on the floor. How did you know that?"

"From a story the teacher read to us in school," Elona said as she settled down onto her heels, like the pictures in the book the teacher had shown to the class.

Amira sat beside her, copying Elona's position. "I say we declare this evening Japanese evening then."

"Can we eat with chopsticks, too?" Elona's eyes grew wide.

Amira put a plate on Elona's lap, then removed a piece of pizza from the box and put it on the plate. "Maybe next time. Be careful and try not to get any on your dress."

Sharon sat on the floor between Amira and Guy and served him, then herself a piece of pizza.

"I can't wait to get everything out of these boxes," Amira said after her first bite. "I think this place is going to be cute once I put a few pictures on the walls and curtains on the windows."

"I remember our first apartment after we got married," Sharon said, looking at Guy, who was already nodding. "A tiny little garage apartment. Your father was teaching at the high school and taking graduate classes at night. I worked at the movie theater. We didn't have a complete set of dishes, much less anything that matched. Mostly things given to us by our parents or as wedding gifts. But I thought it was a grand place. I bought some material and sewed the curtains for the window over the sink in the kitchen and the window by the couch. Remember, Guy?"

"Yes, I do. They looked nice."

"It was an exciting time. We knew our lives were changing; we were growing. We could feel it happening." Sharon smiled at Amira. "As I feel it here with you."

"Am I growing too, Mommy?" Elona asked.

Amira quickly wiped a tear. "Yes, baby, you are. Quicker than I'd like."

After the pizza was gone, Guy and Elona took the empty boxes scattered about the apartment, broke them down, and stacked them in a corner in the dining area. Sharon helped Amira unpack the rest of the boxes of kitchen possessions. When they were done, Amira looked around the kitchen. Although not as big as her previous one, it had the same functionality. She smiled. *Not bad.* The adrenaline she had been running on all day had faded. The pizza sat like a lump in her stomach. Amira went to the couch and sat down with a thud. Just as she did, her cell phone chimed from the kitchen. Since her parents were standing in the same room and John had agreed not to call, she knew it was Ethan. She lifted herself from the couch and retrieved the phone from her purse. She dreaded the thought of a fight over the phone.

"Hello, Ethan."

"I see you have made your pick of things. You could have discussed with your husband the things you were taking," Ethan said.

His voice wasn't raised. Amira thought if anything he sounded tired.

"I tried to talk to you. You just scream at me that I'd get no help from you, so I've made the decisions myself. If there's something I took that you feel strongly about we can talk about it."

"The thing you have taken from me that I feel strongly about is our family."

"I'm not—"

"I'd like to see Elona."

"Sure, you can have her the whole weekend if you want."

"Tonight."

"It's getting late and she has school tomorrow."

"Please. Amira, I haven't seen her in three days. Just for a moment, and you can get the box of food you left in the kitchen from the pantry."

Damn it, Elona's favorite cereal is in that box. Amira looked at her watch.

"Okay, but just for a minute."

UNHOLY

Amira pulled up in front of Ethan's apartment building. Ethan stood out-side against the brick wall at the edge of the sphere of light issuing from the large decorative lamps at the front entrance. His hands in the pockets of his black overcoat, collar pulled up, he huddled against the brisk wind. Amira got out, walked around the back of the SUV, opened the back pas-senger door and unlatched Elona. Now in the lavender coat that matched her dress, she sprang from the SUV to the sidewalk. The massive ponytail bounced with her.

"Daddy!"

She ran to him. Ethan squatted and she ran into his open arms. He lifted and held her to his chest.

"Oh, I've missed you," Ethan said.

"Missed you, too, Daddy."

Ethan leaned her back to get a good look at her. She smiled at him. He smiled too, the first time in the last three days. His child, his daughter, had the power to obscure his sadness. He felt the weight of her in his arms. The most important thing. The only person in his entire life who had given him unconditional love. Unable to betray. "Did you have fun at Grandma Sharon's house?"

"Yes. I slept with Mommy in her old bed."

"I bet that was crowded."

"I liked it, but Mommy says I kick a lot. You should see the new apartment!"

"Do you like it?"

"Yes, I have my own room. We ate pizza on the floor like Japanese."

"You did?"

"Yep, and Grandpa said his knees are broken from it. And my room looks just like the room in your apartment."

Ethan put Elona down and looked at Amira, standing in front of him. Amira thought he looked pale. Mangled beard, disheveled hair, perhaps even thinner in the face. His eyes, bloodshot and puffy, that a moment ago had looked at Elona lovingly, had rage in them.

"I'd like to talk for a moment." Ethan glanced at people passing on the sidewalk and at Frank standing by the door. "Not here. Come up to the apartment."

Amira felt something that she had never felt with Ethan before. The thought of being alone with him made her uneasy. He had slapped her in their last argument; she hadn't expected that, but even then, with his handprint on her face, she didn't feel like he was capable of extreme violence. On that night, it was about control and his loss of it. His hope to regain it. Now, the hope for control was gone. Now, for an inexplicable reason, she felt the whisper of a threat in her ear. "Elona has school tomorrow and I don't want to go back to the apartment."

Ethan looked at Elona.

"You would like to come up, wouldn't you?"

Elona looked at her mother. Amira grabbed Elona's hand. "No, we can't."

"If you want a job, I could talk to Dr. Jones. Perhaps the company could hire you to be my assistant at the lab... maybe a few days a week."

Ethan's tone was as close to a plea as she had ever heard.

"Of course, you would want me to work there with you. You don't want me to do anything that you don't control." Amira let out a sigh. "We're past the point of discussing any of this."

A tear rolled down his cheek.

"Crying, Ethan," Amira said. "Does your desire to manipulate have no limit? Will you give me the box of food so we can go?"

Ethan wiped it away, his face void of expression. "It's your disloyalty to your family that has no limit. I left it sitting in the foyer." Ethan squatted down to Elona and gave her a long hug. Amira held tightly to her hand.

"I love you," Ethan whispered.

"I love you, too, Daddy." Elona looked up at Amira. "I can come back to see Daddy on Saturday, right?"

"Yes, you can," Amira said.

Ethan stood and walked to the front door. Frank opened it for him. Amira picked up a sullen-faced Elona and walked back to the SUV. She placed her in the child seat and closed the door. Elona remained quiet. Amira turned around in time to see Frank opening the door for Ethan, who was carrying the box of food. She met him in the middle of the sidewalk.

"I don't know why you are doing this to us," he said, holding the box in his arms in front of him. "The rabbis of Talmud consider marriage a holy contract, and the dissolution of a marriage an unholy act."

"Ethan... try to understand... I don't love you. I don't know if I ever did. I must move on. I'm not living my life according to something some old men said three thousand years ago."

"The prophet Malachi said, 'The Lord has been witness between you and your wife, she is your companion, the wife of your covenant.' That is what I understand." Ethan handed the box to her and lowered his head. He turned around and walked toward the front doors. Amira did the same towards her SUV.

He pivoted. Shouted, "Even God sheds tears when anyone divorces his wife!" A black automatic pistol came from his right jacket pocket. He raised the gun at her back and pulled the trigger. It did not move. For an instant, he was confused. He hesitated. Then he remembered the safety and flipped it off with his thumb.

Frank lunged, striking Ethan high on the shoulder and reaching for the gun. Ethan squeezed the trigger again.

Amira didn't hear the gunshot so much as she felt it behind her. Thunderous and surreal. Erupting the quiet Boston evening. Her subconscious mind registered a burn on her right arm as the nine-millimeter bullet ripped through her jacket and sweater, passed barely under the skin, then exited. By reflex she whirled around. Frank fell with Ethan to the cement. In Ethan's hand was a pistol; both men struggled with each other. Neither said a word as they pried and squirmed for control of the weapon. What had been an ordinary evening suddenly turned into a fight for life or death.

Amira screamed.

The assistant doorman, David, had heard the shot from the small office in the foyer. He came running out the door. He grabbed Ethan's hand that held the gun, pinning his arm and shoulder to the sidewalk. Unable to move, Ethan went limp.

"You are unholy!" Ethan shouted from underneath Frank. He sobbed.

David pried the pistol from Ethan's grip and Frank forced him onto his stomach, twisting his right arm behind his back.

"Call 911!" Frank yelled at David. David ran back inside.

Amira noticed a warm sensation on her right arm, looked at her jacket sleeve, and could see loose threads and a small amount of red. She placed the box on the ground and wiped at the threads with her hand. *I'm shot.*

"Oh my God," Amira said. She stood, shocked, as people moved around her. An elderly couple came out the front door, dressed for dinner. The woman put her arm around her.

"Are you okay?"

Amira knew her, but only by her last name. "I—I—I think so, Mrs. Schultz."

"Is this your box?" the woman asked, pointing to the box sitting at Amira's feet.

"Yes."

"Why don't we take it inside while we wait for the police."

"No, it goes in the car."

Mrs. Schultz picked it up. Amira's mind re-ran the events of the last sixty seconds. "Okay." She turned back to her SUV to open the front passenger door. She saw the bullet hole in the back-door window.

"Elona!"

JULY 8, 2022

My investment company is up and running well. I am reading all I can about the different tax laws and investment strategies. I have a hundred ideas in my head. Lee is retiring at the end of the year. He and his wife are moving to Geneva. I will miss him. He gave me permission to tug on his ear when needed. Over the last year we have transferred everything to my computers here. It's amazing what can be done with only an internet connection... and days on end with nothing to do because you are waiting on the damn supply boat.

I have been here almost two years. It has been an epic effort to recreate all my work here. Especially because my only means of acquiring the equipment I need is the supply boat. But at least they are reliable, and the man running the boat is dependable. I should be ready for the first cloning in a year.

I remember what sent me down my path earlier than planned. I would have ended up there anyway, eventually. That day started like any other day for me. How was I to know the stone had already been dropped on the smooth surface that was the life I had planned? These ripples will affect me my entire lifetime. No matter how many I get.

THE NEW JOB

It had been a long week for John without seeing Amira. He had not heard a word from her. He understood it would take time. The last thing he wanted was to create more stress in her life. He absorbed himself in his work while he waited. He continued hours of testing and improving the software system for analyzing the brain structure of the cloned monkeys.

On this September day, when John arrived at his lab, he made adjustments to the software parameters and restarted the program. He checked his calendar and noticed a budget meeting with board members in the afternoon. John sighed. It wouldn't be fun. The equipment he had recently purchased impacted the budget for the lab across the hall, and he knew Ethan would aggressively protect his corner of the world. John knew he would probably have to make concessions and pay for most of it himself, leaving Dr. Shinwell with his perceived victory. *If Ethan knew what I was really researching.* It was just the framework of an idea, just the vapor of a theory. Although the process wasn't fully formed in John's mind, he was sure if Ethan Shinwell knew of it, he'd shut him down.

The phone at the desk near the door rang. John looked at the date on his watch. *It's the wrong day for the cleaning crew.* He walked over to the desk and picked up the phone. "Hello?"

"John, this is Phillip. I'm sorry to bother you. Could you come down to my office?"

"Sure, Dr. Jones, what's this about?"

"I'd rather we talk in my office."

"Be right there."

A few minutes later, John entered Dr. Jones' office. He sat down across the cluttered desk from him.

"I received bad news this morning. I got a call from the Boston Police Department, a Detective Garcia. He had questions about Dr. Shinwell."

"What kind of questions?"

"General questions, like did he work here? What was his function here? How long has he been employed?"

"Why are the police asking about Dr. Shinwell? Are they looking for him?"

"He has been arrested. It seems he tried to kill his wife yesterday evening. She's okay. However, it appears that he unintentionally shot their six-year-old daughter in the head. The child died."

"What?"

"He's on suicide watch in the city jail. I had to make calls to a few friends to get the details."

"How is she, his wife?"

"I was told she is in the hospital. Not from her injury. Not from the gunshot wound; it's superficial. Because she's distraught, the trauma of it all." Dr. Jones shook his head. "This really is the saddest thing I've ever heard."

John couldn't think and he couldn't move. The shock mingled with the horror and clouded his mind.

"Why?" John managed to say.

"Yes. It's all too tragic. I wanted to tell you in person because I want you to take over the day-to-day operations of Dr. Shinwell's lab. I don't mean to sound cold about the whole thing. God knows—but regardless of what happens, I think Dr. Shinwell will be away for a significant amount of time. What do you say?"

"Of course," John said absentmindedly, unable to concentrate on Dr. Jones' words.

"Thanks. We'll postpone the budget meeting till next week. It'll give us time to adjust."

John went back to his lab and phoned area hospitals until he found Amira Shinwell as a patient at Massachusetts General Hospital. He all but ran to his car. She needed him.

VISITING

The receptionist at Mass General said, "Room 438. Go down the hallway to the elevators; it's on the fourth floor. Turn left when you get off."

When John found the room, he knocked but got no response. Opening the door, he saw Amira asleep in bed. She had on a hospital gown and he noticed a white gauze bandage on her right arm a few inches above the elbow. He stood at her side and took her hand in his. Her fingers were cold. Under her fingernails, he noticed a brownish crust. *Dried blood.* Her breathing was slow and deep. He lowered his mouth next to her ear.

"Amira," he said. She did not move. "Amira, it's John. I'm here." Again Amira did not move. John stood up straight. The door opened and two older adults entered, each of them with a rolling suitcase. The woman looked suspiciously at the stranger holding her daughter's hand. John released Amira's hand and extended it toward Sharon.

"I'm John Numen. I'm on the board of directors at the company where Ethan works."

"Sharon... I'm Amira's mother," she said, shaking his hand.

"I'm Guy Levitt, her father," Guy said and shook John's hand next.

"I'm so sorry to hear of what happened. I came by to offer my condolences and the company's assistance to Mrs. Shinwell in any way that we can. I seem to have come when she's sleeping."

"Thank you. The doctor gave her something to make her sleep. He told us that's the best thing for her right now. In the meantime, we went home to get a few things," Sharon said.

"How are you doing, Mrs. Levitt?" John asked.

"I'm trying to be strong, for Amira," Sharon said. Her eyes filled with tears. "I just can't seem to stop crying."

"This thing is bigger than any one of us. We're holding on tight to each other and to God to get us through. Our greatest concern right now is Amira," Guy said.

"I'm so sorry. Is there anything I can do for you now?" John asked.

"Thank you, Mr. Numen. I don't think so. Just pray," Sharon said.

🧬

As John drove out of the hospital parking garage, he spoke to his car, "Call Aunt Cathy." In a moment, a ringing phone came over the stereo system speakers.

"John! How are you doing, sweetie?" Cathy answered.

"Okay. Hey, I have the weekend free and am missing your home cooking. How about I come there for the weekend?" John asked.

"That would be great. You've been away far too long."

"Great. I'll see you about seven o'clock."

That evening, John and Cathy sat at the table in the breakfast area of Cathy's house. Bowls of warm tomato soup sat in front of them. Halfway through his bowl, Cathy caught John by surprise.

"I haven't seen you like this since Janet Wilson."

"Janet Wilson... now there's a name I haven't heard in a while." John's mind slipped back to an autumn night his last year in high school, the empty parking lot of the natatorium, after swim team practice. Alone with her in his car. The windows fogged against the crisp outside air. The fumbling, awkward disrobing. He lost his virginity that night.

"I still see her mother at the country club every week. In fact, I play doubles against her every now and then. If you want, I can get Janet's number. Last I heard she had a couple of kids and a couple of divorces. Living in her uncle's travel trailer just outside Oklahoma City."

"Very funny," John replied.

"Her mother says she's been clean months now, working on her real estate license. Probably get you a heck of a deal on some farmland."

"Janet, living in Oklahoma... who knew?"

"How about you start by telling me her name and what she looks like?" Cathy said.

"Aunt Cathy, sometimes you are a little scary."

76

"I raised you. I know you better than you know you."

"Okay, I'll give you the answers to the usual laundry list of questions I get from you... I know you, too. Her name is Amira—she's tall, slender, dark hair, deep brown eyes, smart... went to college at NYU. Does that cover your usual basics?"

"It'll do for now."

"And one other thing... one of the nicest, kindest people I've ever met."

"How long have you been seeing her?"

"About eight months." John looked down at his bowl of soup and filled another spoonful.

"And why haven't I met her yet?"

"She's married."

Cathy's spoonful of soup stopped halfway to her mouth.

"I met her at the company holiday party last year," John said.

"So, she's married to someone at the company?"

"Yes."

"This is so unlike you," Cathy said.

"You can't always stop these things from coming at you. I couldn't help myself, and things have been great. Really great. I've fallen in love with her."

"You're in love... does she know?"

"No."

"Does she feel the same?"

"I think so, although I don't know for sure."

"So, besides the obvious, what else is wrong?"

John told Cathy the whole story. About how they saw each other at lunch and in the mornings. About Amira moving out and the shooting and the death of Elona and that now, as they were talking, Amira lay sedated in Massachusetts General Hospital. And to top it all off, he was in charge of the laboratory that Amira's husband, who was in jail on murder and attempted murder charges, used to manage.

"Oh, my God, John, I saw something about that shooting on the news. Does anyone know this?"

"No, just you, me, and Amira. I don't know what to do. I went to see her. Her parents are with her so I can't just stay there—do you mind if I stay here for a few days?"

"Of course not, this big old house gets lonesome without Robert around to make noise fixing this or that."

"It's been long enough. Don't you think you should sell?"

"This is my home. Robert and I built a life here. Most of your life you were here. It just wouldn't feel right to move."

"You need to get out more. Meet new people. Do new things," John said.

"I do things."

"Have you gone on a date yet?"

"I'm too old to date," Cathy replied.

"You aren't even fifty yet."

"All the good ones are married anyway. Or should I be like you and not let a thing like that stop me?"

"Touché."

John stretched out in his childhood bed. His old room was the same since his visits home during college. Same curtains and same flowery scent to the bedsheets. He slept restlessly, waking before the alarm clock.

John went to the far end of the lab to Ethan Shinwell's second office. On the desk, among the books and papers, stood a family picture of Ethan, Amira, and Elona. John guessed Elona to be about one year old. He picked up the wood-framed photo, took a long look, and threw it in the trash basket by the desk. John gathered the work materials from the desk and moved them to a large table in the middle of the laboratory. When the chemists arrived, they were shocked to hear what had happened with Dr. Shinwell. However, none of them knew him well on a personal level so, without too much emotional fanfare, the work was divided and things proceeded normally. Next was a meeting with Dr. Jones for delivery schedules from the lab and expense reports for both labs to the finance department. When John got back to his laboratory, the monkeys scheduled for a scan were asleep. He spent until ten o'clock that night getting the scans done and setting up the computers for the analysis software to run.

On Saturday morning, his cell phone rang. John looked at the display and saw *Mass. Gen Hosp*. He answered quickly, "Hello?"

"John, it's Amira."

"I've been waiting for you to call. I've been very worried about you. How are you doing?"

"I'm okay, I guess. The doctor says I can go home."

"Did your parents tell you I came by?" John asked.

"Yes, thank you."

"I miss you. Can I come see you?"

"I don't think that would be a good idea. My parents will be here, and I look like a wreck. When my parents aren't around, I'll call you, I promise. I better go now, they'll be coming back to wheel me downstairs." Amira's voice sounded tired.

"Okay, call me when you can."

The phone went dead. He felt better after hearing her voice.

The following week, John checked the obituaries at the Boston Globe website and found the entry he had been dreading:

Shinwell, Elona, 6, entered eternal rest on Sept. 20, 2019. Daughter of Ethan and Amira Shinwell of Boston, granddaughter of Guy and Sharon Levitt of Boston and Rabbi and Rina Shinwell of New York. Services at Temple Ohabei Shalom Cemetery, 147 Wordsworth, Boston, MA, on Thurs. Oct 3rd 4:00 PM.

LATE NOVEMBER 2019

EMPTY SPACES

It was late on a cold Saturday afternoon. The crimson western sky signaled the sun's departure. Amira searched through the ring of keys in her hand, found the right one, and unlocked the door. Inside she switched on the light. Stale air and a chilly apartment greeted her. She looked around the kitchen for signs that anything had changed. She opened the refrigerator.

Empty.

Amira walked down the short hall and paused at Elona's bedroom door. She swung it open. The room was black and silent. She switched on the lamp by the bed. Everything still as she'd prepared. She sat on the bed with Elona's favorite stuffed animal in her hands and looked at the lifeless possessions in the room. They would never move again unless she moved them. The thought of having to throw them away overwhelmed her. Amira curled in a ball and laid her head upon Elona's pillow. She pulled it to her face, hoping to smell her. The tears began, as they had so many times in the past eight weeks. Lying on the bed, the sobs came in waves until she felt shattered. The tears eventually ran dry.

Secretly, she'd hoped something of her daughter would have remained within her room. Something that would bear testimony that she had existed, or perhaps wasn't really gone. Amira had insisted to her parents, and to John, that she come back to the apartment alone. Each of them thought it a sign of recovery, and she let them. But Amira hoped, perhaps, if she was by herself, Elona would reveal herself. Now the weight of the realization that no spirit existed crashed down on her. She went to the kitchen and dug her cell phone out of her purse. After two rings John answered.

"How are you doing today? Gone to the apartment yet?" John asked.

"Can I come over to see you?"

"Certainly."

"I'll be there in thirty minutes."

John opened the door to his apartment, the first time seeing her since their visit to the monkeys. He held his arms out and wrapped them around her in a soothing hug. They stood there, holding each other. Neither one moved or spoke for a long time.

"It's going to be okay," John whispered in her ear. He kissed her on her cheek and could taste the tear that had fallen across it.

"I've missed you."

At dinner, Amira sat quietly and didn't eat much. After the table was cleared, they moved to the couch in the living room. They held each other in the dark. John felt the warmth of her body pressed against him. He didn't know how to say the things he felt. Neither of them moved. After a long while, Amira spoke.

"I got a call yesterday from the assistant district attorney handling the case. He said Ethan had been evaluated by a court-appointed psychologist and found to be incompetent to stand trial, at least for now."

"What are they going to do?"

"A judge placed him in a mental ward. Probably give him medication. If he gets better, they'll take him to trial. The prosecutor told me that Ethan was unresponsive, barely eating, and on suicide watch. So, he didn't think it would be anytime soon—I wish he would kill himself. I really do."

"Maybe it's better this way. Going to trial will be painful. Maybe he'll just stay locked away." John gave her a strong hug.

"I do believe I could kill him," Amira said in a low voice.

Eventually John and Amira moved to the bedroom and fell asleep holding each other, both content knowing she didn't have to leave.

"*Hi, Mommy*," Elona said.

Amira could hear Elona's voice plainly, as if she were talking right in her ear, even felt her breath on the side of her face.

"*Elona? Is that you?*"

Elona floated in front of her. Amira could see her long black hair and purple dress. She was sure it was Elona. Something obscured her view, as if Elona stood on the other side of frosted glass.

"*I just wanted to tell you I love you, Mommy.*"

The frosted glass began to dim. "*I love you too, baby.*"

"*I'm going now; I can't come back,*" Elona said. The darkness began growing inward from the edges.

Amira said the only thing she could say: "*I love you.*" Everything went black. Elona was gone.

Amira sobbed in her sleep. A weight fell on her chest, cutting off her breath, and she gasped for air. She awoke and looked around. *Still in John's bed.*

John opened his eyes to darkness. He wasn't sure what had awakened him. Amira wasn't in the bed beside him and he checked the clock next to the bed. 3:36 a.m. He heard a soft sound coming from the kitchen. A low sobbing. He went toward it. Amira sat, wrapped in a blanket from the couch, at the kitchen table, in the dark.

"I just had a dream about Elona and it woke me." John pulled a chair up next to her. Amira rested her head on John's shoulder.

John held her until the crying subsided. He picked her up out of the chair and carried her back to the bed and lay there with her. Just as the night sky began to glow in the east, Amira fell asleep. John stayed awake. He had thinking to do.

Amira woke to the aroma of eggs cooking. When she entered the kitchen, John was pouring coffee into her cup, his hair uncombed, his face unshaven. She thought he was the handsomest man she had ever seen.

"I made omelets," John said.

"This is most impressive, Dr. Numen."

Amira didn't feel hungry. John insisted she eat. Breakfast over, they remained at the table, drinking their coffee.

"I'm sorry about your dream last night," John said.

"I know it sounds crazy, but I am sure Elona came to me last night to say goodbye for the last time. She can't ever come back. She is really gone."

"I know what it's like to have someone very close to you die."

"Have you ever had a child die?" Amira snapped.

"No, I haven't." John kept his reply soothing.

"I'm sorry... I never thought my life would be without her."

"I don't think you have to be without her," John said.

Amira looked from her coffee cup to John. He sat back in his chair.

"I believe I can clone a human. I've cloned several monkeys, and I believe at this time I can clone a human."

"Clone her? My daughter isn't a monkey in your lab." Amira met his gaze.

"I know she wasn't. She was a wonderful, special child who was taken away too soon. But it doesn't have to be that way. I have the ability to change that."

"You're crazy. They'd put us both in jail."

"Nobody would know."

Amira left her coffee on the table and walked to the bay window in the living room. Outside, the blue sky and golden sun promised a bright but cold autumn day. "Eventually, my parents would know, then the teachers at her school would know."

"We'll go to your parents together. After the child is born. We'll tell them I am the father at first. After a year or so, if they get suspicious, we'll tell them the truth. Your parents aren't going to turn you in to the government. We'll give them time and they'll come around."

"Then what?"

"After the baby begins to grow, we'll have to move away... to a place where nobody knows what the first Elona looked like."

"*We'll* have to move away?"

John walked to her and held her hands. "You aren't going anywhere without me. I'm afraid I've fallen in love with you," he said.

"I love you too." She stared silently for a long time. Finally, she said, "I'd do anything to get Elona back."

"It's a minor procedure to extract eggs from your ovaries. What we need is, say... a hair from Elona's brush. It'll take me a little while to change some things with the machine, but once done, I can build the nucleus of the egg. Four or five days later, perform in vitro fertilization."

"It is really that easy?' Amira asked.

"I just make it look easy. It's a complex procedure. Without my machine, I'd say impossible."

NEW YEAR'S EVE 2019

THE PROCEDURE

Amira lay on her back on the operating table in the primate room, looking at the ceiling. Her head lower than her hips. Her feet in stirrups. A blanket draped across her lower body to keep her warm. If she flexed her neck, she could see the monkeys' enclosure, albeit upside down, above her head. Petri sat perched near the doorway watching through the Plexiglas. John stood at the end of the table. He used an ultrasound machine to guide the tube holding the embryo to the correct area of her uterus. Amira felt the cold handle of the ultrasound and a slight pressure. After a few minutes, John removed the ultrasound handle and wiped the gel from her abdomen.

"We're done. Just stay where you are for a while."

"What a way to spend New Year's Eve, huh? You really know how to show a girl a good time."

"I got your pants off, didn't I?"

John went to the side of the bed, held her hand and smiled. Amira smiled back, but a tear rolled from her eye down the side of her face.

"It's going to be all right," John said.

"I know. I'm just nervous. What if someone finds out?"

"No one will."

Amira looked at the ceiling again and exhaled. "Tell me you love me again."

"I love you."

"Why are you doing this for me?" Amira asked.

"Like I said, I know how it feels to lose someone very close to you."

"Your dad?"

"Yes. If I could've gotten him back, I would have. No matter the risk."

"I'm so sorry."

"So many nights after, I lay awake in my room at night. The house quiet and still, like it had suffered a mortal wound and was dying slowly. My mother's sobs drifted down the hallway. Where he sat at the dinner table, now vacant. The chair outside by the pool where he smoked an occasional cigar sat abandoned. I waited for the smell of his pancakes and listened for his laugh to come up the stairs on Saturday mornings.

"My mother was inconsolable. I didn't know how the pain of it, the shock of it, would change her. How far she would have to go to hide from it. First in a bottle, then in distance from me. I prayed and prayed to God for the longest time to please give him back. Evidently God didn't care." A smile, a bit forced, returned to John's face. "It was a long time ago."

"I just take it for granted—having my parents. They can be a pain, though. I still don't know how they'll take this."

"It'll be all right."

Amira wasn't so sure.

MAY 2020

BASTARD CHILD

Amira hadn't been to her apartment for months. The large walk-in closet at John's, once barren on one side, now held most of her clothes. She created a fictional job to explain to her mother the extended absence from her parents' house. She had been making excuses. Now there weren't any clothes she could wear to hide her condition. Avoiding her mother's phone calls had become a full-time job.

On the counter sat another box of her things, probably the last one she'd need to move before the baby's birth. She stood in the empty kitchen in her unoccupied apartment collecting spices. Her back to the unlocked front door. She didn't hear it open. The first indication she had that she wasn't alone was the sound of her mother placing her purse on the chair in the living room. Amira turned with a start.

"Hi, Mom." Amira gave her the best smile she could manage.

Sharon eyed Amira up and down. "Please tell me you've gained weight."

"I have. As you can see, it's more than that. Please, can we sit and talk?"

"How far along are you, exactly?"

"Just over five months."

"How could you be so irresponsible? Having another child will not replace Elona."

"Mom, please, calm down."

"You want me to be calm? Elona hasn't been gone eight months and you want to try to replace her! You aren't married. You're supposed to be in mourning. Who's the father? Is he Jewish?"

Amira's face flushed with anger. Her heart pounded in her ears. She braced herself against the counter. "Is that what you're worried about? You see how well that worked out the first time—so important that I marry a Jewish boy, he couldn't be Jewish enough! So I did, I married a man more Jewish than you and Dad put together, and you were so proud and so happy. You never asked me if I loved him. Or if he was a good husband. Or father. Or even a good man. You never asked because what's most important to you is how you'd look at the synagogue!"

"That's not true. I wanted you to be happy!"

"Prove it. Be happy for me now," Amira said.

"I can't be happy about you having a bastard child!"

"It's not a bastard! The father is Ethan." The words were out of her mouth before she knew it.

"That isn't possible. Ethan has been locked away for eight months."

Amira's pulse pounded in her ears. Her breathing felt restricted. She paused. Took a breath. "Remember the man you met the day after Elona died? At the hospital?" Amira breathed deep, trying to slow her pulse and catch her breath.

"Yes, from the company."

"His name is John Numen. He specializes in genetics… specifically cloning."

"The baby you are carrying is a clone? Something from a laboratory?" Sharon asked.

"It's Elona's clone. We're going to get Elona back." Her temples pounded.

"Whatever that is you are carrying in your womb isn't Elona. And it shouldn't be there."

"I knew I shouldn't—." A sharp pain stabbed the side of her head with a loud pop. Amira saw a bright flash of light. Nausea swelled inside her. She vomited. She straightened, lost her balance, went to her knees, and put a hand on the floor. Sharon moved to her. Amira collapsed onto her side. Her mouth foamed and her whole body trembled. Sharon grabbed the phone and dialed 911.

Only after Sharon sat down in the waiting room at the hospital did she allow herself to cry. She opened her purse and found a napkin and her cell phone. She selected Guy's number. He answered on the third ring.

"Guy, I'm at Massachusetts General Hospital. It's Amira, she had a seizure, please hurry. I need you here."

"I'm on my way." In all the decades Guy had known his wife, he'd never heard fear in her voice, until now.

A young nurse with a clipboard sat next to Sharon. "Hi, I'm Allison," she said. "Do you know the woman who arrived in the ambulance?"

Sharon wiped her eyes. "That's my daughter."

The nurse took Sharon's information.

Sharon waited alone until Guy arrived, and then they waited together. People came and went from the emergency room. After an hour, a nurse moved them to another waiting room nearer the operating room. The room was empty and quiet. They sat and waited an hour longer.

The door swung open and a doctor wearing green scrubs entered. Sharon and Guy rose to their feet as he walked to them. Sharon could hardly find the energy to stand.

"I'm Dr. Stewart. Are you the parents of Amira Shinwell?"

"Yes, we are. How is she?" Sharon asked.

"Please sit down."

They all sat.

"I'm afraid I've bad news for you. We weren't able to save your daughter."

"Oh, God no, please," Sharon sobbed. Guy held her tight.

"And we weren't able to save the baby, either."

"That baby is the whole cause of this!" Sharon cried. "That thing isn't natural. That baby is a clone, conceived in a lab somewhere. Amira told me herself."

"Are you sure?" asked the doctor.

"You heard me right. Dr. John Numen from The Numen Company made a clone of my dead granddaughter and impregnated my daughter with that abomination. He killed my daughter."

AUGUST 8, 2022

I stood square and numb, in black leather shoes, polished to a translucent shine. My dark blue suit, with a crisp white collar around my neck, tieless. I gazed out the large glass window of the attorney's conference room. From seven stories up, I had a clear view of downtown Boston. The heat from the August sun quivered on the roof of the building across the street. The noisy traffic on the street below writhed as it languished in the summer heat wave. A siren wailed in the distance. I waited.

For six weeks, I had been staying at various hotels since CNN broke the news that the FBI was investigating the first case of human cloning and named me as the focus of the investigation. By the end of that day, it ran on every news outlet. Protesters arrived in front of the company the day the story broke. The livid crowd grew to over two hundred by noon of the second day. A brick broke out a window. The mob blocked the street. The police arrived to control the chanting horde. All the employees went home. After sunset, policemen on horseback pushed the crowd across the boulevard. News vans, smartly dressed reporters, and cameramen circled like buzzards.

"Good afternoon, Mr. Numen."

I looked over my shoulder to see my attorney, David Walston, enter the room. His lean but disheveled appearance was a dichotomy to his effectiveness in a courtroom. Underneath his right arm he carried the same large accordion file he always had for our meetings. "I have good news for you, if you'd like to hear it."

"So far, it's nothing but bad news from you, so yes, that would be a welcome change." My gaze returned to the view of Boston.

"The autopsy report has been released and the medical examiner determined Amira's cause of death to be eclampsia, which caused a massive stroke. The fetus's cause of death has been listed as asphyxia due to Amira's death. I conferred with the district attorney and he has agreed to drop the charges of negligent homicide for both Amira and the unborn child. However—."

"Always a however with you."

"They've released to us the DNA testing results on the fetus and tissue from Elona's exhumed body. It shows them to be an identical match, plus identical matches to the embryos found in the freezer in your laboratory. Confirming they're all a clone. There's a lot of political and public pressure, so I expect them to issue an arrest warrant in two weeks... four tops."

"I'm surprised it's taken this long."

"They want to know where you're staying."

"I think this district attorney is planning on getting his press conference on CNN," I said.

"It does smell that way."

"Tell them The Ritz-Carlton on Avery Street," I said and faced David. "I appreciate everything you've done for me. Do you think your secretary could call me a cab?"

"I thought we'd use this time to begin the preparation of our defense." David removed a thick notepad from the file. "I have a lot of questions about the cloning process."

"Not today. I'll call you tomorrow so we can set a meeting."

David shrugged. "Yes, sir, if that's what you want, but the sooner we get started the better. Things don't get any more serious than this. Twenty years is a long time to spend in a prison cell, and my guess is they'll give you the maximum just to make an example of you."

"You have a staff intern you use for errands, don't you?"

"Yes."

"Can I borrow him for an hour?"

"No problem."

"Would you ask him to come in and bring a piece of paper and envelope?"

David nodded. "I'll call you if I get more information on the issuance of the warrant. I'll see what I can work out to reduce the amount of media present when we have to show up for booking."

"Thanks."

David left. In a couple minutes, a neatly dressed college-aged boy brought paper and envelope. I took a pen from my inside jacket pocket and wrote something on the paper, triple-folded it, and placed it inside the envelope. On the outside, I wrote an address.

"I want you to deliver this to Cathy Edward. The address is on the envelope. Tell her it's from John."

The justice system in America moves slowly. The international banking system does not. They had given me time to make a plan. All that was left to do was say goodbye.

LATE SUMMER 2020

SAYING GOODBYE

Cathy opened the door to find a young man she didn't know standing on her porch. He was well-dressed, and a taxi idled in the driveway.

"Mrs. Edward?" he asked.

"Yes?"

"This is a note from John." He headed back to the cab. Cathy opened the envelope and unfolded the paper.

I need to talk to you. Don't call my cell. Meet me at 494 Lincoln St. Worcester. 8 PM tonight.

John's taxi stopped ten blocks from the small, new Hertz car rental office. One that didn't yet have any security or surveillance cameras. He forced his cell phone down between the seats, paid the fare plus a nice tip. Minutes later he approached the desk, where a young woman greeted him.

"How can I help you?"

"I'd like to rent an SUV."

"I just need a driver's license and credit card."

John handed them to her.

"Mr. Anderson, will you need our insurance coverage also?" she asked.

"No. I won't."

When Cathy stepped inside the Denny's, John raised his hand from his booth next to a front window. He wore a black baseball cap, green T-shirt, and blue jeans. He stood and they hugged for a moment. John already had a cup of coffee.

"Sorry to bring you so far out of Boston."

"The traffic on the highway is horrible. Everybody's driving so fast." Cathy could see a difference in John. "How are you doing?"

"I'm okay. My attorney told me today that he expects an arrest warrant to be issued in a couple weeks."

"This seems incredibly unfair. There is no criminal intent. Haven't you suffered enough?"

"Yes, *incredibly unfair* is an accurate description."

"Can your attorney make a deal?"

"The district attorney seems to think he has found a case to advance his career, so I doubt there will be any offer that doesn't include time in prison."

"I'm so sorry," Cathy said as her eyes filled with tears.

"I'm not going to spend the next twenty years locked up."

"What do you mean?"

"I wanted to meet you tonight because you won't be seeing me again. I have a plan, but the less you know about it the better. I wanted to tell you in person that I love you. You are the best aunt and Robert was the best uncle that any ten-year-old boy could hope for. Both of you did so much for me, to help me through some very tough years, and I'm thankful. I'm sorry things turned out this way. I was hoping to make you proud of me."

Cathy reached across the table and grabbed his hand. "We've always been very proud of you. And still are."

"I won't be around to harass you out of that house of yours. So, I am going to tell you one last time. Let Robert go. Live the rest of your life with a sense of adventure. See things you haven't seen and do things that frighten you a little."

"I'll try."

John's eyes softened. He touched the wedding ring on Cathy's finger. "You were a good wife. You loved him while he was here. And you loved me while I was. We both have to leave you, and neither one of us wants you to spend the time you have alone. Promise me."

"I promise to try." She hated to lie, and this was the best she could do. "Do you think you should call your mother?"

"I see no need. Not much to say, really. She won't miss me much anyway," John said. They stood. Cathy gave him a long hug.

"You can't tell me where you are going?"

"I'm going to make myself a new life." John kissed her cheek and left the restaurant.

Cathy sat back down and watched him through the window and the fog of her tears, as he got into a blue Suburban and drove out of the parking lot.

NOVEMBER 2020

THE ISLAND

John could feel the vibration through his feet and hear the drone of the Cessna's engine through his headphones. A small microphone extended in front of his mouth and an intercom cord contained a button to press whenever he wished to speak to the other two men in the cockpit. Out the window, the turquoise blue of the Caribbean Sea below him spread in all directions. The Bahamian real estate agent, with dark, gold-rimmed sunglasses and a short-cropped afro, dressed in a pale green linen short-sleeved shirt and white linen pants, slouched in the backseat. His voice cracked through the headphones.

"Mr. Taylor?"

John looked back. The real estate agent pointed a bony finger out the window. "You look out the plane to your right, you can see the island, bey. The pilot will make a circle for you."

John shaded his eyes from the sun coming through the plane's window to see a bullet-shaped island below.

"The island be over twenty-five acres, most undeveloped. There be a main residence and three storage buildins, a four-hundred-sixty-meter airstrip and a protected marina with a dock. It has six electrical generators, solar power, full electronic systems, four underground cisterns, fuel storage, fresh water wells, and freezer. The buildin' behind the main house even have a gas incinerator for burnin' trash.

"This island has everything. Privacy, beautiful beaches, surrounded by crystal-clear waters and protected from occasional hurricane winds. The residence and buildin's need some fixin' but have great potential, bey. We be landin' now so you can look." The real estate agent nodded to the pilot. The plane descended.

John waited for the cloud of dust to blow away in the sea breeze. So far, the island appeared to be everything he'd hoped. It was a risk to inquire about the property in person. Risk now played a part in every decision he made. He stepped onto the airstrip.

The sun felt warm on his pale skin and a breeze wafted through his yellow linen shirt and white cotton shorts. He made sure the compact pistol stayed hidden by his shirt in the waistband of his shorts. He thrust on his straw hat and sunglasses. The sandy gravel soil of the airstrip crunched under his leather sandals.

He walked up the hill to the main residence, followed by the real estate agent. The traditional plantation-style house, painted white, had a porch that encircled the entire first floor. The gray wooden planks of the porch, like the rest of the structures, needed to be scraped and repainted. The inside of the vacant house smelled musty. The layout dated the construction period twenty years earlier. John deemed it functional for his purpose.

They walked around to the side of the house and followed another gravel-sand path a hundred yards to a large cinderblock building, painted white, with a tall red brick chimney. It was easy to spot among the palm trees from the air. John pulled the metal doors open. A dusty, barren concrete floor extended a hundred feet long and the same width. Halfway down the right-side wall was the four-foot-wide metal door to an incinerator. John walked to the middle of the room and gave a long look around. The stale air and heat inside the building made him sweat instantly. His body knew he was a long way from Boston. *My new lab.*

"Very sound construction, mon. Has electricity and fresh water," the salesman said.

"I think this place will fit my needs nicely," John replied.

"The price of twenty million dollar be firm, mon." The real estate agent's expression did not change behind his sunglasses. "And that don't include the five-hundred-thousand-dollar payment, per year, to the government officials. You be all over the news. So, if you want to stay down here in these islands, Mr. Raymond Taylor, it be a good place for you, mon."

"Your name... ?"

The real estate agent grinned. "Call me Mr. John Smith."

"Mr. Smith, that's why I've used you for this transaction. I was told you are the man with discretion and the right connections within the government. I'll have the funds wired to your account this week."

"Excellent! I think you be very happy here. As soon as we get back to New Providence, I start the paperwork."

"I was also told you are a man of discretion. I need to emphasize the secrecy of me taking up residency here. There is, of course, a security concern for me."

"Sure, mon."

"And I am hoping you know of another man, like yourself. One willing to make way more than the normal amount for bringing me supplies to this island? One who will keep his mouth shut and can ensure his crew does the same?"

"Yeah mon, I know just the man for you. Gave up the drug runnin', but know all about keepin' a low profile and secrets."

"Mr. Smith, I look forward to doing business with you."

SUMMER 2023

STRANGE THINGS

John liked sailing. He made at least one foray a week to feel the wind and the serenity of the saltwater rushing silently by his boat. From the cockpit of his boat he looked up at the sun in the cloudless sky and scratched at the beard growing on his tanned face. *She would have liked living in the Bahamas... but she wouldn't have liked this beard.* John scratched at his chin again. His boat, a forty-footer, sliced neatly through the waves as he approached his island. He'd bought the used boat in Nassau during his first year on the island. The previous owner said it wouldn't really feel like his until he renamed her. So he did. *Re-Due*.

After docking *Re-Due* at his private pier, John noticed the monthly supply boat from Nassau on the horizon. He hurried to the lab to prepare for the new arrivals. The large wooden door of the cinderblock building had been replaced with metal ones. John entered the access code in the numeric pad on the door and it made a loud click as it unlocked. The interior of the new lab was nearly identical to the one at The Numen Company building.

At the far end of the main room, the newly constructed primate area waited, sparkling clean. John went through the unlocked door, past the operating table. He unlocked the metal mesh door to the cage area, then went to the small refrigerator and retrieved a plastic container of apples and grapes and placed them inside. He opened the small doors that led to the outside to receive the crates used for the journey. John relocked the cage door and left the lab. He removed the large handcart from the nearby storage shed, along with two nylon straps. He quickly pulled the cart down to the dock to meet the boat.

The deckhands were tying the first bowline to the dock when John arrived. The captain came out of the pilot house to greet him.

"I brought some strange t'ings to you, mon, but never somethin' like this."

"Good afternoon, Captain Curry. I expected you'd find this load interesting. Did they give you any trouble?"

"No, sir, Mr. Taylor, the crew liked feedin' them. They seem pretty nice."

Two young shirtless crew members, coal black from the sun, came up from the cargo hole carrying a large metal crate by its extended handles. Primal screams came from inside the crate. Each metal side had a dozen air holes; John could smell the stench of feces and urine ten feet away. The crewmen placed the crate onto his handcart and John secured it with straps. He peered through one of the air holes. He couldn't see anything inside the dark crate. *Yes! Now the real work can begin. As soon as they are sedated, I need to give them a bath!*

"What kind of monkeys them be?" Captain Curry asked.

"They aren't monkeys."

"They look like monkeys to me."

"They're bonobos, part of the chimpanzee family. As close to mankind as you can get in the animal kingdom. Ninety-nine percent of their DNA is the same as ours. They're from the Congo."

Captain Curry stepped onto the dock. John gave him a yellow envelope containing the expected cash payment and the list of items to be delivered the next month.

"I'm going to take them to the house. Have your crew leave the rest of the stuff on the dock. I'll come back to get it later."

"No problem, mon, always a pleasure doin' business wit you." Captain Curry counted the money in the envelope and stuffed it in his pocket. He scanned over the new list. "See you in another month, mon."

John pulled the cart to the side of the lab where the cage opening was located. After securing it next to the opening in the wall, with the crate's door facing the interior of the building, he raised the sliding door. The two female bonobos scampered out of the crate into the primate area of the lab. John lowered the solid metal door over the opening and secured it with a lock. He went through the lab and into the primate area so that he could view the bonobos through the mesh wire wall. Both appeared to be in good health. Females, as he had requested, and they appeared to be eight to ten years old.

"Perfect—time to start testing and completing an improved cloning device."

OCTOBER 5, 2030

It has been about ten years since I bought this island. And finally, I can say it. It is done. The cloning process is perfected.

I have even improved upon the process used to clone Elona. Of course, my mind has been working also on the other process. Without that, there is really no point to all this. I already have written a lot in the journals in the lab, so I won't repeat it here, but only a relatively small amount of software has been written. No sense in starting that work until after the next big step. The time has come. I am ready. I'll write about it when I return. IF I return.

FALL 2030

POINT OF NO RETURN

The early morning sunlight struck the white linen curtains and diffused into the bedroom. The coffee pot in the kitchen clicked on, filling the house with its aroma. Slowly the bedroom became brighter. The black German shepherd, curled up in her bed in the corner, raised her head when she heard John roll over on his back. She walked to the side of the bed and sat down, staring at John. She knew better than to wake her master. That didn't prevent her from staring at him until he woke on his own.

John opened his eyes. The ceiling fan pushed cool air on him. *This is the day.* He looked over at the dog, and she immediately began wagging her tail and tried to reach out with her tongue to lick his face. John sat up.

"Good morning, Frick," John said. "This is a big day."

He rubbed the top of her head and went to the bathroom to relieve his aching bladder. Frick followed him into the bathroom and sat in the doorway. John washed his face at the sink and looked in the mirror.

"Damn, I look old now when I don't shave."

Frick cocked her head to the side. John studied the lines on his face in the mirror and the gray in his beard. The lines on his forehead seemed deeper than yesterday, not yet old, but no longer young. *Ten years. Ten years since I came to this island, ten years of preparing for what is coming next.* He looked at Frick. Gray showed at the end of her muzzle, too.

John knew the next step would change everything. It had to be done if he was to be truly free. There would be no turning back. The last ten years on the island, with an occasional jaunt to New Providence, were a long way from spending them in prison. Which is where John was sure he'd still be. *But I'm not free, either*. The threat of discovery and return to America impended. The yearly payment to the right officials had kept their silence. Who knew for how much longer that would hold?

Every year around the anniversary of Amira's death, a magazine or newspaper published a story searching for the answer to the question: *"Where is John Numen?"*

He knew the way to get free; however, getting caught at the next stage would mean a life in prison or execution.

"Frick, old girl, you and the bonobos are just going to have to make do around here without me for a few days. Don't worry, I'll set the automatic feeder for you and for them."

GUARDALAVACA

John looked over the starboard railing at the setting sun. His latest edition of *Re-Due,* for this trip, had fake registration numbers. Just in case. Twenty-four hours and two hundred and fifty miles ago John had set the sails and entered his course into the computer of the autopilot steering system. He cat-napped during the previous night and even during the day because the swells remained mild, the wind remained constant, and the new fifty-foot cruiser sliced nicely through the open sea. John looked ahead and could see the coastline of Cuba.

The coastal community of Guardalavaca was established in the 1700s. Through the years and the governments that had ruled the island now known as Cuba, it had transformed itself from a farming and cattle-raising community to one dotted with large tourist hotels along its white sand beaches.

Two years earlier, a massive protest swept this island nation and ousted the old regime. The revolutionary protest put large cities like Havana, Santiago de Cuba, and Camaguey into chaos. Even so, the revolution remained bloodless; the national police and army knew they had no way to sustain resistance against a large uprising with the outdated equipment available to them. If they resisted, they and their families would die. Nobody ever liked the government the Castros built that much anyway. When the old leaders fled the country, massive celebrations erupted on the island. The United States government immediately recognized the fledgling democracy and dollars began to flow. In small secluded tourist towns like Guardalavaca, the change from the revolt remained inconsequential. It would take decades for the infrastructure of an island of fifteen million people to be modernized.

Capitalism may have come to the island, but for the many uneducated poor, that didn't mean it brought jobs. In fact, it made the situation for the poor worse. Many things that were free or almost free during socialist rule now came with a price tag. Like many third-world countries, there existed communities living in poverty a stone's throw from where people with excessive wealth played. The islanders who couldn't con or scam sought money in other ways.

Women with no options and one thing to sell paid off hotel security and staff to allow them to ply their trade in the bars, cafes, and restaurants. No matter what government held power, that would never change.

A half-mile off the beach, John lowered the sails and switched on the diesel engine. He could see the terra-cotta roofs of the hotel complex. The white stucco walls were bright against the green of the palm trees, even in the fading sunlight. Along the palm-tree-lined beach, blue plastic lounge chairs and umbrellas dotted the white sand.

The beach was busy with people playing in the surf, strolling near the water's edge. East of the hotel complex, two rock jetties extended into the sea, forming a small, protected inlet. A dozen boat slips, for guests of the hotel arriving by boat, rested there.

John skillfully guided his cruiser into an open slip at the end of the row. Before he could finish tying off the last dock line, a young man in a hotel security uniform approached.

"*Buenas tardes*," the young man said with a smile.

"*Hola*," John replied, happy that life on his island and a satellite internet connection allowed him time to take up interesting things. Like learning Spanish.

"*¿Es usted un huésped en el hotel?*"

"*Si, voy ahora a registrar me.*" John removed a large wad of cash from his pocket and handed a fifty-dollar bill to the guard.

"*No hay problema, miraré su bote.*" The guard smiled.

John went through the gate of the small marina. He walked a hundred yards to the beach. Dressed as he was in a flamboyant shirt and shorts, he blended in with the others walking the white sand, feeling the breeze and watching the last of the day's light fade into the sea. Once in front of the hotel, John walked the sandy path from the beach through the palms. As the sound of the surf faded, he could hear music. He entered a large pool area.

The hourglass-shaped pool, surrounded by yellow, red, and blue lounge chairs, seemed a family affair. Couples and families were scattered about the pool. The main attraction, salsa music played by a four-man band on a small stage, echoed across the pool from an open-air bar on the far side. He selected a stool near the corner of the square bar and had a seat.

"*Hola,*" the bartender greeted John with a smile.

"*Hola, cerveza por favor,*" John said.

"Which kind, pleez?"

"Any will do."

A minute later he returned with a Hatuey, a local brand, and placed it on the bar.

"Five dollar pleez, *señor.*"

John took out the cash and gave him ten. On a small dance area in front of the band, several sunburnt tourists were giving their half-drunken best at salsa dancing. *Those Europeans have no rhythm at all.* The noise of the bar and the indistinguishable conversations of the people around him made the beer go down easy. John waved the empty bottle at the bartender, who promptly brought another. John gave ten more dollars from his roll of bills to the bartender. He watched the crowd and slowly sipped the second beer as the bar continued to fill. Four beers later, the music and crowd had grown loud and large.

She gave the security guard in the lobby and bouncer at the main door their usual payoff and proceeded to the bar. She wore a cotton turquoise top, faded and a bit worn at the seams, which showed her small waist above a pair of white, very small shorts. At the end of her slender legs were worn leather sandals on calloused feet. She swayed just the right amount when she walked.

The older *gringos* were always an easy target. Always willing to pay more. Find the ones over forty and under sixty-five; they had the spare cash. Even if they came with their wife and kids, some would get a second room for their business deal. The young ones had no money or a girlfriend, and they wanted it for free.

She spotted him sitting in the corner. Typical tourist shirt, more of a tan and fitter than usual. *Even better. I'm tired of seeing those round, white gringo-bellies.*

The young woman squeezed up to the bar next to him. Her bare, mocha-colored arm brushed against John's as she leaned on the bar. She threaded her fingers through her shoulder-length black hair. Large gold hoop earrings shone between the ebony strands.

"*Hola,*" she said.

"Hi there." *I'd say mid-twenties. Healthy enough.*

"You stay here, hotel?" She smiled the practiced smile.

"Yes, I am."

"Would you like company?"

John liked the way she got right to the point. He raised his hand to the bartender and held up two fingers. The bartender nodded.

John smiled. "My name is Randy."

"Maria."

The bartender came with two beers. John removed the same lump of cash from his pocket, made sure Maria got a good look, gave the bartender a twenty-dollar bill and waved at him, indicating he could keep the change. John handed one of the beers to Maria and raised the one in his hand.

"To new friends—*amigos.*"

"*Sí, amigos.*" They both drank.

"I have a boat at the dock."

Maria paused. "You have pay to be with me there."

"How much—*cuánto dinero?*"

"Five hundred dollar," Maria said, a good high price point for the negotiating to begin.

"Okay."

Maria couldn't believe her luck. *I usually have to work all weekend to get this much money.* She had seen his cash up close and knew it was far more than five hundred dollars. *With a little more luck, he'll fall asleep and I'll get the whole roll.*

On the walk from the bar to the boat, they drank their beers in silence. The security guard was not around as they walked through the gate down to the last boat slip. When Maria saw the size of the boat, she was sure this gringo wouldn't miss the cash in his pocket. John unlocked the cabin door, went down the ladder, and turned on the lights.

Maria followed him. She had never seen a room so nice. The floor and furniture gleamed from stained and varnished teak. The countertops were a gray, shiny granite. Along the edge were chrome railings. A booth with a table and a tan leather bench seat was on one side, a leather couch on the other, and a flat-screen television on the wall. John motioned for her to have a seat on the couch. When she sat, she could feel the richness of the smooth cool surface. John closed the cabin door and took a bottle of rum from the lower cabinet by a small refrigerator. He placed it on the countertop. He looked at Maria as she took in the whole room.

"Ron?" John said.

"Sí." *I don't mind if it takes longer with this gringo.*

John took two shot glasses from the cabinet and filled each with rum. He handed Maria her glass, sat down on the couch next to her, raised the glass in his hand.

"Salud," they said in unison, toasting each other, and drained the shot glasses.

"Music?" John asked.

"Sí."

John got up to turn on the stereo. She ran her hand over the leather seat cushion to feel how smooth and cool it was to the touch. *I wish I had a room like this, I wish I had a couch like this. A place I didn't have to share with my parents or my brothers and sisters.* She closed her eyes and imagined a room of her own, with a couch of her own. *That would be a nice way to live.* She listened to the soft jazz music now coming around her and rested her head on the back of the couch. She felt sleepy and she let her body sink into the leather.

"Is the music okay?" John asked from the galley.

"Sí." Maria replied with her eyes closed. Her head felt heavy.

"Not too loud?"

He asked again. When he got no answer, he went topside and untied the docking lines. He started the engine and, with the lights off, navigated his boat out of the inlet and into the moonless night.

SUMMER 2031

THE CLONE

Maria lay unclothed on the bed. Her head was shaved for convenience, so he wouldn't have to wash her hair, and it helped keep her body temperature regulated. The monitor on the other side of the bed showed her cardiac activity emitting a rhythmic beep. The feeding tube, in place for the last nine months, had been removed the previous day. The ventilator was still in place. John picked up a hypodermic needle from the tray beside the bed and filled it with Phenobarbital from a bottle. The needle contained a fatal dose of the same medication that had kept Maria comatose for the past nine months while the embryo inside her grew. Now, the fetus had come to term.

"You are going to make history today, Maria."

John pulled on latex gloves and selected the scalpel from the tray. With a long, smooth motion, he cut open the layers of skin and fat covering her abdominal muscles. He placed retractors to hold the tissues open. Next, he cut through the layer of muscle and again placed clamps. Finally reaching the uterus, John made a continuous slice the same length as the others. Amniotic fluid flowed out. He reached in and pulled out his clone, quickly clamping and cutting the umbilical cord. He suctioned out the infant's mouth and nose and massaged the infant's chest until he began crying. John wrapped him tightly in a warm, soft blanket and held him close.

"Hello. Welcome to the world. I've very big plans for you."

John held the infant for a long while. Eventually he knew Maria could wait no longer. *It has to be done.* He placed his clone in a crib under a warming light and returned to Maria on the bed. He picked up the needle from the tray and injected the drug into the IV line and watched until the monitor showed a flat line and emitted a flat tone. John removed the tubes and electrodes that had been sustaining the woman's life and placed them in the bed with her. He wrapped her in the bed sheets and their plastic covering, sealed them with tape, and moved her to a gurney. John rolled her across the room to the furnace, the door already open. John placed her inside. He shut the door, opened the gas valve, and pressed the ignition button. The furnace roared to life. Soon it would be 1,400 degrees inside.

JULY 16, 2031

I have done it. My clone isn't letting me sleep very much, but that is normal, or so I have read. I only need to watch him grow from afar, work on the next process, and bide my time. Tomorrow I am going to Nassau. From there, the next big risk. I have to go back to America.

THE AGENCY

"Hey there, mon, been a long time, Mr. Taylor," said the real estate agent from ten years ago. He shook John's hand from the other side of his desk. "Looks like life be good to you, mon. A little grayer, but you stayin' fit."

"Yes, Mr. Smith, life has been very good to me."

"All them big people in the government are happy, mon, no problems here. So, what you need that boat to go to America for?"

"It's just a quick trip, I'm not staying long. Did you get the other things I asked for?"

"Sure, mon, you got the payment? Has to be cash."

John took the backpack off his back and set it on the desk. Mr. Smith unzipped the top, took a look inside, and placed it in the bottom drawer of his large desk. Out of the drawer above he removed a large envelope.

"There you go, mon. Florida driver license, social security card, and a birth certificate just like you say. The boat is at the marina, registered in the U.S., and all the gas you need. Slip thirty-three. It's got to be back in a week or I charge more money. You have the house at this address," he handed John a piece of paper. "Rented for the week, private dock and everythin' you ask."

"Excellent. Once again it's always nice to know a man with the right connections."

"You take care now, bey? Don't do nuthin' to find yourself in jail over there."

Once back at the *Re-Due,* John removed two large duffle bags from his boat, in slip fifty-eight, to the newly rented forty-foot cabin cruiser in slip thirty-three. One bag contained food items; the other, besides clothing and toiletries, held the infant clone, now two weeks old, sound asleep under a mild sedative. Under a setting sun John motored his rented boat out of the harbor and set the navigation system for Miami Beach Marina, eight hours away.

While still miles away from the coast, John could see the city lights of Miami Beach. At 2:00 a.m. he entered the deep navigation channel south of Miami Beach, passed under the causeway, and around the south side of Hibiscus Island to an unlit dock where he moored the boat.

Carrying the duffel bag with his clone and a briefcase in the other hand, John approached a ten-foot-high aluminum grate gate. An equally high cement wall ran in each direction. He inserted the key labeled "Dock Gate" and it opened. He quickly crossed the yard past the pool to the back door. He found the key labeled "Back Door" and let himself in. The door chimed when he opened it, but the alarm wasn't set. John found a lamp on a table by a chair and switched it on. He found his way to the kitchen and from there to the garage where a rental car, a white Ford sedan, waited, with a baby seat already installed. The keys to the car and garage door opener were sitting on the hood. When John backed out of the driveway, the GPS system acquired its satellites and John entered the address. He punched a number on the cell phone. After a few rings, a woman answered on the other end.

"Hello?"

"Yes, this is Mr. Jacobs. I should be there in about twenty minutes."

"Fine."

The pre-planned neighborhood was nondescript and less than five years old, several of the lots having houses under various stages of construction. John parked the rental by the curb of the house that the GPS informed him was his destination. He removed the infant from the back seat and carried the briefcase. He approached the front door and rang the bell. A short, heavyset woman in her mid-fifties, wearing a blue dress and brown tennis shoes, opened the door a few inches.

"Mr. Jacobs?"

"Good morning, Ms. Lopez. I believe we've business to discuss."

"Come in. This must be the child?" She reached out to take the infant from John's arms. John leaned forward so she could support his head. "My, he's a handsome baby. Any deformities?" She began feeling his legs through the blanket.

"None."

Ms. Lopez motioned with her free hand to a chair in the living room, "Please, have a seat."

John sat in the nearest chair; it had been a long day and the trip wasn't half over yet. "I have the documentation we discussed for the child so that he can be legally adopted through your agency." John opened the briefcase on his lap and removed the forged birth certificate from Nassau, Bahamas. He placed it on the coffee table.

"Good, that should do just fine. And the money?"

John laid an envelope on the table. "In there is the number to a bank account in Switzerland. There's five hundred thousand dollars in there. Every year that you provide the information on the child that I request, I'll deposit another fifty thousand dollars into that account. It has branches in Zurich, Geneva, Lausanne, Bern, and Basel. You can withdraw from this account only in person, at one of these branches, if you wish the existence of the account to remain a secret from the IRS. Understand?"

"Mr. Jacobs, I didn't expect to have to travel to Switzerland for the money. That's an expense we did not agree upon."

John removed a larger envelope from the briefcase. "This is thirty thousand dollars, in cash. It should enable you to make several trips to Europe. Also, with the bank account numbers is the business card of an accountant in Geneva who you will find most helpful."

Ms. Lopez smiled.

❦

Thirty minutes later, John parked the rental car back in the garage. He wiped down surfaces he could have touched and placed the garage door opener and keys back on the hood. As the eastern sky brightened, John removed the dock lines to the idling cabin cruiser and slowly pulled away. John knew the less time he spent in U.S. territory where he was just one fingerprint scan away from arrest, the better. He carefully navigated the boat out of the cut and into the open black water. He set the navigation system for New Providence. Once the coastline of America disappeared behind him, he relaxed. He removed the cell phone from his pocket and crushed it with a hammer, gathered the broken pieces of the phone from the countertop, and threw them into the water. He returned to the captain's station. After the boat cleared the shipping lanes, he allowed himself to nap behind the wheel. By the middle of the afternoon, he was back in New Providence. John removed the items he had brought on board and wiped down the surfaces. He returned the keys to Mr. Smith, who was happy to see him return safely, ensuring annual payments would continue.

John returned to the *Re-Due* and slept till the sun went down. When he woke, the marina was quiet. Without anybody paying any attention, he started the engine, slipped out into the sea, and returned to his island. His mind was already working on the next phase of his plan.

It would take him twenty-five years.

SUMMER 2055

IMAGING

If I had gone to prison, I'd have been out by now, out and free. Although I wouldn't have made the progress on my device. It has to work. John looked out over the ocean from a chair on the porch, morning coffee in his hand.

"It has been a long time, Frick." Frick lifted her head and thumped her tail. "Twenty-five years is a long time. A long time to wait for someone to grow up, a long time to wait to start over again." His hair was now completely white, as was the beard on his face. Deep lines in his tanned forehead and crow's feet radiating from the corners of his eyes bore witness to years in the sun.

"You have been here for the last twelve of them, at least the latest version of you." John looked at Frick lying next to his chair. She was a fine-looking specimen of a German shepherd. Now very gray around her muzzle. "This is a very big day for you." *And for me.* "I mean a Nobel-Prize-winning accomplishment... there has never been anything like it... I don't mean to alarm you, but the last two times, with the previous versions of you, didn't go too well. Hopefully I have it right this time.

"I think I could let them keep their Nobel Prize. It's reward enough that I'll never have to teach you to *sit* again. Not to mention that we'd be insanely rich if we could sell this thing. Okay, we're already insanely rich. Have I told you lately that my investments are doing very well?"

Frick cocked her head, searching for a familiar word.

"Good thing, because I've spent a lot of money over the years on this house, the island, and, of course, mostly the lab. With this invention, I could be the most powerful man on the planet. For the rest of my very long life. That is, if anybody knew." Frick thumped her tail some more. "Let's go get that wild thing out of her crate."

Those words Frick knew and she sprang to her feet. John, wearing swimming trunks, coffee cup in hand, headed to the lab. Frick trotted along by his left side, keeping pace as if the training leash was still there. When John stopped to enter the code in the keypad, Frick sat without being told. John opened the metal door and Frick followed him inside. Directly inside the door was where Frick's clone had spent every night of her one-and-a-half-year life.

"Good morning, Frack," John greeted her as he entered. Frack's tail pounded against the side of the crate, and she pawed at the door. When John released the latch, she bolted from the crate and raced in circles around him, barking wildly. John set his coffee cup on top of the crate, took the tug-of-war rope off the shelf over the crate, and raised it up high in the air.

"Let's go to the beach!"

With that, both dogs ran out of the lab and headed down the path to the sandy beach on the other side of the house. John jogged along behind. The sand was cool in the morning. The clear salt water was warm. Frick stayed close to John while Frack raced up the beach, stopping to investigate an interesting smell here or there. John looked down at Frick.

"Sit."

She did exactly that, as she had been trained, next to John's left leg. Her eyes never left the object of her desire in John's right hand. The surf was gentle, with small rollers coming in. Each wave gave a lazy thud and hiss as it met the beach. The foam swirled and slid back out to sea. John threw the two-foot-long, two-inch-diameter rope as far as he could. As the rope hit the water, John gave the command.

"Go get it!"

Frick sprang from her seated position and sprinted into the water. Frack swam along behind, clueless, following and returning with Frick. Once she had the rope in her mouth, Frick swam and then ran back to John's feet and sat down. The saltwater dripped from the rope in her mouth. John grabbed the rope by one end.

"Release."

Frick released her bite on the rope. Frack rushed in to try to take it from John's hand. He raised it up in the air and Frack leapt up after it, snapping her teeth at the rope. John threw the rope again.

After an hour of beach time, John returned to the lab with the dogs. Each was given a bath at the outside shower area and dried off with towels and brought to the front porch, where the brushing and drying with a hair dryer completed the job. Frack was put on a choke collar and leash and walked back to the lab. Frick followed dutifully.

Once in the lab, John removed a syringe from a drawer in a cabinet along the wall and a bottle of Phenobarbital. John filled the syringe with the appropriate amount and gave Frack an injection in the loose skin of her neck, just behind the choke collar. After he refilled the syringe, he called Frick over to him and injected her as well. In fifteen minutes, both dogs were asleep on the floor.

Across the lab, two beds were next to each other, against the wall. A large table in front of a rack of twenty computers stood to the right of the beds. A monitor and keyboard sat on the table. John moved Frack to a bare metal table in the middle of the room. There he used an electric shaver to remove the fur from Frack's head. Next, he used shaving cream and a razor to make her head completely smooth. The process was repeated with Frick. Each dog was weighed and placed on its own bed. John placed an IV in each dog's foreleg, each connected to a machine that would dispense the right amount of sedative for each dog's weight at the correct intervals, to keep them asleep for the whole process, once John knew how long the process would take.

Hanging on the side of each bed was a metal-and-cloth-mesh helmet. Each helmet had one hundred and fifty-seven color-coded, two-inch-long fiber optic wires. The wires extended from small ceramic-looking sensors in a grid across the helmet. Each wire had a connector in the end. A helmet was placed on each dog; careful measurements were taken to ensure the sensors were positioned exactly right, and then they were taped in place so the sensors could not move. John brought a cable harness from the computer rack, laid along the floor, to Frick's bed. One hundred fifty-seven fiber optic wires were connected to their like-colored connector from the helmet wire. The process was repeated for Frack.

John typed in "Execute" at the blinking cursor. A clock display appeared on the screen with the words "TIME TILL COMPLETE" underneath. The clock display was blank for five minutes while the system collected data to estimate a completion time. When completed, the clock displayed "08:36:37." John went to each of the IV dispensers and entered the time plus five minutes. Returning to the computer monitor, John moved the pointer over the green button and pressed the left mouse button. The clock began counting down.

"Okay, girls, see you in about eight and a half hours."

He looked over at three mother bonobos and their younger clones in the cage at the end of the lab.

"If it goes well, two of you are next."

The day passed slowly. John checked on the progress regularly. Nothing else could be done. As the sun went behind the horizon in a golden sunset, the clock on the computer monitor displayed "00:00:00." The timer on the IV dispenser expired five minutes later.

John took his stethoscope from the table in the middle of the room and listened to Frack's heartbeat. Sounded normal. He removed the IV and mesh helmet. Next, he moved to Frick and listened to her heartbeat. It was faint, and slow, her breathing very shallow. John listened as her heart rate slowed and grew weaker. Three minutes later it stopped.

He removed a large black garbage bag from the cabinet under the table and placed Frick inside, closed it with a zip tie and laid her back on the bed. He opened the lid of the large freezer against the wall. He removed Frick's body from the bed and placed it inside.

"I'll have to take tissue samples from you later, old girl," he said before he shut the lid.

Back at a table in the middle of the lab was a coffee pot. John filled the machine with fresh water, a new filter and grounds, and started it brewing. He listened to Frack's heart and breathing again. Still normal. He placed a blue blanket on the floor, folded twice to add cushion, and lifted Frack from the bed and placed her there. He moved the chair from the computer table and sat.

"Now I just have to wait for you to wake up. And you'd better wake up."

The ache in his back and a numb arm woke him. He straightened from his position slumped down in the chair. He opened his eyes and tried to focus. The blanket in front of him, at first being a blue fuzzy ball, came into sharp focus as John remembered where he was and why he was there. Frack wasn't on the blanket. John sat up in the chair. He heard the tail thumping the floor and looked to his right. There was Frack, bald-headed, sitting at attention, waiting for him to wake up.

"Good morning, Frick, good to see you again."

Frack, now Frick, came over to get rubbed on her very bald head. "I think this calls for a celebration." Frick cocked her head to the side. "We deserve a trip to New Providence. Let our hair down, try our luck at the blackjack table again."

HOME AWAY FROM HOME

John docked the latest model of the *Re-Due* into his usual slip. For this trip he abandoned his usual island attire. He walked off the boat in his best gray suit. The limousine driver placed John's rather large suitcase in the trunk.

"Diamond Palace, please. Back entrance."

Twenty minutes later, they arrived. As the limousine stopped at the curb, John noticed the usual concierge, a middle-aged, slightly balding Englishman, waiting at the doorway.

"Good day, Mr. Taylor."

"Hello, Adam."

"It's good to see you again. I see you have a new dog. What happened to her head?" Adam asked.

"I like it that way."

"Very good. What's her name?"

"Frick."

"Wasn't the other dog named Frick too?"

"Yes. I like that name."

"Certainly." Adam didn't try to figure out the wealthy anymore. "We reserved the penthouse suite for your stay and reservations in the restaurant at nine o'clock, which is about thirty minutes from now."

John, Frick, and Adam entered the private elevator that went to the top floor. The concierge swiped his access card, pushed the top button, and handed the card to John.

"Thank you, Adam. Did you arrange for the same man to take Frick for her walk on the beach?"

"Yes, sir, he said he would be happy to. He should be here before you leave for dinner."

"Great."

The elevator stopped and the doors opened. Directly across the wide hallway was the suite. John swiped the card at the door and the lock released. Adam gave the doors a gentle push and they opened in to a round entry foyer with white marble tiles and domed ceiling with a Murano glass chandelier. Across the foyer was a large living room area with two eggshell-white couches adorned with red satin pillows sitting on a floor of sea-blue carpet with a swirling coral design.

On the black glossy sofa table were three tall, clear, crystal Murano vases with strands of green glass twisting and turning from top to bottom. Beyond the sofas, a glass-paneled wall provided a view of the ocean.

To the right was the kitchen; already on the floor were two stainless-steel dog bowls, one with water, the other with food. Frick went immediately to the kitchen. The porter came into the room, placed the suitcase in the master bedroom, and left as silently as he had entered. John faced Adam, extended his hand with five one-hundred-dollar bills folded discreetly. Adam shook hands and transferred the bills from John's hands into his pocket as smoothly as a magician.

"Mr. Taylor, if memory serves me correctly, I believe the last trip you enjoyed the company of a young lady named Rebecca. Should I enquire whether or not she is available?"

"Not right now, I'll let you know."

"Very good, sir." Adam left the room. Automatically the doors closed and locked behind him. Frick came out of the kitchen licking her muzzle.

"Our home away from home, eh Frick?" She wagged her tail. "Dinner and blackjack for me. And you get a walk on the beach."

JULIA

She strolled through the casino looking for her boyfriend, who had become hard to find since their latest argument. She had hoped this vacation to the islands would help them get back on track. The harder she tried to get close to him, the more elusive an emotional connection became.

During her third trip around the casino floor, her high-heeled shoe bit into the smallest toe on her left foot. She decided a drink at the bar was a better idea, anyway. To her left was a bar just beyond the sign that read "High Limit Room." A lone patron sat there. She passed the sign and sat in the chair at the corner. The bartender came over.

"Mai Tai, please," she said.

"I'm sorry, miss—are you playing at one of the tables in this room?" the tall, black, well-spoken and well-groomed bartender asked.

"No, I just need a drink and my shoes are killing me."

The bartender stated the well-rehearsed line, "I'm very sorry, this bar is reserved for the players in this room."

"Really? Come on, just one drink to relax me, please?"

"I'm sorry—"

"It's okay, she's with me," said the man sitting two stools to her left.

"Yes, sir, Mr. Taylor." The bartender nodded and started on the Mai Tai.

Julia eyed the old man in the nice gray suit sitting at the bar. Whiskey on the rocks on a napkin in front of him.

"Thank you."

"No problem, always ready and willing to rescue a damsel in distress." John extended his hand. "My name is Raymond."

She placed her hand in his. "Julia."

John guessed her age to be thirty. She was nearly as tall as he, athletically built with just the right amount of curves, and tanned. The bartender placed her drink on the bar and Julia opened the small black clutch purse that matched her small black dress.

"Put it on my tab please, Reginald," John said.

"Yes sir, Mr. Taylor."

"Thank you." Julia smiled and with the index finger of her right hand looped strands of her hair behind her right ear.

"It's always better to have a drink with company. Don't you think?"

"Yes, I guess it is," Julia replied.

"What brings you to this bar?"

"My boyfriend. Or I guess I should say the *absence* of my boyfriend. I've walked a hole in my foot trying to find him."

"Ah, I see, we must be in the post-fight time frame."

"Is it that obvious?"

"No, just experienced. Want my advice? Just sit still here and he'll find you eventually."

"Where are you from?"

"Here. Well, not here, but another island near here."

She was pretty sure he was drunk, but one of those practiced drunks who knew how to hide it well. Like her neighbor back in Atlanta, who walked his poodle every evening. "And what do you do there?"

"I do a lot of work in my lab. I run on the beach. Swim. Read. In the evenings, I sit on the porch with a bottle of whiskey and look out at the ocean. Watch the sun go down."

"Sounds a bit lonely."

"Oh, I'm not alone. I have my dog Frick. We've been together a long time. I tell her about my day and she tells me about hers."

Julia took another long drink from her glass, now three-fourths empty. John signaled to Reginald.

"Another for the lady, this damsel is still distressed."

"Yes sir, Mr. Taylor."

"It makes me mad for us to come all this way just to end up in a stupid fight."

"You know what I find the perfect remedy for forgetting about a quarrel with your boyfriend?"

"What?" Julia was suddenly apprehensive the old guy was going to get creepy.

"Blackjack."

John smiled widely. Julia laughed. He was funny and, thank God, not creepy. "I don't have much money with me and know almost nothing about blackjack."

"No problem, I'll teach you, and since you are my student, I think it fair we play with my money. If we win, you keep the winnings. If we lose, it's on me. What do you say?"

The bartender put the second Mai Tai down in front of Julia. "You'd teach me with your money?" Julia took a long sip of her drink.

"Of course. Look, there's a table with nobody at it."

John pointed past her to the right. Julia looked to see an empty blackjack table and a slender Vietnamese woman standing at attention behind it.

"Why not, I need some fun after the last three hours. Let's go."

John and Julia took their drinks and sat down at the two center stools at the semi-circular table. The woman smiled and stepped forward to the center of the table.

"Good evening, Mr. Taylor, good to see you again."

"Good evening, Nhu."

"Does everybody here know you?" Julia asked.

"Better than I'd like to admit." John said to Nhu, "Let's start off with fifty thousand each and see how it goes."

John handed Nhu a card from his pocket, which she swiped through a card reader at the table. She handed it back to John and counted out fifty one-thousand-dollar chips for both Julia and John. Five stacks of ten each. Julia looked at the stacks of dark purple chips in front of her and was speechless. She looked at John, who placed a single chip in front of him.

"It's a thousand-dollar minimum at this table, so let's start with a single chip."

Julia took a single chip off one of the stacks and placed it in front of herself.

"This is crazy. I've never seen fifty thousand dollars at one time, much less have it for gambling money."

"Think of it as Monopoly money."

Nhu reached over to the card shoe holding eight decks to her left and slid the first card out, flipping it face up in front of John. Two of diamonds. Another card in front of Julia. Ace of clubs. In front of herself, five of spades.

"Looks good for you," John said to Julia.

Julia's heart was racing, knowing a thousand dollars was riding on just this first hand. Somehow it didn't matter to her nervous system that it was somebody else's money. Nhu reached to the card shoe again. The first card to John, king of clubs, the next to Julia, queen of diamonds.

"Blackjack," Nhu announced.

Julia gasped. The next card out of the shoe went to Nhu facedown. Nhu reached over to the chip tray and smoothly plucked out a one-thousand-dollar chip and a five-hundred-dollar chip and placed them next to Julia's wager.

"Blackjack pays three to two," John said. "You are a natural. I knew you'd bring good luck."

Nhu retrieved Julia's cards, indicating that she had been paid, and placed them in the discard pile. She looked at John.

"I'll stand," John said.

Nhu flipped over her face-down card to reveal a ten of spades. "Fifteen," she announced.

She slid another card from the shoe and flipped it over. Jack of hearts. "Dealer bust."

She placed a matching one-thousand-dollar chip next to John's. Collected John's cards and placed them in the discard pile.

"Oh my God, I just won fifteen hundred dollars!"

Julia couldn't believe it. She'd never played anything except the slot machines. One time she had won three hundred dollars. She ended up losing it back by the end of the night. She now had twenty-five-hundred dollars in front of her. John reached over and put it in a single stack.

"Let it ride," John said.

Julia's eyes widened. "I'm going to have a heart attack."

John left the two thousand dollars in front of him. Nhu slid out the first card to John. Ten of spades. Next to Julia, eight of hearts. To herself, six of clubs. She slid a card to John. Nine of diamonds. To Julia, eight of clubs. A card, facedown, to herself. Nhu looked at John.

"I'll stand."

She looked at Julia. "Sixteen."

Julia looked at John.

"She'd like to split," John told Nhu.

"I'd like to what?" Julia asked.

"Split. You are going to make these two cards into two separate hands. Of course, it takes another twenty-five-hundred dollars."

"What?"

Nhu took the two eights and moved them apart, John took a thousand-dollar chip and slid it across the green felt table to Nhu, who exchanged it for two five-hundred-dollar chips. John took two one-thousand-dollar chips and a five-hundred-dollar chip and placed them behind Julia's cards. It happened so fast that Julia had a hard time keeping up. In the end, she had two separate eights with twenty-five-hundred dollars behind each. Nhu reached over to the shoe and drew a card and placed it face up with the right hand eight of hearts. The new card was an eight of spades.

"She'd like to split them," John said.

"Again?"

Julia was frozen with fear. Again, the flurry of hands and now she had three eights in front of her, each with twenty-five-hundred dollars in chips. Nhu reached to the shoe and slid out another card and flipped it over. Eight of diamonds. Julia put her hands over her eyes in disbelief. When she looked again she had four separate eights, and ten thousand dollars in chips in front of her. Nhu reached to the shoe, slid out the next card, and turned it over. Two of clubs.

"Oh, thank God, no more splitting." Julia was relieved.

Nhu placed it next to the first eight and smiled. John smiled.

"She'd like to double down."

"What's double down?"

John took another twenty-five-hundred dollars in chips and placed it next to the eight and two. Julia took a long drink.

"You get only one more card for that hand," John said.

Nhu slid the next card out of the shoe and flipped it over. King of clubs.

"Twenty," Nhu announced.

"Stand!" Julia couldn't contain herself. Nhu slid out the next card. Jack of spades.

"Eighteen," Nhu politely announced.

"She'll stand," John said for Julia.

Nhu slid out the next card for the third eight. Three of diamonds.

"She'll double down again," John said.

"Oh, God, really, this is too much, I can't take it."

"It's okay, you're doing great," John said. "Put another twenty-five-hundred next to that one."

Julia did, with a shaking hand. "Great? I'm about to faint." She took another long drink and wiped her mouth with the napkin.

"One card," Nhu reminded her and slid out the next one. Queen of diamonds. "Twenty-one," Nhu smiled.

Julia squealed and bit down on the napkin. Nhu slid out the next card for the last eight. Seven of hearts. "Stand, please God, stand. I can't take it."

Nhu turned over the dealer's down card. King of diamonds. "Sixteen," she announced. John watched Julia, who watched Nhu reach for the next card. Julia's left hand held the napkin she was biting on. Her right hand, again without thought, looped her hair behind her ear. It had been so long since John had seen that gentle movement.

Nhu slid out the next card as Julia's heart pounded in her ears. Nhu flipped the card over. Six of hearts. "Dealer bust," Nhu said with a smile.

"Oh my God, we won!" Without thinking, Julia hugged John, who was smiling bigger than he had in a long time. She jumped up and down in her seat and let out a high-pitched squeal. It was the high-pitched squeal that caught the ear of Julia's boyfriend, Dietrich.

He'd know that squeal anywhere. From the main walkway through the casino floor, he saw Julia sitting at the blackjack table next to a man in a gray suit. He walked up behind Julia just as Nhu finished counting out fifteen one-thousand-dollar chips and placed them in front of Julia. Dietrich stared at the pile of chips in front of Julia.

"Julia?"

She looked over her shoulder to see her long-lost boyfriend behind her.

"Dietrich! Oh, my God, you are never going to believe what happened to me." She had forgotten about their argument for the moment.

"This nice man was teaching me to play blackjack and I just won fifteen thousand dollars!"

"Really? Where did you get the money to play in here?"

John rotated in his chair to face Julia's boyfriend, whose blond curly hair matched his German accent.

"Well, he let me use his money, you know, so he could teach me."

"I'll bet he did." Dietrich looked at John and did not smile.

"No! He was being really nice."

"I'm sure he was." Dietrich didn't stop looking at John.

Julia knew that tone, and that was when she remembered the argument and the three hours she had been searching for him and the blister on her left foot.

"You know what, this man was nicer to me in the last thirty minutes than you have been the whole trip. So just cool your wheels."

"Color up her winnings," John said to Nhu.

Nhu took back the fifteen one-thousand-dollar chips and gave John a ten-thousand-dollar chip and a five-thousand-dollar chip. Nhu took the rest of the chips back. John stood and handed Nhu the card from his pocket which she credited for the chips on the table with one swipe through the machine. John took Julia by the wrist of her left hand so that her hand lay open, palm up.

"It was a pleasure to meet you," John said. He placed the two chips in her hand.

Julia looked at the chips, opened her purse, and placed them inside. She removed a business card and gave it to John.

"It's a pleasure to meet a gentleman. If you're ever near Atlanta, Georgia, I owe you a dinner."

"Thank you." He put the card in his jacket pocket, nodded to the blond German, and walked away.

※

John stared out the window of his dark penthouse. He saw the lights of the office buildings and houses of Nassau, the miniature cars on the streets below him, the moon reflecting off the sea in a thousand tiny points of light as the waves rolled onto the beach below. The room was silent; he could not hear the cars or the surf on the other side of the thick glass. It was 3:00 a.m. He felt tired. He felt alone. He sat on the couch near the end table and switched on the lamp. Frick came over and lay down near his feet. John looked at newly minted, slick-headed Frick.

"Fate?"

Frick lifted his head. John looked again at the business card in his hand.

Julia Watson
Atlanta Zoo
Director of Primate Research Center
Office: (404) 832-7364
Cell: (229) 637-4193

MAY 10, 2057

She has agreed to come to my island and listen to my offer. It took me two years. Wave a big enough carrot and I can get most anyone's attention. Especially if they are having money troubles.

It sure helped finding out she is also an experienced sailor. San Diego Yacht Club champion in 2045. Impressive.

SUMMER 2057

MAKING A DEAL

"This is the *Emerald Green* calling Raymond Taylor," a young woman's voice cracked over the marine radio speaker. Before John could walk from the table to the kitchen counter, the speaker called his name again. John picked up the microphone on the countertop and pressed the transmit button. "This is Raymond Taylor."

"Good morning. I'm about ten miles from your dock. The seas are favorable. I should be there in an hour or so."

"I'll be waiting."

John looked down at Frick. "I should dress better than normal today."

Julia lowered the main sail a few hundred yards from the island while the autopilot kept the bow into the wind, just as she'd done hundreds of times.

The shiny new forty-foot *Emerald Green* glided up to the dock. Julia concentrated as she brought the boat dead in the water inches from the dock. John threw her the dock lines and she skillfully made the boat secure.

"Good to see you." John waved as she nimbly stepped onto the dock. John noticed she was as fit as he remembered from their first meeting almost two years before. Her bronze legs testified to an active life spent outdoors.

"Good to finally see you in person again—I was beginning to think this place only existed on a video conference link," she said. She thought he looked heavier than the last time she'd seen him; his white beard and hair were certainly longer. They shook hands. Julia looked at the sailboat in the docking slip next to the *Emerald Green*. That sailboat was twenty feet longer than the one she'd just sailed in on.

"Nice boat you have there!"

"I bought it three years ago. It's simply amazing the advancements they've made in composite materials. A tenth of the weight of fiberglass and twice the strength. Just like the one you just sailed over, except for the size. She's sixty feet and so automated I can take her out by myself." Frick sniffed Julia's shoes. "This is Frick. We don't get many visitors, so I'm sure she'll make a pest of herself."

"A beautiful dog." Julia tried to give her a pat on the head. Frick shied away.

"I'm glad you like the boat," John said. "As I said, that's the signing bonus if you accept my offer. We can talk business over lunch. First, let's get your gear to your room, and I'll show you around."

"Great."

John and Frick led her past the house and the lab to the beach and the newest addition to the island.

"I had this duplex built last year. I designed them myself with the latest amenities. Had a hell of a time shuttling the contractors in here. I thought they did a good job. Each is one bedroom; they're spacious and have a nice view of the ocean. They're furnished top to bottom." John climbed the twenty steps and stopped at the door of the second duplex. "This is your room." He let Julia walk in first. Frick followed.

Julia admired the cookware hanging over the counters in the kitchen. "This is a really nice place."

"I think you will find the rent very reasonable. I'll leave you to the unpacking and I'll go over to the house and start lunch. I have two nice steaks I've been saving for a special occasion. Lunch should be ready in about an hour."

"I'm hungry already."

🧬

Julia walked up onto the porch. To the left of the door was a wicker chair and foot stool. Beside the chair was a wicker table with two small stacks of books and an empty bottle of Pappy Van Winkle Family Reserve. She studied the label: "Kentucky Straight Bourbon Whiskey." She knocked on the front door. Frick's footsteps were followed by John's. The door opened.

"Come in, please. Excuse the mess," John said.

Julia looked around the living room as she followed John through to the kitchen. Every horizontal surface was covered with stacks of books. Small books, large books, some thick, some less than two hundred pages. The couch had them stacked on one side. The chair in the corner was full. At least half of the wood floor was covered with waist-high stacks. Some of the books were yellow from age. The house smelled like an old musty library.

"I guess living here gives you plenty of time to read," Julia said.

"I guess you could say it is an obsession of mine. Seems like there is always something new to learn."

"It is an astounding collection of books."

"You're just trying to be polite. And I appreciate it. It is a mess. I know. I just have run out of places to put them and throwing them away or burning them seems... sacrilegious."

"Where did they all come from?"

"I order them and have them delivered to the supply boat company in Nassau. They bring them with the rest of my monthly supplies."

Julia sat at the table and noticed that the kitchen was void of books. Only cookware, spices, and utensils could be seen. All the surfaces were clean and shining like new. John moved to the stove and removed a sauté pan from the cabinet.

"Have a seat and watch me prepare the best iron-skillet rib-eye dinner you will ever have," John said.

Thirty minutes later, John served her a rib-eye steak with mushrooms in a port wine sauce and a baked potato.

"It's a pleasure to cook for somebody besides myself for a change."

Julia let the aroma penetrate. "It smells wonderful. Your place here looks bigger than it does in the background when we were talking over the video link. Decorate it yourself?"

"I did, over time."

"What about the details of your very generous job offer that you would only discuss if I came here to see you? Not that an all-expenses-paid trip back to the Bahamas was a problem."

"Very impressive research you have done teaching chimpanzees sign language. And your work in the Congo on primate social structure and the impact of poaching on the resident population is supposed to be the best thing since Jane Goodall, or so the rumors say. The facility also operates as a rescue center. It's very impressive."

"Why does my primate center in Africa interest a reclusive CEO of a Cayman Island investment firm? Especially one living on a private island in the middle of the Caribbean?"

"I'm getting to that. About your research center. One of the things I did find interesting was the shortfall in funds that lies on the horizon. The research center has what... maybe thirty-six months left before the well dries up?"

Julia looked surprised. "Probably more like thirty months. However, a benefactor has promised more funding."

"Please, Julia, may I speak frankly? I do not want to offend you—but I think it would be in the best interest of each of us."

"Please do."

"I know your boyfriend is a successful German banker. And I'm aware, and I know that you know, that recently an outside auditing firm has discovered some abnormalities in the bookkeeping practices of his institution. I'd say the continuation of that cash flow is over. As is, according to a German gossip columnist, the romance between the two of you."

"Yes, well, his degree of dishonesty wasn't confined to just his banking practices. But you also know, nonprofits like mine are always on the edge financially. We make do."

"I have a research project as well, one very important to me—one I've worked on most of my life. My entire fortune depends upon its success and it's about finished.

"My time to leave this island is not far away. Before I leave, I've a problem you can help me with. My research has required the use of bonobos. They reside in a large outdoor compound built on the other side of the island. I've grown very fond of these animals. They, along with Frick, have given me many years of companionship. I've watched each one grow from a baby. They've lived their entire lives here.

"There will be nobody to look after them when I leave. I find it difficult to give them to a zoo or research center. Let me ask you a question. What do you think is the one thing all beings on this planet, from the tiniest bird to the largest whale, want?"

"I... I don't know... food... shelter... a mate?"

"Freedom. However, having been raised in captivity, they know nothing of living in the wild."

"How did they come to this island?"

"The first two, which died years ago, I bought on the black market and had them shipped here. The six here now are second-generation clones of the first two."

"Clones?"

"That is correct. My research here was to develop a perfected, relatively inexpensive cloning process, which I've done. Now I'm ready to leave the island and show the world what I've accomplished."

"Cloning, without assistants or a team? Do you have documentation?" Julia asked.

"Yes, my laboratory is the building you passed walking back to the house. I'll be glad to give you a tour," John said. *After I've hidden the imaging equipment.*

"Let's say I believe, just for argument's sake, that you've accomplished something no one else has been able to do. How do I fit in with this?"

"For the next three months, train these six little souls to live in the wild. At the end of the three months, through your center in Africa, have them transported there to be released."

"Put my life and my job back in Atlanta on hold? Believe what you say is true and to train these bonobos here on my own? Mr. Taylor, that is a tall order."

"I'll be here as your assistant. However, even with my help, you will have to dedicate every waking moment to it. During that time, I'll pay you twenty times your current annual salary, in advance. If at any point you find this endeavor or your stay here on my island not to your liking, you keep that money and the sailboat you came here on and leave.

"On the other hand, if you work diligently and brilliantly and are successful, you will have the salary, the boat, and I'll fund your research and rescue facility in Africa for the next seven years."

Julia extended her hand across the table. "You have a deal, Raymond."

"Great."

They shook hands.

John got up and removed a folder with papers and an optical stick from the desk and placed it on the table next to Julia.

"This is the contract. I had my attorney write it. Take it and read it, use the internet to email it to anyone you like. I think you will find it iron-clad in your favor."

Julia flipped the folder open.

John poured wine in each of their glasses. "The reason it is written that way is that I don't want you worried about the business part of this deal. I want you to concentrate on your work. Tomorrow morning we'll go see your new trainees."

THE BONOBOS

Early the next morning, John and Julia stood outside the front entry gate.

"My goodness, Raymond, you have built an impressive compound."

"After the cloning process was perfected, I built this outdoor enclosure to keep the bonobos. I thought the far side of the island, where their surroundings are undeveloped like a real rain forest, would be the best surroundings. This is as high a place on the island as my house, so if a hurricane comes close, they are protected from storm surge. And, of course, a bigger space for the additional clones. They enjoy being outside rather than the inside of a drab laboratory.

"It's seventy feet by seventy feet, that's five thousand square feet, and thirty feet high. Concrete posts at each corner and stainless steel cables for the grid fencing on the sides and the top." John pointed to the corner across from the gate. "In that corner is a cement shelter, made to look like natural rocks, so they can get out of the wind and rain. They spend most of their time in the large aluminum tree in the center."

Julia's eyes started at the base of the tree, three feet in diameter, the trunk rising out of the ground with small knobs for easy climbing. Ten feet off the ground, four main branches spread out, each heading for a different corner of the enclosure. In turn, each of those branches had a triple fork, each limb still rising higher and forking again until the uppermost branches, which were two feet from the steel cable mesh that covered the top of the enclosure. "That is one damn big metal tree."

"They have an automatic feeder that dumps food pellets twice a day, and a watering station in the far corner."

The largest female bonobo came down from her perch on one of the lower branches and scurried to the door of the enclosure.

"This is Juju, the alpha female of the group. She always expects her banana when I arrive." John removed a banana from the cargo pocket of his shorts and gave it to her through the steel mesh. "I don't go in as much as I used to. I knew they'd have to be removed from this island one day, so I thought it best to reduce the amount of human interaction they receive. The two juveniles on the ledge of the cement cave are her clones. The other original female is named Bobo. She's the one lying on the ground by the tree and her clones are the two juveniles in the tree."

Juju finished her banana and John removed another from the other pocket and handed it to her through the mesh. One of the juveniles came down from the tree and hurried over to Juju. Juju screamed her displeasure and with her free hand pushed the juvenile away and struck her on the back. The juvenile made a hasty retreat to the safety of the tree.

"That's Juju, refuses to share her sacred banana. I'm surprised that juvenile even attempted."

Julia looked at the two clone juveniles in the tree, and then the two clone juveniles by the cave. Nothing out of the ordinary, except she could not tell them apart.

"That's just amazing," she said. "Spend time with these animals and you realize they each have a distinctive look. Just like people, each face and physical build is different. The two clones are exactly the same, and you can tell each pair is just a younger version of the oldest females. Even the moles on their faces.

"First, it was a good idea to reduce your contact with them. I've changes in mind we're going to have to make to the enclosure for their conditioning. The first thing I need to do is make you a list of fruits that are native to the area in which they will eventually be released. Have those shipped right away. We don't have much time for dietary changes." Julia studied the two pairs of clone juveniles in the tree again. "Do you know what this could mean? The bonobos, like the rest of the great apes, are disappearing; there are fewer than ten thousand living in the wild. The silverback mountain gorilla is down to less than three hundred. They're just one more virus outbreak away from disappearing; chimpanzee and wild orangutan populations are dangerously low, too. We've been fighting this problem for decades, tried everything to stop the decline. They're being poached into extinction. The apes just can't reproduce fast enough.

How many embryonic attempts per success to make each clone?"

"One."

"Who knew that a CEO of an investment company living alone on an island in the Caribbean could have the species-saving answer for the primates of Africa? I'd really like to see the lab where you made these."

John pulled open the metal door of the lab. It creaked from the lack of use. The overhead florescent lights came on. Julia passed through the doorway and stepped onto the raised, gray linoleum floor and slowly walked alongside the nearest table. The table was covered with computer circuit boards arranged in rows, covered with clear plastic that stretched over the sides. John followed. The air was hot and stale. The tables had medical instruments arranged in groups and also sealed in clear plastic. Straight ahead she noticed the old primate area at the far end of the room, now dark and empty, the operating table against the wall covered in clear plastic. At the far end of the right wall Julia noticed a large rack of computers. She guessed fifteen columns, each column containing ten computers, each powered off and covered in clear plastic. In the middle of the room in front of the computers was the cylinder-shaped CAT scan machine with its own table, covered in the same clear plastic.

"That's so I can check internal structures of the clones," John said.

Her eyes continued to her right, passing the doors to the incinerator. To the right of these doors was the cloning device. It was in the center of four tables placed together in a square, a large black cylinder as tall as the ceiling. She walked toward it.

"This must be it."

"It is."

"How long since the last cloning?" she asked.

"About ten years."

"Why haven't you come forward before now?"

"I was waiting for the timing to be right."

"What you've done, teams around the world have been trying to do for years."

"I know."

"This could make my rescue center unnecessary one day."

"Could be. You never know how the world is going to react to technology like this. Let's concentrate on saving the six in hand."

"We've got some things to get to the island to begin their conditioning. While we wait on the supplies, we'll need to give each of them a complete physical and photograph them head-to-toe."

"Yes, ma'am."

AUGUST 1, 2057

Julia's work with the bonobos continues. She is working me like a slave. She doesn't know why, but I am very excited. I received confirmation today. He is coming.

THE PROBLEM WITH JUJU

Two months later, the changes to the enclosure were complete. At one end of the enclosure, just outside the mesh cable, a canvas wall blocked the primates' view. A large door at the bottom could be opened from behind the canvas wall by a pulley system anchored at the top of the wall. Two parallel metal tracks entered under the closed door and led to the main feeding area of the bonobos, near the base of the large metal tree.

Julia stood outside the enclosure. She was hidden in the brush with a walkie-talkie in one hand and the end of a rope in the other. John was behind the canvas wall waiting for the command, the walkie-talkie attached to his belt and an earpiece in his left ear. When Julia commanded, he would pull the rope that opened the door and press a button on the ground by the rails that would send a life-sized, full-body-mount, female African lioness down the rails.

It was real lion skin covering a fiberglass body. The lioness had a nasty snarl on her face, her right paw positioned to strike. Beneath her, on the metal chassis attached to the rails, was a small speaker for emitting a digital recording of a lion's roar. A one-second delay was set before the loud roar would happen.

Above the enclosure, suspended in a large container, were the favorite fruits from the bonobos' future home. A rope attached to the latch on the bottom door of the container extended out to Julia's hiding place. It had been two hours since she'd placed the fruit in the container above their enclosure. She pulled the rope, the latch released, and the contents dropped the thirty feet to the ground at the end of the metal rails. The bonobos scampered to the feeding area, except Juju, who stayed on her perch in the tree.

She's such a snob, Julia thought. She waited until the last bonobo was happily feeding in the *kill zone*. Julia pressed the transmit button on the walkie-talkie and whispered, "Now."

John pulled hard on the pulley rope and hit the button with his foot. The electric motor on the rail sled whirred to life and catapulted the lioness down the rails. Just as she entered the enclosure, she let out a roar and John dropped the door behind her. She rushed at the bonobos and roared again. The primates screamed and scampered for the metal tree. Juju came down the tree to face the threat. As the lion reached the end of the rail, Juju struck it across the face with each hand, tearing the lioness's nose and screaming at the strange attacker. Juju ran to the back of the lion and struck it again, knocking the right rear leg loose from its metal mounting plate. Then Juju ran for the safety of the tree.

Julia brought the walkie-talkie to her mouth again. "Okay. Retrieve."

John pressed the button again and the lion reversed at a slower pace. He raised the door to let the lioness through. He lowered the door again and locked it. In his earpiece, he heard Julia's voice again. "Okay, sneak back to my apartment. I'll meet you there."

Julia was already drinking a beer when John got to the front porch. He sat in the chair on the other side of the table, where the cold beer bottle was waiting.

"As we thought, Juju decided to fight. If that was a real lion, she wouldn't have stood a chance," Julia said.

"It's very discouraging. She broke the back leg off the mounting plate. On the bright side, they've taken to the new diet well. Which, by the way, for what I'm paying to have arrowroot, booso fruit, and junglesop shipped here, they could be eating caviar and drinking 1962 Dom Perignon champagne."

"I knew it would be pricy. It'll increase their chance of survival if they know what to search for. What really worries me is that lions aren't the most dangerous predator. It's human poaching. We must teach them to be afraid of humans next."

"So, we need to teach Juju to fear lions and the rest of the group to fear humans. Good luck, they've always been friendly to me. They think of humans as caregivers. How are you going to do that?"

"I've a few ideas swimming around in my head—if I tell you everything, you may fire me."

"I say nothing is better for ideas swimming in your head than swimming on the beach."

"You know me, Raymond. I always have my swimsuit at hand."

"And I'm always in shorts, ready to swim at a moment's notice."

Julia soon emerged from the apartment in her bikini. Beers in hand, they made the short walk to the beach. John finished his beer, placed it on the sand, and took off his shirt on the way to the water's edge. Julia had never seen him without a shirt. The first thing she noticed was how tan he was and fit for a man of his age.

From the back, his long silver hair came down almost to his shoulders, which were still broader than his waist. That was when she noticed the patch of skin just below his right shoulder blade. Darker than the rest of his back, about the size of a quarter, and in the shape of what looked like an ink blob from a psychology exam. Just as quickly as she noticed, her mind moved on to the warm water that was now at her knees as she followed John in. He dove into an incoming wave and began to swim out over the next one. Julia did the same. After a hundred yards they stopped to tread water. Julia swam up next to John. They ascended and descended together like two corks with each passing wave.

"I can't believe I have a job where I can go for a swim at a beach in the middle of the afternoon. Why would you want to leave this place?"

"'I grow old... I grow old... I shall wear the bottoms of my trousers rolled. Shall I part my hair behind? Do I dare to eat a peach? I shall wear white flannel trousers, and walk upon the beach. I have heard the mermaids singing, each to each. I do not think that they will sing to me. I have seen them riding seaward on the waves. Combing the white hair of the waves blown back, when the wind blows the water white and black. We have lingered in the chambers of the sea, by sea-girls wreathed with seaweed red and brown, till human voices wake us, and we drown.'"

"You wrote that?"

"T.S. Eliot. Even a place like this can feel like a prison after a while." John floated on his back, staring at the sky. Bobbing with the waves. He came upright. "I'll race you back to shore. The loser has to go up and fetch the next two beers."

"You're on!"

Without another word, John started swimming to shore as hard as he could. Twenty-five yards out, Julia passed him and reached ankle-deep water five yards in front of him. He was breathing heavily when he stopped beside her and put his hands on his knees. Sea water drained from his hair and beard. He waited for his breathing to slow.

"Getting old isn't for wimps," John said.

"Don't take it so hard. I used to be on a swim team." Julia was used to smoothing the male ego.

John looked up, his hands still on his knees. "Me, too."

The distant hum of the airplane came over the ocean. The distinctive sound of a small Cessna. Julia shielded the sun from her eyes and looked past the palm trees to locate the plane.

"My guest is early," John said.

"Guest?"

"Plan on having dinner at my house tonight. I'll cook you another one of my rib-eyes."

"Who is it?"

"If I tell you everything, you may think this place boring and quit."

SEAN

By the time John got to the house, the two passengers of the plane were waiting on the front porch. John climbed the front steps, extended his right hand, and shook hands with an exact replica of himself at twenty-seven years of age, standing on his porch in a flower print shirt and tan shorts, a blue duffle bag at his feet. Frick, whom John let out of the lab now that the bonobo training was over, approached, wagging her tail.

"It's certainly a pleasure to meet you, Mr. Taylor," John's clone said.

"The pleasure is mine, Mr. Burke." John faced the second man. "And it's a pleasure to meet you too."

Next to the clone stood a black man in his late forties, dressed in white linen shirt and pants. At his feet was a shipping box the size of two shoeboxes. "So, you are the realtor's son. How is your father doing?"

"Them stroke be a bad thing, mon. He be livin' in a home now."

"I'm so sorry to hear it."

"I've been runnin' the family business the past year now, I guess you know? Here be the package you asked me to pick up at the post office, bey."

"It's good to know the family business carries on. I've something for you."

From a table on the porch John picked up a silver metal briefcase, underneath which was a small white envelope. He handed both to the realtor's son. "I appreciate you coming out here with Mr. Burke. Here's your payment." John handed him the envelope. "When you return to New Providence, could you give this briefcase to my lawyer in Nassau?"

"No problem, mon. There's somethin' I'd like to talk to you 'bout, too, if you walk wit me back to the plane?"

As John followed the real estate agent's son down the path to the plane, he was fairly certain what was about to be discussed. Halfway to the plane he stopped.

"My father told me intrestin' things 'bout you lately. His mind started to go the last few months and it wandered and he talked and talked. People couldn't tell silly babble from real stories. But I could. He know you a long time, told me all 'bout them troubles you had back in the States. And who you really be. He told me 'bout the five hundred thousand dollars a year you been payin'. I bet you not know that big-shot government official dropped dead of a heart attack two years ago now, bey? My father been pocketin' that fee, mon. I told him he should raise the price, but he liked you and always say 'Leave the man alone; beside, if squeezed too hard he may go away.'"

The black man shrugged his shoulders. "My father be fed through a straw now, mon. That stroke left nuthin' of his mind. That just leaves me as the only one who know who you really be and I don't think you goin' away. I think you like be here in the islands. I think you want stay here. That's the thing 'bout them arrest warrants, mon, they never go away until the day you die."

"And how much is my 'fee' going to be now?"

"You be wealthy, mon, no trouble for you. I think two million a year be a fair price for you to be free, bey? No electronic transfer, mon, I want it in cash. The government be crackin' down for them taxes."

"I see. I'll need a couple of months to free up that amount of funds. What did you say your name is?"

"Mr. Smith, of course, mon," he said, with the same toothy grin as his father.

"One thing, though, Mr. Smith." John pointed to the briefcase he'd given him. "That briefcase is a neat gadget. On the outside is a fingerprint pad and a combination lock. The person whose fingerprint is registered with it and knows the combination can open it. That would be my attorney in Nassau. If it's pried open, or cut open or tampered with in any way, the contents of the case will be incinerated. Really an amazing device. Just thought you should know."

Mr. Smith laughed. "No problem, mon. I be seein' you in two

months."

John walked back to the house. *Two million dollars, my ass.* His clone was staring at the ocean and Frick was still sitting at attention. "Good girl, Frick." She came over for a rub on the head.

"That's a well-trained dog."

The engine on the Cessna started on the runway and John watched it accelerate and lift into the air and disappear behind the trees.

"Sean Burke, it's good to finally see you in person." John picked up the box from the chair and swung open the front screen door. "Get your bag and come in the house, we've got a lot to talk about."

THE GRANT

Julia dried her hair while her mind returned to the bonobos, in particular the problem of Juju. *How to make her afraid of a stuffed lion? Since a stuffed lion can't hurt her, it is going to be a sticky problem. Fortunately, the other primates were already afraid, if for no other reason than it was just a strange thing moving fast. Juju is the matriarch of the group; she fears nothing. In fact, her lack of fear could affect the other primates. She could actually teach them not to fear the lion either. Her whole demeanor projects authority and entitlement. She even "expects" Raymond to bring her the bananas with every visit.* Julia's mind searched for an answer. None came.

As she approached Raymond's house, she could hear the generator that powered the lab above the sound of the surf and the wind in the palm trees. She wondered what Raymond had been working on in there the last few weeks, when he wasn't busy helping her with the bonobo training. She had meant to ask him and kept forgetting. *Probably not important.* She noticed that the lights of the main house downstairs were on. She could hear Raymond talking inside. She couldn't make out the words. She knocked and heard approaching footsteps. The front door opened, flooding the porch with light.

"Punctual as always," John said.

He opened the door wider and pushed the screen door open. Julia entered. Papers and folders covered the coffee table in the living room. All the books usually piled there were now scattered on the floor. Her attention was drawn to the kitchen table, where she saw a man about her age. Casually dressed, soft brown hair, pleasant smile and nice build.

"Julia, this is Sean Burke. Sean, this is Julia Watson. As I was telling you, she's training the bonobos. Julia, Sean flew here from New York, where he worked for Goldman Sachs. He's now working for me. Sean was a lead investment analyst, a high-level position for someone with the company a mere five years. I was not surprised.

"He was noticed in high school by my company. With a grant from my company, he went to Harvard University, where he graduated with honors. Again, I was not surprised. He has done very well at Goldman. In fact, of all the students my company has helped, he has outperformed them all."

"How many students have received the grants?" asked Julia.

"Quite a few—after he had acquired enough experience, I thought it time to offer him a position with my investment company. You're looking at my new chief financial officer."

"Congratulations, Mr. Burke," Julia said.

"Please, call me Sean. It's a bit overwhelming, this island, this house out here. Mr. Taylor made an offer that was too hard to refuse."

"I know exactly how you feel."

"I believe that you find the high performers and do whatever you can to hire them," John said. He moved to the stove and lit a burner. "Julia, medium-well, as usual?"

She nodded.

John removed three wine glasses from the cabinet and brought them, a bottle opener, and a bottle of red wine from the wine cooler. He opened the bottle and poured three glasses. He handed Julia and Sean each their glass.

"Sean, you are as special as they come. I propose a toast." John lifted his glass and Julia and Sean did likewise. "New friends, new beginnings, and long happy life."

Everyone took a drink.

Two hours later the steaks, mushrooms, and the bottle of wine were gone. The polite small talk began to wind down.

"It's getting late for an old man like me. I'll take care of the cleanup. Julia, would you be kind enough to show Sean the apartment next to yours?"

"Of course. Won't you let me help you clean up?"

"No, no, I can handle this."

John removed a laptop computer from a desk drawer and handed it to Sean. "On this computer, you'll find the information you need to learn about my current investments and the performance of each. There's a power pad station on the coffee table in your apartment. Take a few days to look it over."

"Thank you."

"Julia, am I abusing your kindness if I ask you to show Sean around the island tomorrow? I'm sure he would like to see the bonobos."

"I'd be glad to. I've been meaning to ask you what you've been working on in the lab recently."

"Nothing important, just trying to get things organized for when it's time for me to leave."

"Moving back to the States?" Julia asked.

"Yes."

"Are you leaving soon?" Sean asked.

"That depends on both of you. Julia has to train the bonobos and you have to be ready to take over running my investments. As soon as those things are ready, it will be time for me to leave."

The moon was bright enough for the palm trees to cast shadows on the white sandy path, making it easy for Julia and Sean to follow.

"Did Raymond tell you about his cloning procedure?"

"Yes. I don't know anything about medical science, so most of it was over my head."

"The building to our left is his lab. You should see the inside and the cloning device he built. It's remarkable."

"How long have you been here?"

"Two months."

Sean followed her up the steps of the duplex. Julia pointed to the door to the left.

"That is your place. I'm next door. You should have everything you need. If you have any questions, knock."

"I will. Thank you very much, it's nice to meet you."

"Yes, it has been nice." Julia let herself into her apartment and closed the door.

Sean looked back to the ocean from his vantage point on the porch. The white sand glowed in the moonlight, matching the white foam of the surf. A shooting star streaked above the horizon, silently coming to life and dying in a greenish white light, leaving a sparkling trail which quickly faded.

Not a bad job site, he thought.

A WEALTHY MAN

Sean stood at the stainless-steel mesh and looked up at the morning sun making long golden shafts of humid air through the branches of the metal tree. The bonobos were asleep in the cave and did not hear Julia and Sean approaching with the cart loaded with fruit. Julia tapped Sean on the arm.

"The large one sleeping in the left-most cave is the alpha female. Her name is Juju," Julia said.

"How can you tell them apart?"

"It isn't difficult once you have spent time around them. They each have a unique personality and habits, just like people."

Juju lifted her head and saw Julia. Juju stood to her feet, stretched, dropped to all fours and gracefully descended down the fake stone wall to the ground. On all fours, she ambled over to the mesh opposite of Julia. Juju stopped and sat and held out her left hand. Julia retrieved a banana from her left leg pocket and handed it to Juju through the mesh. Juju peeled the banana and took a bite.

"Look at that, just like a person. How did she know you had a banana?" Sean asked.

"She doesn't know, she just expects it. I have another in my other leg pocket. When she finishes that one, she's going to ask again."

On cue, Juju took the last bite of banana and held out her left hand again. Julia took the last banana and handed it over through the mesh, where it was promptly consumed. Juju walked on all fours to the metal tree, where she climbed up to her usual branch on the left side ten feet off the ground.

"That's the damnedest thing I've ever seen," Sean said.

"She's quite the problem. You see the far end of the enclosure covered with the canvas wall?"

"Yes."

Julia pulled the large four-wheeled cart down to the feeding place. Sean grabbed the handle too and helped. "Behind there is a stuffed lioness. We can make her come charging out of there on those rails that lead to the base of the tree. All the bonobos run from it, except for Juju. She turns to fight. She gave it a couple of good hits yesterday, almost knocked the nose completely off and damaged a back leg. The current problem is to teach her to be afraid of a stuffed lioness. And I'd better come up with a way before I run that lion out there again or she teaches the others there is no reason to be afraid. You've never seen primates before? Ever been to the zoo?"

"I was raised in New York. There is a nice zoo. I haven't been since I was a kid."

Julia reached the feeding station and stopped. The bonobos began making their way over for breakfast, except for Juju. Sean and Julia began removing the fruit from the cart and threw it into the enclosure.

"Your parents still live in New York?"

"No, retired now and living in Orlando, along with every other retired person in America. They like it there."

"How did your parents get Raymond's company to send you to college?"

"They didn't. We didn't even know Taylor Investment Group existed. I graduated in the top two percent of my high school class. There were people with better grades than me. They gave a survey at school my senior year about what major each of us was planning for college and that was when I decided on finance. After the Christmas holiday break, I got a letter in the mail from Raymond's company. They awarded grants to students majoring in finance. It came with an application and I had to write a thousand-word essay. My parents figured we had nothing to lose. Two months later I got a call from an attorney; he told me I was selected for a full scholarship, and the company had made arrangements for me to attend Harvard."

"Wow, that is something."

"My mom and dad were so happy they cried."

"Do you like working on Wall Street? You don't look like a bean-

166

counting geek."

"The hours are long. Not much time for anything else in my life. I have a simple goal: to make lots and lots of money."

Each bonobo had selected the fruit it desired from the pile and absconded with it to their cement cave. Sean noticed that all the bonobos were eating except Juju, still sitting on her perch. "What is wrong with her?"

"Nothing, she knows I'm going to make two more trips and, on the last one, when the others have their fill and have gone away, she can have her pick. Just for the money?"

"Yes. Just for the money. Is there something wrong with that?"

Julia grabbed the handle of the cart and headed back for the next load of fruit, Sean following.

"No higher cause?"

"I don't want money just for money's sake. Like our quirky Mr. Taylor. Be wealthy, so wealthy that you can buy anything, or go anywhere you want. I did research on Taylor Investments before I came out here. Not much hard information out there because it's a privately held company here in the Bahamas. It has investments in stock exchanges around the world. Nobody knows for sure. The obvious investments are worth about $100 million."

"Obvious investments?"

"I'm not bragging when I tell you I am pretty good at what I do. The investments out there for the world to see have a certain pattern to them. They are... too nice and neat."

"Okay, whatever that means."

"Just trust me. So, I kept digging. Being at Goldman gives me access to information most people don't. I kind of made it my own project. I have a theory. I can't prove it, but from what I could glean and with a few educated guesses, from the estimates I found, I'd say the value of the company is over $20 billion."

Julia stopped walking and stood speechless for a moment. "I knew Raymond had money... I had no idea."

"That guy, alone on this island, with no mansion, no corporate jet, no investment team, no brokers, no insider-Wall-Street dealings, no servants, no maids, no chef, and no butler, living in a house furnished like my grandparents'... packed with old books, has quietly made himself one of

167

the richest men in the world."

They began pulling the cart back down the path, away from the bonobo enclosure. Sean continued, "He has been here almost his entire life, at least the last thirty years. Why has he decided to leave now?"

"He hasn't said. I assumed he's going to market the cloning device. That has to be worth a lot of money. I guess he'll have you run the investment part of the company while he focuses on the production of the cloning device."

"Perhaps."

"Is working for Raymond going to make you wealthy?"

"Mr. Taylor made me a very lucrative offer, so good in fact I keep expecting the other shoe to drop. The contract looks solid. If it's as it seems, with the salary and commission from the return on the investments, in six to eight years I should have enough money to start my own hedge fund. And that's where I can make the life-changing money. Who knows, before I'm fifty I could have my own island in the Caribbean.

"What about you? Before you got to the house last night, Mr. Taylor told me about you training the monkeys. What are you going to do when the training is over and you have to leave this paradise?"

"I'm planning to run the research and rescue center I have in the Democratic Republic of Congo, at least for the next three years. That's if the civil war there doesn't force us to leave."

"Why is there a war?"

"Been a war going on there for the last sixty years. I certainly don't see it ending anytime soon; too many factions struggling to assume control."

"I guess it isn't a bad vision, saving the bonobos," Sean said.

"For all my efforts, it's more likely Raymond who will save them. With his cloning device. Once they are being produced, if I could get him to donate one to the center, perhaps I could actually stop their population decline."

"You know, I know a guy who is going to be working very closely with Mr. Taylor. I bet he could present a convincing argument for a tax-deductible donation to a worthy cause."

They had reached the intersection in the path. To the right led back to the lab and the shed that stored the bonobos' food. To the left was the path back to the duplex.

"You would do that for me?" Julia reached out and grabbed Sean's hand.

"You know what they say, 'A worthy cause'—"

"Is a cause worth doing?"

"Is a cause worth a good write-off—at least that's what they say on Wall Street."

Julia threw Sean's hand to his side, put her hands on her hips and gave an exaggerated frown of disapproval. "I can see I've my work cut out to get you to see the bigger picture."

"If I'm going to have any sway with Mr. Taylor, I'd better get to looking at what's on that laptop he gave me." Sean began walking down the path to the left.

"And I need to get the bonobos fed. And the lion needs repairs."

Sean stopped and turned around. "Dinner tonight?"

"I'd like that."

"Great, because you're going to have to show me how to cook it."

"Your place should be stocked with food like mine. Take a chicken out of the freezer."

"And put it where?" Sean asked.

"In the kitchen sink."

"Okay." Sean grinned and continued toward his apartment.

Julia pulled the cart to the shed. Attached to the outside of the door was a handwritten note.

Come see me at the lab – Raymond

Julia loaded the cart with assorted fruits and leaves from the various crates in the building. She pulled the cart around the house and stopped in front of the lab. She could hear the generator running. She approached the large, rusty metal doors with the keypad lock and knocked. In a minute the lock clicked and the hinges creaked as the door opened. John stepped outside, followed by Frick, and closed the door.

"Good morning," John said.

Julia could see the dark circles under John's eyes. "Good morning."

"I need a favor. I'm going to be very busy in the lab for a couple of days and I'm not able to be a very good host. I thought it would be nice for Sean if you took him sailing."

"Today? I don't know. He's back at his apartment going over the data you gave him last night. He seemed anxious to look at them, and I

169

need to repair the lion."

"How about tomorrow? I insist. You've been working hard for weeks now and everybody needs a break."

"He has probably never been on a sailboat."

"You are probably right about that. You'll convince him to put the work off for a day. Tell him I insist. There's a nice cay about twenty miles to the southwest. On a bearing of about two hundred and thirty degrees. Very pretty spot. Take him there."

"Okay, a day off it is," Julia said. *I have been itching to take out my new boat anyway, just been afraid to ask for a day off.*

"Great. I'll even feed the bonobos in the morning so you can get an early start."

DINNER

When Sean answered the knock on the door he had been showered, shaved, and dressed in his nicest pair of shorts and shirt for over an hour. When he opened the door, Julia stood there in a pink dress, the setting sun behind her, the tan lines from the bikini top around her neck disappearing under her silky brown hair. She was holding a covered black cooking pot with an insulated mitten in one hand and a carton of milk in the other.

"Hi! I thought we were having chicken?" Sean said, looking at the pot.

"We are. This is just mashed potatoes. It will go well with the fried chicken we're going to make."

"Come in, please." Sean stepped to the side so Julia could pass. "Fried chicken and mashed potatoes and milk?"

Julia walked into the kitchen and set the pot and the milk carton on the countertop. "There are a few things I have learned while working in Atlanta. One of them is that the traffic is horrible no matter the time of day or night and another is an appreciation for Southern cooking. And, no, we are not having milk."

Sean closed the front door. Julia looked in the kitchen sink to find the now-thawed whole chicken in the sink. Sean walked into the kitchen.

"What's the first thing to do?"

Julia reached over and pulled the largest butcher's knife out of the wooden knife set holder and turned to Sean.

"We clean the chicken."

Sean looked at the knife, then back to Julia's smiling eyes. "How about you clean this one and I'll do the next one?"

"Okay, city boy, I'll let you off the hook this time. How about you get the flour, salt, pepper, and cooking oil out of the pantry and put them by the stove."

"I like the sound of that kind of helping a lot better."

Forty minutes later, the skillet on the stove was full of pieces of chicken covered with flour and frying in the hot oil. Sean stood proudly in front of the stove with his hands covered in pasty flour, watching the pieces fry.

"That wasn't too bad," Sean said. "I like the dipping them in milk and putting them in the flour part best."

"Yes, that is the most fun part; it's the part my dad let me do, starting when I was about ten."

"What? You had to go rain on my moment of glory like that?"

"I'm just saying."

Sean raised his hands up in front of his face and looked at his palms and then the backs of each hand. "You know," he paused, still rotating his hands, "I bet you wouldn't have that know-it-all attitude if you had flour smeared all over your face." Sean lunged at her.

"No!" Julia grabbed Sean by the wrist of each arm and tried to keep his flour-covered fingers from her face. Laughing, Sean pushed her back into the corner of the kitchen counter, where she had no escape. She pushed hard against his arms, but Sean gently leaned his weight into her. Julia could see the inevitable defeat coming and closed her eyes and pushed as hard as she could, but soon the cold, sticky fingers of each hand were pressed against her cheeks. Julia was laughing too hard to resist. She let go of Sean's wrists and lowered her hands to the countertop in surrender. Sean stood there, his fingers still pressed against her face until she opened her eyes and looked into his. His hands now gently touched her face. He lowered his lips to hers. Julia closed her eyes and pressed her lips back against his. When he pulled back and placed his hands on top of hers, she exhaled and opened her eyes.

"I didn't think I should pass up the chance to give you a kiss," Sean said.

"I'm glad you didn't." Julia could feel her pulse racing.

Sean stepped back and smiled. "And now that you have flour on your face, I think we can celebrate with a glass of wine."

"Only if you rinse your hands off before you get the glasses." Julia laughed and wiped the flour from her cheeks.

"Deal." Sean quickly rinsed his hands clean of flour, dried them, then removed two wine glasses from the overhead cabinet and a bottle of white wine from the wine cooler under the countertop near the refrigerator. "I noticed this in there yesterday."

"I know. Mine is fully stocked too."

Sean uncorked the bottle and poured two glasses, and Julia used tongs to turn the still-frying chicken over in the grease.

"The chicken doesn't have that much longer."

"How long have you lived in Atlanta?" Sean asked.

"About four years now."

"You're from there?"

"No, I was raised in Spring Valley, California. It's just outside San Diego."

"Did you like your job in Atlanta?"

"It was okay. It paid the bills, as they say. Of course, I was living like a monk so I could send as much money as I could to my research office."

Sean handed Julia a glass of wine. "A toast."

Julia raised her glass.

"To not living like a monk." Sean grinned. Julia smiled and they both took a drink.

"Okay, let's set the table."

The chicken continued to fry, tended to by Julia. They drank the bottle of wine and Sean opened another.

"Okay, the chicken is about done," Julia said.

"Sounds great, I'm starving."

Sean placed the plates on the table while Julia retrieved the chicken pieces from the grease and placed them on a napkin-lined platter. She heated the mashed potatoes in the microwave and joined Sean at the table. Sean selected a leg and Julia served him a helping of potatoes. He bit into the crispy fried meat and let the flavor soak in. "This may be the best fried chicken ever made by mankind."

Julia selected her chicken and took a bite as well. "I told you that Southern cooking can sure grow on you."

They ate in silence until each had finished their first piece of chicken, then Sean got his second piece and took a breath. "Do your parents still live in Spring Valley?"

"My mother and dad divorced when I was about a year old," Julia said, as they finished the chicken she had fried. "She moved away and never came back. I know she was in San Francisco for a while. I don't know where she is now. So, it was just me and my dad. He died of a heart attack about a year and a half ago."

"I'm sorry," Sean said.

"It's okay. I do miss him. We were very close. Dad and I used to go sailing together. We used to compete in races. We had a very fast J-twenty-four sloop, and a great crew. San Diego has a great sailing community. Everybody around there knew my dad. He'd won more of those club races than anybody. Speaking of sailing, in fact, Raymond insists we take a day off tomorrow and I take you sailing."

"Really, he's giving me a day off on my second day of work so a beautiful woman can take me sailing in the Bahamas? I think I'm going to like working for this man."

"How'd your work go today?"

"The information on that computer was just the investments in the Asian stock market, the Shanghai, Hang Seng and Nikkei exchanges. It's very extensive and I haven't got to the property investments. I assume he's going to start me out in Asia to see how I do. I don't see anything I don't think I can handle."

"Have you told Goldman Sachs you have a new job yet?"

"Technically right now I'm on vacation for a few weeks. Gives me time to evaluate this job."

"Are you going to have to move?"

"Mr. Taylor said I could work from anywhere I want. A simple internet connection will do it. Maybe I could spend a few weeks a year at this place. Maybe Paris in the spring or the Amalfi coast in the summer."

"I'd love to go to Paris."

Sean finished the last of his potatoes, drank the last of his glass of wine, and poured each of them another.

"If I end up there, I'll give you a call so you can join me."

"That sounds great." Julia tried to imagine what Paris would be like. She knew Paris only from pictures and television. She was sure it would be romantic. "For now, the cooking lesson is going to continue. You can join me in the kitchen for the final part: dishwashing."

"You mean no waiter to come and just take them away?"

Julia brought her plate to the kitchen counter and started filling the right-hand side of the sink with warm, soapy water. Sean obediently followed. Julia placed her plate in the soapy water and found Sean standing behind her empty-handed.

"Your plate?"

"Oh, sorry."

Sean retrieved his plate. Julia began washing the pot the mashed potatoes were in. Sean stopped directly behind her and reached around and placed his plate in the sink. Julia smiled at having him standing so close to her. Sean gently kissed the top of her shoulder near the base of her neck. Julia stopped washing the second plate.

EAVESDROPPING

It was well past sundown on the second day that John had been working on the imaging helmets. He had a few more of the new sensors to put in the helmets. He was tired and happy because the new sensors eliminated the need to shave the heads of the imaging source and target. Tomorrow he'd be able to run a test. While he worked, he had been listening to the conversation coming from the speakers next to the computer monitor.

After ten minutes of silence from the speakers, he put down the helmet and looked at the screen. He held his hand in front of the screen and moved the pointer to the volume icon and spread his fingers. The volume increased. Still he could not hear anything. He moved his hand so that the pointer moved over the window labeled "Apartment 1," then moved his hand down until the pointer was over the button labeled "Kitchen." John pinched his thumb and index finger together and the button was selected. He listened. He believed he could just barely hear the softest noise, not voices. It was a rustling sound. He moved his hand again until the pointer was over the button labeled "Bedroom." John heard moaning.

John moved his hand so that the pointer was over the "Quit" button and touched his thumb and index finger again and the speakers went silent. John stared at the screen for a minute. He remembered a feeling from long ago. The fumbling of clothes in the bedroom of his Boston apartment. He wanted to have that feeling again. John looked down at Frick sleeping at his feet.

"Looks like things are moving faster than I anticipated. I hope the test tomorrow goes well."

AUGUST 29, 2057

It is late, almost midnight, but the new helmet is ready, just in the nick of time. I'll do a test run with it tomorrow. I'll need the island to myself, so I have sent them away. The lovebirds should enjoy a day-trip on Julia's new boat. There's nothing like being young and finding a new lover. The carefree thrill of the whole thing. You don't realize that it's a flash in the pan.

Juju's attitude will finally become useful.

TEST RUN

The sound of the surf woke him up. He slowly opened his eyes and peered through the window above the bed's headboard. The sun was not quite yet above the horizon. Sean blinked his eyes open and gave them a few seconds to adjust. That was when he noticed Julia lying next to him, resting her head on her hand and smiling.

"Did you know you make a soft snoring sound when you're on your back?"

Sean smiled. "No, I didn't know that. And what other flaws did you observe while I was sleeping?"

"Nothing else, really. Well, just one other."

"Yes?"

"Obviously, you've been finding your way to the gym." Julia lifted up the sheet covering them and looked underneath. "However, you've got to be the whitest white boy I've ever seen."

"I told you I haven't had a day off in the last five years." Sean lifted the sheet and looked at Julia's naked body. "Besides, I'm not sure that is a bad thing coming from Sheena, Queen of the Jungle."

🧬

John poured his first cup of coffee and went to the porch, Frick following. He looked at the sun. At least two fists above the horizon. *Damn it, must be after nine o'clock.* The wind blew through his hair, and he looked to the east. A high, thin haze of clouds covered the sun. He had slept for ten straight hours. He still felt tired. He could see the *Emerald Green* three hundred yards off the beach. Its tall white sails were slanted and stiff in the wind, surrounded by waves of turquoise. White foam appeared at its bow as it sliced through the waves.

John looked down at Frick. "Looks like we'd better get started. We don't have that much time."

He went to the storage building. The cart was parked outside and he brought it in and filled it with fruit. He put two bananas in the cargo pockets of his shorts. He pulled the cart to the laboratory, left it by the path, and unlocked the laboratory door. Frick followed him inside.

John searched for a small bottle of clear liquid. He pulled out a syringe and removed it from the sterile packaging. He stuck the needle in the bottom of the small bottle and drew out a syringe full. He removed the banana from his right leg pocket and in three places stuck the needle through the banana peel and injected a portion of the liquid. John repeated the process for the other banana. He went to the front door, Frick behind him. John stopped.

"Stay," he said to Frick.

He returned to the cart and pulled it down the path to the bonobo enclosure. Juju, of course, was the first one to greet him. She held out her left hand. John gave her a banana through the wire mesh. He moved a few more yards down and threw fruits through the mesh. The other bonobos came over for breakfast. The oldest Juju clone came near the mesh. John looked over at Juju. She had finished her banana and was sitting where she had eaten it, not moving. She raised a hand up to wipe her mouth and let it fall back to the ground as if it was too heavy to hold up. John removed the next banana from his pocket and waved it at the oldest Juju clone. He handed it to her through the mesh. She quickly peeled it and ate it in two quick bites. John threw the rest of the fruit through the mesh. The remaining bonobos gathered there to eat. John brought the cart back to the main gate, entered the code in the keypad, and let himself into the enclosure. The bonobos ran for the caves. *Good. I guess they are getting wary.*

Juju was now lying on the ground. John grabbed her under each arm and lifted her into the cart. He pulled the cart over to the unconscious clone and lifted her into the other half of the cart. The cart was much heavier now, so it took John twice as long to get back to the lab, and his shirt was damp with sweat when he got there. He unlocked the door, allowing Frick to come out. She immediately went to the cart to smell and inspect the bonobos. John pulled the cart inside, and Frick followed.

John first lifted the clone out of the cart and placed her on a scale on the center table and recorded her weight. Then he carried her to the CAT scan table. The machine was already on, in standby mode. He placed the straps across her legs, stomach and chest, and placed two brace blocks on either side of her head to keep her face straight up. The computer started the scanning process and John watched its progress on the screen. It lasted thirty minutes. John untied the straps and moved the Juju clone to the table by the imaging computers near the wall. Once she was strapped to that table, John started an IV in the clone's leg that was hooked up to the sedative dispenser machine. John took a fresh syringe from a drawer and drew a small amount out of the bottle of clear liquid. He gave her an injection in the thigh.

Don't want her waking up during the scanning.

Next was Juju on the scale. Once the scan was done, he carried her to the other table by the imaging computers and placed an IV in her leg too. He fitted imaging helmets on her head and that of the clone, and set a timer for three hours and thirty minutes.

THE CAY

Julia stood behind the wheel of the *Emerald Green*. She looked down at the display on the top of the wheel mount, which gave a distance in nautical miles and bearing in compass degrees to the point she had entered in the navigation system. The imaginary point the system was directing her to was the cay Raymond had described the day before, three miles away. The computer said she was directly on course, and they would be there in nineteen minutes and forty-eight seconds.

Sean was seated on the starboard side of the cockpit wearing a white T-shirt, dark blue swim trunks, and dark sunglasses. He had been there for most of the trip, relaxed and smiling, feet propped up. He was looking at the clouds and sun and water like he had never seen them before.

Julia lowered the sails with the touch of a button. The boat slowed and flattened in the water. She started the engine and directed the boat closer to the beach. Sean noticed the change, lifted his head from his reclined position, and began watching Julia. He moved his feet from their propped-up position to the deck.

"Can I do anything to help?" he asked.

"It's okay, I've got it."

She dropped anchor and moved the gear lever to "neutral" and killed the engine. The boat rocked awkwardly for a minute before the anchor rope tightened and the boat steadied. There was no sound apart from the waves breaking on the cay, the wind through the rigging, and the crystal-clear water lapping against the hull.

"Sheena, oh mighty Queen of the Jungle, is there anything you can't do?"

Julia walked over and stood in front of Sean. With her right hand, she reached up and pulled the string of the bow around her neck, and with her left hand pulled the string of the bow behind her back. Her bikini top fell to the deck. The untanned flesh of her breasts glistened bright in the sun. She shook her bikini bottom off and let it fall to the deck of the cockpit.

"If you can catch me, you can find out!"

She used the bench seat next to Sean to leap over the cables of the safety railing behind him and into the gin-clear water below with a splash. When she came back to the surface, Sean stood in the boat and peeled off his T-shirt and swim trunks. He stood up on the seat to look over the side of the boat to the water below.

"Woo! Look at that whiteness!"

Sean jumped over the safety railing into the water. Julia began swimming as hard as she could for the beach. She reached it first and stood in waist-deep water and began splashing him furiously when he reached water shallow enough for him to stand. He tried to bull-rush his way through the wall of water Julia sent his way, but being unable to see, every time he lunged for her she would side-step and he would miss.

"What's wrong? Big strong white man not quick enough?" She sent a series of even harder splashes as she tried to extend her range.

Sean ran at her through the waist-deep water. She turned to dive away, but Sean grabbed her by the ankle. She tried to kick his grip free but knew it was too tight. Sean pulled her to him so that she was straddling his hips. Then, as her chest came next to his, he wrapped her in a bear hug as she put her arms around his neck and locked her feet behind his back. Sean stood up but not all the way, leaving his knees bent so that their shoulders were out of the water. The salty ocean water ran down from their hair over their faces. They kissed each other. Then they pulled their mouths apart and took a deep breath.

Julia took her arms from around his neck and combed her fingers through her hair to get it out of her face so she could see. He kissed her again. He could taste the salt, but he could taste her too. He moved his head to the side and kissed her neck and then her shoulder. He lifted her higher out of the water and kissed her nipples. Her breasts were firm and the nipples erect. Sean lowered Julia back down into the water where his erection was waiting for her. Julia rolled her hips, arched her back, and took him inside.

Julia nudged his leg with her hand.

"Hey, white boy, we'd better get you out of the sun."

He sat up and looked to see if he was burnt yet. They'd fallen asleep at the water's edge. He looked up and saw white puffy clouds moving in front of the sun.

At first Julia thought it was a bit of stubborn sand, so she splashed some water on the spot below his right shoulder blade. When she wiped it with her hand, she could see that it wasn't sand. She turned Sean so the sunlight was on his back. That was when she could tell it was a birthmark, a darker patch of skin. It looked familiar to her.

"It's a birthmark. Been there my whole life. Come on."

They swam back to the *Emerald Green* and put their swimsuits back on. Julia went down into the cabin and said, "Hey, catch," and threw him a green plastic tube labeled "Sun Block SPF 50."

"Thanks. It's getting cloudy."

"Better not take any chances. I can't have you being too sensitive for me to touch."

They ate leftover chicken and drank beers. Sean felt very content as he looked out over the green water to the horizon. "I've wanted to come to the Bahamas for years. If I'd known it was this nice, I'd have come a long time ago."

Julia looked out at the water too. "It's nice here." The water had a dark green tint now that the clouds were thicker. She looked at the sky and noticed there were fewer patches of blue left. "Would be a nice place to vacation."

"Vacation isn't the reason I was wanting to come. Remember I told you my parents raised me in New York and they now live in Orlando? That is true, except that they aren't my biological parents. I was adopted."

"How long have you known?"

"They told me when I was ten. It isn't a problem for me. They're my parents as far as I'm concerned. When I was in high school, I found the adoption papers in my dad's file cabinet. From an adoption agency in

Miami. The folder had my birth certificate inside. It was a Bahamian birth certificate. It gave the name of the mother, but not the father. There was no last name for me. I had the first name of Sean.

"I thought maybe I'd come to Nassau and dig around in the census records or something and maybe see if I could find my mother in there. If those records are even available to the public."

"You should at least try before you go back to New York."

"You're right, as long as I'm this close."

"Either way, you'll feel better if you tried."

"I'll give it a try before I go home."

Julia looked to the northeast and didn't really like the shape or color of the clouds. She went back down in the cabin. At the navigation station, she switched on the computer and in a minute linked to the satellite. Sixty miles to the northeast of their boat's location, green blobs showed a developing squall line. It wasn't bad, yet her experience told her that it had potential. Julia stuck her head out of the cabin door.

"We'd better go. Looks like there's weather building to the northeast."

Julia had to take a long tack against the rising wind and waves, intentionally bypassing Raymond's island and tacking back to starboard for the final leg. The waves were now coming at them from the port side as the boat climbed up and down each swell. The wind was gusty and strengthening and beginning to blow the tops off the waves, causing whitecaps. Julia was sure they'd reach the dock before the rain started. Barely.

Soon they were at the dock. Julia looked up at the house and could see lights on in the living room. Swiftly they secured the boat to the dock and jogged up the path to the house. The sky was growing darker. Lightning flickered on the horizon. As they came to the front of the house, they found John standing on the front porch with Frick.

"Good evening, you two. Any trouble finding the cay?"

"Julia's something else with a sailboat," Sean said. "It's really beautiful there. Too bad the weather made us leave early."

"I'm glad you had a good time."

Sean and Julia came up onto the porch.

John said, "I have bad news. Especially for you, Julia."

"What is it?"

"When I went to feed the bonobos this morning, I found Juju dead."

"What? How?"

"I wish I could say. No physical injury to her that I could tell. She was just lying there at the base of the tree."

"That is terrible," Sean said.

"I can't imagine what could have happened," Julia said. "I'd like to see her, see if I can detect anything. Where is she?"

"I gave her a complete examination. I thought you would want to see her so I put her in the freezer."

Julia looked concerned. "I hope it isn't a disease. Especially one that could infect the others."

"Good point. We'll keep a closer eye on the others."

The first few raindrops hit the roof of the porch with loud clicks.

"We'd better get back to our place," Sean said.

"Sean, there are stocks I'm considering in the European markets—I know I had you looking at the Asian information—could I get your opinion on a few things?"

"Sure."

John said to Julia, "We may be awhile, if you don't mind."

The rain began tapping harder on the roof.

"I'd better hurry back to my place if I want to stay dry," Julia said. "I'll see you guys tomorrow."

It was a downpour as Julia ran to her apartment. She showered, put on a T-shirt and shorts, and poured herself a glass of red wine from a half-empty bottle on the counter. She went and curled up on the couch. Darkness came quickly outside. She couldn't see the beach or hear the surf. Sheets of rain blew against the windows and splattered across the porch.

She sat in the dark living room and listened to the rain and sipped the wine. Although she had only known Sean for two days, there was something very familiar about him. *If someone had told me I would have a blind date with a stockbroker from New York City who had never been on a sailboat or south of the Mason-Dixon line, I'd think he wouldn't be my type. Somehow, he is my type. Of course, his looks help.* Part of her wished he'd come over tonight, that any minute he would knock at her door. She knew things were moving fast and perhaps it was best to slow down a bit.

Poor Juju. Her mind searched for any possibility that would explain the sudden death of an adult bonobo in captivity. None came to mind. However, she realized now with Juju dead, her problem with the lion was solved. The other bonobos had a healthy fear of the lioness.

The wine was working. She could feel herself sinking into the couch. She looked at her glass and was surprised it was empty. The rain beat at the windows and the roof. She left the wine glass by the sink, brushed her teeth in the bathroom, and climbed into bed.

THE MORNING AFTER

The sky was clear and the sun was up when Julia woke. She made her usual protein shake for breakfast and changed into a tank top and BDU pants to feed the bonobos. Sean's door was closed and she listened for any movement within. She heard none. The sand on the path was wet and the footprints that had been there in the loose sand were washed away. Julia passed near the main house on the way to the storage building and it, too, was quiet and still. The generator behind the laboratory building, which had been running for the last two weeks, was turned off. *Those two must have been up late deciding what to do with Raymond's money. A nice problem to have.*

Julia moved from crate to crate, inspecting each of the fruits before she put them in the cart. None smelled bad or had any unusual coloration. When the cart was full, she pulled it outside and closed the doors to the building. Then she headed down the long path to the bonobo enclosure. The bonobos were in the metal tree. The oldest Juju clone sat on the lower left-hand branch, just as Juju had. When the clone saw Julia approaching, she climbed down from the tree, came to the wire mesh, sat on her haunches and extended her left hand to Julia. The other bonobos stayed in their places. Juju's clone peeled and ate the banana Julia gave her and extended her left hand again. Julia handed her a second banana, and it was consumed also. The clone returned to the tree on all fours and climbed to the lowest branch on the left side of the tree. Julia was dumbfounded. The clone had replicated Juju's request for the bananas, moving and acting exactly like Juju.

When Julia got back to her duplex, Sean's front door was still closed and his apartment quiet. She changed into her running shoes and shorts and decided a good run along the beach would help her think about the behavior of Juju's clone. After her run and shower, she went back to the porch. She went quietly over to Sean's door and listened. No sound. She knocked lightly three times. No sound and no movement. She knocked again. Still no response. She turned the door knob and gradually opened the door and looked inside.

"Hello?"

No sound came from inside the apartment.

"Hello?" she said louder.

Sean's swim trunks and T-shirt from the day before lay on the kitchen floor, still wet and sandy. Through the doorway of his bedroom, she saw Sean lying on top of the bed naked, without covers, his back facing the door.

"Sean?"

He didn't move. Julia came into the bedroom and sat down on the edge of the bed. She could see him breathing deeply. She touched him on the back.

"Sean, are you okay?"

Sean startled awake. "What?"

"Are you okay? I was worried about you. It's almost lunch time."

"I'm okay." Sean sat up. "I was just tired, I guess."

"Were you and Raymond up late last night making big investment plans?"

"Yes. We were up very late."

She leaned over and gave Sean a kiss on the ear. Sean kissed her back, a deep, longing kiss. Julia pulled away.

"So, you were missing me?"

"Yes, I was."

He pulled Julia down onto the bed beside him. He moved on top of her and pressed his body against hers. Julia could feel that he was hard as he pressed his hips into her. His hands pulled up her shirt and Julia held her arms over her head so Sean could take it off. She was glad she hadn't bothered with a bra. Sean sat up and undid the string on her shorts and pulled them and her panties off at the same time and threw them to the floor. Then he was back over her and let out a deep moan. Sean kept going. Then, without warning, Julia felt him climax. He let out a garbled moan into the pillow and went limp on top of her, all of his weight resting on her. Julia tried to look at his face that was buried in the pillow, but couldn't. She rubbed his back with her hands.

"Hey? Are you okay?"

Sean moved his arms to take some of his weight off her.

"Somebody was missing me, weren't you?" Julia smiled at Sean as he lifted his face from the pillow. He rolled off beside her.

Sean was silent. Julia waited for him to recover.

"I've had an interesting morning," Julia said. "Remember yesterday Raymond telling us that Juju had died?"

"Yes," Sean said, smelling her hair.

"When I went this morning to do the feeding with the fruit from the storage shed, Juju's oldest clone was sitting on Juju's branch on the tree. Also, when she saw me, she came down from the branch and came to the fence and held out her left hand for a banana the exact same way that Juju used to!"

"I'll be damned. That is something. Did you talk to Raymond?"

"I didn't see him and the lab is quiet. So I assumed he was sleeping."

"He's probably awake by now. Maybe we should go tell him?"

"It isn't just that the clone was doing the same things that Juju did. It was that she was acting like Juju. Same facial expression, same mannerisms, same damn snobby attitude."

"Perhaps the clone learned them from Juju?"

"Maybe."

They reached the main house. It was quiet and the front door was closed. Julia and Sean approached the door and Julia knocked. They could hear Frick trot across the living room floor to the door and bark, just once. Julia knocked again. Frick barked again.

"Hello?" Julia called out.

Sean opened the screen door and tried the doorknob. The door was unlocked. Sean pushed it open.

"Hello?" Sean called out into the house.

"Raymond?" Julia called loudly.

Julia walked toward the bedroom on the other side of the kitchen. The door was open and she could see someone on the bed. Raymond was lying face up in the bed, the sheet covering him up to his chest. He was wearing a blue pajama top. His eyes were closed, his skin pale and grayish, lips blue, and dark circles were under his eyes. He was perfectly still. Julia reached out with the back of her hand and touched his cheek; it was cold and leathery. Julia buried her face in Sean's chest.

"Oh, my God, he's dead."

DETECTIVE ROLLE

Sean and Julia sat on the front porch of the main house, Frick lying at Sean's feet. Her ears pricked up and she lifted her head. In another minute, Sean and Julia heard a Cessna approaching. As it came in for a landing, Sean saw on it the emblem of the Royal Bahamas Police Force. Julia sat with her hands folded in her lap, one holding a handkerchief. Her eyes and nose were red from crying and she was pale.

"It's the police."

Julia nodded.

Soon they could see three black men walking up the path to the house. The first two wore jackets, dress shirts, and dress pants. The younger of the two, in his early forties, carried a large black case. The third was carrying a backpack and wore green surgical scrubs. The lead man came up to the porch where Sean and Julia stood and extended his hand toward Sean.

"Chief Detective Bill Evans. We spoke over the phone."

"Sean Burke. And this is Dr. Julia Watson."

"This is Detective Rolle and Dr. Nicks. Royal Bahamas Police Force, as a matter of policy, investigates every death that occurs outside of a hospital. That's why we are here. To be honest, when it's the death of someone with the status in the business community as Mr. Taylor had, that is why *I* am here," Chief Detective Evans said.

"We understand."

"Detective Rolle will have questions for you. Where is the body?"

"Inside the house, in the downstairs bedroom," Sean answered.

Evans took Rolle's black case and entered the house with Dr. Nicks.

Detective Rolle removed a small notebook and pen from his inside jacket pocket. He flipped the notebook open and looked at Sean.

"You said your name was Sean Burke? S-E-A-N?"

"Yes, sir. B-U-R-K-E," Sean answered.

"Your name is Julia Watson?"

"Yes."

"When was the last time you saw Mr. Taylor alive?"

"About midnight," Sean answered. "We were discussing business here in his living room."

"You are a business associate of Mr. Taylor?"

"I'm the chief financial officer of Mr. Taylor's company."

The detective said to Julia, "Do you work for Mr. Taylor as well?"

"Yes. I'm here to—to care for primates Mr. Taylor has on the island."

"Primates?"

"Bonobos specifically. I was preparing them to be shipped back to Africa to be released."

The detective continued writing. "Where on the island are you two staying?"

"In a duplex near the beach on the other side of the house," Sean answered.

"Were each of you there last night?"

"Yes," Sean answered.

"Together?"

"No. She was in her apartment and I was in mine."

The detective looked at Sean. "How long have you been staying on the island?"

"This is my third day here."

The detective looked at Julia. "You too?"

"I've been here about nine weeks."

Sean and Julia could hear the clicking of a camera coming from inside the house. The physician came out to the front porch. He had a latex glove on each hand.

"Had he complained of any pain or discomfort lately?"

"No," Julia said.

"Last night during our meeting, he complained of heartburn. And the reason we stopped at midnight was because he said he was feeling tired," Sean said.

"Did he take any medication for it?" the doctor asked.

"Not while I was here."

"Thanks." The physician headed toward the air strip.

"I'd like to see where you two were staying last night," Detective Rolle said.

"Of course, this way," Sean said.

They walked the path to the duplex, the dog following them. Sean and Julia waited on the porch while he inspected their apartments.

"Okay, we can go back to the main house now," the detective said. When they got to the lab, the detective said, "What's that building?"

"That's his laboratory," Julia said.

"I'd like to look inside."

"Only Raymond knew the combination to the lock," Julia replied.

"I know it," Sean said.

"You do?"

"He showed me last night. There are a few things in there for a business venture." Sean punched the combination on the pad and the lock clicked. He swung the doors open and the lights inside kicked on, running on battery power. Detective Rolle and Julia stepped inside, and Sean followed. Julia saw that the equipment that had been wrapped in plastic was gone. The tables were bare. The cloning device too was gone. In its place, sitting on the floor along the wall, were black plastic shipping crates, stacked three high. The matrix of computers against the far wall was no longer wrapped in plastic.

"Mr. Burke, what were you and Mr. Taylor discussing in here?"

Sean pointed to the rack of computers. "Those. Mr. Taylor wanted to sell them. He was wondering about their value."

"Was he planning to leave the island?"

"Yes," Julia said. "He never really said when he was going to leave. He said that it would be soon."

"Okay, I've seen enough."

Sean and Julia sat and waited on the porch as the detective went inside the main house. Julia felt tired. Mainly she felt sad. Frick went to the edge of the porch and looked out over the ocean. Sean and Julia heard the engine of another Cessna plane. In a few minutes, the pilot throttled back the engine as it landed. The three men inside the house came out. Dr.

Nicks approached Sean.

"I found some phenobarbital pills in his bathroom, on the counter. Do you know if he was taking this for some reason... maybe to sleep?"

"Not that I know of."

Detective Rolle and Dr. Nicks got the stretcher and went back inside. Chief Detective Evans stood by Sean.

"Are you expecting anybody today?" Evans asked.

"No," Sean said.

"What time today did you discover the body?"

"Just after noon. We hadn't seen him the entire morning, so we came to check on him," Sean said.

"Both of you were together when you found him?"

"Yes."

Chief Detective Evans removed two small white cards from his jacket pocket and handed one to Julia and the other to Sean. "I've seen plenty of these in my career, and this is a death by natural causes if I've ever seen one. We'll do an autopsy and toxicology back in Nassau just to make sure. If either of you need to contact me, you have my business card."

"Thank you," Julia and Sean said in unison.

The detective went back inside the house. Sean saw Mr. Smith hurrying up the path. As Mr. Smith reached the house, Detective Rolle held the screen door open so that Chief Detective Evans and Dr. Nicks could carry John's body out on a stretcher. He had been wrapped in a white sheet.

"What the hell happened to him?" Mr. Smith said.

"He just died," Sean replied.

"Oh, mon, I can't believe this. I can't believe this man up and die on me like this."

Detective Rolle said to Mr. Smith, "Did you know Mr. Taylor?"

Mr. Smith suddenly realized he was talking to the police. "I talked to him once. A few days ago, when I brought that mon here on the plane." Mr. Smith pointed at Sean.

Detective Rolle removed a fingerprint scanner from his jacket pocket. "Place the fingers of your right hand here." A few seconds passed. "Mr. Earle Charlton," Detective Rolle said, taking a note in his notebook. "Did you and Mr. Taylor do business together?"

"No. Mr. Taylor was an old friend of my father's."

Detective Rolle looked at him suspiciously, as if he might be holding something back. Nonetheless, he didn't press the point. "If you need to contact me, this is my business card."

Detective Rolle handed Mr. Smith the card and followed the stretcher to the plane. Mr. Smith looked at the ground, his body tense, his hands clenched. He glared at Sean and Julia. He waited until the engine on the detective's plane roared to life.

"Fuck!"

Without a word to either Sean or Julia, he walked back down the path to his plane.

Sean smiled slightly, but Julia didn't notice.

SOMETHING
DIFFERENT

Julia brought two plates of pasta to the table and placed one in front of Sean. She didn't feel hungry. Sean insisted she eat something and he twirled his fork in the noodles. She watched him for a minute.

Frick was beneath the table, at Sean's feet. "You have a new best friend," Julia said.

"She must be feeling lonely and lost."

"What do you think we should do now?"

"Good question. I suppose I should go to Nassau and talk to the company's attorney, see what legal ramifications this has for the company."

"I don't mean to be cold about it, but do you think there's a chance Raymond's company could still fund my research facility in Africa?"

"Do you have a contract with Raymond for that?"

"Yes."

"Anything in there covering this situation?"

"Not that I remember."

"We'll see what the lawyer has to say."

Julia stopped twirling her noodles and looked at Sean. He was finishing the last of his pasta and smiled at Julia. She forced a smile back. When Sean cleaned his plate, he brought it to the kitchen. Frick followed. Julia had lost what little appetite she had and pushed her plate away. Sean came and got it and returned to the kitchen with Frick. Julia took a drink from her wine glass and watched Sean in the kitchen. Something was definitely different about him.

JUJU'S CLONE

Julia could see Raymond walking ahead of her on the beach, heading toward the water. He put his empty beer bottle down in the sand and took his shirt off. He looked at her over his shoulder and smiled. She could see it there, on his back. The birthmark. Julia heard Raymond's voice: *"… even a place like this can feel like a prison after a while…"*

Julia startled awake. The sun was up and the room was lit. She looked at Sean lying on his stomach next to her. On his back below the right shoulder blade was the same birthmark from her dream. The same birthmark she had seen on Raymond.

Julia blinked until her head was clear and slowly slipped out of bed. She put on her tank top and BDU pants and got her boots from the closet. She went out on the front porch to put them on. She went to the storage shed and removed the cart from the side of the shed and loaded it with fruit.

Julia pulled the fruit cart to the end of the metal rails near the bonobos' tree and pushed the cart over, spilling the contents on the ground. She exited the enclosure and ran through the brush until she was behind the canvas wall. The bonobos were rummaging through the fruit. Julia grabbed the rope that opened the lion's door and placed her foot over the switch on the ground. She pulled hard on the pulley rope. The electric motor on the rail sled started and the lioness jumped down the rails. Just as she entered the enclosure, she let out a roar. The bonobos screamed and ran for the metal tree. Except for Juju's oldest clone. She came down from the tree, stood on two legs at the end of the rails, and as the lion reached the end of the rails, Juju's clone struck it across the face. The clone circled around behind the lioness and struck it again. Julia's stomach knotted. *It isn't possible, it just isn't possible.*

Julia dropped the lion's door, leaving the lion inside, and ran down the path back to the lab. *Whatever happened to Juju and Sean happened in that lab.* She tried the front metal doors. They were locked. She tried the same combination used on the bonobo enclosure. It didn't work.

"Damn it."

Julia circled the building, looking for a way to climb up and maybe get in through the roof. The brush was thick and the walls were vine-covered. She could see no way up and no windows. As she got near the back corner, she saw through the brush and vines the outline of a small door. She pulled the vegetation out of the way. A latch at the top with a rusty padlock held it closed. Julia grabbed the lock and pulled. The years of salty air had done a job on the screws securing the latch to the brick. The latch shifted. Julia grabbed it with both hands, pulled again, and it came free.

The rusty door hinged at the bottom dropped to the ground. Julia bent down and entered the old primate area. She gave her eyes a minute to adjust to the dark. The light coming in through the small door behind her helped. She pushed open the mesh door leading out of the primate cage to the old operating room. She felt along the wall till she found the door into the main room of the lab. The overhead motion sensors detected her and the lights in the lab turned on, illuminating the stacks of black crates.

She went to the nearest crate and unsnapped the four buckles holding the top down. Inside was foam packing and assorted tools and computer circuit boards. Julia looked at the rack of dark, silent computers. In front of them was a crate twice the size of the others.

Julia unsnapped the six buckles holding the lid in place. She raked the packing foam out and dug inside, first pulling out a computer monitor wrapped in bubble wrap. She threw it to the floor. A laptop was next, also wrapped in bubble wrap. She threw that to the floor. Her hand felt something that wasn't made of hard plastic. She pulled it out of the packing foam. It was wrapped in bubble wrap also. She unwrapped it until she held in her hands a wire-and-cloth-mesh helmet. It had one hundred and fifty-seven sensors, with each sensor attached to a fiber optic cable bundled together into a harness. The chin strap hung down on each side. The knot in her stomach got tighter. She dropped the helmet to the floor. She ran back out the small door. *I have to get out of here.* She hurried past the main house toward the dock. As she passed by the front of the house, the screen door swung open.

"Good morning," said Sean and smiled at her. Julia stopped in her tracks. She didn't wave or smile and for a moment it seemed as if she was going to run. "I was wondering where you were."

"Feeding the bonobos."

Sean came down off the porch and gave her a kiss. She attempted to give him a kiss in return.

"Everything okay?"

"Yes, fine. I was just feeding the bonobos."

"I heard you the first time. How are they doing?"

"Well."

"Where you heading?"

"I thought you were still asleep."

"I was just gathering papers. For our trip to Nassau to see the lawyer—when would you like to go? How about today?"

"The sooner the better." Julia tried to sound nonchalant. "The weather looks good."

"Today it is. Go pack your things and I'll finish gathering papers and we can take off."

Julia walked to the duplex, her heart racing. She reached her apartment and got her bag from the closet. *Just act normal.* She packed her clothes, her lab notes and her tablet. She came to the kitchen. Sean was standing in the front doorway, Frick behind him. Sean wasn't smiling.

"What were you doing in the lab?"

Julia's stomach turned. She quickly reached for the wood block of knives and pulled out the largest butcher knife and held it out in hand.

"Stay away from me!"

"I don't know what you think you know— you're mistaken."

"You aren't Sean, you're Raymond."

"It's going to be okay. Just give me the knife."

"I'm leaving."

"I can explain everything."

He lunged at Julia. She side-stepped to the kitchen counter as his left hand grabbed at her wrist. She lost her grip on the knife and it fell to the floor as Sean's grip threw her off balance. She grabbed a pot from the stove top, and as Sean was correcting his balance to grab at her hands again, she hit him with the pot on the side of the head, knocking him to the floor at the entryway to the hall. Frick barked at her and snapped at her leg.

Julia picked the knife up off the floor just as Frick sunk her teeth into her calf. Julia screamed in pain and thrust the knife into Frick's side. Frick released her bite and snapped at Julia's hand as she removed the knife in time to keep from being bitten again. Frick retreated to stand between Julia and Sean and growled. Blood dripped from the wound. Julia ran out the front door and down the steps, taking two at a time. Sean came out of the front door running, followed by Frick, who was barking.

Sean sprinted to catch up to her. His legs ached. Julia was twenty yards ahead, running hard, her arms pumping, the knife blade in her hand flashing in the sun with every stride. Frick snapped at Julia's heels. Julia tried kicking the dog away, landing one deep kick in its throat. Her leg tangled with Frick's and she fell. Sean got to Julia just as she rolled over. The butcher knife was buried to the handle in Julia's chest. Her eyes were wide with pain, her left hand grabbing at the handle. She took a deep ragged breath and coughed blood out of her mouth and nose. Frick tried to get to her feet but was unable. She lay back down and went still.

"No!" Sean knelt beside Julia, panting. Julia arched her back and tried to take another breath. She clenched her teeth in pain. Julia let out her last breath in a gurgle and didn't move again.

DEEP WATER

John lifted Julia's body into the incinerator. He took the belongings from her apartment, the ones that weren't metal, and placed them inside also. Tears streamed down his face, clouding his vision. He wiped them away. He walked back down the path and carried Frick's body back to the laboratory and placed her inside the incinerator also.

John opened the crate that contained the bottles he needed. He took three bottles and a syringe to the storage shed. He removed eight bananas from one of the crates and injected each with a lethal amount of liquid. He returned from the bonobo enclosure with the cart holding five dead bonobos. He placed the bonobos in the incinerator with Julia's and Frick's bodies. He went to the house and gathered the two boxes of files and a large black suitcase waiting in the living room and put them aboard the *Re-Due*. Next, he removed the emergency locator beacon and the computer from the *Emerald Green*. He brought those back to the lab and put them in the incinerator and closed the door. John set the timer on the wall to twelve hours, more than twice the time required to turn the contents to ash. He pressed the ignition button. The furnace roared.

He untied the *Emerald Green* and fastened a tow rope to the bow and pushed her out of the slip. He fastened the other end to the back of the *Re-Due*. He pulled away from the island as the sun sank below the horizon. He looked back at the *Emerald Green* to make sure it was following nicely. It was. He looked back at his house, sitting tall and white on the hill. The smoke from the incinerator billowed, erasing the things John needed to hide. He set a course east. Before he went to New Providence, he needed to find deep water. Very deep water.

THE ATTORNEY

Late in the morning two days later, John pulled the *Re-Due* into its slip in Nassau. The Bahamian chauffeur and black limousine were waiting. After tying off the boat, John placed the boxes, the navigation computer from the *Re-Due,* and a blue duffle bag on the dock. The chauffeur put them into the trunk of the limousine. John locked the cabin and stepped off the *Re-Due* for the last time. He got in the back seat of the limousine. The chauffeur got behind the wheel.

"Where to, sir?"

"Number 20 George Street."

At 20 George Street, the sign to the right of the door read, *Thompson & Thompson, Attorneys at Law.*

"Would you bring the two boxes and the computer, but not the suitcase, into the office, please?"

"Yes, sir."

A young Bahamian woman sat board-straight behind the reception desk.

"I have an appointment with Mr. Thompson. I'm Sean Burke."

She pressed a button on the phone on her desk. "Mr. Burke is here to see you."

A second later, the door to the office to John's left opened. Out stepped a sixty-year-old, white-haired Englishman. Mr. Thompson.

"Very good to meet you." They shook hands.

The chauffeur came through the door with the first box.

"Please put the boxes in Mr. Thompson's office," John said.

"I'm so sorry about the passing of Mr. Taylor," the attorney said.

"I've been on retainer with Mr. Taylor for many years."

"He told me."

"Mr. Taylor spoke very highly of you. He said you were his most trusted friend. We do have a lot of things to discuss."

"The sooner we get this legal ball rolling, the better."

The chauffeur delivered the final box, with the navigation computer sitting on top. John tipped him with a hundred-dollar bill.

"If you won't mind waiting for me to finish with Mr. Thompson?" The chauffeur nodded.

The attorney invited John into a small, well-organized office. "Let us get down to business, okay?" he said once they were seated. "Last month I received a package from Mr. Taylor by secure briefcase. It contained papers to designate you as the chief financial officer. He and I spoke about it over the phone, and everything is in order. I've papers for you to sign to be filed at the courthouse. It's very routine."

John nodded.

"Also, three days ago Mr. Taylor delivered to me his Last Will and Testament. I'm required to videotape the reading of the will to you and submit it to the court."

"Okay."

The attorney picked up a remote control and pointed it at a video camera mounted on the wall in the corner. The attorney opened the folder on his desk and began.

"I, Raymond Taylor, being of sound mind, declare this to be my Last Will and Testament. I revoke all wills and codicils previously made by me. I appoint Adam Thompson as my personal representative to administer this Will, and ask that he be permitted to serve without court supervision and without posting bond. If Adam Thompson is unwilling or unable to serve, then I appoint his son, Charles Thompson, to serve as my personal representative, and ask that he be permitted to serve without court supervision and without posting bond. I devise, bequeath, and give all of my business and residuary estate as follows: One hundred percent to Sean Burke. Under penalties for perjury, we, the undersigned Testator and witnesses declare: That the Testator executed this instrument as his Will; that in the presence of witnesses, the Testator signed or acknowledged his signature already made, or directed another to sign for him in his presence; that the Testator executed the Will as his free and voluntary act for the purposes expressed in it; that each of the witnesses, in the presence of the Testator and of each other, signed the Will as witness; that the Testator was of sound mind; and that, to the best of his knowledge, the Testator was at the time eighteen or more years of age. All of which is attested to this 28th day of August, 2057. Signed, Raymond Taylor."

The attorney picked up the remote and stopped the recording. "I don't know if you are aware that there's no inheritance tax in the Bahamas."

"I am aware."

"Mr. Burke, you have just become a very wealthy man."

"How long will it take to clear the Will through the courts?" John didn't feel like giving him the smile he was expecting.

"I'd say a couple weeks."

"Let's get to signing what is necessary. And there are a couple of things I need you to do for me."

"What are those?"

"As soon as the sailboat is in my name, I'd like you to commission the manager at the marina to sell her. And as soon as the island is in my name, I'd like you to find a real estate company here in Nassau to sell it. However, look at the original paperwork from Mr. Taylor's purchase of the island, and be sure not to use that real estate company."

"I understand."

"Also, I'd like you to contract a crew and boat to go to the island and get all the crates that are in a large building near the main house. It has large metal doors with a keypad lock. I'll leave you the combination so you can give it to the captain of the crew. However, there's no rush; I'll call you in a few weeks with an address to ship them to. You can hire the crew after that. I know that these tasks are a bit outside of your past services for Mr. Taylor. I'll make sure you are well compensated for them. I need someone here on the island I can trust and count on. For instance, if I should call you for anything by phone, I'll want to speak to you personally. Can I count on you, Mr. Thompson?"

"Of course," said Thompson, taking notes.

"These boxes contain the personal papers and effects of Mr. Taylor, most of them regarding the company. Rent a small storage unit for them. Have the monthly rent charged to the company account. As soon as I know the address for shipping the crates, you can also send me the details of where this storage unit is and any combination or key to gain access."

"Yes, sir."

"One last thing. I know Mr. Taylor requested that you hire a private investigator last month to locate people in Boston and New York. Do you have the report from the investigator?"

The attorney pulled a folder from the bottom right drawer of his desk and removed a plain white envelope. It was sealed. He handed it to John.

John took the envelope and held it in his hand for a moment. He had waited to get this information for a long time. He would only allow himself to have it if the imaging had been successful, if in his new body he was sitting in front of the attorney, asking for it himself. He ran his finger under the flap and tore it open. He took out the two sheets of paper and unfolded them. He looked at the pages and refolded and put them back in the envelope.

"All right. Let's complete your paperwork. I need to get to the airport."

The jet was bigger than the ones John remembered; this particular one was from the third generation of the carbon-fiber fuselage made by Boeing. That difference didn't change the appearance of the plane. Soon one of the flight attendants closed the cabin door. He could hardly believe he was going back to Boston.

Soon he felt the wheels of the jet lift from the runway. He was leaving the Bahamas, knowing he was never coming back. John closed his eyes, for the first time in two days allowing himself to think about Julia. The memory of her gasping last breath on the sandy path came rushing back. John wiped away a tear. "I'm so sorry," he whispered. He thought about watching the mast of the *Emerald Green* sink below the surface in the moonlight. The water boiled as the boat's interior quickly filled with seawater, beginning its long drop to the ocean floor more than five thousand feet below. *I had hoped for such a different beginning to my new life. You're as much collateral damage of my mess as I've been to Ethan's.* "I am truly sorry," he whispered again. *Retribution is coming.* The flight attendant brought him a double whiskey and a pillow. Eventually he fell asleep.

"Sir?" John felt a gentle shake on his arm. He opened his eyes to see the flight attendant leaning over him.

"We are about to land. Could you bring your chair upright, please?"

John pressed the button and the chair back came upright.

"Thank you." She continued down the aisle. John looked around, foggy from sleep. Passengers were moving around, putting away things in their bags.

The flight attendant came by on her way back to her seat.

"Ma'am?"

She faced John.

"What day is it?"

"It's the first."

"What month?"

"September. You were in the islands a long time?"

"A lifetime."

John realized his birthday was almost here and he hadn't known realized it. He reminded himself of his new birthday: July 10, 2031. He repeated it to himself again so he could say it without hesitation if anyone should ask. John looked out the window to see the lights on the ground rushing up in the window. He was back in Boston. He was back home.

LATE SUMMER 2057

BACK HOME

"Auto-drive engaged," the computer in the taxicab said.

The driver took his hands off the wheel, and the cab accelerated up the ramp and perfectly merged into the fast-moving Boston traffic.

"That's a pretty neat gizmo."

"I didn't like it at first—now I do," the taxi driver said.

The taxi went into the tunnel that ran under Boston Harbor. Every fifty yards were orange-tinted lights overhead, illuminating the roadway. John looked at the speedometer. It read seventy-five miles per hour. He looked at the cars in the lanes to the left, and they were traveling at the same speed. None of the drivers had their hands on the steering wheels; one driver read a book. The taxi came out of the tunnel back into the night.

"Exit approaching," the computer voice said again.

A mile later, the taxi took an off-ramp.

"Prepare for manual operation."

The taxi driver put his hands back on the wheel. John could see another large yellow overhead tube approaching and when the taxi went under, the computer spoke again.

"Manual operation resume."

Soon they went over the bridge leading into south Boston, taking John past the ferry landings and bending around until the Boston Common was on his right.

"It won't be that long before you can ice skate on Frog Pond," John said.

The taxi driver looked in the rearview mirror. "In the Common?"

"I used to go there when I was a teenager." As soon as the words were out of his mouth, John knew his mistake. *This is going to take some getting used to.*

"Nobody goes in the Common any more. Unless you are a homeless drug addict or a hooker."

"Really?"

"You've been away for a long time, haven't you?"

John looked at the dark empty park until the taxi turned and it disappeared from view. A block later, the taxi stopped in front of the hotel, obviously in need of repair. John could see, through the glass doors, a dimly lit foyer. A homeless man slept on the sidewalk.

"This is it," the driver announced.

John looked out the window at the dark windows on the floors above him.

"Do you know a better place?"

"I was hoping you'd ask. You don't seem like the kind of guy who would want to stay here. I'm a people person. I deal with people all day long, and I can tell you don't belong here. There's a five-star hotel on Interstate 90 up near Watertown."

"Sounds great."

Soon the computer-aided taxi got on Interstate 90 and took the appropriate exit. It was another half-mile to the Charles River. Ahead, a large, well-lit, new hotel sat beside the easy-flowing river. The taxi turned into the front driveway, and John saw the sign, "The Wynn of Massachusetts." The taxi stopped at the front door.

"Fifty-seven dollars and forty-three cents," the driver said.

John handed him a one-hundred-dollar bill.

"Keep the change."

"Have a nice stay in Boston."

"Thanks."

An hour later John was in his suite, showered, shaved, sitting in the living room in his underwear, looking at the white envelope in his hand. He took out the first page and read it again.

Cathy Edward
Age: 84
DOB: 3-22-1973

No outstanding debt. No living relatives.

Current Residence: Donald Village of Assisted Living, 1690 Adams Street, Boston, MA; Room 274.

No current phone number.

AUNT CATHY

The new shoes felt nice. The hard, fresh leather on the soles made loud taps on the tile floor. He liked the feel of the new dress slacks and shirt, and cardigan sweaters were still in style in Boston, if you wore a tie. Some things never changed. The new cell phone in his pocket felt weird. John checked the numbers on the doors as he passed each one, stopping in front of 274. He knocked on the door and soundlessly pushed it open. Cathy sat in a wheelchair facing the television. She didn't hear him knock or notice the opening door. Her shoulder-length hair was completely white and thin, neatly combed back from her face. Her skin was pale and splotched with age. She wore a simple blue dress with long sleeves and pink slippers with blue socks. She squinted through her thick silver-framed glasses at the television screen six feet away.

"Aunt Cathy?"

Cathy knew instantly who it was as the sound of his voice rushed back over the dim expanse of years. She turned her head. Standing in her living room was John.

"John!"

John came to her, knelt down, and wrapped his arms around her. She hugged him around his neck. Tears fell on the back of her blue dress. Neither of them moved for several minutes. John pulled back so he could see her face. Behind those wrinkles, glasses and watery eyes, John could see the Cathy he'd left in Denny's decades ago.

"Aunt Cathy, it's so good to see you. I've so missed you."

"I've missed you too, John. I didn't know you were coming home from school today or I'd have made you roast beef."

"School?"

"You've been at school so long, and we haven't heard from you, so we didn't know when you'd be visiting."

"We?"

"Robert and I. He'll be so happy to see you when he gets home."

The color drained from John's face.

"Help me to the kitchen and I'll make tea, and you can tell me about school."

A nurse came through the open door holding a tray with a plastic bowl and a drink.

"Time for lunch, Mrs. Edward."

"Look. My son is here from medical school."

"I didn't know you had a visitor," the nurse said, giving John a hard look. John smiled.

"I don't remember seeing you visit Mrs. Edward before."

"This is my first visit. May I talk to you outside?" John asked.

The nurse placed the tray of food on the coffee table and said to Cathy, "I'm going to step out to the nurse's station for a minute. Finish your chowder and I'll be right back."

Once they were in the hallway, John asked, "How's Mrs. Edward doing?"

"What's your name and how do you know her?"

"Sean Burke. I'm the son of a family friend. He asked me to check on her since I was in town for a couple days. How long has she been here?"

"About five years."

"She seems to think that her husband is alive, when I know he died over forty years ago."

"Most of the seniors living at this faculty are in the advanced stages of Alzheimer's. In an hour, she won't remember you've been here today. It's nice that you came to visit her. She doesn't get any visitors, at least not in the last three years."

"I'd like to give you my cell phone number so you can call me if there's anything she needs, or her condition changes."

DISTANT
RELATIONSHIPS

John slid the key into the lock. The apartment building in the middle of New York City's financial district was modern and trendy. The kind of place where the young professional on the rise wants to be *seen* living, more than they actually want to live there. Sean's apartment was on the third floor. A one-bedroom. The lock clicked open. John found the light switch and the recessed lighting above the kitchen cabinets came on. At the far end of the kitchen was a small dining room with a glass table. John looked to the right, around the corner to the living room, and saw that the left wall was completely glass above waist height. The light from the sunless evening sky shone through. Below, in the busy street, the headlights of electric cars moved in silence. The furniture was sleek, understated, and expensive. A chair, a couch, and a glass coffee table. On the coffee table was a remote for the combination television and computer mounted on the wall opposite the couch. The screen was less than an inch thick, slightly curved, and occupied most of the wall. To the right of the screen was the doorway to the bedroom. John stepped in front of the screen and it came on, the wide screen turning a pale blue.

"Good afternoon, Sean," a female voice said.

"Show email please."

"Email." The screen showed a long list of unread mail. John scanned the list and found the one that looked like it came from Sean's workplace.

"Open." John commanded. It was from Sean's supervisor, asking him to attend a meeting the next week.

"Reply."

A new screen opened, showing the email body for the reply.

"Mr. Holmes, it's with deep regret I must inform you of my resignation from my position with Goldman Sachs, effective immediately. There has been a sudden illness with my father and I must immediately move to help my mother, who is also ill. I'll not be returning to the office. Please reassign my work as you see fit. It has been a great pleasure working with you and for Goldman Sachs. Sincerely, Sean Burke." The perfectly composed email hung in front of him on the screen.

"Send." With that, it was gone. *It's best if Sean doesn't just disappear without a reason,* John thought. He scanned the list again and found one from Sean's parents. It was from Sean's mother, reminding him that his Aunt Charlene's birthday was the next week.

"Reply." John waited a second for the page to come up. "Mom, I have been offered a new position with a new company. It is an exciting opportunity for me. I have already started work for them. It will require me to travel extensively, however. Tell Aunt Charlene 'Hi' for me. I'll be in Europe for the next couple months. I'll write more later when I have time. Love. Sean."

This relationship is about to become very distant, John thought. *No way I can show up at Christmas or something. Way too many things I don't know. They will certainly be able to tell. If Julia could tell after just two days with me, I could never get past close family members or friends. The Burkes don't know it yet, but they have lost their son. If they send a private investigator or the police, all they'll find is a perfectly healthy, sane Sean, choosing not to see his parents. 'Yes, Detective, I know they seem like a nice old retired couple, but that's because they're not your parents. You have no idea how controlling they are. Over my life, trying to control my money. Take this, for example. I wouldn't obey them, so they sent the police to talk to me. I just couldn't take it anymore so I moved away. No crime in that.'* John scanned the list of emails again, looking for a girlfriend or anybody who might really become concerned if Sean broke off all contact with them. He didn't see any. *Too bad there isn't a girlfriend, I could have had fun with that. 'Hey, Karen. There's something I've been meaning to tell you. Your pussy stinks. Go fuck yourself.'*

He entered the bedroom and sat down on Sean's bed. It felt nice; memory foam. John opened the bottom drawer of the bedside dresser, saw fitness magazines and condoms. He opened the top drawer, and a black matte-finished Glock pistol slid into view. John took it out of the drawer, felt the weight of it in his hand.

This solves one of my problems.

MR. SANCHEZ

John stood outside the large complex of storage rooms and punched the attorney's number on his cell phone. After two rings, a woman's voice answered.

"Thompson and Thompson law office," she said with a Bahamian accent.

"Hi, this is Sean Burke. I'd like to speak to Adam Thompson."

"One moment please, Mr. Burke."

In a moment, the attorney spoke. "Mr. Burke, good to hear from you. How are you doing?"

"I have a shipping address for the crates."

"Go ahead."

"I've rented ten units at this address: 725 Atlantic Avenue, Brooklyn, New York. The name of the business is Sanchez Storage."

"Got it."

"I'd like for you to personally go to the island and supervise the loading of the crates onto the private transport. If you'll get the ball rolling on your end and give me an estimated arrival date, I'll let the owner of the storage facility know so he can secure the units after the crates arrive."

"Yes, sir, I should have something for you in a few days. I'm expecting the paperwork to clear the courts soon, by the way. I greased the process, you might say."

"Thank you, Mr. Thompson."

"Is there anything else?"

"I'm sure there will be, but not now." John ended the call. The owner of the storage facility stood beside him. They had just finished inspecting the units.

"Thank you, Mr. Sanchez. The contents from my apartment will arrive in two days and more crates later. I'll leave you my number so you can call me if there are any problems. And once the crates arrive and you secure the units, call me. I'll come back here and inspect the units, and if it's satisfactory, I'll give you another five thousand dollars," John said.

"No problem, sir," Mr. Sanchez answered.

EMPIRE SUITE

"Good evening, sir, welcome to the Langham Place," said the Asian woman behind the check-in counter.

"I'd like the best room you have available."

"How many nights?" Her smile gave no clue that she was surprised at this request by a man of John's age.

"Two months should be fine."

"Our Empire Suite is available at a rate of three thousand dollars a night."

"Sounds perfect."

"It has a nice view of the Empire State Building."

"Even better."

"I just need a driver's license and credit card."

She began typing information into the computer in front of her. The bellhop arrived with a cart filled with five large suitcases from the taxi.

"Empire Suite please," the clerk said to the bellhop. She looked back at John. "If you will place your right index finger on the scanner, please."

John did as requested.

"Will there be anybody else needing access to the room?" she asked.

"No."

"Okay. You are all set. Simply place your right index finger on the scanner by the door; it will let you in."

After the bellhop left the room, John opened the first suitcase and took out the large envelope full of cash. $52,246.35. John grinned as he recalled the look on the bank teller's face when he told her he was closing his savings and checking accounts and would like the money in cash. *Not everything can be done with a credit card.* After the clothes were put away, John pulled out the white envelope and took out the second piece of paper.

Ethan Shinwell
Age: 77
DOB: 11-22-1979

On lifetime parole from Massachusetts Depart-ment of Correction since 2053. No outstanding debt. No living relatives. Currently living off in-heritance from parents and the sale of their house. Regularly attends worship service at Emanu-El of New York, 1 East 65th Street, New York.

Current Residence: Holmes Towers, Upper East Side. Apartment 492.

Phone number: 212-615-3854

RETRIBUTION

The enormous gray limestone building that is the temple of Emanu-El had been reaching skyward for almost a hundred and thirty years. Its monolithic mass dwarfed the surrounding buildings. On the front of the temple was an enormous wheel-like window. This window contained twelve spokes that represented the twelve tribes of Israel. The Star of David adorned the center. The entrance, below the window, consisted of three sets of bronze doors. Each bore symbols of the twelve tribes of Israel. Beyond the entrance, the temple engulfs a person with a monstrous sanctuary capable of seating two thousand members, under ceilings more than a hundred feet high.

For the past month, John had followed his prey into the temple many times.

Ethan Shinwell always sat in the center of the vast room. Shafts of sunlight streamed through the great round window and washed over Ethan while he sat in silence and prayed. He came to pray almost every day. John knew what Ethan would do next. So, he waited.

Ethan came out of the synagogue and shuffled to the curb. He buttoned his coat. The arthritis in his hands made it a struggle. He looked to his right, raised his hand, and a taxi parked at the end of the block switched on its lights, moved forward, and stopped in front of him. Ethan opened the back door and got in behind the driver. A Plexiglas shield divided the driver from the passenger.

"Holmes Towers," Ethan said.

The driver pulled away from the curb and took an immediate left onto 66th Street. Ethan stared out the window. Dark figures moved down the sidewalks. He couldn't make out their faces. He didn't really care to.

Ethan didn't notice the driver pull up a clear plastic oxygen mask to cover his mouth and nose and reach beneath his seat and turn the valve of the oxygen bottle. The driver flipped a switch mounted under the console. From the trunk of the cab, valves opened on two large cylinders filled with halogenated ether. A piece of foam covered the end of the hose that ran under the back seat and came out at Ethan's feet into the passenger compartment of the car, which had been specially sealed to be as airtight as possible. The foam reduced the hissing sound of the escaping gas.

Ethan felt tired. A strange taste filled his mouth. Suddenly he was slightly nauseous. He pressed the button to lower the window. It didn't work. He tried the button on the other door. It didn't work either.

"Could you stop the car, please?" The driver didn't respond. Ethan knocked on the Plexiglas. "I said stop the car." The driver ignored him. "I don't—"

Ethan slumped against the door, his head resting against the window.

The driver flipped the switch off.

Ethan opened his eyes. Things were blurry. Dark. He sat in a chair, his head slumped forward. It seemed tremendously heavy. He tried to focus. It was quiet. Ethan's throat was dry. He coughed. The echo told him he was in an open space of some size. A battery-powered lamp sat on the wet, bare concrete floor to his right. The sound of dripping water came from behind him. He lifted his head. Directly in front of him sat another man. The man put Ethan's glasses back onto his face. He came into focus. A young man, dressed in jeans and a blue sweater.

"Who are you?" Ethan asked.

The man didn't answer. Ethan tried to move, and that was when he realized his arms and legs were bound and a rope around his chest held him against the back of his chair. Ethan strained against the bindings for a moment.

"Why am I tied to this chair? Who are you? I'm a poor man, I've no money."

"Don't you remember me, Ethan?"

Ethan focused on the man again. "No, I don't know you. Where am I?"

"In an abandoned building scheduled for demolition in a few days."

Ethan tried to look around, but the man grabbed him by the face and made him look forward. "Think about it for a minute... I certainly remember you. I've been waiting a long time to see you again."

Ethan studied the man again. "Son, nobody your age is worth remembering."

The man slapped him. Not terribly hard, just enough to make it sting. The pain brought the rest of Ethan's brain into focus. The man set Ethan's glasses straight again. "Oh, yes, you do. Don't I look like somebody you worked with a long time ago?"

Ethan stared at the young man and his mind moved back to a time that it was very seldom allowed to go. "You look like John Numen, or at least when he was young."

"In fact, I look exactly like him. Don't I?"

Ethan's eyes grew wide. "Oh, my God!"

"Yes. You believe what you are seeing. Think about it for a moment, and I am sure the answer will come to you."

"You are his clone?" Ethan asked.

"This body is a clone." John stood from the chair and turned a circle. "It's something, isn't it? That isn't the truly amazing part. I also have an exact image of John's brain taken from John himself. So, basically, I am John."

"That's impossible."

"Ethan, we are men of science. Certainly you know such a thing isn't impossible. Very difficult, I'll give you that. It requires that the two brains have the exact same physical structure, but it's not impossible."

"John sent his clone here to play this cruel joke on me."

"Okay, test me. Ask me something that only John would know."

"Where did we meet for the very first time?"

"In Dr. Jones's office. You were very rude, of course. The next time was in your office; we got in a thing over the budgets of the labs. You were always such a prick."

Ethan stared blankly at the man in front of him.

"Yes, it is true. I have done it. An idea that began long ago in my lab across the hall from yours has achieved perfection. I've achieved immortality. You don't need to go to church, I can be your deity. Observe my apotheosis. You should feel privileged. Besides me, you are the only person on this planet who knows this is possible."

"Where is the old John?"

"His body died in the brain imaging process. After you remove the information from it, the brain quits functioning."

"And the mind of the clone?"

"Wiped clean. Whoosh! Replaced by John's—mine."

"You killed him."

"I replaced him."

"You are the devil. I pray God has mercy on your soul," Ethan said.

"As if you are an oasis of virtues. You should be the last person to judge me for killing. I've been watching you for the past four weeks. Hardly a day goes by that you don't go to that synagogue. Seems you do a lot of praying these days, Ethan. The great Emanu-El. The biggest, most important place is required to hold the sins you carry, huh? You need a God that big? I've seen you there, alone, sitting in a pew for hours. Praying and reading from that book of myths and fables you call the Tanakh. What is it you are asking your big God for?"

"Forgiveness," Ethan said, his eyes downcast.

"And do you feel forgiven? Has this God of yours shown mercy and relieved you of your burden? Of your guilt?"

"No."

"Good. Neither have I. You didn't know Amira and I were having an affair." Ethan raised his eyes to meet John's. "An affair that started long before she moved out. For the very first time, we both felt loved. And you knew she didn't love you. You didn't care. You clung to your pride. Your God. Your religion, and you refused to let her go."

"I was her husband!"

"When the chips were down, when you couldn't get what you wanted by force or threat or prayer, you chose a gun. And Elona paid the price."

"I was going to kill myself," Ethan said.

"Why didn't you?"

"I don't know. I—I wasn't thinking clearly. I couldn't bring myself to do it."

"It's my belief that when a man is under pressure, that's when he shows what he really believes. So, you can pray and preach and put on that look of quiet distain at the unholy world. But you don't fool me. We are no different.

"You ended Elona's life and set mine and Amira's off in a direction that ended hers. And you made me spend the rest of that life waiting for a chance to start again. And that's where I am."

John moved the chair he was sitting in to the side and turned his back to Ethan. He took a couple steps and inhaled. "I'm beginning again." He faced Ethan again, a slight grin on his face.

"You are nothing more than Dr. Frankenstein and the monster rolled up into one. What apotheosis have you achieved? What are you going to do with immortality?"

"I'm going to have a life, not one in hiding. One out in the open."

"A life. That is all? You're a self-made god only abiding by the laws of nature. Accountable to no one. Killing other humans for no other goal than to extend your time aimlessly seeking little more than amusement, comfort, and pleasure. Who would want a god that doesn't know what he wants?"

"Unlike you, I will never die," John said.

"Mankind is not ready to live forever. We do enough damage to this fragile planet and each other in a single lifetime. Why are you telling me this?"

"Two reasons. The first is closure. You're the last artifact left from that life. I needed to tie it up and put it away. I needed to show you what I've done."

"And the other reason?" Ethan asked.

John looked down at Ethan. Old, pale, long gray beard, blotchy skin, almost bald, and tied to a chair. Exactly how and where he wanted him.

"Retribution."

John reached behind his back and from his waistband removed the pistol. "You killed the woman I loved... I've never forgiven you for that." He pointed the gun at Ethan's chest. "Now you can talk to your God in person about what you did."

Ethan closed his eyes.

John pulled the trigger; a flash came out of the barrel. Ethan's body jolted. The brass casing echoed with a metallic cling when it hit the cement floor. Ethan's head slumped forward. He did not move. John picked up the lantern and left the building.

Dawn was breaking when John parked the cab in the handicapped parking spot at a closed liquor store two miles from his hotel. The oxygen and ether bottles and the tubing he removed from the car and threw them away in the dumpster in the back of the store. He wiped clean the surfaces he or Ethan Shinwell may have touched. He made sure his untucked sweater covered the pistol in the small of his back and walked to his hotel.

He'd paid cash for the cab, and the title was in a fictitious name. By this time tomorrow it would be sitting in a tow yard, where it would stay for three years until the tow company sold it for scrap metal.

HIDING PLACE

John opened the door to the last of the storage units. Mr. Sanchez waited outside. The last one, like the others, was full of crates from his island, stacked three high. John smelled the scent of the ocean in the room. He unlocked one of the crates and took the pistol from under his coat, placed it inside and locked the lid.

Once outside, he placed the lock on the last unit's door, retrieved an envelope from the inside pocket of his jacket and handed it to Mr. Sanchez.

"My company will be sending you a check every month for the rent. Also, you have the name for the company's attorney should there be any problems."

"Yes, sir. Thank you." They shook hands and John returned to the waiting limousine.

"Where to, sir?" the driver asked.

"Airport, please." John's cell phone rang. He looked at the display and saw it was Mr. Thompson.

"Mr. Thompson, I was going to call you. I just got through looking at the crates in their new home. Everything looks fine."

"I've good news for you. The legal paperwork has been completed, and you are now the sole owner and CEO of Taylor Investments."

"Yes, that is good news. Thank you for your hard work. You'll find something extra in your Christmas bonus."

"If there's anything else, just let me know."

"I'm sure there will be," John said.

A GOOD LIFE

"Now boarding Flight 2840, nonstop service to Barcelona, Spain," John heard over the airport speaker system. He had been in the bar waiting for his plane to be de-iced. It hadn't taken as long as he'd thought.

John's cell phone rang again. He looked at the number and could tell from the area code it was from Nassau; however, it was not a number he knew. John answered the call. "Hello?"

"May I speak to Mr. Burke, please?" the man's voice said.

"This is Mr. Burke."

"This is Detective Rolle with the Royal Bahamas Police Force."

"Yes, Detective Rolle, what can I do for you?"

"I'm investigating a missing person's report. It's about a Ms. Julia Watson. You were on Mr. Taylor's island together back in September at the time of his death."

"Yes, we were."

"I was wondering if you've heard from or spoken to Ms. Watson since?"

"No, I haven't."

"She's overdue at a research facility in Africa, and the administrators there contacted us because they are concerned. The last they knew or heard from her was when she was staying at Mr. Taylor's island. Do you know where she may have gone from there?"

"After Mr. Taylor died, she said she was going to sail back to Florida. I don't know when she left, because I left before her and came to Nassau on Mr. Taylor's boat. She was still on the island when I left. We said goodbye at the dock."

"I see."

"If I do hear from her, I'll let you know right away."

"That would be helpful," Detective Rolle said. "I have another unusual thing to talk about. The toxicology report on Mr. Taylor showed a high amount of phenobarbital; not a lethal dose, but a significant amount. Did you see him take any medication while you were there?"

"No."

"Either pills or with an IV?"

"Not in front of me, and Julia never mentioned anything like that to me either."

"When will you be coming back, Mr. Burke? I'd like to ask you a few more questions."

"I'm not sure, but I'll let you know as soon as I do."

"You can reach me at—"

John ended the call. He'd not thought about Julia for weeks. He stared at the empty glass in front of him, remembering the curves of her face and the way the sun glinted off her hair. *I'm sorry.*

"Now boarding all rows all seats for 2840 nonstop to Barcelona, Spain," came over the speaker system again. John stood from the bar stool.

"You have a good flight," the bartender said.

"I intend to have a good life. I'm due one."

And he would, for the next twelve years.

SPRING 2070

RETURNING TO AMERICA

John could tell from the light coming in around the edges of the curtains that covered the large glass door to the terrace that the sun was up. However, it was not yet at its zenith. He pushed the covers off and swung his feet to the carpet. The woman beside him stirred; her hair covered most of her face except for her thin nose and full lips. The creamy skin of her back disappeared under the sheets. He got his robe from the back of the nearby chair and threw it over his shoulders. Stepping over the discarded clothing, he drew the curtains to the side and pushed open the heavy glass door to the salty ocean air and stepped onto the cool white marble tile of the terrace. Slowly, he moved to the iron railing. The sunshine hurt his hungover eyes, all the way to the back of the sockets.

John took a deep breath and closed his eyes. It was warm for this early in the spring. He thought about his dream. It was coming more often now. White sand beaches, so white it hurt his eyes to look at them, and glistening surf and blood on the sandy path beneath the palms.

Below him was Monaco Harbor, where all manner of yachts rested in the crystal water. None of them ever seemed to move. To his right was a panoramic view of the Prince's palace and many other hotels and large houses built on top of each other into the hillside that rose high above the harbor. To his left, beyond the mouth of the harbor, the emerald Mediterranean Sea stretched to the horizon.

He had done well at the roulette table the night before. The casino had banned him from the blackjack tables the day before. He didn't think they knew for certain he was counting; he was good at camouflaging it, except when he didn't control the whiskey, like in Venice.

They were probably tipped off by those cocksuckers in Venice. They would want him to stay for a while longer for a chance to get their one million Euros back. *Serves them right. I wouldn't ever risk that big a take at blackjack.* He stared at the horizon. He closed his eyes. Even though he liked Monte Carlo, and he liked the suite, it was still time to go. The plane tickets were bought.

It had been twelve years since he'd left, even longer since he had left his island. Between then and now he had been to Barcelona, Pamplona, Madrid, London, Prague, Istanbul, Munich, Vienna, Rome, Capri Island, Venice, and Paris. For the past six months, he had been here, staying in the Place Du Casino in Monte Carlo. Oliva followed him here from Paris.

"Let's go to Monte Carlo," he said one day as they strolled along the wet sidewalk beside the Seine. John knew it was time to go back; winter was coming, and his time was about up. For the previous few weeks, even Paris seemed to be awash in grayness.

"Why?" she asked. Like him, she was dressed in a heavy leather coat and knit cap. Behind her, gray clouds hid the top of the Eiffel Tower.

John grinned. "Because I've never been."

"*Bien.*"

She was easy like that. They had met at a party; donate to enough charitable organizations and you eventually get invited to the right ones. She still lived at home with her parents and went to college part-time, trying to break her way into the Paris fashion scene as a model. She had never been outside France. She looked mature for twenty. She believed everything John told her.

He recalled the day he asked her to move into his apartment, while they were seated at a sidewalk table at the café near her parents' flat. She was wearing a bright yellow dress on a sunny spring day. She was excited and hugged him hard around the neck. John was sure that he was going to miss Europe.

Shuffling footsteps came from behind him. He opened his eyes and turned to see Oliva wrapped in the white sheet from the bed walking up behind him. She came to his side and leaned against him to hide from the cool breeze, her chestnut hair blowing in the wind. She looked up at him. Slightly hungover as well, she squinted her light blue eyes from the mid-morning sun.

"*Bonjour,* Sean, my lover," Oliva said, proud of the English she had learned in the past year.

Oliva liked being with a man older than she. He told her he was thirty-two. He was really thirty-eight. He acted much older. She assumed that was a side effect of wealth and affluence. During the past year, he had shown her many things and taught her a lot, even about Paris. Places and parties she could have never gone to. It was a very pleasant change from the boys her age.

"*Bonjour, mon amante,*" John replied in perfect French. He had gotten used to the name Sean. "We need to finish packing and have breakfast. You don't want to miss your plane."

"I know. Are you sure I can't go with you to London?" Oliva said, switching to French.

"We've talked about this. I'll be a few days, a week at the most. You'll stay with your parents until I get back to Paris. In the meantime, you can look for our new apartment."

"If you say so." She looked out across the harbor with a slight smile. She liked the idea of picking out a new place for them to live together.

The driverless limousine ride to the airport in Nice was quiet. When they reached the checkpoint, beyond which only ticketed passengers could proceed, she faced him.

"I don't like it when you are this quiet. I'm nervous enough about flying alone."

"Sorry, I was just thinking about my trip and business." John handed the ticket to her. She hugged him tightly.

"I'll miss you. Call me as soon as you get to London. How long before your flight leaves?"

"I will." John looked at his watch. "Less than an hour."

She kissed him and walked away, passing through the checkpoint gate manned by a large security officer. John stood and watched her as long as he could until she disappeared in the mass of people. She didn't know, just as the others over the last twelve years hadn't known, that she would never see or speak to him again.

John worked his way through the crowd to his terminal. All departing passengers passed through a long gray tube that scanned every man, woman, and child for any prohibited items in their carry-on luggage, in-

side their clothes or inside their body. He didn't miss the days of long security lines and removing his shoes. At the end of the gray tube, security
personnel would hand-check anybody who had suspicious or prohibited
items. There were always a few lined up, usually the people who flew in-
frequently and didn't know the rules. Outside the window at his gate sat
the long, sleek passenger jet. A ram-jet engine hung beneath each wing, a
slender black cone protruded from the air intake of each engine. An hour
later, John reclined in his first-class seat. After the plane leveled off, the
captain's voice came over the speaker.

"Good afternoon, ladies and gentlemen. This is your captain. We've
reached our cruising altitude of fifty thousand feet. The computer shows a
flight time just under six hours, making our arrival time in New York at
three in the afternoon local time."

The flight attendant busily served drinks under the familiar hushed
hum of the jet engines and the thin air outside rushing over the plane. She
put the requested glass of water in front of John. *Time to dry out.*

Soon enough it would be time to kill again. He felt very tired. John
closed his eyes. He needed sleep to prepare himself for what was coming.
The plane wasn't over the ocean long when he fell asleep.

The feeling of the plane starting its descent and the increase in aisle
traffic woke him up. Monte Carlo and Oliva were now thousands of miles
behind him. As routinely as the most seasoned business traveler, in less
than forty minutes after he stepped off that plane John was seated on a
rented jet scheduled to fly from New York to Vail, Colorado. Soon the
plane was airborne, and John chased the sun westward for another five
hours. When the wheels of the plane touched down at Eagle County Airport, the sun had sunk behind the mountains to the west.

"Good morning, Ms. Dale." John stood from his seat at the breakfast table
to greet her. She looked slightly older than the picture on the internet.
Same blue blazer and tan briefcase in her hand.

"It's very nice to meet you in person, Mr. Burke." She smiled her
best real estate sales smile as she shook John's hand. "When did you arrive in Vail?"

"Last night."

"Nice choice of hotels. The Four Seasons has been one of the best for decades."

"Would you like breakfast?"

"No, thank you. I'm fine," she said.

"Let's get started."

"Excellent. We can use my Suburban. I've other properties we can look at besides the one we emailed about. If you would like."

"We'll see."

Forty-five minutes later, Ms. Dale stopped at the end of a long gravel road that wound its way over a ridge and into a valley, hidden and far from the highway. She removed from her briefcase a large topographical map, which, once unfolded, was almost as large as the dashboard. She placed her well-manicured fingernail at the end of a twisting gray line.

"We are here. It's almost two hundred acres, bordered on three sides by state wildlife areas. It has senior water rights and over one-half mile of private fly-fishing with this creek to the south, along with twenty acres of irrigated meadows. You won't find a more secluded spot in the whole state."

John opened the door and stepped into the mountain air. Patches of snow hid from the sun in the shadows of the trees. It was still cold at this altitude. The sky was clear. The mountain ridge to the east kept the meadow in shadow until late in the morning. He stood at the front of the Suburban and looked into the wilderness. Bare trees towered over the road and stood silently staring back at him. Ms. Dale stepped out as well. The rocks crunched under her high heels. John let out a deep breath and watched it become mist in front of him. *A nice change from an island to reconstruct my lab this time.*

"Ms. Dale, it's perfect. I'll take it."

"What offer would you like for me to give to the owner?"

"I'll pay their asking price, sixteen million."

"Very well. You have financing arranged already?"

"It'll be a cash sale. The sooner we close, the better." John was pretty sure he heard a pause in Ms. Dale's breathing. He looked at her. She was standing like her feet couldn't move. "Is there a problem?"

"No, sir." She gathered herself. "The closing shouldn't take long."

SUMMER 2070

IRINA

Irina's blonde ponytail bounced behind her head as she walked down the sidewalk. Her skin was cotton white, her eyes a light blue. The physique of an athlete moved under baggy sweatshirt and sweatpants. She was eighteen years old. A duffel bag full of judo gear hung from her shoulder. She pulled open the door of the gym and moved down the narrow hallway.

"Hi, Uncle Pavel," she said through the doorway to his office.

He sat in a small, cluttered office, the walls covered with pictures of Pavel with famous Russian boxers. Now his hair and thick mustache were mostly white, and the lines on his face ran deep. Papers, needed and unneeded, covered his desk.

"Good afternoon, Irina. How is the beauty of my gym?" He smiled, crow's feet radiating from the corners of his eyes.

"Good, just here for a quick workout. I'm tired of sitting around the house."

"I talked to your father, and he's beaming about the regional tournament."

"It went well," she said and shrugged.

"Come in here for a minute. I want to talk to you."

Irina sat down in the chair by the door. Pavel pulled a poster out from the middle drawer of his desk. It was large and folded in half. He handed it to her.

"Look what's coming to Kirov in two weeks."

The poster announced a mixed martial arts contest. A women's preliminary fight, no names were given, followed up by the main fight between two heavyweights she had never heard of.

"It's all the rage in Moscow, so they're branching out. A big promoter is going to set it up at the old warehouse by the river."

"About time somebody used that old building for something," Irina said.

"The two guys are a couple of nobodies trying to work their way up," Pavel said. "There are two women fighting, too. I'm the local promoter. I'm going to put these posters all over town. Have you ever seen an ultimate fight?"

"On TV."

Pavel leaned back in the oversized metal chair; it creaked under the weight of the barrel-chested Russian. "I'm meeting the promoter to see about doing this in Kirov on a monthly basis. Train local fighters, both men and women, and have them fight ones from other parts of Russia. They pay fifty rubles a fight to the winner, twenty to the loser."

"Fifty rubles?" That was almost as much as her father made in a month working at the mine.

"Yes. If you're really good, you can get a contract with the company, go to Moscow and make twice that every month. And if you win a championship, the payout is ten thousand rubles. And maybe even go to America and make the big money."

"How much money?"

"For the women's bantamweight world championship last year, the payout was five million U.S. dollars."

"Do you think I could do this?"

"I do. You would have to train differently. I'd have to train you, not your father."

"He'd never agree. He wants me to go to the national tournament next year."

"I watched you train for the regional tournament. I've been doing this for a long time, and I know burnout when I see it. Do you want to go to the national tournament?"

"Not really."

"I didn't think so. Have you told your father?"

"No."

"I didn't think so. Come with me in two weeks; I'll introduce you to the promoter and you can watch the fights. If you think you want to do it, *then* you can talk to your father."

"Okay."

"Friday night in two weeks. I'll take you there in my car. For once can you dress in something else besides sweats?"

"I thought I was the beauty of your gym."

"You're the beauty of all of Kirov. It's just nobody can tell. I want you to impress this guy from Moscow. It's easier if he sees a sophisticated woman. Not a party girl and not a gym rat."

"Okay, okay."

ROMAN

In the middle of the old warehouse sat an octagonal cage with a mesh-wire fence two meters tall, surrounded by metal bleachers. It looked out of place in the otherwise rotting interior. A large assembly of floodlights hung from the ceiling to illuminate the cage. The bleachers were full of workers sitting shoulder to shoulder. With so little to do in Kirov, when word spread that mixed martial arts from Moscow had come to the town, the miners showed up, hungry for entertainment. Especially entertainment that involved fighting.

Pavel worked his way through the crowd, and Irina followed close behind. At the back corner of the room, near the door that led to the fighters' preparation area, Pavel approached a man. He was sedate, in his late forties, with dark hair, dark eyes, and a dark suit. He had a narrow face with a crooked smile. They shook hands. His eyes immediately went to Irina.

"Irina, this is Roman Churkin. He brought this event here from Moscow. Roman, this is Irina Popova."

"So, this is your judo girl?" He eyed Irina's tight blue jeans and snug sweater. "She certainly is a looker. Can she fight?"

Irina began to speak. Pavel beat her to it. "She won the regional judo championship last week."

Roman looked her up and down again.

"Train her up, and I'll see what I can do from the Moscow end."

He shook Pavel's hand again and went through the doorway behind him.

"I thought I was here to see if I'd like it?" she said.

"No harm in advanced promoting. Besides, I know you're going to like it. I think you could beat either of the two girls fighting here tonight without any training. This could be your golden ticket. Think about it. Even if you win a national judo championship, what are you going to get? A medal, a handshake, and see you later. I know there's nothing after that life. That's how I ended up in Kirov. So, then what are you going to do? Marry this boyfriend of yours? What's his name?"

"Mak."

"Mak. I've no clue what you see in this guy. He's what, ten years older than you?"

"Nine. What I see is that he has his own place and his own car."

"Beside the point. You're just going to stay here and have little Mak babies? Is that what you want?"

"No."

"You've been coming to my gym since you were a skinny ten-year-old. I'm very proud of what you've done and how hard you've worked with your father—he can take you, and judo can take you, just so far in this world. You're a woman now, and you have to think about making your own future. Just think about that while we watch these fights to-night."

Pavel and Irina made their way to the first-row reserved section. Soon two women fighters came down the pathway to the octagon. Once in the ring, the referee introduced each fighter. The crowd cheered equally for each since nobody knew them. The fighting was sloppy. Throughout the first round, each fighter swung wildly at the other. They pushed and pulled in an awkward dance, and the round ended with them in a standing grapple.

Midway through the second round, the taller woman pinned the shorter to the mat with a headlock and choked her until she tapped her hand on the forearm around her neck to signal submission. The referee stopped the fight. The taller woman stood and held her hands over her head and pumped her fists. The crowd whooped their approval. Pavel looked at Irina with a knowing smile.

By the time the main fight between two heavyweight men ended, the crowd thundered in a frenzy. The vodka bottles that had been hidden in the men's coats and boots were drained and the cigarette smoke hung thick under the floodlights as a bloody victor held his hands high while his opponent lay on the floor with his trainers holding smelling salts beneath his nose. Pavel watched the screaming crowd and knew he could sell this out every time.

THE TALK

Irina's father worked in the mines, like most of the men in Kirov. In the foothills outside the city was one of the few places in the country that Volkonskoite could be found. It had been mined for decades, a green mineral that was used by painters and ceramic potters worldwide for its unique deep forest green pigment. It is dug up and loaded onto ships at the port on the Vyatka River, and it leaves Kirov, unlike the residents. Irina's mother died of cancer when Irina was ten. Irina became the housekeeper and cook after school.

She waited for her father at the kitchen table. He would arrive just after dark, if he didn't go drinking first. Payday was weeks away, so she was sure he'd come straight home from work. She wasn't going to tell him if he had been drinking. He came through the door in his orange jumpsuit, the usual amount of gray dust covering his legs and boots. His hardhat was cocked to the side. She had made his favorite soup. She waited until his bowl was half empty.

"I've decided not go to nationals."

He looked stunned. "Why? We've worked so long and so hard for this. It's what you want."

"No, it's what you want. You never asked me what I want."

"What do you want?"

"I've decided to try mixed martial arts instead. If I can get good at it, I can make a lot of—"

"Ultimate fighting? That is no sport. It has no elegance. Two brutes trying to beat the shit out of each other in front of a drunken crowd. Who's telling you to do this, your Uncle Pavel?"

"He says he can train me. He says if I can do it professionally I could make—"

"I heard you." He laid his spoon on the table and glared at her. "What makes you think you can do that for a living? Nobody around here does that."

"There's a promoter from Moscow bringing fighters here once a month."

"You should forget about this. Focus on training for nationals."

"I don't want to go to nationals."

"I said you'll forget about this foolishness and focus on nationals."

"I don't want to go to nationals!"

"As long as you live here, you'll do as I say."

"Fine. Mak wants me to move in with him. I'll go there." She left her bowl of soup on the table.

"You spend most of your time with that loser anyway. You can both go and be losers together!"

She grabbed her purse and slammed the front door behind her. Standing at the bus stop, she dialed Mak's number.

"Hey," Mak answered.

"Hi, I was wondering if you are busy?"

"Not really, just hanging with friends."

"Can I come over?"

"Sure."

Mak sat up in bed, lit a joint, and took a long draw on it. He handed it to Irina, who was lying naked next to him. She took a long draw on it and handed it back. She exhaled at the same time Mak did. Except for the glow of the joint, the one-room apartment was dark.

"Why are you so quiet?" Mak asked.

"I had a big fight with my dad. He wants me to go to nationals. I'm tired of judo. I want to do something else—ultimate fighting. Uncle Pavel says I could make a lot of money. Fifty rubles a fight."

"Not bad. You're going to do it?"

"Can I stay here for a few days until this blows over with my dad?"

"Sure."

SPRING 2071

THE CRATES

John stood in the kitchen of his nearly completed house, looking out the window at the mountainside. The construction had taken longer than expected. It had been slowed, first by bitter ice and snow, then again by warm mud. *The thaw came late this spring. I'm running behind.* John punched a number on his phone.

"Good afternoon, Mr. Sanchez," John said. "I'm calling to make sure the crates in seven of my storage units were picked up in a timely manner."

"Absolutely, Mr. Burke. They were loaded on the eighteen-wheeler without a problem," Mr. Sanchez said.

"I should be shipping them back to you in a year or so. I'll keep renting the same units even though they're empty, along with the other three, of course."

"No problem, Mr. Burke."

John ended the call.

I must have the lab ready and the cloning done before the snow starts.

THE CONTRACT

The room was quiet except for the sound of the tape coming off the roll as Pavel wrapped Irina's left hand. They could hear the crowd outside the room. Men laughing. Heavy boots on the aluminum steps. Pavel finished the hand. Irina slid off the table, flexed her hands and gave a few jabs into the air at an imaginary opponent.

"Remember, your opponent is faster than anyone else you have fought. You have the reach advantage. Stay outside and work her with your jab to set up your overhand right. Don't let her get inside on you. She knows your judo skills. She probably thinks it's best for her for it to be a boxing match. After she discovers her error, watch for her to go for your legs for a take-down."

Irina continued to throw combinations at the vision in front of her.

"All of a sudden she'll want to make this a wrestling match. Don't let her. Once you have her hurt, sweep her legs and find an arm bar."

The door to the room opened. The sound from outside grew and dimmed when the door slammed shut behind Roman. Same dark suit, same crooked teeth behind the same crooked smile. Irina could feel his eyes on her immediately.

"How is the Kirov Queen?"

"She's ready," Pavel said.

"The winner of this fight will get a two-year contract with the company. You'll come to Moscow to continue your training and fight in any matches arranged by the company anywhere in Russia. Before the end of the contract, we expect you to be in the position to fight for the world championship bantamweight title. If you don't meet our expectations, at any time we retain the right to release you at our sole discretion. I have the lawyer and the papers here for signing after the fight. Any questions?"

"No," Pavel said.

"I'd like her to answer," Roman said.

"I have none," Irina did her best to smile.

"Good luck," Roman replied and left the room.

Irina closed her eyes and took a breath. The door opened again. The ring official was there.

The official said to Pavel, "Anthony will be your cut man, as you requested."

"Thanks," Pavel said.

The door opened again. "It's time," Roman yelled through the doorway.

Irina gave Pavel a long hug. When they released each other, he looked at her.

"Now let's go kick her ass," he said.

Irina, followed by Pavel, came through the door into the arena area and followed the barricaded pathway to the ring. Cheers began with the local crowd, most of them there just to see her fight. She stopped at the bottom step and looked to her right at the first row. Mak was there. He gave her a thumbs-up. The official gave her and her attire the required inspection. When she stepped onto the platform and through the gate in the cage, the cheering grew louder.

A murmur grew in the crowd from the opposite end of the arena. Anna was tall, with stringy arms showing every fiber. She seemed to grow in size as she approached. Soon she was in the cage, too, along with the referee, who raised the microphone to his mouth.

"This fight is three five-minute rounds. Break clean on my command, and protect yourself at all times. Return to your corners."

Each of them did, and the crowd cheered. The referee handed the microphone through the cage. He went to the center of the cage, looked at each woman, raised his hand and with a downward motion yelled, "Fight!"

Irina circled around to her right. Anna threw a jab. Irina stopped it with her left hand without thinking. Anna lunged head-first at Irina's thighs. Irina side-stepped. Left-right-left to the top of her head. Anna straightened up, Irina circled, *jab-jab*. One glanced off Anna's cheek; the other missed. They orbited each other, traded jabs, and attempted kicks.

Anna lunged again, swung a looping right hook, attempted to move in close, wanting to wrap her arms around Irina's legs for a take-down. The looping hook and forward lunge left her unprotected. Irina side-stepped to her left and landed a stiff left jab to Anna's jaw. Her head snapped back while her body's momentum carried her forward into Irina's overhand right to the bridge of her nose.

An orange flash of light went through Anna's vision, and her arms dropped. The skin across her nose split open. Irina moved back to her right and centered herself in front of her opponent. The jab glanced off Anna's forehead. Anna brought her hands up to block the follow-up right to the side of her head. Blood streamed from Anna's nostrils. She stepped back to distance herself from the punches that were coming from unseen places.

Irina stepped forward, *jab-jab*, seeking the injured nose. Anna re-treated, her eyes wide, trying to weave her way backward out of the maze of punches. Irina moved in, her left jab slicing between Anna's gloves and landing on her cheek.

Back to the center of the cage they circled. Irina knew she had the speed now. She didn't wait. She moved left and flicked her jab through the opening in Anna's hands and landed on her right eye. Anna countered with a glancing right off Irina's forehead. Irina circled left, jabbed to the right eye, followed with an overhand right that drove the blocking hand back onto Anna's nose.

Anna swung and missed. Irina front-kicked to Anna's lead leg, and a right-cross found the nose cleanly. Blood dripped onto the canvas mat floor. Anna charged, head down. Irina gave her a left-right-left to the top of her head.

Irina side-stepped and stopped to kick. Anna charged again, coming into her as she raised her leg. Irina couldn't side-step in time and twisted to avoid the contact. Anna lunged into Irina, high on the torso, and slipped her left arm around Irina's neck to attempt a standing headlock. Irina pushed Anna over her head and twisted her head free of the lock. She grabbed Anna by the right wrist and pushed on her left shoulder. Irina used her left foot to sweep Anna's feet, sending them both crashing to the mat, Irina on top.

The crowd yelled and cheered. They stomped on the aluminum

steps and clapped their hands.

Anna went to a defensive position, wrapping her legs around Irina in a quick writhing motion that Irina could not control underneath her. Irina pried herself loose and wedged her body to gain control of Anna's left arm. Anna rotated to keep Irina from gaining a leverage position. Anna convulsed like a worm on a hot-plate. It was already too late. Irina stretched Anna's left arm, pinning Anna between her legs. The arm was across Irina's upper thigh. Irina could feel it giving way and hyperextend. The referee moved in.

"Over!"

Irina released her grip. The crowd cheered. Irina stood and Anna rolled onto her knees, holding her left arm off the mat. Pavel rushed through the gate and lifted Irina in the air, her hands raised. Irina looked out across the cheering crowd. Pavel let her down. Irina walked the circumference of the cage with her arms raised.

Her father stood at the end of a bleacher.

"Daddy! Daddy, I did it!" she yelled through the cage and the cheers of the men.

They looked at each other. He wasn't clapping. He wasn't smiling. He stepped off the bleachers and walked away.

Pavel, Mak, and Irina were waiting in the preparation room when Roman came through the door with another man in a dark suit, holding a brief-case.

"Congratulations." Roman shook Pavel's hand and Irina's. "This is Vlad, a lawyer for the company."

Vlad shook their hands. "Congratulations," he said. He placed the briefcase on the table, opened it, and removed two papers.

"This is the contract as Roman explained to you earlier." He took a pen out of the briefcase and handed it to Irina. "All I need is your signature."

Pavel was smiling as big as Irina had ever seen. She leaned forward and signed her name to each sheet and handed the pen back to Vlad. He handed one of the copies to Pavel, put the other paper back in the brief-case, and closed it.

"I'll be seeing you in Moscow next week," Roman said.

"I can't wait," Irina said.

Roman and the lawyer left the room. Irina looked at Pavel again, tears in her eyes.

"Uncle Pavel, thank you so much!" Irina hugged him, her arms barely able to reach around his large frame.

"It was nothing."

"I'm going to miss you in Moscow."

"I'm going to miss you, too."

Irina hugged Mak. "We did it, baby. We're going to Moscow!"

"How about we go out to Lexior's and celebrate?" Mak said.

"Yes, we should celebrate. Uncle Pavel, you can come too," Irina said.

"Not me. That place is for the young people. I'm going home to a nice dinner, a glass of cognac, and my leather chair."

LEXIOR'S

Mak cut through the back streets on the way to the club. Irina used to like going to the club; they got in using fake IDs when she was in high school. It was fun. She'd met Mak there. Without a doubt, the coolest, sexiest man she had ever met. Standing three inches taller than she, with broad shoulders, dark hair, and chiseled chin. Older. Confident, and had his own place. Instant mutual attraction. She hadn't been to Lexior's since she started training with Pavel. She could smell the cigarette smoke on Mak when he came home. It was the only happening place in Kirov.

"We're going to meet a guy tonight, okay? A guy who I can do business with," Mak told Irina.

"I thought we agreed you'd stop after I won."

"I'm supposed to get a job waiting tables? You know there's no way I'm doing that shit. This is what I'm good at."

"You're just a fucking liar. You never do anything you say. You didn't want to go out because I won. You wanted to meet this guy."

"I don't tell you how to run your life, and you don't tell me how to run mine."

She could hear the music inside when they parked the car across the street. Irina skillfully navigated the potholes in the street in her high heels and tiny red dress. The line to get inside was a half-block long. The guy at the door wore a black T-shirt stretching mercilessly across his chest and shoulders. He nodded. Mak already had a small plastic bag in the palm of his hand. The bouncer unclipped the entry rope and shook hands with Mak. In one smooth motion the baggie was passed. Irina followed Mak through the door.

Cigarette smoke glowed blue and green in the lights above their heads. The front dance floor to the left was a mass of bodies. People at the bar were lined up three deep. Mak tried to hold Irina's hand as they moved through the crowd. She wrenched her hand away. He stopped and grabbed her by the arm and pulled her close.

"Lose the fucking attitude. Don't fucking embarrass me in front of these people."

She gave him a cross-eyed look. "I'm supposed to act like I think you shit gold?"

"We're going to act like we don't need to do business with them, like we don't need their money, like we're doing *them* a favor. If they don't think I can control my woman, they won't make any deal with me. So you are going to smile, be charming, and do whatever I fucking tell you to do."

"So, I'm smiling and being charming and doing whatever you fucking tell me to do. You're hurting my arm."

"I'll do more than that if you fuck this up." He released her and grabbed her hand. She didn't pull away. They started through the crowd again, past the dance floor, through a doorway into a room with a larger dance floor that was jam-packed. They moved through the tables to another bar just as crowded as the first. Beyond the bar were private semi-circle booths along the wall. Mak made his way to the one nearest the bar. A man at least a foot taller and seventy pounds heavier than Mak shook hands with him, while the other hand felt around Mak's waist for a weapon.

"Good to see you again, Mak."

"Same to you, Andrei."

Andrei leaned across to check Mak's waist on the other side and in Mak's ear whispered, "Remember, he doesn't like to shake hands." He slapped Mak on the shoulder, ran his hand across his back, and grinned.

"No problem."

He pointed to the right side of the booth and Mak slid in.

"Let me see the purse, please." Andrei pointed at Irina's clutch. She handed it to him. He opened it, examined the contents, felt the sides for anything that could be concealed inside the lining, and handed it back to Irina, who then slid in beside Mak. Across the table sat a man so fat he could hardly fit in the booth. His round face sat on top of his round body with no neck in between. He was about the same age as Mak and dressed in a white shirt and tan suit. He had long brown hair pulled back into a ponytail. In front of him was a plate of bread, an empty bottle of vodka, and a shot glass. He was chewing on a piece of bread, the remaining bite held by the thick fingers of his hand resting on the table. He smiled at Mak, his eyes becoming tiny slits.

"Irina, this is Yuri," Mak said.

"Bringing a woman here is like bringing sand to the beach," Yuri said.

Mak laughed along. "If we can work out a deal, she'll be working for me, so I thought you would like to meet her."

"She's very pretty sand. Andrei's cousin tells us you know your way around Kirov. You have a bit of play here working with Leo," Yuri said.

"Me and Leo have made good deals. It's been good business."

"How much are you moving here?"

"Two kilos a month, when I can get it," Mak said.

"Yes, when you can get it. Two kilos is very good. As you probably know, Leo has become unreliable, perhaps using his own stuff too much. Who knows. I'm looking for someone I can count on. Somebody who'll do what he says."

"You can ask around, I'm solid."

"You seem to be a guy looking to move up." Yuri stuffed the piece of bread he was holding in his mouth and chewed. "If we can do good business in Kirov, that could be a possibility."

"Everybody is looking to move up in the world. I don't see why we can't help each other out. You front me the stuff, we split the profits. I take sixty percent, you take forty."

"I take forty percent when I'm fronting for you?" Yuri said.

"I have the local distributors in place, and I'm taking the risk."

"I'll tell you what I'm considering… a fifty-fifty split for the first few one-kilo deals. We'll see how that goes. Once we move up to two kilos a month, then I'll agree to sixty-forty."

Mak shrugged. "I don't see a problem with that."

"I don't make any deals with someone I haven't drunk with yet. Send your sand for more vodka."

Mak pulled two one-hundred-ruble bills out of his front pocket and handed them to Irina. "Get a bottle of the best they got."

Irina smiled and nodded, put the bills in her clutch, swung her legs out and went to the bar. Mak knew this was her way of saying, *I am not talking to you, asshole.*

The long bar was crammed with people standing and talking. Most were trying to elbow their way to the front and get the attention of one of the two female bartenders. By the time Irina got through to the bar, she ended up on the opposite side from where she had started.

She looked beyond the glare of the overhead lights at Mak and Yuri talking and laughing in the booth. A young woman with long, dark hair and a black dress as short as hers stood at the booth. She seemed to know Mak and gave him a friendly hug around the neck before she sat down beside him. Mak quickly glanced toward the bar, looking for Irina. He didn't find her in the crowd since she had moved around the bar.

The bartender looked Irina's way. "What do you need?"

"A bottle of your best vodka."

The bartender walked toward the other end of the bar.

"Is that just for you?" a man's voice asked from beside her, a voice she knew.

Irina looked to her left to find Roman standing next to her, same dark suit, same crooked smile. An attractive brunette in a plunging dress and dangling silver earrings held his arm. She smiled at Irina without sincerity.

"Hi, Roman. What are you doing here?"

"It's the only place with a decent crowd in Kirov. You fought well tonight. I talked to the man who runs the company back in Moscow, and he's impressed."

"Thank you. I expect us to get there next week," Irina said.

"Good. I'll set you up with our trainers, and we'll see about arranging a fight soon."

"How many glasses?" the bartender asked, now back in front of Irina holding a bottle of vodka.

"Four."

The bartender put the bottle and four shot glasses on the bar and said, "One hundred and eighty-six rubles."

Irina looked back at the table. Mak and the woman were still talking.

"Good, the whole bottle isn't just for you," Roman said.

"No, it's for the table."

"Training will be demanding in Moscow. It'll be a full-time job. We're expecting great things from you. Come prepared and determined."

"I'll be ready."

Irina looked back over at the booth. Mak and the woman were not there. Irina handed the bartender the bills, put the clutch under her arm, grabbed the bottle with one hand and four shot glasses with the fingers of her other. Irina made her way from the bar to the booth and put the bottle and glasses on the table.

"Where's Mak?" she asked.

"I think he stepped out for some fresh air." Yuri picked up the bottle, twisted the top off, and began pouring shots.

"And the woman who was talking to him, did she go too?"

"I didn't see any woman. Did you, Yuri?" Andrei said.

"No. No woman."

Irina walked toward the back of the club. She could hear Yuri and Andrei laughing as she left. She passed the dance floor, stopped and took a long look out there. She didn't see Mak, although she thought she could hear him laughing. To the right, a hallway led outside to a small courtyard. She followed the dark hallway, past a couple groping each other against the wall. The courtyard had long strands of lights strung overhead, going from a center pole out to the edges. It was mostly couples, drinking and smoking. A man and a woman sat in the back corner on the edge of a bench. The woman had long dark hair and a black dress. The guy on the other side was obscured. She made her way over, expecting the worst. The woman pulled back from the kiss, and she could see it wasn't Mak.

Irina went back to the hallway. She stopped and leaned against the wall. It was just too crowded to find him. To her right was a side hall to the bathroom, a steady flow of people moving in and out. Two drunk guys sauntered by laughing.

"Oh, man, I need to find me a chick who will let me fuck her in the bathroom stall."

They laughed more. Irina looked down the short hallway. The men's restroom door was open. Nobody was moving in or out. She went down the hallway. Guys were standing around, not making much noise. She squeezed through the doorway. A couple of guys were at the urinals.

She passed them on her way to the row of stalls. She could hear something. A clicking and another noise she could barely hear over the thumping bass of the music from the dance floor. Something else caught her ear. She moved down until she was at the last stall. She could see the door moving. Each time it moved, it clicked, and she could hear a low moan, a woman's voice. She waited outside.

Inside the stall the woman was bent over, bracing her hands on the stall door, her dress pulled up around her waist. Mak stood behind her with his pants around his ankles. He thrust into her for the final time. When the orgasm ended, he took a long breath. She looked over her shoulder at him and giggled. She got some toilet paper and wiped between her legs and threw it in the toilet. She straightened and lowered her dress, turned around and kissed him. She held out her hand. Mak pulled up his pants, took a small baggie from a pocket and gave it to her.

"Call me... we'll party together," she said.

"Yeah, I'd like that," Mak said.

She unlocked the door, straightened her dress, and walked out to find Irina standing there. Irina didn't move.

"Oh, shit," the woman said as she hurried by and made her way through the crowd of guys waiting to see who came out of the stall.

Mak came out, looking down, buckling his belt. When he looked up, Irina was three feet in front of him, her right arm cocked back like a spring. The last thing he remembered was the sound of his teeth clashing together. A sharp pain streaked to the back of his skull. Mak didn't know it, but his face was the first thing to hit the floor. Irina's fist gashed open both lips. The floor left a purple contusion on his right cheek. Irina turned around to leave. Roman stood directly behind her, in front of the group of laughing, high-fiving men.

"I'll be coming to Moscow by myself. I'll leave tomorrow," she said, massaging her right hand.

"Obviously."

NEW THINGS

Pavel unlocked the door of his gym at 11:45 a.m., like every Sunday morning. He passed the office to the main room and switched on the light. He knew the Sunday group would start showing up soon. A high school boxing match was a month away, and the coach had them coming in on Sundays. First things first, he needed coffee. He opened the door of his office to find Irina asleep, wrapped in a blanket. Curled up in his chair. When he turned on the light, she woke up. Mascara streaks ran down her cheeks. Her purse was on the desk and her high heel shoes on the floor. Her eyes were puffy and her nose red.

"Irina, what are you doing?"

She squinted from the overhead light. "Hi, Uncle Pavel. I needed a place to sleep."

"What happened, did you have a fight with your boyfriend?"

"Worse than that." Her eyes began to fill with tears. "I caught him with another woman."

"I never liked that guy. What happened?"

"I knocked him out."

Pavel laughed. Tears fell from Irina's eyes. Irina laughed too. The more she tried to stop, the more she couldn't. Pavel had to sit in the chair by the door.

"You finally knocked someone out. I told you. Wait for somebody to make you mad. Couldn't have happened to a better guy." Pavel took a deep breath. "I'll make coffee."

Empty coffee pot in hand, Pavel left for the water fountain. Irina used the tissue on the desk to wipe her eyes and blow her nose for the hundredth time. She took her cell phone from her purse and turned it on. She found a voice message from Mak. She selected it and listened.

"Don't you ever come back to my apartment, you fucking bitch! I took your shit and threw it in the fucking dumpster and set it on fire! If I ever see you again, I don't care where, I'll fucking kill you!"

Pavel came back in the room with a pot full of water and a damp towel. He handed the towel to Irina. She put her phone down and wiped her face.

"How did you get here?" Pavel asked.

"I took a cab from the club."

Pavel poured the water into the coffee machine and switched it on. He sat back down in the chair by the door. They heard the front door open and shut, and one of the high school boxers passed by the doorway. He looked through the doorway and stopped.

"Hi, Pavel." He looked behind the desk. "Hi, Irina. What happened to you?"

"Go get warmed up," Pavel snapped, and the boy disappeared from the doorway. They heard the door open and close again and could hear more high school boys talking to each other as they filed past the doorway.

"I need to go get these guys started." Pavel stood and left the office, shutting the door behind him.

She heard more boys come in the front door, talking and laughing. The light punching of the heavy bag as somebody began to warm up. Pavel giving directions. The normal noise of the gym. So many Sundays she was part of it, but now it felt distant to her. Pavel came back in the office. He poured coffee in a mug and placed it on the desk in front of Irina. He poured himself one and sat in the same chair as before.

"How will I make it in Moscow without anybody there with me?"

"You're better off alone than with that guy."

"You're probably right… Daddy was at the fight last night… I saw him. He just left, wouldn't talk to me."

"Your father is bitter. At me, at you, at life. He thinks the way he knows is the only way. My brother is the most stubborn man I've ever known."

"Mak left me a voicemail… besides calling me a bitch, he says he burned my stuff in the dumpster."

"I'll take you shopping for whatever you need. The farther you stay away from him, the better."

"You're the best uncle any niece could ever ask for."

"I have one condition. As soon as we are done with the shopping, I put you on a train to Moscow. I don't want Mak finding you. I'll call Roman and tell him you will be arriving tomorrow, in the morning."

"I don't think he'll be surprised. He was at the club last night and saw the whole thing."

"Good. He'll understand. I'm sure he's flying back this morning. He can take you to the place you'll be staying. Deal?"

"Sounds great to me."

THE TRAIN

Irina and Pavel worked their way through the crowd at the train station. She was carrying her new gym bag full of new fighting gear, wearing new jeans, a sweater, and leather shoes. Pavel rolled a very large suitcase stuffed full of new clothes, shoes, and makeup. Its shiny metal exterior looked out of place among the dingy floors, walls, and people of the station. The train, long, metallic, and sleek, looked out of place too. They stopped at the entrance to the correct car. Pavel lifted the suitcase onto the top step inside the car in one large motion.

"All right, this is it," Pavel said.

She hugged him around the neck and kissed him on the cheek. "Thank you for everything." She held herself around his neck.

"Try to sleep. Roman will be there at the station to take you to your new place."

A woman's voice blared over the speakers overhead, "Last call for all passengers on 892 to Moscow. Last call for all passengers."

"I'll call you and let you know how things are going."

"You'd better," Pavel said.

He patted her on the back, and she released her grip. She stepped up through the door of the train to the top step, beside the new suitcase. Her eyes watered as she faced Pavel. "If you see my dad, tell him goodbye for me," she said through the open door.

"I will. I promise."

She grabbed the handle of the suitcase and pulled it down the aisle until she found her seat. She rolled the bag into the luggage holding bin opposite her booth and sat down. She kept her gym bag close because it held her food for the trip. The train car was scarcely populated. Nobody looked at one another, their faces impassive, dreading the boredom of the monotonous trip ahead.

"Closing all doors," a man's voice on the speakers said.

A loud hiss came from outside, and the door that she came through closed. Suddenly it was quiet inside the car. She looked through the window to see if Pavel was still there. He was gone.

The train silently glided forward without vibration, gradually picking up speed as it moved into the orange glow of the setting sun. Things outside the window seemed to pick up speed. Kirov went by with increasing rapidity. Soon the space between the houses increased as they passed through farmland, followed by long stretches of forest. As sunlight faded, the light inside the car faded with it. She could spot only an occasional house with the lights glowing. Irina knew at long last she was out of Kirov.

ۤ

Just after midnight she woke. She looked out the window. Opaque blackness. The train slashed through the vast night of the countryside under the immense, timeless sky. She thought about her father as the train slid down the track. He would live the rest of his life alone, she was never going back, and he would never leave Kirov. What lay ahead she couldn't know as the train hurtled down the track.

People moved past her down the aisle, lovers in the night, the man's voice low and comforting, the laughter of the woman, silky and sensual, fading as they continued to their seats, out of sight. Irina laid her head back down. She wished Pavel was there. She wished she knew what waited for her in Moscow. She fell asleep.

She couldn't know the twists of fate that the train carried her to, but if she did, she would have gone anyway.

MOSCOW

Irina looked out at the city passing by her window in the mid-morning sunlight. It stretched out as far as she could see, tall buildings in every direction. When it seemed the train was moving no faster than a man walking, it entered a dome tube with white skylights that diffused the sunlight, giving everything a soft glow. The train stopped.

The people in the car began moving to gather their luggage. Irina waited. The doors opened and soon the car was empty. Irina removed her cell phone from the docking station, picked up her gym bag, and slung it across her torso. She rolled her suitcase down the aisle and lifted it out the door.

Even the air in the train station felt different. People were flowing in the direction of the main building. Irina followed them. She passed through large round doorways, down domed hallways, and over shiny tile floors. She went up two escalators and crossed the massive main terminal room, dodging through throngs of people. Her cell phone rang. It was Roman with instructions on how to find him.

After she put the suitcase in the trunk, she got in his car. "After I show you the apartment, I'll take you to the gym five blocks away. You'll be able to walk there, once you know where it is. You'll get to meet your trainers," he said.

"I have more than one trainer?"

"Each with a specialty. You're our newest and most promising investment. We'll give you every chance to succeed. However, you'll work hard, and you'll start today."

Without another word, Roman drove through the streets of Moscow. People were everywhere. Cars clogged every street. The streets became narrower as he drove through the neighborhood. They turned down a street that paralleled a river and took a right turn onto a large, busy street. To the right was the apartment building with pastel green columns separated by beige brick.

The first thing that struck Irina about the apartment was that it was about the same size as the one she had shared with Mak. It was clean. Green couch past its prime, no television, small kitchen table with three chairs, beige carpet, pictureless walls painted beige, a single window with curtains that matched the carpet. The kitchen area had a sink, a stove, a microwave, and a small white refrigerator.

Past that, she could see into a room with a bed. The door had been removed. There were no sheets or blankets on the bed. Neither she nor Pavel had thought to buy linens. Irina placed her gym bag on the green couch, let the suitcase stand on its own, and looked around. She loved it.

Roman held out a blue plastic access card with a key attached. "This is your building access card and your key," he said.

"Thank you."

"There's a grocery store three blocks up the street from where we parked. The refrigerator is empty, so you go there first thing after you leave the gym today. The dietician will meet with you today. She'll tell you what you need to buy."

"Dietician? Thank you. I will," she said.

"Grab what you need for the gym, and I'll walk you there."

Irina picked up her new gym bag from the couch and slung it over her shoulder. "I'm ready."

Roman led her down a street lined with identical redbrick buildings. They were once industrial buildings, but now were a mishmash of different businesses. A shoe shop, a play house, a furniture repair shop, a bicycle repair shop, and a warehouse. Roman crossed the street in the middle of the block. Above a brown metal door was a sign that read "Rolling Thunder Gym."

The smell of the gym was the first thing she noticed. It made her think of Pavel's gym. It was busier and louder. Trainers yelled instructions to two men boxing in the sparring ring. Roman went down a hallway, and she followed him. A few meters later he entered an open office door, where a man sat behind a desk. A woman sat in a chair opposite him.

"Good to see you again, Roman." Roman and the man behind the desk shook hands.

Irina glanced around the room at the pictures of fighters on the walls. None of them had a younger version of the man behind the desk in them. She guessed him to be about Roman's age; however he was much taller, athletic, with short, thick blonde hair and blue eyes. Irina nodded politely at the woman, who stood and stared expressionlessly. She could be Irina's mother, with graying hair to her shoulders and a business suit tailored to fit her lean physique.

"This is Irina," Roman said. "Irina, this is Alecks Klokov. He manages the gym."

Irina shook his hand and beamed a smile.

"And this is Roza Sizy," Roman said.

Irina shook her hand too. "It's nice to meet you."

Roza nodded.

"She's your dietician," Roman continued. "And she has diet plans to give you. She'll be tracking your physical statistics, such as weight and body fat percentage. If you have any food allergies, you should let her know. Ms. Sizy, please show Irina to the women's locker room. You can talk things over with her there."

"Yes, sir, Mr. Churkin," Roza replied.

"Irina, when Roza is finished, change into clothes for sparring. We have head gear and gloves that will fit you; you'll need little else. Warm up with the speed bag. We'll meet you there," Roman said.

"Yes, sir," Irina replied.

Roza picked up a briefcase from the floor beside her chair and walked out of the office. Irina followed her. Once outside the office, she guided Irina back the way they had come, past the sparring ring, past the speed bags down another hallway and into the women's locker room. The sound of the gym faded behind them. Lockers lined each wall, with a single bench down the middle. At the end of the room was a counter with a mirror and beyond that she could see a doorway to the shower area.

"This is the locker room," Roza began. "Always keep a lock for your locker; you may choose any one you want. Down that way is the shower area. Bring your own towel and shampoo and soap; the toilets are to the right. Please sit down."

They both sat on the bench. Roza opened the briefcase and removed a clipboard and a pen. She handed Irina a large manila envelope stuffed with papers.

"There's general information about a proper diet in there. The important part is the grocery list and meal plan. There's a credit card for the grocery store. Each week the store will have a list of items for you to purchase and pay for with that card. The cash that you get each month is for living expenses besides food. Please follow the meal plan strictly. Begin with the page titled 'Week 1' for both the grocery list and meal plan. Next week go to 'Week 2' until you reach 'Week 5.' After that you'll start over again. Depending on how things go, I'll give you a different five-week plan in a few months. Understand?"

"Yes."

"Good. Do you have any food allergies?" Roza picked up the clipboard and pen.

"No."

"Are you pregnant at this time?"

"Excuse me?"

"If you are pregnant I need to know so we can decide what to do about it."

"No, I'm not."

"If I were you, I'd stay that way. You have the good fortune of being given the opportunity to train at an elite professional level. This is the best training facility in Russia. A pregnancy that you would be unwilling to terminate would end that abruptly. Are you using any form of birth control now??"

"Yes."

"Continue to do so, whether you have a boyfriend or not. Understand?"

"Yes."

"When was your last menstruation?"

"A week ago."

"Any chance you have become pregnant in the last week?"

"No."

Roza wrote on her tablet.

"You don't use an electronic pad here?"

"Electronic records can be stolen without the thief even being in the same country, much less in the building. Sometimes the old ways are the best ways. Now I need you to take your clothes off and stand on the scale by the doorway to the shower so I can get your weight."

While Irina undressed, Roza continued to write on the clipboard. The tile floor was cold to Irina's feet. She stepped on the scale and the digital display showed "58.87 Kg." Roza wrote on her pad again. Irina stepped off the scale. Roza handed Irina a black plastic device the size of a cell phone with two metallic handles sticking out each side.

"Hold a handle in each hand."

Irina did as she was told. After a minute, a voice from the box said, "Twelve point six eight percent."

Roza wrote on her tablet. Irina handed the device back to her.

Roza took another device from her briefcase and clamped it onto Irina's index finger. "There will be a stick."

The device drew out a tiny amount of blood from Irina's finger. Roza removed the device and watched the display. Two minutes later, the indicators were green. "Good, you have no immune disease of any kind, no genetic diseases that will affect you later, such as ALS, and you don't have any banned substances in your blood. It's important that you stick to the supplements on the approved list in your packet. We can't have you failing a blood test before any of your fights. You can get ready for your workout now."

Roza put everything inside her briefcase. Irina opened a locker near her bag and placed her street clothes inside. She opened her gym bag and removed her workout clothes. Roza picked up her briefcase.

"I'll be in touch in a week or so to see how things are going," Roza said.

"Thank you so much."

"You'll find my number in the packet. Call me if you have any questions."

"Yes, ma'am."

The clicking of Roza's high heels disappeared into the sounds coming from the gym down the hall. Irina sat on the bench. She looked around at the empty locker room, at the packet of diet information. The knot that had been in her stomach all day grew tighter. Suddenly she wasn't sure she was ready for this.

When Irina came out of the locker room, she could feel the gym watching her. Nobody was obvious about it; nonetheless, the other fighters in the gym were watching. She pretended nothing was unusual and, with her hands already wrapped, went to the speed bag and began her warmup, taking her time between strikes. Each strike was crisp and on the mark.

Ten minutes later, the bag and her hands were a blur, and she had forgotten about the others in the gym. She felt someone beside her and gave the bag an extra-hard strike. She turned to see Roman, Alecks, and two other men she didn't know. The closest man was tall and slim, with salt-and-pepper hair; the other was younger, late twenties, handsome, and wearing fighting shorts and a T-shirt. Irina thought she recognized him, but couldn't remember from where.

Roman pointed to the man with the salt-and-pepper hair. "Irina, this is Sergej Laskin. He'll be your boxing trainer."

"I hear you are Pavel Popova's niece?" Sergej asked. "Your father trained you in judo, too, they tell me?"

"Yes."

"I never met your father, but I do know Pavel. He was a good fighter in his day. I've been told about your judo championships. What I want to know is, can you be a good boxer?"

"I think I can become a good boxer."

"I have a sparring partner waiting for you in the ring. Let's get gloves and headgear on you and see if I agree."

Sergej helped put the gloves and headgear on her. A young man, shirtless, already gloved and with headgear, was waiting in the ring.

"It's a pretty face, let's not mess it up on the first day," said Sergej. "All right. Let's go for two minutes." He clicked a button on a stopwatch.

The young man met her in the center of the ring. He was shorter than Irina. He was the same weight. He threw a jab that she avoided, then another. He constantly moved in front of her, his head never a stationary target. They traded jabs; he threw a combination, and the follow-up with his right hand glanced off her forehead. Irina counter-punched and landed a solid right to the side of his head. Irina knew this was a straight-up boxing match, so she didn't have to worry about this guy trying a takedown. They circled, dodged, and jabbed at each other. She threw a jab, and it landed. She circled right, threw another. It landed. He counter-punched and missed, tried another that she blocked with her glove, and without thought she came with her right-hand square on his chin. He staggered back a half-step and covered. She threw a jab that struck his glove against his face and lowered it just enough for her next right to find his temple. He backed into the ropes. She moved forward, left and right hands striking his gloves. Some of them slipped between to find flesh or head gear. He could find no escape from her pounding fists. Another right landed on the side of his headgear. He wavered.

"Time!" Sergej shouted.

Irina stopped. When she went to her corner, she noticed several other men in the gym had stopped their workouts and stood watching.

"We won't need another round," Sergej said.

Irina spit her mouthpiece into her glove. "I was just finding the zone. I can do better."

"Better? I can't wait to see that. You just staggered the University of Moscow men's featherweight champion into the ropes in less than two minutes. I've seen enough for now." Sergej looked at Roman and both men smiled. Sergej removed her gloves and headgear.

"I did?" Irina said. She smiled too.

"Yes, you did," Roman said.

The younger man in the black fighting shorts and white T-shirt stepped forward. Irina liked the way he looked. Roman looked at the young man. "Your turn."

Erik stepped up through the ropes and into the ring. He extended his hand.

"Hi, I'm Erik Lyadov," he said.

When Irina heard the name, she knew where she knew him from.

"You're a fighter! I know you. I've seen you fight on television. You're ranked like fifteenth in the light heavyweight division." Irina shook his hand. His grip was strong and gentle.

"More like twentieth now, after his last fight," Roman said from behind the ropes.

"Yes, more like twentieth now." He looked past Irina at Roman. "Roman has told me about your judo background. I'll be helping you add other aspects to your mixed martial arts repertoire, mainly kicking, jiu-jitsu, and grappling. Today I'm going to spar with you for grappling to get a first-hand assessment of your skill level."

They went to the center of the ring, held their hands up, shoulder-high, palms toward each other. Their hands engaged each other and they leaned into each other, their heads resting on the other's shoulder. The standard grappling position.

Erik had to hunch over to match Irina's height. He placed his left hand on the back of her neck, and her right hand went under his arm, grappling the back of his shoulder. His right hand rested on the front of her left hip, and her left arm around his neck. She leaned her weight into him and applied pressure with her legs. He didn't move. She could tell that he only matched her resistance; he could easily overpower her if he wished.

Erik attempted a leg sweep, which she avoided. They broke free from the hold and backed away from each other several steps. They approached each other again and resumed the standard grappling position. Erik applied pressure to her, wrapped his arm around her waist and tried to take her to the mat; she spun with him but stayed up. He forced her to bend forward at the waist as he moved beside her, now facing the same direction as her, his right arm around her waist, her left arm still around his neck. He extended his right leg to sweep her left foot; she avoided it and remained on her feet.

Irina's feet were now poorly positioned. He reached over with his free left hand and grabbed her left ankle and pulled it out from under her as he leaned into her upper body. She pulled him toward her, rolled underneath him, placed her left foot between his legs and hooked it to the back of his right leg. In an instant she somersaulted him over the top of her onto his back, her legs locking him in place.

The gym crowd, which had remained silent since the previous boxing match, cheered. When he came to a stop, she had his right arm by the wrist, stretched it across her pelvis and applied an arm bar. He immediately tapped her leg to submit. She released him. The gym crowd clapped their approval.

"All right, very good job," Erik said.

"Thank you," she replied.

"Like Sergej, I've seen enough for today. Your judo skills are very strong, very impressive. I'll come up with a training schedule; the problem will be finding you sparring partners. I'll see what I can do."

Erik and Irina left the ring. Roman and Sergej stepped down and the crowd dispersed. Irina's face was flushed and her hair a mess and she was breathing much harder than Erik. And she had just earned the respect of everyone in the gym. They gathered outside the ring, and Roman spoke to the group.

"Alecks will work with Sergej and Erik on which days you'll work with each, and which days will be conditioning. Alecks will be your conditioning coach. This is our team. I'll work on getting you fights, so that we can plot our path to the title fight. Work hard and nothing can stop us."

"Yes, sir, I will."

Roman nodded his approval and left. Alecks spoke next.

"Since this is your first day in Moscow, we will start your training tomorrow. You need time to get unpacked in your new place, and I know you have a grocery list. Be here at 7:00 a.m., and I'll have your schedule."

"Yes, sir. Thank you."

"You don't need to call me 'sir,' just Alecks will do."

"Thank you, Alecks, I'll see you tomorrow."

When she left, Alecks spoke to Erik. "What do you think?"

"Unbelievable. The only way I could beat her was to resort to out-muscling her. She's very quick."

"Her judo skills?"

"Certified top black belt level, I'd say. She'll need to work with Jiu-Jitsu skills to teach her how to fight from her back. Her attitude seems humble, too. My guess is she'll be a quick learner," Erik replied.

Alecks looked at Sergej, "And you?"

"Good skill set. Quick hands, and a stiff natural jab. I know Pavel, he is a good trainer... he's even had a couple guys go to the Olympics from his gym. But that right hand didn't come from some trainer in Kirov. A right hand like that comes straight from God. She's got a solid foundation. She needs to work on her combinations, add a good upper cut. She has naturally fast hands. When I am done with her, they'll be invisible to her opponents."

Alecks cleared his throat. "I talked to Mr. Norin on the phone this morning. He's taking a personal interest in this girl. Have you ever seen him send Roman to pick up a fighter at the station? So, we need to train her right and keep it strictly professional. With those looks and fighting skill set, they are expecting to make a big international celebrity out of her. We're going to be watched very closely."

THE OLD MAN AND THE CATHEDRAL

Irina woke from a deep sleep. She was achy. It had been two months of hard work since arriving in Moscow. They had worked her harder than she had ever worked in her life. Three training sessions a day meant a life of eat, sleep, and train. No time for anything else. Today was Sunday, her day off, her day to sleep in and do whatever she wanted. What she wanted more than anything was a breakfast full of bacon fat and sugar. The dietitian wouldn't allow it.

After breakfast, it was time for a trip to the grocery store. Outside, the ascending sun promised a pleasant summer day. The sky and the empty sidewalks were clear. Instead of her usual route, she headed in the opposite direction to explore the neighborhood. She crossed the street to the sidewalk that followed the Moskva River. A cathedral, with its white walls and gold onion-domed tops, stood tall against the blue sky across the river. She had noticed it the first day Roman drove her from the train station to her apartment. It seemed you could see it from anywhere in Moscow. She had never seen such a church before. She decided to visit. Above her a footbridge crossed the river. She climbed the staircase. At the top of the arch of the bridge she could see the heart of Moscow and the Kremlin in the distance. The cathedral grew as she approached.

At the end near the cathedral an old man with long white hair sat in a metal chair behind a small table. He stared straight ahead, his clothes dirty and oversized. Both hands rested on the top of the table. Stacks of books covered the table. He didn't look her way as she approached. She hadn't seen real books since she was a child; everything was electronic now. Irina liked the feel of a real book. She remembered her father reading to her from one that was filled with fairy tales. The books on the table were stacked six or seven high. Eight stacks were on the table. No two books the same.

"Good morning, young woman. Used books for sale," the man said. His voice was low and rasped from too much vodka.

Irina looked at his leathery face and crooked hands, deformed with arthritis, resting on the table. Now that she stood directly in front of him, she saw that his eyes were foggy with cataracts.

"I love real books," Irina said.

"Anything in particular you like?" His voice vibrated from his chest. It seemed stronger than the man it came from.

"I haven't read much since high school. I was heading to that church—I've never been before. Do you have any books about the church?"

"You don't need a book about that church. I can tell you everything there's to know about it."

"What's its name?"

"The Cathedral of Christ the Saviour. It's the tallest Orthodox Christian church in the world. It was destroyed in 1931 during the rule of Joseph Stalin."

"Destroyed?"

"Its demolition was supposed to make way for the Palace of the Soviets. That was never built, so this church was reconstructed in 1990 on the same site for thirteen billion rubles. The footbridge you are on was constructed in 2004."

"So, that's not the original church?" Irina asked.

"No."

"Why was it destroyed?"

"'State atheism,' it was called. The government's anti-clericalism opposed religious power and influence in all aspects of public and political life, including the involvement of religion in the everyday life of its citizens. Certainly, that period of history you studied in your high school history class?"

"I must have been absent that day."

"You're young. Still plenty of time to learn about the past. It's important you know what happened in the past. Everything has a past: people, places, governments… nothing affects a thing's future more than its past. Like this cathedral, for example. In 1882, it was the location of the world premiere of the famous 1812 overture by Tchaikovsky."

"Since you seem to know everything, what book do you have that you think I should read?" Irina asked.

"Have you ever read any of the literary classics?"

"I don't know. Maybe, if I heard a title?"

To his left in the stack closest to him he counted down three books. He pulled one out of the stack. The cover was black and the pages slightly yellow.

"*Dead Souls,* written by Nikolay Gogol. Originally published in 1842. This copy was printed in 2020. The last hardback printing."

"What is it about?"

"Do you know what a serf is?"

"Yes, it's a servant."

"Yes… but more than that. A serf isn't only a servant. He's legally bound to a landed estate."

"That sounds cheery."

"Most likely not for the serf. Being as they were property, the lord of the estate had to pay taxes on them. Each estate had a property register. In these registers, to count serfs and people in general, the measure word 'soul' was used. For example, 'four souls of serfs.'"

"Sounds very archaic," she said.

"This novel was set just after the war of 1812. Censors didn't come and count too often, so many times a serf would die, but the lord would have to pay taxes for the dead serf for years until the next census. The main character of the novel, Paul Ivanovitch Chichikov, travels the countryside and begins buying the dead souls from the landowners. Alleviating them of the tax burden."

"Why would he do that?"

"You'll have to read the book to find out."

"How much?"

"I consider it a public service to advance the education of our great country's youth, so I ask only five rubles."

She removed a five-ruble coin from her purse and placed it in his hand. He handed her the book.

"Anything else I need to know about the church?"

"In 2012, five members of an all-woman music group named Pussy

Riot held an impromptu performance in the cathedral and were sent to prison for a year and a half. They won't say that in the tour." The old man grinned.

Irina crossed the cathedral square and followed the signs to an entrance. Just inside the doorway was a large wooden box, waist-high, with a slot in the top for donations. Placed on top was a sign stating there were hourly tours. She entered through an open gold-leaf gate that was four meters high. She moved into the nave of the cathedral. Small groups of people were standing about the room. The floor was a checkerboard of multicolored marble. Light came through the blue stained glass windows, and sconces ringed the room, four meters high. The domed ceilings rose high above her, joined by gold-leaf arches. Each section contained an elaborate mural. She eased forward to a brass gate barrier that spanned the width of the main room and prevented anyone from getting too close to the altar.

The altar, against the wall opposite the doorway she entered, was raised by six steps. It was like a small-scale model of the cathedral itself. Brilliant white, a gold cross on each top corner, and a larger gold cross on top of the main cone roof. The walls were covered with small arches, an icon painted inside each. High above her was the interior of the main dome. Past the ring of windows was a mural of God, bearded and in a robe. He stood in clouds filled with winged angels. Rays of light shone from his head, and he had both of his arms stretched with palms facing out, like he was giving a blessing. In front of him was a small infant. Irina assumed it was Jesus. A white dove was just above the infant's head. The gold leaf on the arches and ceiling shone with a light of their own. People moved quietly about, and everyone spoke in whispers. Irina closed her eyes and took a deep breath. She slowly exhaled. *If there's a place that looks like heaven, this must be the place.*

As she approached the bookseller on her way back, she saw him cock his head slightly as she got close.

"How did you like it?"

"It's beautiful, the most beautiful building I've ever seen. And the government tore it down to rebuild it fifty years later?"

"Not the government. Over a million Muscovites donated money to build this church. No better way to give Stalin the finger." The same grin came to his face again.

Irina cut through the side streets, passing two blocks from the gym. When she reached the next main thoroughfare, she went left. Five blocks later, she arrived at the grocery store, where her order was not ready.

At a café, she bought a small coffee, the only one she would have all week. The tables were empty except for one occupied by an old woman and her cup of coffee. She retrieved the book from her purse, placed it on the table, and opened it. The binding creaked. She turned the yellow-tinged pages carefully, feeling the smoothness of each page with her fingertips. At first, the reading went slowly. The old grammar seemed awkward. After two chapters, it felt better and the book took her in. The people moved around her unnoticed for two hours.

"Where did you get that old book?"

The question from a voice beside her jolted her out of the movie playing in her head. Standing beside her was Erik. She wished she had fixed her hair before she left the apartment.

"I bought it from an old man on the street."

Erik sat in the chair across from her.

"I almost didn't recognize you without your hair pulled back. I like it this way."

"Thanks."

Erik looked different in regular clothes, his shoulders broader, his brown hair neatly combed to the side. She suddenly realized she was looking a bit too long. She found a scrap piece of paper in her purse to mark her place in the book.

"What's it about?" Erik asked.

"It's about a man traveling about, buying dead servants from landowners," she said, hoping that would do.

"Is it good?"

"It has interesting observations about human nature."

"Such as?"

Irina opened the book, flipped back a few pages. "'Countless as the sands of sea are human passions, and not all of them are alike, and all of them, base and noble alike, are at first obedient to man and only later on become his terrible masters.'"

Erik nodded. "I used to do mixed martial arts because I loved it; now I need it to make a living."

"When's your next fight?" Irina asked.

"They haven't scheduled one. Since my ranking has slipped, I think they might have other fighters they are focusing on." Irina knew he meant herself. "Tomorrow they are going to tell you they have a match set up for you," Erik said. "A girl from Australia, Chloe Hogan. She's on the fast track to a title shot. Currently ranked tenth in the world. They think you can beat her, and that would put you on the fast track. This Australian girl thinks you're going to be a nice warmup fight with a big payoff. She's in for a surprise, and you are going to get instant international exposure. Mr. Norin put up a purse of a million Australian dollars to get this fight. He's betting big on you—Afanasiy Norin."

"I've heard the name from Alecks. Who is he?"

"He's the big boss. Roman's boss. He runs everything, the gym and most of what goes on in Moscow. Very well-connected and extremely rich. A guy that seems to be everywhere and nowhere. I've never met him."

"How much do I get when I win?"

"You didn't read that contract you signed with Roman, did you?"

"No."

"Nobody does. I haven't seen your contract, but I'm sure it's just like mine. It basically says you belong to them. You get whatever payment they say. Only after you're champion, then maybe you can get them to bargain with you. But you'd have to threaten to stop fighting or something like that. I don't know… they probably have a way to make you fight anyway. Not with this fight, especially with this fight, since Norin is putting up the fight money."

"When do I fight?"

"Two months. This is why we've been having you do so much sparring. You are a difficult student to train. You need experience. It's your biggest deficit. There aren't any women except maybe the top five in the world who can match your skill level. So, that's why we've been having men spar with you. You are going through the ones that are somewhat close to your size in a hurry. We are running out of options, so it's time to accelerate the timetable for you."

The man behind the service counter waved to get Irina's attention. "I need to pick up my groceries now."

"Let me help."

"I can manage. Thanks anyway."

"If you won't let me carry your groceries, how about if I take you out to dinner tonight instead?"

Irina felt her face flush. "I'd like that."

"Great. I know a nice place near the Kremlin. I'll come pick you up at 6:00. Ever ride on the back of a motorcycle?"

"No."

"Don't wear a dress."

THE ELK

John climbed from the basement below the garage to the kitchen. The lab was coming along nicely. All the crates were unpacked, and the jigsaw pieces of the island lab were now being put into place. The cloning device, now fully assembled, stood in the center of the lab. It was almost time to connect the computers and start the software. He took a drink from the refrigerator and looked across the meadow. Green and flush. Dainty flowers budded in the patches in a multicolored mural. At the far end, a small herd of elk fed in the center of the meadow. *Fucking elk. They're setting off the motion sensors almost every night.*

A bull elk stepped from the tree line into the clearing. His head and neck were a chocolate-brown, his body a saddle-beige. Massive velvet-covered antlers arced up to the sky on each side. He gave a casual glance to the cows, feeding a hundred yards away, and started browsing on the phorbes at his feet.

Fucking elk.

THE DATE

Shortly after 6:00 p.m., Erik and Irina were on his motorcycle, zipping through traffic three blocks from the Kremlin. Irina's arms were wrapped around his chest. She could feel the pavement under the tires and held on tight. Suddenly Erik swerved out of the traffic and parked the motorcycle in front of a small cafe. Erik hopped off, and Irina took a moment to gather herself.

Inside it was busy, cramped, and smoky, with small metal tables arranged in rows, each a bit too close to the ones beside it. They seated themselves at a table near the door.

"How did you like that ride?" Erik asked.

"It was fun."

"Remember to lean into the turns with me, okay?"

"Sorry."

The waiter approached. "Anything to drink?"

Erik asked, "Will you have wine?"

"Wine sounds wonderful, if you won't tell my trainer."

"Two glasses of red, please," he said to the waiter. Erik pointed to something on the menu Irina couldn't see. "We'll each have that." The waiter nodded.

The meal came, and the rich purple beet soup and sour black bread were warm and tasty. The wine was a nice treat in contrast to Irina's strict diet. When they left the café, the sun had set, and the Sunday evening street was slow-paced. They got back on the motorcycle, and Erik drove five blocks and made a right. Irina remembered to lean. At the next intersection, he made a left.

At the end of the block, Erik stopped next to the curb. On the cornerstone of the building was a brass plaque with faces of Russian soldiers wearing helmets. The plaque was inscribed, *General Erik Lyadov – Hero of the Soviet Union – 1945.*

"You and he share a name," Irina said.

"He was my great-great-great-great grandfather. What that plaque doesn't tell you is that he killed thousands of German prisoners of war. If they tried to surrender by raising their hands, he would hack them off with a sword and shoot them."

"So that show-no-mercy attitude is a family motto?"

Erik laughed. He drove the motorcycle through traffic back to Irina's apartment. They took the elevator to her floor and walked to her door.

"Thank you for dinner. I had a great time," Irina said.

"Me too," Erik replied. "I'd like to take you out again soon if you'd like."

"Yes, I'd like that."

"There's a problem. Nobody at the gym can know. Norin gave a strict 'hands off' order. If they find out, they'll fire me. The last thing they want is for your social life to get in the way of your training."

"I can keep a secret if you can."

"I'll see you in the morning. Just as your trainer."

"Yes."

THE PLAN

The alarm clock went off just as Irina drifted back to sleep after lying awake for most of the hours after midnight. That was nothing unexpected. She never slept well the night before a fight. Erik hit the snooze button. It had been months since their very first date. She'd felt him restlessly tossing most of the night as well. She slid closer to him and laid her head on his shoulder, and he wrapped his arm around her.

"How did you sleep?" Erik asked.

"Okay," Irina said and took a deep breath.

"You're going to be fine. You're more than ready."

"I know."

"You're going to dominate her. The world is going to see it, and buzz is going to start. We are going to shock the MMA world today. That's why the gym has been closed to the public for the last two weeks; they are keeping you under wraps. After you win tonight, you're going to be all over the Internet. Worldwide."

"And then a title fight?"

"No, then you'll have to fight the current number three or four probably. Then a title shot."

"In America?"

"Yes, in America, because that's where the current champion lives. When you win, the next championship will be here. Unless—"

"Unless?"

"Do you want to come back to Moscow?"

"You mean rather than stay in America?" Irina asked.

"Yes. As long as you stay here, you'll have to fight for Norin. If you go to America, you can get the manager you choose, who works for you. Not the other way around. You'd get to call the shots."

"Yes! That is exactly what I'd like to do."

"I've a friend in America. Jovan. We used to train together. He had a gym in Moscow until Norin bought him out. He took that money and moved to America and started over. Now he lives in Houston, Texas. If you can get us there, his company might give us work visas. We'd just stay there, use the money from the fight to set us up. Start our own gym. Get sponsors. What do you think?"

"I think Texas sounds great. Are you sure your friend will do that?"

"Especially if you are the current world champion."

Irina closed her eyes and tried to imagine life in America.

"First things first. Dominate today, and the buzz can begin," Erik said.

THE AUSTRALIAN

The old Olympic stadium was full, as expected. The tenth-ranked woman in the world was fighting. The one on the fastest track to challenge the champion, as Roman put it, "carrying all the buzz." The under-card fights were entertaining and the fighters enthusiastic; however, not that skillful. Now it was the evening's main event. Irina stood on her side of the cage while the announcer introduced her opponent, and the audience cheered. Erik was in her corner, along with the usual cut man from the gym. Behind them, sitting in the first row, was Roman. He told her Mr. Norin planned to be there, but she didn't see anybody next to Roman other than a slender blonde-haired woman in a form-fitting pink dress.

Erik gave her a confident smile. Across the ring, Chloe Hogan, her challenger, looked fit and determined in her lime-green fight clothes. She glared at Irina across the empty space. The knot in Irina's stomach felt like a fist. The referee approached the center of the cage, raised his hand, and said, "Fight!"

Irina circled her opponent, shuffled her feet, and flashed a left jab. The people in the audience and the sound in the stadium faded as she focused on the form in front of her. Chloe returned a jab, which Irina avoided. Irina's mental clock sped up; she watched Chloe's head and hands. Chloe stepped forward to punch, putting weight on her front left leg, and Irina came quickly with a roundhouse kick with her right foot, striking Chloe hard in the thigh just above the knee. Chloe winced and stepped back. Irina moved forward, *jab, jab.* Her right hand followed up and found the side of Chloe's head.

Chloe stopped, changed directions, and then shifted weight on her front left leg to strike. Irina struck the leg in the thigh above the knee with a kick. Chloe moved back, and Irina moved forward. Jab, right-cross, jab.

Chloe was backed against the fence. She tried to clench Irina around the shoulders. Irina backed away. The Australian threw a right hand that grazed the top of Irina's head. In a flash, Irina's right hand found its mark, square on Chloe's nose and upper lip. The opponent bent forward and to her right. Irina's left upper cut found its mark, and she heard Chloe groan. The crowd sensed that Chloe was hurt, and they rose to their feet.

Chloe moved to Irina's right. Irina's punches came in a hurry, most of them slipping between the gloves and finding flesh. The Australian was in full defensive mode, just trying to survive. She knew another hard right to the face would put her down. Blood dripped from her lips. She tried moving right again to escape the punches.

Irina moved forward and pinned Chloe against the cage. For a second the opponent felt relief; she thought she could hold Irina here for a minute and gather her wits. Irina didn't give her time. She swept her outside leg and pulled Chloe over the top of her to the mat. Chloe kept rolling and for an instant gained leverage on top of Irina by getting up to her knees. Irina rolled onto her back and shoulders, brought her legs behind her head, and wrapped them around Chloe's chest. Irina rolled with her and sat up, changing her grip to the nearest arm. It was pinned between Irina's legs along with Chloe's head. Irina pried the arm free, leaned back, and stretched Chloe's elbow across Irina's pelvis, putting the torque on the joint and bending it in a direction it doesn't go.

Chloe didn't have time to submit, and in an instant Irina dislocated the elbow. The referee rushed in and stopped the fight. Irina released her grip and stood. She looked as if not even a hair was out of place. Her opponent, bleeding from the nose and mouth, stayed on the floor and cradled her arm. Her trainers rushed to her side.

Irina raised her arms in victory. The clock said a minute and forty-five seconds were left in the first round. She smiled at Erik through the wire cage. The crowd roared their approval of the newest star of the cage.

Let the buzz begin.

NUMBER THREE

Irina had studied English in high school and could pick out enough words to get a general sense of the conversation with the reporter from ESPN, although she still needed the translator. Roman sat beside her. There were the usual standard questions about her background, detailed in her online biography. And always the question about how it felt to defeat the tenth-ranked fighter in the world in her first professional fight.

Irina answered them with the scripted responses Roman had taught her, meant to sculpt her image as a confident and humble beginner. Irina was sure the translator could answer the reporters' questions herself by now. Just as the interview was about to end, Roman spoke in English to the reporter.

"Our organization here in Moscow has extended an invitation to Belinda Wells' camp in England, the current number-three fighter in the world, to fight Irina here in Moscow. We made the offer yesterday. We will put up a two-million-pound purse, winner take all."

"Have you heard back from Wells' camp?" the man on the screen asked.

"Not yet. I'm expecting a reply before the end of the week."

Irina could tell by the tone that something important was being said. Still on camera, she longed to whisper to the translator, "What did Roman say?"

"Thank you for your time," the reporter said.

"Thank you," Roman answered.

The screen went blank. Roman nodded at the translator, and she stood and left the room.

"Very nice job with the interviews," Roman said. "Things on the public relations front are going well. Nothing can happen now to cause a problem."

Irina wondered if Roman knew about her and Erik. She concentrated on maintaining eye contact and remaining expressionless.

Roman continued, "Be extra careful when you are away from the gym. No going out at night, no clubs, no behavior that could cause an issue, and of course no drinking. I'm saying this so it's clear between us. We've been thrilled with your behavior and your work ethic."

"You'll have no problems. I have one goal and that's to be world champion."

"Good. See Sergej and begin studying the Wells videos."

"Belinda Wells will fight me?"

"We've extended an open offer and a purse."

"How much of a purse?"

"Two million pounds. Wells must be pushed out of the top five. There's a rumor that the American champion, Kim Fontenot, is about to announce a fight with the number-two challenger. We want you waiting in the wings when that fight is done."

THE BRIT

The stadium was filled. Everybody who was anybody in the world of ultimate fighting in Russia, Europe, and America came. High priced seats went to promoters, managers and fighters, all were eager to see the prodigy from Kirov. This blonde fighter with a face out of a fashion magazine, who had dislocated the elbow of the world's number-ten fighter. They had to see for themselves. They were polite to each other, they knew each other well. The real purpose was to look for weakness in either this new fighter or her team.

The crowd was rowdy and vocal for the preliminary fights. Irina stood on her side of the cage, Belinda Wells on the other side. Belinda looked bigger than on the videos. The announcer gave Irina a longer introduction this time, and the cheering was huge, at least equaling the noise made for her British opponent.

Wells charged at Irina from across the cage. Irina retreated, protecting herself from the punches until her back was against the cage. Irina moved right and threw a jab that missed. Wells closed the distance and wrapped her arms around Irina's chest, swept her right foot behind Irina's calf, and took her to the mat. She tried to position herself on top of Irina. Irina countered and got enough leverage to get to her feet.

Wells kept her arms wrapped around Irina's shoulders and pushed forward, throwing Irina off balance and taking her to the mat again. Irina landed on her back, Wells on top of her, grappling for a head lock.

Irina backed out of the hold and scrambled to her feet. Wells forced her forearm under Irina's chin. Wells threw a couple of knees at Irina; they missed their mark. She pushed Irina back again, drove forward with her legs. Irina retreated and allowed Wells to get slightly off balance, coming forward and dropping her upper body.

Irina shifted her position to the left and wrapped her right arm around Well's neck. For an instant, each had the other in a standing head-lock. Irina threw her right knee to Wells' forehead, causing Wells to lose her grip. Irina slipped her head out as Wells pushed her against the fence.

With a slight height advantage, Irina tightened her grip around Wells' head. She straightened her back and attempted a guillotine hold, putting downward pressure on the back of Wells' head with the underside of her upper arm while her forearm cut off the air supply. Irina stood tall, arched her back, searching for enough leverage to maximize the torque on Wells' neck.

Wells felt Irina's balance shift. She moved to her right and swept Irina's leg again, sending them both to their knees. The fighters separated as they scrambled to their feet. As they rose, Wells threw a right hand that landed squarely on Irina's cheek. Irina threw her own that missed, and Wells came forward again, sending left and right hands at Irina's head. Irina retreated until she hit the fence again.

Another punch found Irina's face, knocking her against the fence, another punch and Irina felt her knees quiver. Her legs got heavy.

The crowd roared.

Irina felt Wells' body shift in front of her and knew instantly where the punch was coming from. She slipped under it with her head, came up behind it and wrapped her arms around Wells, bending her forward at the waist. Irina held her for a moment, long enough for her mind to catch back up to full speed.

The fighters struggled to gain the leverage, pushing or pulling to gain a tactical advantage. They ended up against the cage's fence, each trying to use it to their advantage for leverage or to grind the opponent's face into the wire mesh, and went to the mat.

After a minute on the mat, Irina broke free of Wells, and each fight-er got to her feet. Wells rushed at Irina again. She threw punches, and Iri-na found herself retreating again, slipping or blocking punches. Just as she reached the fence on the opposite side of the cage, Irina's right hand found its way to the side of Wells' head. In the slightest pause in the for-ward rush, Irina threw her left. It found Wells' chin.

Wells came forward, trying to grab Irina. Irina was able to get Wells to bend forward and again got her in a forward standing head-lock. Wells pushed and pulled and jerked from side to side to keep Irina from applying pressure. When Irina knew she could not keep the hold, she released and simultaneously threw a left knee to Wells' face as her arm cleared her throat. Irina felt it land solidly. Wells straightened up, took a slight step back and came at Irina with punches again. Irina sensed less precision behind them now. She dodged them more easily as she retreated. Irina shifted her direction slightly, *jab, jab*; both found her opponent's chin. Wells shifted to account for the slight shift in Irina's position, and the right hand of Irina came again. It struck the left cheek with a thud. Wells' forward motion stopped, and space grew between the fighters. Irina shifted her feet and sent the jab. It found mostly glove.

The horn sounded, ending the first round. For the first time, Irina lost the first round.

Erik and the cut man were waiting for her. Erik took out her mouth guard and gave her water. The cut man put a towel to Irina's bleeding nose.

"She's good," Irina said.

"So are you."

"I hit her hard. I don't know how she didn't go down."

"That's experience. She knows how to take a punch. You hurt her. It isn't showing on her face, but I could tell, she hasn't taken a right hand like yours before. She knows you are younger, stronger and quicker. She wants to turn this into a grappling match. Don't let her. Use the whole cage."

Irina nodded. The cut man moved a cold compress around Irina's face.

The ring official came over. "Thirty seconds," he said.

Erik put the mouth guard back, Irina stood, and Erik and the cut man left the cage. Across the cage her opponent was standing too.

"Fight!" the referee yelled.

Wells charged at Irina again and attempted a front kick. Irina blocked it and moved to the side. As soon as Wells landed, she charged again, coming with a roundhouse kick that struck Irina's hip as she backed away. Wells came forward again, and Irina circled left, *jab, jab,* and a right hand that struck glove and the top of Wells' head. Left jab, stiff enough to stop Wells' advance.

Irina shifted back to the right, *jab, jab*. Wells came forward, right hand again solid to Irina's left eye. Wells stepped back out of range, let her hands drop and bounced on her toes.

Irina could see her thinking. Wells came forward, faked a left jab and dove for Irina's knees. Wrapped her arms around them and brought Irina to the mat. They tumbled together, and Wells lost her hold on Irina's legs. Wells was on her back, Irina over her, facing her. Irina's arms were free, and she punched Wells in the face, landing three solid punches. Wells covered her head with her arms and squirmed to find leverage with her lower body.

Irina found the leverage position first and put her weight on her opponent to push her into the mat, striking her again in the face. Wells tried to turn facedown and find a place to hide her head against Irina's body to escape the pounding. Irina squirmed with her and pried her onto her back again. Wells held Irina's right hand in a lock against her body. Irina's left hand was free, and she pounded on Wells' face and head again. Blood flowed from Wells' nose and mouth.

Wells tried to roll facedown again and cover her face with one hand. Irina gained leverage again; she could feel her opponent weakening and rolled her on her back again, using her body weight to pin her. Irina pulled her right hand free, let fly two hard punches to Wells' face, and again Wells rolled over to block her face. Blood from her nose smeared on the mat. Irina punched with her left hand again. Wells could find no escape and was constrained to blocking with one hand. Wells got her knees under her and tried to stand as Irina kept up the left-hand strikes to the bleeding face. Panic crept into Wells' thinking. Her plan wasn't working; she needed to escape to regroup.

As Wells tried to stand, Irina was over the top of her. Irina pushed herself up off Wells' back, standing first, and as Wells came up, Irina landed a left knee to Wells' face. Wells stumbled sideways. Irina held her up and held her in place for the second knee to the face.

The crowd groaned together, and the volume grew louder. The prodigy was taking control. Wells stumbled to her right, and both fighters went into the fence. Irina grabbed Wells behind the head and brought it forward to meet her rising knee for the third time. Wells' hands dropped. She was stunned from the blows, her face half-covered in blood below the nose.

Wells' brain began shutting down even before Irina's right hand landed flush on the chin, snapping Wells' head to the right. Sweat and blood flew from it. Her knees buckled, and she went down on them. She paused there for an instant and fell over.

The referee rushed in and waved his hands, stopping the fight. Irina held her hands in the air. Wells' trainers rushed to her. Erik grabbed Irina around the thighs in a bear hug and lifted her up over his head.

Let the buzz roar. Let it roar all the way to America.

Erik lowered her. "I thought I told you to stay off the mat with her?"

THE ACCIDENT

Irina strolled the footbridge. The grand white cathedral towered in front of her, its golden domes shining even under the gray August sky. A quiet Sunday morning walk was what she needed more than anything

A month after her victory, the buzz had reached a fever pitch with interviews, photo shoots and, of course, training. Roman had to close the gym. And she was furnished with a bodyguard to drive her to and from the gym. This made getting Erik in and out of her apartment more of a challenge.

The old man sat at his usual table. Same dirty, baggy clothes, same table covered in books. She stood in front of his unseeing eyes.

"Good morning, young woman. Enjoy *Dead Souls*?"

"It was very good. I didn't mean to take so long to finish. Life got busy and complicated. You can have it back now. Perhaps you can sell it again to somebody else."

He gave a knowing smile. "When a young woman like you gets a busy life, there's usually a new man at the root cause."

"Maybe," Irina said.

"I remember young love. I was in love once, met her when I was about your age, in the fall. It was our first semester at Moscow University. I saw her sitting on a marble bench, reading a book in the sun by the long reflecting pool. I knew the book she was reading because I was carrying the exact same one. I had the same assignment from my professor. I sat down on the bench, and she looked at me.

"'Very unfair of them to give us that book as an assignment our first week of class without even telling us where a good pub is to read it,' I said. She smiled at me, the most beautiful smile. I do believe we both fell in love that afternoon—it didn't last. You know how love is. It ended way too soon."

"How long did it last?" Irina asked.

"Fifty-seven years." The old man put his crooked hands on the book and felt its edges. "Thank you for giving it back to me, that's very kind of you. What do you think the author was trying to say in his story?"

"Do you mean why would Chichikov buy dead servants?" Irina asked.

"Well, we'll start with that. Why did he buy those dead servants?"

"To fake the ownership of a large estate so he could borrow money against it, using it as collateral. And of course, disappear with the money," Irina answered.

"He spent a great deal of time and energy with his swindle to try to make that happen. Why would he do that?"

"To be rich, I guess." Irina shrugged her shoulders.

"Chichikov was pretending to be somebody he wasn't, pretending to be somebody of importance. He dressed himself in the outward signatures of a noble. That wasn't enough for him. What was Chichikov's ultimate goal?"

"To live a happy, carefree life, I suppose," Irina replied.

"Exactly. Very good, you're a bright young woman. So Chichikov believed if he was rich he could obtain happiness, he could purchase it, he could buy his way to nobility."

"Yes, he did believe that," Irina said.

"Do you think that if Chichikov had been successful in his fraud, he'd have been happy for the rest of his life?"

"No, I don't think he'd have been. I doubt he's capable of that."

"Me either," the old man grinned. "It's true what they say, you can't buy true happiness in life. It has to come from inside."

"I'm ready for another book," Irina said.

The old man felt down a column of books and pulled one out.

"*One Day in the Life of Ivan Denisovich* by Alexander Solzhenitsyn, published in 1962. This copy isn't that old; it was printed in 2009. In 1970, he was awarded the Nobel Prize in Literature. He was expelled from Russia in 1974." He handed the book to Irina.

Irina studied the thickness of the book. "Not a very long story."

"Two hundred pages or so. But believe me, they're a powerful two hundred pages. The story happens in a Soviet labor camp in the 1950s and describes a single day of a prisoner named Ivan Denisovich Shukhov. I think you'll find him an interesting contrast to Chichikov."

Irina opened her purse, removed a five-ruble coin, placed it in his palm and continued to the cathedral with her new book.

As Irina sat, her eyes followed every line of the gold-leafed edges of the walls. She studied every detail of the murals on the ceiling above her and the smaller altars along the wall to her left. She took two deep breaths in and out, closed her eyes and absorbed the beauty of the building. She felt the peace, calm, and holiness of the place, and she liked it. She sat quiet and still for the next hour.

It was like Pavel's gym early in the morning, when she let herself in just as the sun peeked over the eastern horizon. The gym held a sanctity while the city slept. But a sanctity that burned away with the rising sun. Not here. It was always here. She opened her purse, took out her new book, and turned the pages until she found the first chapter. She had finished reading the first page when her cell phone in her purse vibrated. She looked at the display and saw Erik's picture.

"I was hoping you would call soon. Finished at the gym so soon?" she whispered.

"Where are you? I'm at your apartment." Erik's voice sounded tense.

"At the cathedral."

"I need you to come home right now," Erik said.

"What is the matter? Is something wrong?"

"Nothing's wrong, but something has happened."

"Tell me. You're worrying me."

"The number-two contender who was supposed to fight Kim Fontenot in a month, Cecilia Rodriguez, was in a car accident day before yesterday. She was killed."

"Oh my God."

"Kim's manager is supposed to call Roman this morning," Erik said.

"I'm on my way."

Irina opened the door to her apartment to find Erik sitting in the kitchen, staring at his cell phone on the table. He got up and gave her a long hug.

"My friend in America, Jovan, was the one who called and told me. He didn't say how the accident happened. He heard it on the news. He called Kim's manager because they are friends, and it was Kim's manager who told him they were going to call Roman this morning."

"My God, Erik, I can hardly believe it."

"I asked Jovan about the work visas and he said no problem. He'll call his lawyer as soon as the fight is announced."

Erik and Irina sat down at the kitchen table and waited for Erik's phone to ring. They watched the phone until hunger made them cook dinner. After three more hours, they moved to the couch, taking the phone with them. Irina laid her head on Erik's chest and fell asleep. At 6:00 a.m. Erik's phone rang, startling them both out of their sleep. Erik saw that it was Roman's number.

"Hello?"

"I have something to talk about," said Roman.

"Yes, sir," Erik answered, not wanting to say too much.

"Meet me at the gym early." Roman hung up.

"What did he say?"

Erik got up and put his shoes on and hugged Irina. "Remember, we need to act normal this morning and be surprised when he tells us anything."

"I will."

They kissed and Erik left just as the morning noise of the street below began its daily rhythm.

An hour later, Irina got into the bodyguard's car and another burly bodyguard opened the gym door for her. The gym was empty except for Erik, stretching by the body bag.

"Irina," he yelled at her across the gym.

She looked in his direction.

"Roman wants to talk to us."

When Irina got to the gym's office in her workout clothes, Erik was already there. Roman was behind the desk.

"I've news for you, Irina," Roman began. "As you know, Kim Fontenot planned to fight Cecilia Rodriguez in a month for the world championship. There has been a sad development. Cecilia was killed in a car accident."

"That's terrible," Irina said.

"Yesterday I got a call from Kim's manager. They would like to defend her title against you. They want the fight to be the first Saturday in October in Denver, Colorado, in America. A short five weeks away. Of course, I agreed."

"That's short notice," Irina said.

"You'll be ready. I've no doubt about that."

"Well, I have a lot of doubt about it," Irina said stubbornly.

"Now we need to talk business. By that I mean money. In America, when they're dealing with a fighter who is not an American citizen, they will only make a contract with you once you are in America. In this case, Denver. The arrogant American fighters association has deemed the standard contract provides eighty percent of the purse to the fighter and twenty percent to the manager. The percentage of the proceeds from the televised broadcast is negotiable. I am here to represent Mr. Norin in this matter. Mr. Norin has invested a lot in you, your training, nutrition, and the apartment that you live in rent-free."

"I doubt he has lost money on me."

"Good point," Roman said. "The purse is eight million American dollars. Kim is guaranteed three million. If you lose, you get one million and Kim gets seven million. If you win, you get five million and Kim gets three. That's what it's going to say on paper. But once the money is wired to the bank account I have set up for you, a VTB bank, all proceeds will be transferred to Mr. Norin. All money from televised broadcasts go to him too."

Irina nodded, thinking about five million American dollars.

"However—" Roman continued, "when we return from America with the title belt in hand, you'll move out of the current apartment to a much better one and be given a Mercedes.

"It's important not to let the business side of this distract you. This gym is officially closed to everybody except Irina's team."

"It won't. I am just grateful for you giving me this chance." *You thieving bastard.*

Irina and Erik rose from their chairs and left the office. Irina wanted to hold Erik and laugh until she cried. She knew Erik felt the same. Instead, they didn't look at each other and went through their normal workout together. When Erik was sure nobody could hear, he whispered to her, "I'll call my friend as soon as I leave."

"Be at my place early. I want to make love to you all night," she whispered back.

SEPTEMBER 2071

THE SPOOFER

John entered the bar at midnight. It reeked of stale cigarette smoke and beer. Several men sat at the bar. Several more played pool at the other end of the room. John got a beer at the bar and sat in the last booth against the far wall, as he had been instructed.

The hard metal of the pistol under his jacket pressed against his lower back when he leaned back in his seat. Halfway through his beer, a man sat down across from him. Twice the size of John, leather hat pulled low, keeping his face in shadow. A sleeveless T-shirt displayed enormous tattooed arms that he rested on the table.

"You're Thomas?" the man asked.

"Yes," John replied.

"I hear you have work for me."

"It's parked outside." John slid the remote to a Toyota sedan to the middle of the table. The man glanced at it and let it stay there.

"The price is twenty thousand."

John slid an envelope beside the remote. The man opened it and examined the contents.

"You're five thousand short."

"There's a Canadian cold front moving through next week. The mountain passes will be treacherous. It looks like an early start to the winter to me. I have a timetable I'm working to. I need the work done before next week. I'll give you another fifteen thousand if you have it done in three days."

The meaty hand collected the remote. "Meet me back here in seventy-two hours," the man said and slid out of the seat.

GOING TO AMERICA

Irina and Erik stood in the private terminal at the Moscow airport and looked through the large window at the plane parked on the tarmac. It was enormous and shiny, standing like a white elephant against the black predawn sky. A truck-mounted boarding ladder led up to the plane's door.

"Is that Mr. Norin's plane?" Irina asked Erik.

"I do believe it is."

"You've got to have a lot of fucking money to have a plane like that," Irina said.

"I hear he's got more than one."

The door to the room opened and closed. Roman, dressed in a tuxedo, with a very tall woman hanging on his shoulder, entered the room. The woman had black hair to her waist and dark brown skin, perhaps Indian. She wore a black cocktail dress with white trim and lazily carried expensive high heels in one hand. They were followed by four bodyguards. As usual, the guards were dressed in black jackets, white shirts, no ties, black pants, black shoes, and an earpiece in their left ears.

Irina recognized the guards. From one time or another they had driven her to or from the gym, or were there to open the door to the gym after Roman restricted access to it. She didn't think she had ever heard any of them say more than two words. She certainly had never seen the woman before. She could now tell by her unsteadiness that she was intoxicated.

"Isn't she a beautiful plane?" Roman said.

"It is," Irina said. "Is it a formal occasion to fly on this plane?"

"That's your plane?" the drunk woman slurred.

Roman escorted her to the nearby seat and placed her there. "Wait here for me." He went back to Irina and Erik. "Late night party, sorry. The plane is very fast too, latest jam-jet technology. We'll be landing in America in nine hours. In fact, when we land in Denver, by the hands on the clock we won't have left Moscow yet. Just in time for our second sunrise for today. I suggest everybody get their sleep on the plane. Everybody have their passports?"

Irina and Erik nodded. Roman looked back at the woman passed out in the chair.

"Good, the crew is already on the plane, so we're ready to go," Roman said. He looked at the tallest bodyguard. "Leave her."

It was a short walk to the plane and a long climb up the boarding stairs to the plane's door. Irina went down a hallway to the main room. The main bar was to her right. On each side of the plane, next to the windows, was a table and two chairs. At the far end was a semi-circle couch with a coffee table in the middle. On the right side of the couch was another hallway. The upholstery was cream-colored leather, the wood chocolate-brown, the tabletops black laminate. The carpet on the floor matched the chairs. Irina sat on the couch; she was followed by Erik.

Roman stood by the bar and the smiling flight attendant went behind the bar and began mixing a drink. When she was done, she handed it to Roman. Each guard found a seat at one of the two tables. Irina heard the fuselage door shut.

"Miss Popova," said the flight attendant, "the first door is your room. If you have trouble sleeping, there's medicine and a bottle of water on the nightstand."

"Mr. Lyadov, your room is the third door. My name is Yana if you have any questions."

"Thank you," Erik replied.

"Personally, I'm not going to wait for us to reach cruising altitude. I'm going to take my drink and retire to my bedroom." Roman walked across the room to the hallway on the right side of the couch. He paused and raised his glass. "See you in America." He disappeared down the hall.

Irina watched through her window as the lights of Moscow dropped away beneath the plane. She couldn't believe she was going to America.

She felt a gentle shaking and a soft voice, "Miss Popova, wake up."

Irina opened her eyes to see Yana leaning over her, smiling.

"We're almost to Denver," Yana said.

Irina flung back the covers and sat on the edge of the bed. She was in panties and an oversized T-shirt.

"I wanted to tell you that I wish all the luck for you."

"Thank you."

"Can I get your autograph?" Yana asked. "Please don't tell Mr. Churkin, I probably shouldn't be asking you."

"I don't have anything to write with."

Yana took a small notepad and pen out of her pocket and handed them to Irina.

"Your name is Yana?" Irina asked.

"Yes."

Irina wrote on the pad,

"To Yana,

Thanks for a wonderful flight.

Irina Popova"

"Thank you," Yana said and placed it in her pocket.

"I'm glad you like it. It's my first autograph."

Yana left and Irina quickly dressed. When she went to the main room, Roman and Erik were seated on the couch, and the bodyguards were in their chairs. As far as she could tell, they hadn't moved.

"Sleep well?" Roman asked.

"Very well."

As Irina finished her breakfast, she felt the wheels of the plane touch the ground. It was dark outside, so Irina could not see what America looked like yet. The jet rolled to a shuddering halt. Porters carrying their luggage, they left the plane and headed down the tunnel and out into the terminal, much larger and brighter than the one in Moscow. They waited in line and had their passports scanned. A chauffeur helped with the luggage as Roman, Irina, Erik, and the largest bodyguard got into one limousine. The other three bodyguards took the other.

The sky was bright from the rising sun. It silhouetted the mountains in the distance. A large jet roared overhead as it departed the airport. The highway was full of cars she had never seen before.

THE HOTEL

The floors of the foyer of their hotel were marble, and glass and crystal chandeliers hung from the ceiling. Roman spoke to a man in a suit and signed papers. One by one, each of them had their index fingers scanned. They followed Roman to the elevator, and Roman put his finger over the scanner on the panel and selected the solitary button on the panel, the very top floor.

"This is the elevator that services the penthouse. To get to our floor, you must scan your index finger and press the button," Roman instructed the group.

They exited the elevator and turned right, down a short hallway. The rooms ahead occupied the entire floor. Near the end of the hallway the two bellmen waited with the luggage on a cart. Roman pointed to a door.

"Marat and Gleb," Roman said.

Two of the bodyguards stopped; one of them scanned his finger, and the door opened. They pointed to their luggage on the cart, and the bellmen took them off and put them in the room. They waited in the hallway. Across the hall, Roman pointed at another door.

"Irina," he said.

Irina placed her finger over the scanner on the door. It clicked open and the lights inside came on. The bellmen were back, and she pointed to her luggage, which they removed and took into her room.

"Erik, you're next to Marat and Gleb," Roman said.

Erik scanned his finger on his door, and the bellmen retrieved his luggage.

"Next to Irina is Anton and Viktor."

One of them scanned his finger, and the bellmen moved in their luggage.

"I'm in the last room at the end," Roman said.

He scanned his finger on his door, the door clicked open, and Marat and Gleb went inside. Anton and Viktor remained in the hallway. When Marat and Gleb came back out, the bellmen were allowed in the room. Gleb went in and came back out with them. Roman waited for the bellmen to leave with the cart.

"We have this floor to ourselves," said Roman. "At the opposite end of this hall is a workout room. It has a nice spacious area for Irina to get in a light workout this afternoon and tomorrow. We have a meeting in Conference Room 5 with the American promoters at noon. We'll go over the payout contracts with them over lunch. Irina, I'm assigning Viktor to you, for your own safety. He speaks fluent English. Whenever you leave your room, he must accompany you. It's important that you remain safe. Without you there can be no fight."

"Thank you," Irina said. *Safe? So you can keep an eye on me.*

"After the meeting, we'll go see where the weigh-in will happen. Tomorrow afternoon is the official weigh-in." Roman's cell phone rang. "Excuse me," he said, heading for his room.

Irina and Erik exchanged glances and went to their rooms. When Irina entered, the lights came on again, and the sheer white curtains over the windows opened. The sun lit up the mountain range in the distance. The sky was clear and vibrant blue. The mountains had snow, cotton white, more than halfway down from their peaks.

Irina opened her backpack and removed her fighting gear, laying it out on the bed. From her suitcase, she hung her clothes and put her makeup bag on the bathroom counter. She heard a knock on her door. When she opened the door, Erik was standing there.

"I thought I'd help you get your gear ready for the workout this afternoon," he said.

Irina looked down the hall toward Roman's door, where one of the bodyguards sat.

"Of course, come in," she answered.

Erik came in and she shut the door. They hugged each other for a minute without moving. He kissed her.

"It has been so difficult to be near you and not touch you," Erik said.

"I know. Me too."

"Can you believe it, Irina? We're actually in America," Erik asked.

"What about Viktor? Isn't he going to be a problem?"

"I don't think so. He's not that smart. Just stick to our plan after the fight, and remember we are to meet Jovan at the bus station, two miles from here by taxi. You have your American money. It will get us tickets to Houston."

"I love you," she said.

"I love you too."

🧬

"Not much left to do now except win the fight," Roman said after the meeting where the contracts were signed, and a scanner took an image of Irina's iris, which would allow her to access her post-fight bank account for transfer to the Russian bank.

"And this is just the beginning. You'll have many more championship fights. You are young. You could be champion for the next decade. With the face you have, the money we are going to make in the ring is nothing compared to the money we are going to make in endorsements. Since your last fight, five major brands—from cars to clothes to athletic shoes—are interested in signing you as a spokesperson. They want you to make commercials for them for television and magazines."

"Why didn't you tell me?" *And cut the "we" crap.*

"First things first. I didn't want you to get distracted from your training. Now I want you to know, so you know it's all right there for us to take. We can own the whole fighting world. All you have to do is win the fight."

🧬

An hour later they were riding in a limousine with the man who represented the American bank. He spoke perfect Russian. "Will you be staying in America a few days after the fight to see the sights?" said Mr. Arnold.

"We'll be leaving that night," Roman answered.

305

"That's too bad. Denver and the state of Colorado are beautiful, especially during the fall season. It's the perfect time of year to drive up into the mountains. That high mountain air can cleanse your soul," Mr. Arnold said.

Office buildings of polished stone and glass passed by outside Irina's window. She hoped Houston was as nice as Denver. The limousine pulled into a restricted parking garage and stopped. They exited the vehicles and followed Mr. Arnold through a set of glass doors.

"We will have a woman at these doors to meet you at noon tomorrow. She'll be easy to spot because the staff here wear red blazers. She'll take you up these elevators to the second floor. They will keep you backstage until you are announced. There will be a lot of television and Internet cameras. After the weigh-in, the announcer will ask you a couple questions. There will be an interpreter there for you. The whole thing shouldn't last a half-hour.

"Saturday night you'll come in the same way. Your fight should start about nine o'clock. Our drivers will have you here at seven o'clock. There will be someone to escort you to your dressing room, where you can do your prefight preparations."

"We're supposed to be provided a cut man," Roman said.

"We've a highly regarded one for you. He'll come to your dressing room about an hour before your fight. His name is Rafael Cámbara. Been in this business for thirty years and was the cut man for two world champion boxers."

"Sounds good," Roman said.

Mr. Arnold shook everybody's hand. "It was a pleasure to meet you. I usually don't attend these fights; however, there is such excitement over Irina that even my wife wants to see her fight. I'll see you Saturday night."

THE WEIGH-IN

Irina got out of the limousine first, dressed in her robe, her fighting clothes underneath. The parking garage was empty. The bodyguards, Roman, and Erik walked to the glass doors.

A woman in a red blazer met them at the door. She held open the elevator doors, and everybody got in. She got in with them. She exited the elevators and made a left turn. The group followed her to a large room. The backstage area was in front of them.

Irina could hear the media and an announcer on the other side of the stage. Tall curtains blocked her view. Eventually she heard her name announced, and Roman motioned for her to enter the stage. An audience of three hundred was waiting for her. Strobes of cameras flashed, and she could see a television camera on a long boom. In the center of the stage was a weight scale. A man, also in a red blazer, stood on the other side. Irina did her best to keep an emotionless face.

"Take off your shoes," Roman said to her from behind.

Irina did. Erik helped her remove her robe. She stepped onto the scale. The man in the red blazer adjusted the scale.

"One hundred thirty-five," he said.

The announcer repeated it to the crowd. Cameras flashed nonstop. Irina stepped back off the scale. The announcer came and stood beside her, holding a microphone.

A woman came and stood on the other side of her. "I'm your interpreter," she said in Russian.

The announcer said something in English to the interpreter, who repeated the question. "To what do you attribute your quick rise through the professional ranks to have a chance at a world championship so soon?"

"To hard training, a good support team, and being prepared when the opportunity came," Irina said.

The interpreter repeated her words. Then translated the next question: "What's your plan for facing such a skilled opponent who has dominated those who have fought her?"

"Stay focused, stay quick. Use her strength against her when I can."

The interpreter repeated her words. The announcer stepped away and began talking loudly again. Irina heard the name of her opponent mentioned.

"Kim Fontenot."

The American came through the curtains on the other side of the stage. Her eyes met Irina's instantly. They were glaring and furious beneath a protruding forehead with no eyebrows. Her hair was shaven next to her scalp on one side; the other was in braids. She jerked on her sweat top and bottom, and they broke away at Velcro seams. She threw them into the crowd. Underneath was a bikini. She rotated her muscular and tattooed back to the audience and flexed her arm muscles. Tattoos wrapped around from her back and partially covered her abdomen in a swirling jumble of meaningless shapes.

Irina leaned over to Roman and Erik. "Is she going to fight in that bikini?"

They shrugged.

Kim stepped onto the scale; the red blazer man made adjustments.

"One hundred thirty-four and a half," the announcer said.

The American flexed her arm muscles again, and the cameras flashed. She stepped off the scale and the announcer stepped over.

"What's your thought on how to approach your opponent tomorrow night?" the announcer asked.

"I'm going to dominate her. She shouldn't be here after three pro fights. It's an insult to me and the other fighters who have worked their way up," Kim answered, glaring at Irina across the stage. "I'm going to show her what a real beating feels like."

The interpreter standing next to Irina repeated her words into Irina's ear. Irina's face remained emotionless. Inside, the anger grew.

"What the fuck are you doing here?" Kim yelled at Irina, pointing her finger, ignoring the man attempting to interview her.

Irina stood expressionless and stared back as the interpreter talked in her ear.

"You don't even have the fucking right to be on this stage with me!" Kim abruptly left the stage. Erik put the robe back on Irina. Irina's face was flushed with anger. *Roman was right about one thing... the Americans are arrogant.*

OCTOBER 3, 2071

THE CHAMPIONSHIP FIGHT

When Irina got out of the limousine, she could hear the crowd inside cheering for one of the preliminary fights. Erik got out carrying his gear bag, and Viktor carried Irina's backpack and the post-fight interview dress and shoes Roman had bought for her. The bodyguards and Erik surrounded her and Roman from the limousine to the elevator. The same woman in a red blazer held it open for them and followed them inside.

They went to the second floor just like the day before. When the elevator opened, two policemen were waiting for them. The group exited the elevator and made a right turn; one policeman was in front, another in the back of the group. Irina could feel the crowd above her. The woman stopped and opened a blue door and held it open for the entourage. The policemen stayed outside.

The room was bright from the overhead lights. There was a training table and two metal chairs. An area to the side was covered with mats for the fighter to warm up and stretch. Near one corner was a door; one of the bodyguards opened it to find that it was a bathroom.

Erik and Viktor put the gear bag and backpack on the table. Viktor hung the skimpy lavender dress covered with sequins on a hook on the wall, along with the cloth bag containing the shoes.

"I want everybody outside," Erik said.

None of the bodyguards moved. They looked at Roman. Erik looked at Roman. "I mean everybody, including you."

Roman nodded. "Everybody out."

The door opened and shut and Erik and Irina were alone.

"Did you get what we need?" Irina asked.

"Yes, it's in the bottom of the gear bag I brought."

Irina came to Erik and put her arms around him and her head on his shoulder. "I'm so nervous."

"It'll be all right. Nothing's going to stop us. Let's concentrate on winning this fight, then our new lives can start," Erik said.

"Okay." Irina looked up. "Let's get ready."

Irina took her fighting shorts and tank top out of her backpack. She removed her jewelry and changed from her street clothes to her fighting clothes. Erik waited for her on the mats.

"This fight is no different than the others. You're prepared, you're trained to the best of our abilities, and we're going to go through our usual prefight stretch and warm-up," Erik said.

When Roman knocked on the door with the cut man, Irina had her hands wrapped and was striking pads on each of Erik's hands.

"This is your cut man," Roman said. "He wanted to meet you."

Rafael Cámbara was short, with ghost-white hair, dark skin, a leathery face, and large hands. He shook hands with each of them. He looked at Irina's face. He said something.

"He says you have the skin of a child," Roman said.

Rafael put his hand on Irina's forehead, around each eye, and her cheekbones. He said something else to Roman and smiled.

"He said it doesn't look like you've ever even been hit. He thinks you'll not start tonight."

Again, he spoke to Roman.

"He says he'll see you at the cage, and he thanks you for letting him be in your corner."

Irina smiled and nodded. Rafael and Roman left and Irina went back to striking the pads being held by Erik. Just as a few good beads of sweat formed on Irina's forehead, Erik stopped her and gave her a drink. After a few more stretches, she put on her robe to stay warm. The door opened. A ring official in a red blazer stepped into the room, with Roman.

"It's time," Roman said.

The bodyguards formed a ring around Irina as she came out of the room. Roman moved inside the ring, and Erik stepped behind Roman. A line of security guards blocked the walkway. A man with a television camera walked backwards in front of the group, led by another man in a red blazer.

The group made its way through the entryway to the floor level of the arena. Irina had her hood pulled over her face to hide from the flashes of cameras. She could hear the announcer in the cage. None of the words were familiar. Regardless, she was sure it was the best introduction she'd ever had.

When they came through the entryway, two white-hot spotlights shone on them from above. The crowd roared. Irina could feel the floor vibrate. Cameras flashed from every direction. The Russian entourage made its way to the cage, and the bodyguards fanned out. Irina approached the cage door. Erik removed her robe and put her mouthpiece in. He stepped back. The cut man was already there. The female official gave her the cursory pat-down to ensure there were no sharp edges or anything illegal about her attire. She stepped away, and Irina entered the cage. The vibrating crowd roared their approval.

Irina stayed in her corner and bounced on her toes. The announcer began talking again, and the spotlights swung to the opposite side of the arena. Now that the lights were off of her, Irina could see how massive the inside of the arena really was. The lights overhead scanned out across the sea of people that arched up in every direction.

The music blared, and the crowd cheered. The spotlights followed Kim down the aisle. She was surrounded by her own entourage, one of them directly behind Kim holding up the metallic championship belt. The spotlights followed them until they stopped outside the cage door. After a pat-down, Kim stepped into the cage, and the crowd began to settle. The American glared at Irina across the cage. She paced back and forth like an animal, never taking her eyes off her opponent.

Irina went to her side of the cage. Erik and Rafael were there on the other side of the wire fence. Erik motioned her closer.

"There's nobody here except you and her. She'll try to get in close and get you to the mat to stay away from your punches. You have the reach advantage. Strike from a distance! Stay sharp, stay quick!" Erik yelled into her ear.

Irina nodded. The referee came into the ring. He was a muscular black man wearing a black T-shirt and black pants. He went to the center of the ring, looked at each fighter, raised his hand, and in a downward chop yelled an English word Irina did understand: "Fight!"

Each fighter closed the distance. The American tried a front kick at

Irina's chest. Irina side-stepped it and, in a blur with her long, left jab, struck the American on the cheek. The American counter-punched and Irina delivered what she had been working on as a surprise: a roundhouse kick aimed at her opponent's head. It was blocked by the American's left hand; however, the force of it drove the hand back into her head and made the American take a step back. Irina advanced, throwing another left jab to the face, lowering the American's left hand, followed by a right that landed above her browless left eye with a hard thud. The crowd came to its feet. The American ducked and protected and dove for Irina's leg in an attempt to take her to the mat. Irina pushed her down and away and moved back out of reach. The American scrambled to her feet and Irina kicked again, this time a sidekick with her left foot, striking the American in the abdomen. The American leapt forward again, grabbed Irina's arms and hands, closing the distance before another strike could be delivered. The fighters locked in a standing grapple, each jockeying for leverage. The crowd sat back down as the contest became a defense struggle. The fighters went back and forth along the fence. The American pressed her body weight into Irina to attempt to tire the younger opponent. Irina tried to find a way to break free, to get some distance. The American struck Irina in the thigh with a knee and bull-rushed her back into the wire fence. Irina twisted the American into the fence with her, swept her leg closest to the fence and took her to the mat, landing on top of her. The crowd cheered. Irina held her there and tried to find a way to pry the American's arm and position for a submission hold. The American knew what Irina was attempting and became a mass of arms and elbows, working her way around and on top of Irina. They rolled together, and Irina found herself on her back with the American straddling on top, facing her. The fists came at her face in rapid succession. Irina blocked most; however, too many found their way through. Irina grabbed the American's hands so she couldn't strike. The American lowered her torso and ground her forearm into Irina's face, getting her face close to Irina's ear.

"Fucking weak bitch," the American said in perfect Russian.

She spit in Irina's ear. Irina felt rage rise inside her like a tidal wave. Irina released the American's hands as she rose up to strike at Irina's face again. Irina rolled farther onto her shoulders, got a foot hooked on the front of the American's neck, pulled her off balance and rolled her off. Irina rolled with her and got to her feet.

The American was up too. From a half-crouch, she threw a punch. It landed on Irina's left eye, snapping her head back and cutting her on the side of the eye with the sting of a wasp. Irina covered her face in time to block the next blow. Irina retreated.

The American came at her, throwing combinations of punches at Irina's head and ribs. Blood came from the cut and dripped down Irina's cheek. The crowd's volume increased, as did the rage inside Irina, fueled by pain.

Irina forgot about the title. She forgot about the crowd. She forgot about escaping to Houston. For the first time, she felt rage while in the fighting ring. All she wanted to do was hurt this American as badly as possible. She would show how the arrogant can be shamed. As Irina backed to the fence, she knew the American would try to move in to take her down. She anticipated the lunge. She saw it coming in slow motion. Irina shifted to the side, rotated her shoulders, and threw her right hand with perfect precision and power. It landed on the American's nose with a crunch. Irina heard her exhale, and the forward lunge stopped. Blood flowed from both nostrils. Left jab and a stiff right to the same browless left eye, this time cutting open the skin. The crowd leapt to its feet.

Irina circled the American and backed her against the fence with a flurry of jabs, kicks, and uppercuts. The crowd's volume became deafening. Irina was unaware of them. She could see her opponent and nothing else. She could hear her own breath and nothing else. An uppercut sliced between the gloves and found the American's chin. The bobbing and ducking slowed. Irina's hands moved faster, her mind anticipating the American's movements. The American threw a weak left hook that was too slow and too short. It missed Irina's chin. That miss left the American's face exposed to Irina's right hand. The rage morphed into power. Power that came from Irina's legs as she calculated the opening for the blow in a nanosecond. Muscle memory took over. On her toes, she rotated her hips through her right hand. The punch struck the American on the sweet spot of her chin. The sound of leather striking skin and cutting to the bone could be heard three rows deep. It happened at such speed that most of the spectators wouldn't see it clearly until it was replayed in slow motion on the overheard jumbo screen. The American's legs collapsed, and she landed in a seated position, her back against the fence.

Irina pounced, landing punches to her head. At first the American vainly covered with her hands, but as she slumped to the side her hands fell away and she was defenseless. Irina didn't care. Her rage burned and she continued to punch the head that wagged on the end of the neck. The referee grabbed Irina from behind, pulled her away, and signaled the fight was over.

Erik was there, wrapping his arms around her and lifting her in the air. That was when Irina realized what she'd done. She raised her hands in victory. She could hear the crowd now, and they were chanting "KI-ROV QUEEN!"

THE ESCAPE

Irina sat in the limousine wearing her tiny post-fight dress and high heels. The title belt rested on her lap. The city outside looked different at night. The limousine stopped at an intersection. Steam came up from the drain by the curb into the cold night air. She looked at a woman standing near the curb. Her dress was shorter than Irina's, and she wore tall, spiked heels. She looked tired. She noticed the limousine and stood a bit straighter and smiled. She looked at the opaque windows and said something at the car. The light changed and the limousine started again.

The streetlights reflected off the large metal plate of polished silver and gold. "World Champion" was engraved across the top. Irina lightly touched her left eye. The cut man had given her a cold compress for the swelling. She looked over at Erik. He was looking at Roman as if he was interested in what Roman was saying. Trying to pretend to be normal. Irina could tell his mind was racing. This was it, they had to make their escape when they got back to the hotel. Roman talked in the front seat with the tall guard about the fight; they laughed and smiled and poured another drink from the minibar. The limousine stopped in front of the hotel.

"Wait for us. We'll be back in twenty minutes," Roman said to the driver.

Everybody exited and moved through the lobby toward the elevator. The doors were open and they got in. Erik had his duffel bag with him. Irina had her backpack in one hand and her title belt in the other. When the elevator doors opened, they moved down the hall to their rooms.

"Everybody pack and be ready to leave in fifteen minutes," Roman said.

Irina entered her room. The bodyguards, Erik, and Roman went to their respective rooms. She dumped out the contents of her backpack onto the floor and gathered the clothes, hers and Erik's, that were already prepared and sitting on her bed. Also in the pack she put the title belt, their passports and identifications. She heard a tap on her door. She opened it, and Erik was standing outside with a large bundle of rope in his hand.

He snuck to Roman's door at the end of the hall, tied one end to the large looped handle, and passed the other end through the looped handle of the door to the first guard's room. He secured it with an overhand knot. At the second guard's room, he secured it with a double overhand knot. Irina moved out into the hall and silently closed her door.

They both quickly walked down the hall to the elevator and pressed the button. Irina could feel her heart pounding in her chest. No sound came from down the hall indicating any of them knew they were trapped in their rooms yet. Erik held her hand. The elevators doors opened. A man stood inside.

"Jovan?" Erik said.

The man raised his hand and fired a small gun at Erik. Two small darts penetrated Erik's clothes and buried deep in the flesh of his chest. Irina turned to run to the stairs behind her. She heard the pop of the gun and felt a sting in her back. She took another step, and her legs stopped moving. Everything went black.

MR. NORIN

Irina heard a distant voice.

"Wake up!"

Irina tried to open her eyes.

"Wake up!" The voice was louder.

She could feel a stinging on her cheeks.

"Wake up!!" It was Roman's voice.

She opened her eyes. They were heavy. She felt the slap on her cheek. She opened her eyes wider from the pain. Things came into focus. She was seated in a chair at the end of the table in the dining room of Roman's suite. Her chair wasn't facing the table; it was turned ninety degrees. Roman stood in front of her. He held a small gun in his hand. She looked to her right and saw Erik slumped over onto the table in the chair beside her. His hands were tied behind his back.

"Erik!"

Irina tried to move before she realized her hands were tied behind her back.

"He woke up before you. Very angry at Jovan." Roman nodded at the man standing behind him, along with one of the bodyguards. "Kept cursing, mad as hell, so I shot him with the darts again—he should wake up again in a while, I think. These are new to me. I don't really know how they work. I don't know how many times you can shoot someone with one of these things before they die.

"You have no idea how disappointed I was when Jovan called me to tell me you and Erik were going to leave me. Hiding in Houston. Houston? Didn't you think I'd find you? Did you think I was just going to let you run away from me?"

"I don't want to fight for you or Mr. Norin anymore," Irina answered. "I want to make my own fights… my own money."

Roman said to Jovan and the bodyguard, "Wait outside."

They left through the door to the hallway and shut the door. Roman faced Irina.

"Mr. Norin—have you ever seen Mr. Norin?"

"No."

"Of course you haven't, but you have. I'll give you one guess who Mr. Norin really is," Roman said, leaning forward and cocking his head to the side.

"You are?"

"Do you think I could move around like I do with only four guards if the world knew I was the one running it all? Mr. Norin has made his share of enemies. And some of them are very bad people, make no mistake. And just like everybody else, Mr. Norin has people who are on his shit list. Right now, at the top of that list are you and your boyfriend. After all I've done for you, gotten you out of that crappy town, this is how you show your gratitude?"

"You have made way more money off my fights than for anything you have paid for me."

"The money I've made so far is nothing compared to the money I'm going to make from your future fights and endorsements. Let's not forget those. Now that you have won, the deals waiting are worth over ten million American dollars."

"Fuck you! I won't fight for you."

Roman slapped her hard on the side of her face, re-opening the cut over her left eye. He leaned down, putting his face inches from hers.

"I'm glad you brought up the subject of fucking."

Roman put his hands on Irina's thighs, slid her dress up around her waist, and moved his hands down to her inner thigh. He brushed the side of his hand against the outside of her panties.

"Let us get something straight. I own you. I own your whole fucking life. I own your boyfriend's life and everybody in your family's life. From now on, if I want you to fuck me, you'll fuck me. You'll fuck me as hard and as long as I want you to, and in whatever position I want you to. If I bring another woman to bed with us, you'll fuck her too."

Irina glared at him.

Roman took his hands away and stood up straight. "I'm looking forward to that long plane flight back to Moscow. I think that blonde flight attendant, I believe Yana is her name, is particularly cute, don't you?"

"Asshole."

"You'll fight for me. And you'll win. Didn't you think it was an enormous stroke of luck that when you became the number-three-ranked fighter in the world, the number-two-ranked fighter died in a car crash?" Roman shrugged his shoulders. "You're a bright girl... you figure it out. Wouldn't it be sad for an accident to happen to Erik? Or your father? Or poor Uncle Pavel?"

Irina's face changed from anger to fear.

"Do everything I tell you to do, and they live normal lives. Never knowing the danger you have saved them from." Roman looked over at Erik, still slumped over on the table, unconscious. He slid the gun into his pants' waistband. "Let's start now and see if you're as smart as I think. I'm going to untie your hands, and we're going to see if you can follow instructions. One word from me and the guard just outside the door will be here in a second."

Irina nodded. Roman leaned over her shoulder, behind her. He could smell her perfume. His forearm rubbed against her back. He struggled with the knot in the rope for a minute before it came free. Irina brought her hands in front and rubbed her wrists. "See, that's good," Roman said. "Stand up."

Irina stood. She was close to him, and he put his nose next to her neck and inhaled.

"I'm looking forward to our new understanding."

Irina stepped to her left and back. "I'll do what you want as long as you don't hurt my family."

Irina bent at the waist and unbuckled the strap on each of her shoes and stepped out of them. She reached behind her back and unzipped her dress, pulling it off her shoulders and letting it fall to the floor. Standing in her panties and bra, she unsnapped her bra and let it fall to the floor. She slipped her thumbs under the strings of her panties, pulled them down over her hips, and let them fall to her feet. She stepped out of them in a delicate maneuver.

THE APOTHEOSIS

"My God, you are beautiful." Roman's eyes worked their way from her feet to her face. "I've always had a thing for natural blondes." Roman smiled that crooked smile. Irina took a step toward him, and Roman froze with anticipation.

The rope quickly came down from overhead, and before Roman could utter a syllable, Erik used his strength to cinch it around Roman's neck. Roman's eyes bulged. Erik lifted him off his feet, and his mouth gaped open. No sound came. Roman pulled at the rope. The rope cinched tighter. Roman reached for the dart gun in his waistband. Irina removed it. Roman wiggled his smaller frame against Erik's, his wide eyes locked on Irina's. He kicked his feet at the air. He reached back and grabbed at Erik with one hand while he tried to get the fingers of the other hand under the rope. His face turned a deep red, with a tint of blue. The wiggling slowed. Erik didn't let up. Roman's eyes went glassy, and his tongue protruded from his mouth. His whole body went limp. Neither Irina nor Erik moved for another sixty seconds. Erik slowly lowered him to the floor.

Jovan was standing outside the door to Roman's room, the dart gun at the ready by his side. He heard the click as the door opened behind him. He turned to see Irina's hand with the dart gun. Irina fired, lodging two darts in his neck. He fell to the floor with a thud. Irina and Erik moved into the hall. The door to their right opened, and a guard stepped out. Erik lunged at him, and they grabbed each other around the shoulders. Erik pinned him against the door, forcing his forearm into the guard's throat. The guard twisted to the side to reverse his position with Erik. Irina raised the dart gun and pulled the trigger. Nothing happened. Irina took the dart gun lying on the floor by Jovan's side. The guard pulled a gun from under his jacket. His back was now to Irina. She fired the dart gun at the same time she heard a louder bang. The guard fell. Lying on the floor on the other side, resting against the door, was Erik. The door behind him was splattered with blood. He held his hand to his upper abdomen.

"Erik!"

"I'm shot." He tried to get up. His legs wouldn't move.

"Oh, my God. We've got to get you to a hospital." Irina knelt by his side.

"I can't stand."

Irina tried to lift him. After she had him less than a meter up, he became too heavy and dropped back to the floor. She tried again, using all her strength with the same result. They heard a voice over the earpiece of the guard lying in front of them. "Is everything okay there?"

Erik looked up at her. "The other guards will be coming soon. You have to go."

"I'm not going without you."

"You have to." Erik took a sharp breath. "They'll kill you. I can't stand, so I certainly can't run. Go now, take the stairs." Erik picked up the guard's gun that was on the floor next to him. "I'll kill them if I can—you have to go."

"No! I won't leave you." Irina's face twisted like she was going to cry.

"Irina, listen to me. We will not be living in America together as we planned."

Irina started to cry. She said nothing but laid her head on top of his and sobbed.

"Listen to me." Erik knew they were wasting time, and he could feel his breathing becoming difficult. "You have to go now!"

"No, I'll stay with you," Irina sobbed.

"No, what I have to do is what must be done if we are to be free. Hurry now, take the stairs. You must go, for both of us. You must live."

Irina held him tightly and sobbed. Tears came to Erik's eyes too. He grabbed her arm and pulled her back. The voice over the earpiece came through louder.

"There's no more time, go, run!"

Irina hugged him and sobbed, "I love you."

"I love you too."

She kissed him on the lips and held his face in her hands. This would be their last kiss. She knew it. He knew it. She lingered for a long moment. To feel every essence of him. To hold him in her heart and soul and imprint the feel of his lips on her mind. To taste the last breath of him in her mouth. Like ripping the bandage from a wound, she broke away from him. She sprinted down the hall. She didn't look back because she knew if she did she wouldn't be able to keep going. She ran past the elevator to the stairs, pushed open the metal door and ran down the stairs. The door automatically shut behind her and locked. She couldn't get back to him now no matter what happened.

Erik's breathing got shallower. He was sure the bullet must have hit his spine. There wasn't much pain, and his legs wouldn't move. He looked at the pistol in his hand. He pressed the button to eject the clip and saw that it was full except for the one round the guard had shot. He put it back in the gun. He would wait; they would come off the elevator, and when they rounded the corner he would shoot. If he was lucky, he'd get them by surprise. *Just don't pass out. Even if I get only one of them, it could make a difference.*

Jovan groaned and moved his arm.

Erik held out the gun, pointed at Jovan's head and pulled the trigger. Blood and brains splattered on the wall and floor. He did the same thing to the guard on the floor in front of him. Erik's breathing sped up, and sweat dripped from his forehead. *If they take too long, I won't be able to stay conscious.* The gun felt incredibly heavy in his hands. He heard the elevator ding and the door open. He had the gun ready. The tall guard was the first one who came around the corner.

🧬

Irina heard the first shot and stopped. Another shot. Even though they were muffled, she knew what they were. She paused a moment more and didn't hear anything else. She began running again. Then she heard gunshots, too many to count. Her bare feet were numb from the pain of running on the concrete stairs. She moved faster. She was halfway to the first floor. She had descended three more floors when she heard the door at the top open.

"She's running down the stairs! You go down the elevator, I'll take the stairs."

Irina continued running, using the handrail for balance. She heard a loud bang and a bullet ricochet off the cement wall above her. She ran down the stairs, legs pumping, feet barely touching the floor. She reached the bottom floor. She could hear the guard running down the stairs above her. She couldn't go through the lobby; the other guard might come from the elevator.

Looking to her right, she saw the exit to the street outside. She ran for it and threw the door open. The night air was frigid and sharp in her lungs. She was in the alley on the side of the hotel. She could see the street a half block away. She ran down the alley as fast as she could. The cold pavement flew under her feet. She ran around the corner of the building and down the deserted sidewalk.

She looked behind her. A taxi was coming down the street. She ran into the street and held up her hand. It slowed and pulled up beside her. She climbed in the back seat, slammed the door, and lay down so she couldn't be seen. The driver accelerated. She waited for a gunshot to shatter the glass. None did. She felt her heart pounding and heard her panting breath. She felt the taxi make a corner. She saw the driver look back at her over his shoulder. She didn't say anything. She hoped he could tell she was hiding.

What she didn't see was the driver flip a switch that opened the valve on a cylinder of halogenated ether.

OCTOBER 4, 2071

AGENT BOUDREAUX

Agent Troy Boudreaux stepped off the elevator, showed his badge to the uniformed policeman standing in front of him, and took a sip from his coffee cup. He wore a suit and tie because the FBI required it, a heavy overcoat to fight off the cold air outside, and a large tablet in his left hand because it was the information source for just about anything he might need to know.

"Agent Boudreaux, FBI, here to see Detective Kevin Provost."

The officer spoke into the microphone on his collar, "Detective Provost, the FBI is at the elevator."

"Be there in a second," the voice over the radio answered.

Agent Boudreaux noticed the bullet holes in the wall behind the officer, a bloody palm print on the stairway door, and to his right, the body of a tall man in a black jacket and pants. He was lying face down on the floor at the corner in the middle of the hallway. A black pistol was on the floor beside his head. Small yellow cardboard tents littered the floor, marking shell casings. A few minutes later Detective Provost came around the corner.

"Hi, Troy," Detective Provost said.

"How are things, Kevin?"

"Work is driving me insane. You?"

"About the same. As you can tell, I'm here on a cold Sunday morning," Agent Boudreaux replied.

"Has to be better than when we worked the graveyard shift for the PD."

"Well... yeah."

"Got something here we thought the Bureau needed to be in on from the very beginning. And since I know you were stationed in Moscow for a time, I asked for you. How's your Russian?"

"Passable. Especially for somebody born and raised in Southern Louisiana."

"None of these guys are going to talk to you. What we do have are documents you could translate for us. Follow me." Detective Provost stood over the tall man lying on the floor. "Dead guy number one, two rounds to the chest, has a radio, an earpiece, and a pistol. We assume he's a bodyguard."

"Guarding whom?" Agent Boudreaux asked.

"We'll get to that."

They walked together to where three more bodies lay on the floor. The Denver police department crime scene analyst was still there taking measurements and photographs.

"Dead guy number two, dressed just like dead guy number one. Tacker darts in his back and single gunshot wound to his head. Looks like the head shot was while he was already on the floor.

"Dead guy number three has Tacker darts to his neck and a single gunshot wound to his head. He doesn't appear to be a bodyguard. Like the others, he appears to have been shot by dead guy number four.

"Dead guy number four has a gunshot wound. One to the forehead, two in the chest and one in the upper abdomen. I think the one to the forehead was just to make sure. In his hand is the pistol from the dead bodyguard beside him. Also, beside him are two Tacker guns. We don't know who they belonged to."

Agent Boudreaux looked at the bullet holes in the door and wall and the spent shell casings. "Hell of a shootout."

"Now is when it gets a bit weird."

"It's weird already."

They entered Roman's room.

"Dead guy number five: Roman Churkin, according to the passport. Strangled here in the dining room. Suite is his, so we assume he's the guy who needs bodyguards. Near the body is a woman's bra and high heeled shoes. Besides the rope around his neck, there's an identical length of rope in the chair. This guy is the reason you're here."

"I can hardly wait."

"All of these guys are Russian; one of the guys in the hallway lives in Houston now. He's from Russia. They were here because Churkin had a fighter in a world championship fight at the arena last night. Dead guy number four, Erik Lyadov, was the trainer."

"And the fighter?"

"That's who left the bra and high heel shoes. Irina Popova. She won the bantamweight world championship last night." Detective Provost led Agent Boudreaux to a tablet computer lying on the dining table, a stack of passports and papers next to it. "Here is the security camera video of the exit on the south side of the hotel. The one at the bottom of the stairwell at the other end of the hall."

Detective Provost hit play and it showed a black and white, infrared video of Irina exiting the building and running down the alley to the street in the distance.

"She just won a few million dollars hours before this happened."

"Where is she now?" Agent Boudreaux asked.

"We don't know. This video is the last seen of her."

"Whose bloody palm print is on the stairwell door? She doesn't look shot in that video," Agent Boudreaux asked.

"That would be one of the two missing bodyguards."

"There's also a blood trail that leads down the stairs. Here's the video of him." Detective Provost hit the play button again and the video played, showing the bodyguard with a bloody wound to his left shoulder exiting the hotel. He left the camera view in the opposite direction as Irina.

"And where are they?" Agent Boudreaux asked.

"We believe he's on a private jet back to Russia, as far as we know. They must've had their passports with them because they weren't in any of the rooms. The other bodyguard went down in the elevator. Security video doesn't show him to be wounded. They got in a limousine out front, which is how they got to the airport. The limousine driver is being held at the station till I get there to interview him. They probably got to the airport about the same time the first marked unit showed up here at the hotel. The police chief has called the governor, who has called Senator Dean, who has called the State Department to contact Russian authorities to intercept the plane when it lands in Moscow. I wouldn't hold my breath for that. Yet another good reason to have you here. Maybe the Bureau can apply pressure. The media is camped out across the street, but the chief wants a total media blackout until we figure out what happened and why."

"Give me a few minutes and I'll work the background on these guys and the diplomatic end and see what they say, and see if any of the Russian embassies have been contacted by this girl. She can't leave the country, you have her passport." Agent Boudreaux sat down at the dining table and pulled over the stack of passports, cell phones, and papers. He switched on his tablet.

"Businesses are about to open. I'm going to go to the street behind this hotel, see if any of them have a security camera," Detective Provost said.

"I'll call you as soon as I have something."

Detective Provost took the elevator down to the lobby and walked down the alley to the street where Irina was last seen running. The sky was gray, and clouds hung low among the tall buildings. Small delicate snowflakes drifted down to the pavement. Detective Provost reached the street and looked in each direction. Nothing much to see. He looked across the street from the alley at a jewelry store. He crossed the nearly empty street and peered through the storefront glass. A camera was mounted on the ceiling inside, pointed out to view the front display cases, sidewalk, and street. A man was busy bringing items out of the safe for the display windows. The detective knocked on the glass door of the jewelry store until he got the man's attention. Detective Provost held up his badge.

Back in the suite, Agent Boudreaux entered the names and passport identification numbers for the entire stack and requested a full history on each. He took another sip of his coffee and sat back to wait. The tablet chirped. The report was back. He began reading. Obviously, this wasn't an ordinary group of Russians. His cell phone rang. It was Detective Provost.

"Hi, Kevin. I was about to call you. I just got the reports back on your Russians. This is a serious bunch. The dead bodyguards are ex-Russian military, special forces. The one from Houston was military too, regular Army. Churkin is an employee of a company named Rolling Thunder Promotions. It's the company he charged these rooms on the penthouse floor to. Nothing on the girl or the trainer. And no contact from the girl at any of the Russian embassies," Agent Boudreaux said.

"I'm looking at security video from a jewelry store across the street from the alley. It's a bit grainy and dark. It looks like the girl got into a taxi. I'm getting a copy now, and I'll send it to our video department for enhancements to see what taxi company it is. They should have a record of where they dropped her off."

THE NEW PATIENT

John ran the electric razor over the last bit of blonde hair and let it fall to the plastic sheet on the floor. That was the last task. His new patient lay on the hospital bed, naked, with the needed equipment and computers hooked up to keep her hydrated, fed, and sedated. Not so sedated that she needed a ventilator, just sleeping. The latest equipment was computerized and automated. In theory, John wouldn't have to do anything else except check the monitors until the soon-to-be-implanted embryo came to full term.

John looked her over. Very fit for a prostitute. He examined the cut over her eye. *Must have got smart-mouthed with her pimp or a customer. Didn't have time to put her shoes on.* He checked her arms for needle tracks. *None.* He clamped a device to her index finger and pressed the button. In a minute, the small screen gave the report: the only drug in her system was the one John was administering. John was surprised.

Next, he gave her a blood test to determine when she would ovulate. He gave her an injection to help the ovulation process along. *I'll check again in a couple days.*

John put the electric shears on the plastic sheet with her hair and her clothes. He folded the corners of the sheet in and took the bundle to the furnace, where the other packaging had already been placed. He closed the door, set the temperature and timer, and pressed the ignition button of the furnace.

He rolled the bed, Irina, and her instrumentation to the elevator and lifted her to the second floor. He pushed her down a hallway to a bedroom on the corner. Inside the bedroom, he placed her against the wall opposite a bank of windows and plugged in the power supply.

He took the elevator down to the first floor, down a hallway that led past a storage room, packed with provisions he'd need for an extended snowy winter. He went up a small set of stairs to the kitchen and the main living area of the house. From there John had a panoramic view of the meadow, the drive leading to the front gate, and the mountains on either side. Fresh snow had fallen to a depth of six inches, and it was still snowing. He was tired. He had been up for twenty-four hours. He ate a bowl of fruit and climbed another flight of stairs for a shower. Afterwards, he dialed a number on his phone. While the phone rang, he observed the mountain behind his house, standing majestic beyond the solar arrays, half-hidden in low clouds, even though it was in the afternoon.

"Good afternoon, Sean," a woman's voice said.

"Good afternoon, Lynda. I wanted to call to congratulate you on last quarter's fiscal report. Very nice job-reducing cost. The agency's almost operating without loss. Much farther along than I anticipated, for such a new organization."

"Thank you. I'm glad you called. Will you be back to visit us soon?"

"Yes, in a month or so."

"I'll arrange a luncheon with the city council members. A meet and greet, establish our reputation."

"Get their names and their political organizations' contribution information, and I'll send a check for each of them beforehand. It can't hurt for the agency to be associated with healthy campaign contributions. And there's one other thing I need from you. I'd like for you to send me a list of candidate couples who are highly qualified wage earners."

"Any particular case interest you?"

"No, I'm brainstorming. See what it would take to establish our organization in that market. Have it ready for me when I see you in a month."

"Yes, sir."

John ended the call. He checked the weather forecast and saw that another snowstorm was predicted in seven days. Twice the snow this one had brought. He lay down to sleep, confident he had the pieces in place. *All I need is a quiet winter in the mountains for my clone to incubate.*

He hoped he didn't dream. Years ago, he had stopped dreaming of

Amira. Nor did he dream of accomplishments or science or his imaging system. Now he dreamt of places he had been. He wanted his mind to rest and shake the feeling of unease. He fell asleep and dreamt of the bulls running the streets in Pamplona, the green water of the canals in Venice, and the cobbled streets of Paris glistening under the street lamps after a summer night's rain. He dreamt of ashen beaches with turquoise surf in the sunrise. He dreamt of the deep blue ocean with a dying moon sinking to a watery horizon and blood on a sandy path beneath palm trees. He walked the path to the beach. More blood appeared on the ground. He tried to walk around it, but it stuck to his feet. He waded into the surf to wash it off. His feet wouldn't come clean. It was on his hands. It wouldn't come off. He scrubbed harder. The surf became red. He looked down the beach in both directions, and the red water rolled onto the white sand, leaving a bloody stain.

THE CIA AGENTS

Agent Boudreaux's phone rang as he was parking his car. He looked at the number on his car's display. "Hey, Kevin, what's new?"

"Plenty, and none of it makes sense. The guys in the video lab sent me back the enhanced version of the security video. The cab is from J&L Taxi, so I went there and talked to the manager. I showed him a still image from the video, which had the cab identification on the side, so he could pull the record. That cab has been in the repair shop for the last three days. He showed it to me. It's been up on a stand being repaired from a front-end collision. So, the taxi on the video is an imposter."

"Why can't things be easy anymore?" Agent Boudreaux said.

"Things finally did. I had two detectives scan traffic cams at that time shown on the jewelry store video to determine where the taxi went. Since there isn't much traffic on the streets that late, they found it on three different cameras. It was last seen by the camera for the auto-drive engagement station entering Interstate 70 going west. We got the license plate number from that camera, and it's a fake also; the number isn't in the DMV system."

"That's nice work," Agent Boudreau said.

"It gets better. I got somebody at the transportation office to get the electronic signature registered from the auto-drive system, to see whom the car belongs to, and tell us where they got off the interstate. The auto-drive system has been spoofed. It came back to a pickup truck from Boulder. If it's a proper spoofing, it will be a totally different vehicle when it exits."

"I get to add to the mystery. I got a call from my section chief to meet him at the office. I can't remember the last time I saw the section chief in the office on a Sunday. I assume it has something to do with this. I'll check in with you when the meeting is over," Agent Boudreaux said.

Agent Boudreaux took the elevator to the section chief's floor and headed down the hallway to the corner office. The door was open, and the office administrator's desk was empty. He looked through the door.

"Come in, Agent Boudreaux, and shut the door, please," Section Chief Landry said as he pressed his finger on the computer screen on his desk. The screen on the wall behind him came on. A black man with a chiseled chin, a thick mustache, and wearing a blue suit looked into the camera, obviously in an office judging from the furniture in the background. "This is Deputy Director Carona of the CIA's Counterintelligence Center in Washington D.C. He's joining us by secure video link."

Agent Boudreaux sat in the chair on the other side of the desk.

"Good afternoon, Agent Boudreaux," the man on the video screen said.

"Good afternoon, sir," Agent Boudreaux said.

"I'm interested in why you requested a background check on Roman Churkin?"

"He was a homicide victim in a penthouse suite of a downtown hotel last night. Also, two of his bodyguards and two other men were killed in a shootout on the top floor. Churkin was strangled to death. The others were shot."

"They're the other ones you ran checks on?"

"Yes, sir. The only one I requested who wasn't killed is Irina Popova. She's currently missing. Denver PD is trying to find her now."

"You were at the crime scene?" the CIA officer asked.

"Yes, sir."

"Did it look like an assassination to you?"

"Hard to tell for sure. If I had to guess, I'd say it was something within the group. Probably over money because the Popova girl won a professional fight last night. Not a trivial sum either, a few million dollars. So, my early guess is that it was over money."

"The reason we are having this conversation is because Roman Churkin isn't his real name. He's really Afanasiy Norin. He's a retired colonel in the Russian military and ex-KGB. He runs a billion-dollar criminal enterprise in Moscow: drugs, prostitution, and extortion. He has high-ranking political friends, so he has a clean exterior."

"That fits what we're seeing here, judging by the hotel suite he was in. His group had the entire top floor," Agent Boudreaux said.

"He also owns several legit businesses. Shipping, export, a casino, a couple of restaurant chains, and sport gyms. He has never come to the United States before. We don't think he was doing anything here more than bringing his fighter to the fight. However, since he showed up dead, we are naturally curious. Not that a gunfight in a high-rise hotel isn't unusual, but is there anything else extraordinary about the circumstances?"

"I just got off the phone with Detective Provost from Denver Homicide Division. He's the lead detective on the case. There's security video of the girl running from the emergency exit of the hotel. She flees to the street behind the hotel. She was being chased by a wounded guard. He went the wrong way, and she got away. Security video from a business behind the hotel showed the girl getting into a taxi. It's a fake, with a fake license plate and a spoofed auto-drive system. It was last seen getting on Interstate 70 going west."

CIA Director Carona's face stiffened. "Section Chief Landry, I'd like for your man to take over this investigation. I'll be sending two men from my agency to assist. I'll send you their credentials over secure comm. Expect them at your office by eight o'clock tomorrow morning. I'd like to determine the nature of this homicide and the people involved to see if it has any implications in the intelligence community.

"I'll have the Attorney General call the Denver Police Chief within the hour to inform him that the FBI will take over the investigation. I'm sure he'll want to speak to you also. I'd like to have Agent Boudreaux lead the case, since he's the most familiar with it. I don't want any information released to the media. Of course, this conversation, and the CIA's involvement, is considered top secret. No information about our involvement should be given out without my approval."

"Yes, sir," Section Chief Landry replied. The video screen went blank.

🧬

Deputy Director Carona rotated his chair to the two agents sitting off camera.

"This stinks! Fake taxi, fake license plate, spoofed auto-drive, it has *hit* written all over it. Secretary of State Franklin is supposed to go to Moscow next January to negotiate a trade deal with the Russians. Our strategy is based on information Norin has given us over the last five years. If he was compromised, we need to know, I don't care what it takes." He stood and went to the window and looked out at the courtyard. The neatly cut grass and sidewalks were empty on a Sunday afternoon. "Now I must make a very uncomfortable call to the director, who will have to make a very uncomfortable call to the Secretary of State, who will have to make a very uncomfortable call to the President." He faced the two men. "Let me make this clear, all of our careers could be finished over this fuck-up. I'm too old to go back to being a safe-house keeper in Ecuador. I want a full background investigation on Irina Popova. Assign your whole team to it. Full cell phone, bank accounts, credit card, the works. I want our assets in Kirov and Moscow on it immediately. I want to know everybody she knew since grade school. If she had a couple of fucking goldfish named Mango and Tango, I want to know. I want you two to get your asses to Denver and find her. Find out who did this, and find out why. However, first and most important, before you do any of that, I want you to go out to the waiting room and tell Agent Price to come to my office because I want to know how Afanasiy Norin was in Denver, Colorado, and nobody fucking knew!"

OCTOBER 5, 2071

CLOSING IN

Section Chief Landry and Agent Boudreaux sat in the conference room at the FBI building waiting on Special Agents Baker and Cutshaw to arrive. The table of the conference room was covered with crime scene photographs and drawings and three different computers. Video screens on the walls were ready with the surveillance videos from the hotel, the videos from the jewelry store security camera, and videos from the traffic cameras and the entrance ramp camera at the auto-drive engagement station on Interstate 70. Just after nine o'clock in the morning, the CIA specialists were escorted into the conference room. They were mid-thirties, bearded, wearing blue jeans, dress shirts, and jackets. Each had a large metal suitcase in his hand. Everybody shook hands.

They placed the suitcases on the table and opened them. Inside each was a large computer. The blond-haired officer spoke. "I'm Agent Baker, from the Special Activities group in Langley. My partner is Agent Cutshaw from Counterintelligence. We reviewed the photos and videos on the flight here, so there's no need to go over that again."

Agent Boudreaux and Section Chief Landry looked at each other and regretted the two hours it had taken to prepare. "What we're interested in is the recorded radio transmission from the auto-drive system of the taxi as it passed through the engagement station. It wasn't in the electronic package sent to us earlier. Does anyone here have that?"

"I do," Agent Boudreaux said and handed him an optic stick.

Agent Baker inserted it into the computer in the case. He made selections on the display screen and waited.

"The identification number of the computer that installed the spoofing software is right here." The officer pointed to a long string of letters and numbers.

"You can do that?" Agent Boudreaux asked.

"We can do that; I can't tell you how. Now I'll perform a search to see if that computer has ever been connected to the Internet."

Less than a minute later, he said, "682 Curtis Street here in Denver." A few more swipes on the screen. "That residence is occupied by Mark James Burris. The computer is connected and on right now."

Agent Boudreaux typed that name into his computer on the table. "He has an arrest record. Ten years ago he did two years in county jail for drug possession and was paroled six months ago after another two years for auto theft."

"There's nothing in our system on him, besides what Agent Boudreaux listed," Agent Cutshaw said.

"Now let me see if the data on his machine is encrypted."

"We'll need a warrant," Agent Boudreaux said.

"I appreciate your desire to follow legal procedure. However, time is pressing, and we are not after a prosecutable arrest here. There's no way in a court of law that we are going to expose the capability we just used to locate Mr. Burris. Our goal here is to locate Irina Popova and determine what she knows about the events at the hotel. Everything else is secondary.

"The software system Burris used to spoof the auto-drive on that taxi will have recorded the original identification number. I'll get it out of the system. Once we obtain that, we can find the owner of that vehicle." Agent Boudreaux looked at his Section Chief, who just shrugged. Agent Baker kept manipulating the display in front of him.

"It's encrypted. Luckily, it's a system we know." Agent Baker continued to sort through the data on his display for ten more minutes. "Here it is. These are the files from the spoofing software; it's an illegal copy of what the manufacturer uses. The black market is full of them. They're kind of expensive. He has been busy. More here than I expected. Somebody should tell the Denver PD there's an auto-theft ring in their city." He cut his eyes over to Agent Boudreaux. "That taxi was a Toyota sedan, it looked about two years old to me. Here is it. Are you ready?"

"Yes. Go ahead," Agent Cutshaw said.

"Alpha, one, three, four, six, zebra, zero, dash, three, seven, seven, zero, dash, foxtrot, dash, four, four, whiskey."

Agent Cutshaw clicked away and then stared at his screen. The room was silent for two minutes.

"Got it," Agent Cutshaw said. "The vehicle belongs to Sean, spelled S-E-A-N, Burke, spelled B-U-R-K-E. I've got an address in Eagle County just outside Vail."

"I'm out of Burris's computer clean. I'm searching on Sean Burke... I've got his date of birth and his social security number," Agent Baker said.

Agent Boudreaux entered the name in his computer. "Nothing on him here."

"CEO of a company named Taylor Investments," Agent Baker said. "Corporate headquarters in Nassau, Bahamas." More swipes on the screen. "It looks like he was in Europe for a long while, up until about a year and a half ago. This is the first residence he has had in America in almost twelve years."

"Section Chief Landry, could you plug this into the monitor on the wall?" Agent Cutshaw held out a small black device that fit into the input port on the side of the screen. Once plugged in, an aerial map of Eagle County showed on the screen. Sean Burke's passport photo was in the bottom left corner of the screen.

"That's the photo from his passport." Agent Cutshaw made more swipes at his display, and another photograph appeared on the bottom right of the screen. "And this is his picture when he arrived in Boston Logan International a year and a half ago."

The photographs matched. A few more swipes on the display and the map zoomed in to a lone house sitting in an open meadow. The satellite view didn't reveal its true size.

"This is the house. He owns a considerable bit of acreage around it too," Agent Baker said.

"Wait a minute—" Agent Boudreaux interrupted. "You're telling me that a CEO of an investment firm conspired with an ultimate fighter to wait until a Russian mobster was in America to kill him and escaped in a fake taxi to a mansion in Eagle County?"

"You're assuming he's really a CEO and she's really an ultimate fighter," Agent Cutshaw replied. "Do you have a better explanation for this?"

"I guess I don't. What bothers me is that on the video of her running out of the hotel, she looked frightened. Not like a professional assassin."

"Judging from the mess at the hotel, I'd guess things didn't go as planned. She may have very well been scared and running for her life from the bodyguards who survived," Agent Baker replied and stared at the monitor intently.

"I'll call Langley and see what assets we have in Europe that can check on the list of places Burke has stayed over the last ten years or so. Section Chief, I need you to call the Legal Attaché Sub-Office in Nassau by secure video comm. Tell them that I'm going to be at their office in nine hours; that's about eight o'clock in the morning Nassau time. I'll need someone to break the ice for me with the Royal Bahamas Police Department, get them to give me access to their records," Agent Cutshaw said.

"What? No hacking the Nassau police?" Agent Boudreaux asked.

"We will if required. Since it's a friendly foreign government, we like to ask politely first."

Section Chief Landry nodded. Agent Baker got up and approached the monitor.

"I'm going to search the computer of the construction company that built the house to get the blueprints and find out what kind of alarm system it has. Agent Boudreaux and I are going to set up surveillance. We'll cut through the forest here. Come over this ridge and set up somewhere along the side of this mountain, just inside this tree line. That should put us within seven hundred meters." Agent Baker pointed to a place on the monitor.

"That is still pretty far," Agent Boudreaux said.

"I have long-range optics we can use and laser microphones that will work well on any of the rooms that have glass windows. Since we want to keep this operation as covert as possible, even among the FBI, we'll use Section Chief Landry for logistics so that only he knows where we are." Section Chief Landry nodded. "We'll pick a resupply point along this road." Agent Baker pointed at the monitor again. "We'll meet there every other day, so you can keep us fed and hydrated. Also, you'll have to set up a tailing detail in each direction on the main highway leading to the residence. We will notify you if any car leaves the house or visits the house. We want it followed and pictures taken of the occupants. If they go to the airport, they'll have to stop them and take them into custody. Put enough personnel on it so that it's available twenty-four-seven."

Section Chief Landry nodded again, his mind racing to keep up with the CIA agent.

Agent Baker continued, "I want them in place by the time we are. Radio communications must be through encrypted channels. If we are dealing with Russian intelligence, they will be listening. We'll keep twenty-four-hour surveillance until Agent Cutshaw gets back from Nassau and we assess our options. I want us to be in place after dark tonight, so we have about ten hours before we need to leave. Since we don't have time to get our own, we'll have to steal cold weather gear from the local Hostage Rescue Team supply. There's snow on the ground at that altitude, so we'll need camouflage to match that."

SURVEILLANCE

The fresh snow crunched under Agent Boudreaux's boots as he reached the top of the ridge in the dark. His breathing was labored. Through his night-vision goggles the dark forest around him was easy to see, albeit in shades of green. Agent Baker was already on the way down the opposite side of the ridge, twenty yards ahead, making his way silently through the trees.

Agent Baker's backpack was twice as heavy as his. Boudreaux moved twice as slowly. Agent Boudreaux adjusted the sling to the assault rifle on his shoulder and looked to the east, through the aspens. He could see a faint glow to the sky. The cold north wind hissed through the trees. He looked down and couldn't see Agent Baker. He looked down at the snow. Elk tracks crisscrossed the snow. He looked for boot tracks. *There they are.* He started down the ridge, following Agent Baker's tracks in the snow.

Agent Boudreaux stopped beside Baker ten yards inside the tree line. Agent Baker dropped his pack and rifle, removed a hatchet, cut branches of evergreen brush and built a small wall. He removed a shovel and raked away the snow till bare ground showed in a six-foot by six-foot area behind the wall of brush. He placed a waterproof white tarp on the ground and set up two small folding stools and a sleeping bag.

They both removed their night-vision goggles. The house stood black against the white meadow in the distance. They set up the tripod and a thermal camera with an enormous lens, another spotting scope with an equally big lens, and the laser microphone. The driveway that led to the stone-and-metal entry gate was to their left. Elk tracks crossed the snow in numerous places. There were patches where they had pawed away the snow to get to the growth underneath. The sky above had brightened; at ground level it was still dark. A bull elk bugled from across the meadow. He was somewhere in the distant tree line. The long trumpet echoed through the valley. Along the opposite tree line there was movement. A herd of ten elk cows, followed by the lone bull, scampered through the trees, moving in and out of sight. The cows stopped and then trotted again, dodging and darting, trying to stay away from the bull attempting to find a receptive cow. One that would stand to be mounted. Eventually, before the mating season was over, they all would. All that was required on his part was persistence.

Agent Boudreaux looked through the spotting scope that was still in night-vision mode; it was too bright, so he switched it off. Agent Baker handed him the thermal camera, then moved the laser microphone in front of him, put the headphones on, and peered through the aiming sight. He directed the laser at a large window on the second floor. He squeezed the trigger that activated the laser and began recording. He listened and heard nothing. He switched to a window on the nearest corner of the house and squeezed the trigger. He heard a rhythmic beep. He listened for a minute, took off the headphones, and handed them to Agent Boudreaux.

"Listen to this," he said.

Agent Boudreaux listened for a minute. "It sounds like a heart monitor, like in the hospital."

OCTOBER 6, 2071

MR. SMITH

Agent Cutshaw walked into the Royal Bahamas Police Department's main building with Nassau's current legal attaché. They were escorted to the chief's office.

"Good morning,'" the chief greeted them with a smile.

"Thank you for seeing us on such short notice," Agent Cutshaw said.

"No problem. What we can do for you?" the police chief asked.

"We'd like to search your records for any information on a man named Sean Burke. He was in Nassau about fourteen years ago. Also, any information on the company he owns, Taylor Investments. It's based in Nassau."

"What's this about?" the chief asked.

"He's a friend of a high-ranking senator in America, so before this senator appoints him to a position, we'd like to make sure there aren't any skeletons lying around that could embarrass the senator later. You understand why we couldn't go through the regular channels for this?"

"Go down the hall to Records on the left. I'll call Sergeant Gerver to let him know; he'll help you."

Once in the records office, Sergeant Gerver typed in the information in the computer and waited a couple minutes.

"There's one record on file from a long time ago. He's listed as a material witness to a death. Ruled natural causes or possible overdose," Sergeant Gerver said.

"Could you print me out a copy of that report?"

"Already done." Sergeant Gerver retrieved a stack of papers from the printer and handed it to him.

"What about Taylor Investments?"

"It's listed on only one report too, the one I just gave you. The man who died in that report was the CEO of Taylor Investments."

Agent Cutshaw looked at the bottom of the report.

"Is Chief Detective Evans around?" he asked.

"He's been dead... must be five years," Sergeant Gerver answered.

"How about Detective Rolle?"

"He's Chief Detective Rolle now. Back out the door, go left at the end of the hall."

Agent Cutshaw and the attaché entered the open office door to see Chief Detective Rolle staring out the window. He stood when he heard them enter.

"Good morning. I'm Agent Cutshaw. I'm sure you know Mr. Thomplate, the attaché."

"Yes, I do. Good to see you again, Mr. Thomplate. Can I help you?"

"I'm doing a background check on a man named Sean Burke, and he was mentioned in a report you did fourteen years ago. It was a natural death or accidental overdose case." Agent Cutshaw gave the papers to him. Detective Rolle read the report.

"I remember this. A strange case. One of those that stays with you. You have this feeling you missed something. Raymond Taylor was a wealthy local businessman. He owned a small island south of here. We got a call that he'd died overnight, so Chief Detective Evans, me, and Dr. Nicks flew out to investigate. He was mid to late sixties I believe, dead in his bed. Nothing seemed unusual. Sean Burke and the woman listed there, Julia Watson, were staying on the island at the time. They were both employees of Raymond Taylor. There were no wounds, but the toxicology report came back with phenobarbital in his system. We found some pills in the bathroom. But we also found an IV puncture wound on his ankle. It could have been self-administered. We considered the possibility that Sean Burke could have overdosed him, since he was the sole inheritor. It was only a theory we kicked around the office. No evidence whatsoever.

"Six months later, I got a few calls from friends of Julia Watson. They were concerned about her. We checked, and she wasn't on the island anymore. In fact, the island had been abandoned; the place had been cleaned out. I called Sean Burke and asked him, and he said the last he knew she was sailing back to America. I kept checking back with friends who reported her missing for the next year. Nobody ever heard from her again."

"What about this other witness listed at the end, Earle Charlton?"

"He came there as we were leaving with the body. He seemed mad about Raymond Taylor dying. I just assumed he was trying to scam Mr. Taylor out of money. He's one of our resident... what is it you call them in America... wise-guys." Chief Detective Rolle swiped at the computer screen a few times. "I thought I saw his name come across my desk." A few more swipes. "He's being held now awaiting trial on a fraudulent paycheck cashing charge. Currently residing at Her Majesty's Prison."

HER MAJESTY'S PRISON

Earle Charlton sat on a plastic chair at a plastic table, in an orange, threadbare jumpsuit in an interrogation room. Agent Cutshaw entered and closed the door behind him. The agent sat at the table opposite a man whose record said he was fifty-nine. The gray hair, leathered, creased skin and hollowed eyes made him look ten years older. Agent Cutshaw put his briefcase on the table, opened it, and removed the police report.

"You are Earle Charlton?"

"Ya, mon, who are you?"

"I'm Agent Cutshaw with the United States Government. Your name came up in a police report from fourteen years ago. It had to do with the death of Raymond Taylor, a businessman who owned an island south of Nassau." Agent Cutshaw noticed him sit up a bit in his chair.

"Raymond Taylor, keep hauntin' me still."

"How did you know him?"

"I did work for him. Find things for him. My father did the same thin'."

"Your father knew Mr. Taylor?"

"He's the one who sold him the island he bought. My dad could sell anythin'."

"Did you know another man who was there that day, named Sean Burke?"

"I brought him there a few days before."

"Had you ever seen Sean Burke before that day?"

"No."

"Ever seen him since?"

"No."

"On the day Mr. Taylor died, you showed up at the island. Why?"

"I had—a deal with him. I was gonna be a rich man except that bastard up and died on me."

"What kind of deal?"

Earle gave a broad yellow grin and leaned forward, putting his elbows on the table. "I know somethin' about Mr. Taylor. Somethin' nobody else on this earth knows. Somethin' he didn't want nobody else to know. Somethin' very bad. Somethin' you don't know or you wouldn't be here askin' me about Mr. Taylor."

"What's that?"

Earle shook his head. "Why should I do somethin' for you? You got to do somethin' for me. Get this case against me dropped. You the big agent from America, should be no problem. Get this case dropped and I'll talk."

Agent Cutshaw took his phone from the briefcase and touched the screen. In Washington, D.C., Deputy Director Carona answered.

"This is Cutshaw. I'm interviewing a man in the Nassau, Bahamas, prison about our problem. He wants to exchange information for dismissal on a fraudulent check charge." Agent Cutshaw paused to listen. "His name is Earle Charlton, case number six, eight, one, one, five, three." Agent Cutshaw paused again. "Yes, make the call, get an agreement, and have them call me back on my phone."

Agent Cutshaw put the phone back down on the desk. "I'm going to get an agreement to have your charges dropped by the attorney general's office. If what you have to tell me impresses me, I'll tell them to go ahead. If it doesn't, you go back to your cell to wait for trial."

Earle sat and smiled. Agent Cutshaw's phone rang, and he pressed the speaker button.

"This is Agent Cutshaw, who am I speaking with?"

"This is Attorney General and Minister of Legal Affairs Wallace," a woman said over the phone.

"Do you know Mr. Charlton?"

"Yes, everybody in my office is familiar with Mr. Charlton. I've been bringing him to court since I was a first-year prosecutor."

"I'm here with Mr. Charlton in an interview room at the prison. I've got you on speaker. I want you to tell him that you agree to drop the case against him if I call you back in the next three minutes and tell you I'm impressed with what he tells me."

"I agree," the woman said.

"Thank you." Agent Cutshaw ended the call and looked at the smiling man across the table.

"Raymond Taylor wasn't Raymond Taylor. Him a big-shot rich doctor from America. He come runnin' to this island from the law. He got caught clonin' a human, a baby girl. They gonna put him in jail for it. So he come here."

"When was this?"

"When I was a boy. My father helped him hide here."

"What was his real name?" Agent Cutshaw asked as he took a tablet from his briefcase.

"His real name be John Numen, N-U-M-E-N."

Agent Cutshaw entered the name on his tablet. A picture appeared on his screen with the label "Fugitive – Assumed Deceased." The picture was of John Numen from almost fifty years before. It was an exact image of Sean Burke. Agent Cutshaw checked the date again. He couldn't believe it. He pressed the screen on his phone.

"Yes?" the woman's voice said.

"I am impressed."

OCTOBER 8, 2071

THE RAID

It was midafternoon when Agent Baker's secure phone lying on the tarp beside him rang. Agent Boudreaux, who was napping on the ground, opened his eyes. It was Cutshaw.

"Talk to me, man," Agent Baker said.

"Big things to tell you but not over the phone, not even this one. What have you got there?" Cutshaw replied.

"We've got plenty of video of him moving about the house. He hasn't left, and nobody has come to visit. We haven't seen or heard the girl. This is a guess, but we think she's unconscious in a second-story bedroom. We can hear a heart monitor in that room, and he comes and goes from it pretty regularly. How long before you are back? It's damn cold here at night."

Agent Cutshaw was standing outside a storage unit holding a mesh helmet with a fiber optic harness in his hand. "I'm in Brooklyn right now. I found interesting things in a storage building in Nassau and here in Brooklyn. The rent at both places is being paid by Taylor Investments. I'm on my way to the airport. I expect to be back in Denver in five hours. Leave Boudreaux there, and meet me in Denver."

"Okay." Agent Baker hung up.

"I'm going back to Denver, gotta leave you here for a while."

"How long?"

"I'm not sure." He put the secure phone in his empty backpack and removed a radio from it. He got his rifle that was leaning against the tree. "Keep doing what we've been doing, keep your radio handy in case we need you." He pressed the transmit button on the radio.

"Baker to Landry, do you copy?" Agent Baker said into the radio.

"Go ahead."

"Meet me at the usual place in one hour."

"Copy."

He laid the radio beside Agent Boudreaux and disappeared into the forest.

The sun sank in the sky behind the mountain. The sky turned golden. The sun continued its descent, and the sky transitioned to orange. A bull elk bugled at the far end of the meadow. Agent Boudreau could see him standing in the middle of the field. He brought the lens to his eye. The bull's breath misted as he bellowed again at the cows standing fifty yards away.

Agent Boudreaux watched Sean move about the house and listened with the laser microphone to the music playing in the living room. The sky faded to ink, and the stars came out. The interior lights of the house gave a soft amber hue to the snow around the house. After ten o'clock, the lights inside the house went out. Ten minutes after eleven o'clock, Agent Cutshaw's voice came over the radio.

"Cutshaw to Boudreaux."

"Go ahead," Agent Boudreaux replied.

"We're parking just out of sight on the main road. We're going to cut through the trees to your position. We'll be coming up behind you in about forty minutes."

"Copy."

Agent Boudreaux put on his night-vision goggles, and the night turned to bright green day. He waited. Soon he could see the silhouettes of the men moving through the trees until finally they were beside him. Agent Cutshaw, Agent Baker, and Section Chief Landry were in tactical gear and night-vision goggles. They carried Tacker rifles and pistols in holsters on their belts. Agent Baker also carried a rolled-up body bag. He handed the body bag to Agent Boudreaux. Then he handed Boudreaux a bulletproof vest and an extra Tacker rifle he was carrying. Boudreaux put on the vest. Agent Baker spread a blueprint of the house on the tarp.

"We are going to make entry," he informed Agent Boudreaux. "He has an alarm system that isn't monitored. Let's hope he isn't using it. We've made a master key for the brand of lock he has on the front door. We'll enter there and split into two teams. You and Section Chief Landry will take the stairs in front of you. You must move slowly and quietly; we don't want to wake him. He should be sleeping in the master bedroom here." Agent Baker pointed to a place on the diagram. "You two move down the hall to the bedroom on the corner where we think the girl is. Use the body bag to carry her out of the house through the front door.

"Wait there. Once Sean Burke is secure, we'll meet you there with him. After that we'll search the rest of the house. If you have to shoot, use the Tacker rifle. We want them alive. Do you have any questions?"

"It sounds so easy when you explain it that way. I'm willing to do anything to get out of this cold," Agent Boudreaux said.

Agent Baker put the blueprint back in his pocket. "Let's go."

The four men moved at a slow jog across the open meadow, being careful not to trip on anything unseen below the smooth surface of the green-hued snow. Everybody kept their fingers away from the triggers of their rifles. The elk behind the house stood for a moment and stared at the men. Then they all ran for the near tree line like the devil himself was on their heels, kicking up snow in their wake.

The motion sensors at the rear of the house dinged an alert on the panel next to John's bed. The screen came on. John woke, rolled over, and looked at the infrared video feed on the screen. Six elk cows ran out of view. *Fucking elk.* He silenced the alarm and closed his eyes.

Slowly and quietly, they went up the stairs to the front door. Agent Baker removed the master key from his pocket and inserted it in the dead bolt.

The motion sensors for the front porch dinged an alert. The screen came on again. This time it showed an infrared image of the porch leading to the front door. John opened his eyes again and prepared to absentmindedly silence the alarm when he noticed the image on the screen. Four men in tactical gear, with rifles, were at the front door of his house. John swung his feet to the floor. His eyes widened with surprise. He grabbed the assault rifle lying under the bed.

Agent Baker turned the lock, and it made a soft click. He eased the door open. No alarm sounded. He clicked the safety off his rifle and stepped inside. He motioned Boudreaux and Landry toward the staircase in front of them.

They made their way up the stairs. Agent Boudreaux went first, slowly taking each step until he reached the second floor. Section Chief Landry stopped at the halfway point to wait and cover for his partner until he reached the top. Then Landry ascended the rest of the stairs. They moved slowly down the hall to the open door at the end, silently leaving snowy-wet boot prints on the wood floor. Before they reached the door, they could hear the rhythmic beeping coming from the room. Agent Boudreaux stopped at the door and leaned his head past the door frame to peer inside.

A woman lay on a hospital bed, covered with a sheet from the shoulders down. She had tubes coming from two different machines into IVs in each arm, and electrodes from the heart-monitoring device were taped to her chest. Agent Boudreaux went in and stood beside the bed. The woman was Irina Popova. He could recognize her even though she had no hair.

Landry moved to the other side of the bed. He found the power switch on the heart monitor and switched it off.

"What should we do with these IVs?" Section Chief Landry whispered.

"We can't take them out; we don't know what he's giving her. It might kill her. Unhook the dispensers, and put them in the body bag with her. We'll take the sheet off the mattress underneath her and take everything out like that," Agent Boudreaux replied.

They slung their rifles across their chests. Agent Boudreaux removed the electrodes that were taped to Irina's chest. Next, he unhooked the dispenser on his side of the bed, and Section Chief Landry did the same. Agent Boudreaux placed the body bag on the floor and then pulled the sheet off the mattress at the head of the bed. Section Chief Landry did the same at the foot of the bed. The sheet enveloped her like a cocoon when they lifted her from the bed and slowly placed her on the floor inside the body bag. Agent Boudreaux zipped it halfway, and they grabbed the handles at the head and foot of the bag. Quietly and carefully, they carried her back down the long hallway, down the stairs and out the front door. They moved out eighty yards and laid her in the snow. The body bag was thick and would protect her from the cold for a short period of time.

They each knelt on one knee beside Irina and watched the house. It was dark and quiet. The front door was wide open. They stared at it and waited for the CIA officers to exit the front door. Each tried to slow his breathing and listen for any sound. Everything was silent. A half-full moon hung above the mountain to the east.

A shot from inside the house echoed across the meadow. Before it faded, automatic gunfire intermingled with pistol shots rang out. Agent Boudreaux and Landry stood, rifles at their shoulders pointed at the front door. The house was still dark through their goggles.

"Stay here, I'm going to the front door," Agent Boudreaux said. His gun ready, he took a step toward the house.

The explosion knocked them to their backs, a bright green flash blinding them. They lay on the ground, stunned. Agent Boudreaux jerked the goggles from his eyes and looked at the house. Flames rolled out of every window and the front door. Burning debris was scattered around them and Irina in the snow. They could feel the heat from the house on their faces. They got to their feet and grabbed the body bag and pulled her through the snow, away from the house.

Section Chief Landry was breathing hard, his breath in clouds in front of his face. The second explosion came. A ball of fire rose from where the roof of the garage used to be. It mushroomed into the mountain air, lighting up the mountainside like a setting sun. Shadows of the trees danced on the mountainside snow. More burning boards flung themselves across the meadow.

"Do you see Cutshaw and Baker?" Section Chief Landry asked.

Boudreaux shook his head, looking grim. "They're still inside."

FEBRUARY 2072

DOUBT AND A PRAYER

Agent Boudreaux took off his hat, shook the snow from it, and stepped inside the cathedral. The tall white walls and arched ceiling of buttresses were in front of him. He slowly moved down the center aisle toward the altar; dark wooden pews were on each side. Halfway to the altar, he saw a woman with short blonde hair sitting in the middle of a pew to his right. She was wearing a pale pink dress, matching shoes and jacket. She was praying and didn't look at him. He sat beside her. She finished her prayer and glanced at him. She looked down at her hands folded on top of a book resting in her lap. He could still see the remnants of the cut under her left eyebrow.

Agent Boudreaux spoke to her in Russian. "They told me I could find you here."

"I like it here. Do you have more questions for the FBI?"

"No, no more questions." Agent Boudreaux looked up at the ivory ceiling and the tall white walls. "This place reminds me of a cathedral in Moscow, near the river; it's called Cathedral of Christ the Saviour. Ever been there?"

A tear slowly rolled down her cheek. "Yes." She removed a handkerchief from her purse and wiped it away.

"I wanted to offer you my congratulations. My section chief told me you were given special approval to stay in America if you want. And the agency has released the hold on your bank account."

"Yes. Thank you."

"Are you going to go back to Russia?"

Irina inhaled and blinked her moist eyes. "I don't think so. Erik wanted to come to America. It seems like it would be a disservice to go back to where he wanted so badly to leave. Even without Roman there, it seems like a bad place." She wiped away another tear.

"I think that's a smart choice."

"They told me you were the one who rescued me from the house in the mountains."

"It was me and another agent."

"Thank you for risking your life for me." She smiled at him. "And tell the other agent thank you for me. I wouldn't be here if you hadn't. They told me he had the whole house rigged with incendiary explosives."

"You're welcome. I was told the same thing."

"Did you know the two CIA agents who died?"

"No, I didn't."

"Do you know if they have families?"

"Sorry, I don't know." Agent Boudreaux felt badly for not knowing more about them.

"I hope their families are strong. I pray for them." A single tear fell from her bowed head and landed on the book in her lap. Irina wiped it away with her hand.

"I hardly ever see a real book anymore. What are you reading?" Agent Boudreaux nodded to the book beneath her folded hands.

"*One Day in the Life of Ivan Denisovich* by Aleksandr Solzhenitsyn. Do you know classic Russian literature?"

"No."

"It was a book recommended to me by a very wise man. In the beginning, before they let you question me, I told the men from the CIA everything that happened at the hotel, how Erik and I had planned our escape and how it went wrong. They questioned me for a long time about it. I begged them to tell me what happened to Erik, but they wouldn't say. No matter how much I cried and begged, they only kept asking me questions. It went on for many, many days.

"There is a line in this book that helped me through those days. When I didn't know what was going to happen to me. 'You should rejoice that you're in prison. Here you have time to think about your soul.' I had many days to think about my soul... and Erik's. After a while they believed me. From then on, they have been very nice to me. The big man tried to break the news about Erik to me gently. It was still hard knowing for sure. I cried until I was exhausted. He tried his best to comfort me. He reminded me of my Uncle Pavel."

"I'm sorry about Erik."

"Roman wouldn't just let us go," she said and wiped another tear. "He was a very bad man. What he got he truly deserved."

"I'd agree with that."

"They told me about Sean Burke. It's difficult to understand how this man could abduct women. They say he's responsible for the deaths of many women. Impregnating them, delivering the babies, incinerating the mothers' bodies and selling the babies through his adoption agency... a wealthy man like that, just for a sick fetish. Of all the taxis I had to get into, it had to be his."

"That is bad luck." Agent Boudreaux didn't tell her about the massive CIA presence they'd mounted before the next sunrise after the explosion. They'd sealed off the area. Removed all evidence. All information about Sean Burke had disappeared from all his sources. Agent Boudreaux had more questions now than before the raid. He didn't know much more than what the newspapers published from a scripted news conference his boss gave two days later. He did know Sean Burke's body, as well as the bodies of the CIA agents, didn't go through the county morgue.

"You know, besides my life, you saved many other women's lives. It is good he's dead too."

"Yes, it is," Agent Boudreaux said. He closed his eyes and said a prayer of his own.

The End

ABOUT THE AUTHOR

Darrell Lee

Darrell Lee, born and raised in Port Arthur, Texas, received his BS in Computer Science and moved to Houston for a job on the Space Shuttle program.

He has been an avid reader all his life, especially science fiction. He holds a great respect for the talents of the tellers of the tales. Their ability to suck the reader into their imaginary world and hold them captive there, making the reader see things differently or things not even considered and how the cerebral journey changes the reader in some way.

Another lifelong trait, is that he craves a creative outlet. Down through the years it has taken many different forms. Painting, charcoal drawing, photography, chess and computer software. His ultimate goal as a writer is simple and challenging— leave a mark on the reader.

By day he currently works on assorted software systems for the International Space Station. By night he writes, secluded in his home office, with a wife that softly brings him snacks and falls asleep on the couch waiting for him to go to bed. He is a member of the Houston Writer's Guild and the Houston Writer's House.

The Apotheosis is Darrell's second book with Progressive Rising Phoenix Press. His debut science fiction novel, *The Gravitational Leap*, is one of nine pieces of work to make the final cut for the 2018 Cygnus Science Fiction Book Award, a division of Chanticleer International Book Awards.

For more information about Darrell Lee:
Visit his website: www.authordarrelllee.com
Contact him via email: authordarrelllee@gmail.com

Progressive Rising Phoenix Press is an independent publisher. We offer wholesale discounts and multiple binding options with no minimum purchases for schools, libraries, book clubs, and retail vendors. We also offer rewards for libraries, schools, independent book stores, and book clubs. Please visit our website to see our updated catalogue of titles and our wholesale discount page at:

www.ProgressiveRisingPhoenix.com

CPSIA information can be obtained
at www.ICGtesting.com
Printed in the USA
LVHW040741080719
623418LV00005B/857